Romantic Suspense

Danger. Passion. Drama.

Deadly Mountain Rescue
Tara Taylor Quinn

Undercover Cowboy Protector
Kacy Cross

MILLS & BOON

DEADLY MOUNTAIN RESCUE
© 2024 by TTQ Books LLC
Philippine Copyright 2024
Australian Copyright 2024
New Zealand Copyright 2024

First Published 2024
First Australian Paperback Edition 2024
ISBN 978 1 038 90267 2

UNDERCOVER COWBOY PROTECTOR
© 2024 by Kacy Cross
Philippine Copyright 2024
Australian Copyright 2024
New Zealand Copyright 2024

First Published 2024
First Australian Paperback Edition 2024
ISBN 978 1 038 90267 2

MIX
Paper | Supporting
responsible forestry
FSC® C001695
www.fsc.org

Published by
Harlequin Mills & Boon
An imprint of Harlequin Enterprises (Australia) Pty Limited
(ABN 47 001 180 918), a subsidiary of HarperCollins
Publishers Australia Pty Limited
(ABN 36 009 913 517)
Level 19, 201 Elizabeth Street
SYDNEY NSW 2000 AUSTRALIA

Cover art used by arrangement with Harlequin Books S.A.. All rights reserved.

Printed and bound in Australia by McPherson's Printing Group

Deadly Mountain Rescue

Tara Taylor Quinn

MILLS & BOON

Dear Reader,

Welcome back to Sierra's Web, where a firm of best friends, all experts in their fields, help solve crimes! *Deadly Mountain Rescue* is particularly close to me, literally! It's set in a fictitious town fashioned after the small town I live in, situated in the far east of Phoenix valley!

I sit and look at the mountains as I write, and finally, I'm up in them, too, while in this story! I've climbed to the top of the highest peak of the great Superstition Mountains, spent a lot of time in them and can promise you that everything you read here, in terms of mountain description and challenges, comes straight from those experiences. I've driven on the road mentioned in the first chapter. And have seen a car go over the side of the mountain, too.

But wait, I don't want to give too much away! Just one more little tidbit. Stacy's last name, Waltz. She's named after a famous German from these parts, Jacob Waltz. He mined in these mountains, brought out a lot of gold, but never told anyone where his mine was. People still come to our little town every year to go up in the mountains and hunt for the Lost Dutchman Mine!

As for the rest of the story...I fell in love with Jesse "Mac" MacDonald from page one. And would love to grow up to be Stacy. They have a very special bond, beyond just romantic, but it sizzles, too. I hope you enjoy spending time with them as much as I have. Happy reading!

Tara Taylor

DEDICATION

For Timothy Lee Barney, the man who challenged me
to climb to the top of the mountain. And who
holds my hand through every challenge we face.
I love you. Then, now and forever.

Chapter 1

"How is it possible that we grew up in the same town and I feel like I've been breathing lore and stories since I was born, and you are only half aware of a few of them?"

Saguaro Bend police corporal Jesse Macdonald listened to his partner of five years through his truck's sound system as he headed toward the gated community he called home. "I guess by the time you came up, they'd run out of interesting things to teach," he said, with a tired grin. They'd had a long night on duty—responding to three shooting calls, all unrelated, two resulting in victims being hospitalized.

But no matter how tough the shifts were, these respective drives home, the way he and Stacy always stayed on the line until they were both on their own properties, put him in a better mindset to get some rest.

"There's no way you didn't know that Geronimo ruled our mountains until the late 1880s…"

"I didn't," he admitted truthfully, while knowing full well he'd have denied knowing just to hear her exasperated reaction.

"Jesse Macdonald, you don't even try to learn!" she said, right on cue, bringing on his full smile.

"And you, Stace, need to join us here in the twenty-first century," he drawled. Words he told her often enough, but not ones he meant. Not only was Stacy the finest cop he'd ever worked with, she was also very much present in her daily life.

Aware of those around her. Aware of the world's struggles.

And deeply caring about both.

"It was a rough one tonight, huh?" Her soft tones came over the speakers, hitting him straight in the gut.

"Yeah. But, hey, we won two out of three." They'd apprehended two of the three shooters. Nothing beat that feeling. Which was why, at thirty-eight, he was still on the street. And planned to turn down the offer he'd heard was coming his way from the county sheriff's office. Just as he'd chosen not to take the lieutenant's position within the Saguaro police department.

He and Stacy had brought in more bad guys than any other duo in the state during their five years together. The invitations they received from other Arizona police departments to help with particular situations was a testament to that.

"I heard you have an offer coming in." Her words were upbeat.

He'd wondered if someone had said something to her. "You ready to take on a young pup? Bring him up?" He had to ask. At thirty, she'd proven herself. Should be moving up in the ranks, even if he chose not to do so.

"No."

He was alone in his truck. The satisfied nod, his hint of a grin, wasn't hurting anyone.

But holding her back would.

"You know, whenever you're ready, I'll support you completely."

Turning onto the short drive leading into his community, he slowed as he approached the gate, waited for the sensor to read the chip in his windshield and allow him access.

He'd drive around the neighborhood. Do a quick check. And by then Stacy would be home as well. Just outside city limits, on the desert property willed to her by her grandfather.

The smart, athletic brunette had been living there alone since her husband's death seven years before.

When she didn't respond, his gut sank. She *was* ready. And he would do everything in his power to make the transition easy for her. "Stace?" The present was as good a time as any to take the first step of the breakup. Admitting that it was time for her.

Helping her feel good about moving on. Joining in her anticipation of a new phase in her career—her life.

When she still didn't answer, he pushed again. "Stacy, it's okay…"

"What? Oh… Sorry, Mac. For a minute there, I thought someone was following me. But when I turned to take the long way home, just to be sure, they sped right on by…" Her tone was off.

Senses honed, Mac sat up straight. "Following you? For how long? What kind of vehicle?"

"Headlights higher than mine. Could still be an SUV. Maybe a truck. Dark. I couldn't really tell. Brights were on."

Driving in the desert in the dark, the high beam lights were a must. It needed to happen for safe driving. Javelina, coyotes, other animals hunted at night. But coming up behind someone?

"Head back to town," he said. "I'll meet you at Rich's."

An all-night diner they frequented not far from the station.

"No need." Stacy's voice came over the system, sounding more like herself. "I'm a big girl, Mac. And I'm fine."

He heard the warning tone. She was a damned good cop. Didn't need looking after.

And he didn't blame her. With her big brown eyes and long dark hair, she gained some attention. And there were still those who thought of women as needing protection.

Because some did.

Which made it hard for Stacy to hold her own sometimes.

"I know how to lose a tail," she said then, and he heard the irritation in her tone.

"No one's completely immune," he replied. Still not liking those bright lights. "We're human."

"And if I was worried, I'd be the first one to ask for help."

He knew that, too. One of the reasons they were such a good team was because they each brought something different to the page. And they talked things through, always.

"I don't like the brights on, coming up on your tail."

"Yeah, that's what triggered me to begin with. But the vehicle backed off. I made my turns, watched the response. I'm guessing the dude just forgot he had them on."

It happened.

"Whoa!" A hiss followed the exclamation.

"Stacy!" Foot immediately on the brake, Mac met his seat belt with some force as he made a U-turn on a street not made for one.

"Yeah, wow. I need some sleep. I almost clipped a van. Had to swerve to miss it."

"I'm on my way."

"Don't be ridiculous," she said then. "I'm serious, Mac. I'm half a mile from home. I'm going in and going to bed and if you show up, I'm not only not opening my door, I'll be royally pissed."

"Just tell me this…is there any possibility that the van is the same vehicle that was behind you earlier?"

"No. A van's skinnier than a truck or full-size SUV,

lower to the ground. Now quit demeaning me and go to bed."

"I'd hope you'd do the same for me, if your radar was on alert." He wasn't in a joking mood all of a sudden.

"Of course I would. You trust me with your life, right?"

"Implicitly."

"Then trust me with mine."

Right. "Point taken." They were both tired. And had seen more than the usual amount of abhorrent behavior that night.

"I'm turning into my place now," she told him. "And Mac?"

"Yeah?"

"Whenever I'm ready to move on, you'll be the first to know."

Hanging up from her partner as she waited for her automatic garage door to open, Stacy Waltz couldn't imagine a life that would be better than being Mac's partner. Which was why, every time she heard about an offer coming his way, she panicked a little bit.

That's what had caused her little bout of paranoia on the drive home—the pending promotion she'd heard about before their shift started the previous night. She'd waited all night for him to mention it. And when he hadn't, she'd had to bring it up.

A truck with headlights didn't scare her.

Losing Mac as a partner did.

Maybe not a healthy realization, overall. But understandable. They were great together.

Garage door up, she slowly moved her red SUV inside. In some ways, her years with Mac were the best of her life.

Hard to believe they'd been born and raised in the same

town, but she hadn't met him until after the worst days of her life. Joining the force after she'd lost Brett had been the only thing that kept her going. The first person she'd met, on her first official day of duty, had been Jesse Macdonald.

Shaking off the night, and the drive home, Stacy pushed the button to close her garage door and unlocked her glove box, grabbed her small clutch purse, and opened her driver's door with a promise to herself to branch out and spend off duty time with some of the other officers who were always inviting her to do things with them. She went occasionally. It was time to go more.

Just so she'd be prepared when Mac did get an offer he couldn't refuse.

As she well knew, nothing lasted forever...

What was that?

A shuffle on the pavement behind her vehicle?

Desert roof rats again? She hadn't checked the live trap before work.

Shaking her head, she was debating whether to do so before getting some rest. She made a move toward the door into the house and heard the garage door start to go up again.

Startled, she spun around.

A strong arm wrapped around both of hers.

Pulling her back against a much bigger body.

Even as she was shoving her elbows into abs of steel, she felt the prick. Saw a gloved hand pulling a syringe away from her arm, removing a long needle that had pierced her uniform sleeve.

She threw a heel back and straight up. Caught him right in the crotch.

A wave of sickness spread over her.

She had to puke.

Was dizzy.

Couldn't let herself lose consciousness.

Arms snaked beneath her knees, around her back. Lifting her.

She had to fight it. To be aware.

She kicked out. Hard. With both feet. Flailed her arms.

Her captor didn't let go.

Take note of every clue.

The cowboy boots on her garage floor.

No voices.

Her head swam more with every step.

The back of her SUV, open.

She was dropped to the carpet. Her time to escape. Legs...wouldn't move. She had to kick. Nothing happened.

Ropes wrapped around ankles. Pulled tight.

Arms jerked behind her, shoulders on fire.

Mac home in bed.

And then...nothing.

Chapter 2

Mac didn't go to bed. Those bright headlights were bothering him. He'd learned long ago to trust the tingling in his spine. Someone forgetting to turn off their high beams would surely have noticed when the blinding brightness reflected back at them from Stacy's shiny steel bumper. They'd have been nearly blinded.

Unless the driver had planned to follow a cop…hadn't wanted to be identified.

Still in his truck, he was backing out of his garage, and headed to Stacy's without a second thought.

She'd never have to know.

He'd drive by, see the lights on in her house and go home to bed.

One thing he knew about Stacy, at least the Stacy who'd come out of her husband's tragic death and joined the Saguaro police force, was that she was a creature of habit. She never went right to bed after a shift. She got changed, and then sat up and watched at least one episode of a sitcom.

There'd still be lights on at her house.

He just had to see the lights.

He repeated the words to himself all the way out of town, while he paid attention to every inch of ground he covered.

He just had to see the lights.

There were no lights.

Struck with panic, Mac quickly shut it down as he pulled into Stacy's drive. Grabbed his gun and went around the side of the house. To the back, the other side, and then, gun still in hand, watching his back, he strode toward the keypad outside her garage door.

Punched in the code.

Heard the hum of the garage motor, waited for it to rise enough for him to bend down and see inside.

And had his radio out before he'd straightened up.

"Possible officer in danger," he bit out. "Repeat, possible officer in danger." He quickly rattled off Stacy's address. And his phone rang.

It wasn't Stacy. Declining the call from their lieutenant without picking up, he dialed Stacy instead. The phone rang. Six times. And went to voice mail.

"Stacy, it's Mac. Call me, dammit."

She could be out. Might have had a hot date for the morning. Their sex lives, dating lives, were the one thing they didn't talk about.

What if she'd hooked up with a psycho?

They were going to amend their "no date" talk policy the second they were back together.

Jim Stahl, their lieutenant, was calling in a second time as Mac left his message.

Needing all the hands on deck he could get, Mac picked up.

In and out of consciousness, Stacy twisted her head, pulled her arms as far as she could to the side behind her and glanced at her watch. The lighted digital readout gave her a focal point. Half an hour had passed. She was pretty sure they'd been driving the entire time.

Driving in circles?

There'd been turns.

But not full ones. That she was aware of.

No streetlights at all.

Driving up the mountain was more like it. The crude road known as The Trail—which led from Saguaro Bend to a mining town on the other side of the mountain sixty miles away—was only half a mile from Stacy's property.

Judging by the bumps and the less than stellar condition of the road, they weren't on the newer highway just south of the trail that also went east, to the other side of the Clairvoyant Mountain range.

Keeping her fingers busy, she alternated between working the ropes binding her and pinching herself the only places she could reach. Her butt. Her hips. She had to keep herself awake. Aware.

Active at all times.

And quiet.

Only one door had opened before they'd pulled out of her garage. The car had dipped with the weight of one entry, and the door had immediately slammed shut. One captor.

Her key fob was in her front breast pocket.

Wasn't it?

Rolling, she tried to feel the push of plastic against her breast.

It wasn't there.

Staring at her breast, waiting for another turn, flashes of moon to illuminate her jail, she saw the unbuttoned shirt pocket and her stomach sank.

He'd taken her fob without her knowing. Had touched her breast.

What else was she unaware of?

What other clues had she missed?

And what was he planning to do with her when he reached his destination?

* * *

While he was still on the phone with Jim, relaying what he knew about the bright lights behind Stacy on her way home and the van that she'd nearly hit, Mac let himself into Stacy's house. Went from room to room, smelling her scent, trying not to notice the personal things that they didn't share with each other. Like…all of it.

They were work partners. They knew where each other lived. Knew how to access each other's houses in case of emergency.

But they'd never actually been inside each other's homes.

Her comforter was untouched. Gold and maroon.

She made her bed. There were throw pillows on it.

As he walked through, noting everything he could, he tried her cell again, his jaw tightening as it went straight to voice mail.

Stahl was already having someone put a trace on her number.

The entire place—two spare bedrooms, one set up as an office, both bathrooms, living room, kitchen, dining area—all spotless. Not a single sign that she'd been in it since she left that morning.

Sirens sounded, and he ran outside to meet his work mates. Fourteen out of the twenty Saguaro officers and detectives were either there or arriving—some in uniform, many still in plain clothes—with weapons on. Along with both lieutenants, all three sergeants and Chief Benson. One of their own was in trouble.

The sight relieved him. They'd find her.

And tightened every nerve in his body with fear. All of them there. A fact that indicated that she was in serious trouble.

As he was heading out to the team meeting he knew

would be forthcoming in seconds, Mac stopped, his gut sinking. "Chief," he called, knowing everyone else would follow. He couldn't take his gaze off the indentation in the hard desert earth just to the side of the end of Stacy's drive. "Someone was here and left in a hurry," he said. Tire marks wouldn't show. Someone burning rubber did. "The tire width is too large to be hers," he said, stating the facts he knew.

He'd been with Stacy when she'd bought the new tires on her SUV. He'd picked her up when she'd dropped off her vehicle.

"So are we thinking she was forced to drive her own car someplace?" Stahl asked.

It looked that way. But forced how? And why hadn't she called him?

Unless someone had been in the car with her, holding a gun on her—

"It's too early to know what we're thinking," the chief interrupted Mac's thoughts before they spiraled in a direction that was not going to help. "Let's split up. In twos. I want eight of you on foot, on her land, and surrounding acres as well. The rest get out there. Let's find her and bring her home safe."

Mac didn't have his "two" to jump in the passenger seat of his truck as he ran toward it. No one mentioned the lack. Or offered to drive with him. "Macdonald!" Chief Benson's voice came from not far behind him.

He stopped. If the chief thought he was going to keep Mac back...

"Her phone's not pinging," the older man said, his face looking more concerned than Mac had ever seen it. Which put another rock in Mac's gut. He'd known the man his entire life. Benson was a friend of Mac's father. Had sided with his dad during his parents' rancorous divorce.

"It rang the first time I called it," he said, his voice, his look, urgent. *Do better.* He wanted to bite out the command.

The man nodded. "And pinged off a local tower. Now it's not."

He stopped breathing. Stared. "You think she's close."

"You know her best since Brett was killed. What do you think?"

"I think if she's nearby, she'll be okay." He said the first thing that came to mind. But wasn't sure if he was talking like the respected, decorated cop he was, or just a desperate man trying to reassure himself.

Almost an hour had passed since she'd pulled into her garage. Dawn was breaking fast. She could see rock walls whizzing past.

Wherever he was taking her, it was remote.

Would make it harder for anyone to find her. The Clairvoyant Mountain range encompassed nearly two hundred thousand acres. Had she just dreamed that?

She was drifting in and out.

Anxiety, thank God, had left her.

She had to think.

To plan.

There were flares.

She loved the mountains. Had climbed to the top of the highest peak in the Clairvoyants once. With Brett. Or Mac?

Flares.

Inner sidewall storage. Driver's side. Above back wheel.

Plastic embedded knob to turn.

She was playing tag in the street with the neighbor kids. Brett ran fast. Caught her. She squealed.

He laughed.

Her shoulders screamed with pain. Bumps in the road.

Had to use her foot to turn knob. Get flares.

Couldn't let it show in the rearview mirror.

Shoes up. No good. Use rope.

Sweat. In eyes. Burning.

Couldn't close. Couldn't sleep.

Flares.

Flares.

Rope. Use rope. Angle foot.

Rope hooked. Push.

She didn't have a momma like the other kids. Her momma died. But she had the best daddy.

Your mom and I...we loved each other so much. And that love made you little belle of mine.

The flare. The rope had worked. She could see the flare.

Couldn't she?

Brett, can I see?

Our love was so strong because we grew up together. Knew each other our whole lives. We knew the good and the bad, too. Shared all the important memories. There were no ugly surprises, just more love, every single day.

The toes of her shoes. They had to be grabbers. Like tongs.

She liked that. Toes as tongs.

Alliteration.

And home. Tongs on the stove.

She put her shoes on at home.

Home. Mac.

No, Brett. No Brett.

Blood everywhere. Right in front of her.

No! A whimper? Hers?

Waking her up. Wake up!

The flare.

A plan.

Toes together. More sweat. She got it!

Rolled to her belly, bent her legs back, dropped the flare. Rolled to her side, her back to the flare.

Grabbed it.

Gotcha!

Abigail. Best puppy. Daddy brought her home. Called it gotcha day!

Puppy licks on her nose in the morning.

Wake up!

Flare, be ready. Flare in one hand. Other hand on cap.

The sun was shining through the car's window. Too hot.

She and Brett. Water. The sand. Honeymoon.

Slowing down.

Wake up!

Sleep felt so good.

Bumpity bump bump.

Wake up!

Stopping! Roll on back! Hide flare!

Feet toward hatch. Open.

Kick!

Body slam.

None of it mattered. He was bigger than her. Giant-sized. He took her hits. Overpowered her.

He was pulling her. Her hair caught.

She tried to fight. Was thrown over a shoulder. Hung there.

She might die.

Mac would never forgive himself.

Mac. She unscrewed the cap. Tossed the flare.

Saw a vehicle up ahead. In front of hers. Mountain car. There to rescue her?

Or was she just imagining it? Did she see it with her eyes opened or closed?

Her captor, facing forward, walking…did he know?

He plopped her down.

Oh! She was sitting in her own driver's seat. Was he going to…

With eyes barely able to focus, she tried to assess her dash. Was there enough gas?

His hand brushed her breast.

Oh God, no.

The seat belt came over her chest. Hand at her thigh.

Click. Belt locked in place.

She had to keep her eyes open.

Ropes.

No way to put her hands on the wheel.

Or push the pedals.

Open your eyes! Was that Mac telling her? No, Mac was home. She'd said she was fine.

She wasn't fine.

As she felt the car start to move, Stacy opened her eyes.

Saw the vast openness of space in front of her. Felt like she was floating.

Some part of her vaguely realized that she was going over the side of a mountain.

And pretended Mac was going to catch her.

Just like her daddy had always done when she was little.

Chapter 3

He'd made a mistake. Listening to Stacy's personal need to take care of herself, to protect herself, rather than his own instincts. He was a cop. Her professional partner. Not a personal one.

As Mac ran to his truck, got in and started driving, he prayed to whatever fates might hear him that his own lapse hadn't cost Stacy her life.

Shift fatigue gone with the sunrise, he scoured every inch of roadway between town and Stacy's place, and then past her place. Running cases through his head the entire time with one thought in mind. Who, of all the people they'd taken down, had run-ins with or generally made enemies of, would want Stacy, but not him?

Why just her?

Who would know what shift she was working? And where she lived?

If he could find the kidnapper, assuming there was one, he'd find her. It was basic cop work.

Tuning the police radio in his truck to the private channel the chief had designated, listening to every one of his fellow offercer's reports of places searched and found empty, he grew more and more focused.

Focused like a crazed being with only one goal.

He would not rest, would not stop until she was found.

And if she was hurt, God help whoever had harmed her.

When he'd exhausted the miles around Stacy's acreage, including knocking on doors and getting neighboring property owners out of bed, or talking to the early risers as the case was, he turned to what locals called The Trail. A sometimes one lane, partially paved road over the mountain.

Without any idea of who'd taken her, or why, he had to think like a kidnapper. He'd want all traces of evidence gone forever. Three hundred twelve miles of rugged, desert-covered mountain with cliffs that dropped off more than a mile down sheer rock face to boulders below. The minimal chance of covering all that inaccessible ground made the area a great dumping area for something one didn't want found.

Ever.

And something else was bothering him. Those tire marks at the end of Stacy's driveway. They'd been wide, but that didn't mean high. Maybe it wasn't Bright Lights who'd gotten to her. Maybe, like she'd said, the driver of that vehicle had been lax in turning off his brights. Not a danger to her. She had finely honed cop instincts, too. Her captor could have been someone lying in wait for her to get home. Not on the road, where she, a trained cop, would notice. But an off-road vehicle sitting in the dark in the desert...

Radioing in to have everyone on the lookout for a four-wheeler, he let those who'd been assigned up the mountain know that he was joining them and took the miles up the trail an inch at a time, looking for anything that might speak Stacy to him.

Where am I? Stacy came to with a sense of unreality. As though she'd been transported to a new dimension. One where people lived in clouds made of cotton.

When she tried to move, to ease the burning pain in her shoulders by bringing her hands around, nothing moved. Her muscles were clenching, but nothing more. Bands on her hands. Band on her body.

What universe was she in? Did she need to fight?

Lifting her feet to kick out, she felt her entire world rock precariously. The seat beneath her. The pillow upon which her face had been lying.

And knew she had to rest some more.

No one had found Stacy's SUV. Her clutch purse. Her phone. Anything to give any hint as to where she might be.

An hour into the search for her, then two, Mac was beginning to hope that she was off somewhere on some clandestine date—maybe in Phoenix, in a snazzy hotel room. He'd happily pay out of his own pocket for all the overtime being spent to search for her if he knew she was safe.

She hadn't been in her home. Hadn't changed out of her uniform. There hadn't been a dirty one in the washer or in the laundry basket he'd seen in her bedroom.

Maybe the guy had a thing for women dressed in cop uniforms and she'd gone straight from work, only telling Mac that she was on her way home. That she'd arrived there.

But then, why tell him about Bright Lights?

Or the van she'd nearly hit?

On the radio again, he asked the chief to have someone check vehicle ownership of every one of Stacy's neighbors, looking for a van. Just to be sure that Stacy's near miss had really been just that.

He asked for a check on all local businesses open to the public at six in the morning, too. Surveillance tapes at the grocery store, all gas stations, Rich's...just in case she'd decided, after she'd hung up with him, after she'd reached home, that she wanted something she didn't have.

The granola bars with chocolate on top that she loved.

Or something else with milk chocolate.

It would be just like her to turn around, go back to town and take care of her craving. That was Stacy, self-sufficient and willing to do whatever worked, put forth whatever effort necessary to take care of any issue in front of her. Rather than let it hang there, in the background, unresolved.

But she'd never have gone without her phone.

Or turned off her phone.

It *could* have run out of battery.

But only if the battery was failing. Something she'd have noticed and taken care of immediately.

He also called in a list of names—the ones that were most prominent in his mind—of past cases to look into. Benson and Stahl already had detectives and their two tech people looking into all his and Stacy's cases. Checking them against jail and prison release records.

Looking for any evidence that someone who might have moved out of state had come back.

And they were looking into her credit card usage, too. Had gained access to account information from the office in her home.

She'd hate that.

"Have you notified her father?" he asked the chief on a private channel. Benson and Mac's father had been in high school when Stacy's father was in grade school, but pretty much everyone in town knew the man. An Army Ranger, one who'd made the news for his heroism, had lost his wife, a Waltz, in childbirth—the day Stacy was born. He'd given up his career to stay home and raise his baby girl.

And when Stacy was grown and married, settling down

on her grandfather's property, Adam Sorenson had joined the Peace Corps and had been stationed overseas ever since.

"Not yet," the chief said. That was it, nothing more.

But Mac heard the rest, with lead in his gut. They didn't know if they were giving a missing person report or preparing a death notice.

As he drove, Mac passed parked police vehicles in the various pull-offs along the trail. And he heard reports come in after searches of areas were complete. He wasn't focusing on those areas. He was looking along the parts of the road where most people would not stop. Areas where, if he stopped, no one would be able to pass him. As the morning wore on, there was traffic on the road, making his check points more difficult to maneuver. But he still made them.

Finding absolutely nothing.

Growing tenser by the minute, he wondered if he was in the wrong place. Benson had put a call into the Phoenix police, and they were sending a helicopter up to search the area. An expense, with no evidence that Stacy was even in the vicinity.

Or officially missing.

She'd been gone four hours. An eternity to Mac.

But not even enough to report to the police in normal circumstances. If Stacy was a civilian who simply hadn't returned home as expected, her family would either need evidence of bizarre behavior, or wait another twenty hours before police would even put out a report.

For good reason.

Some people didn't return home on purpose. And couldn't be hunted because of it.

But Stacy wasn't people.

She was a cop who'd arrested two shooters that night alone.

A woman who put her life in danger every single day she went to work.

She was predictable. Dependable. Set in her ways. Not one who'd just disappear without telling someone or keeping her phone on.

She was also his partner.

They had to find her.

Why in the hell am I sleeping sitting up?

Stacy came to, thinking her upper arms and shoulders hurt so badly because she'd fallen asleep in a chair in her living room.

She didn't ever sit in that chair.

Her spot was the right end recliner on the couch.

And her pillow stunk.

Opening her eyes, she was still kind of floating in a sense of 'everything was going to be okay'. Until she noticed that her pillow didn't have a case. That it wasn't a pillow at all.

Her head was resting on an airbag.

Fear shot through her.

She'd been in an accident? Her fault?

Was anyone else hurt?

Raising her head slowly, not sure how badly she was hurt, she felt her SUV rock. Forward and back. Fear shot through her.

And bits of a nightmare surfaced. She'd been in the back of her vehicle. Bound.

She'd hit her head. Had a nightmare.

Was she still having it? Was she asleep dreaming that she was awake?

Pulling her arms, feeling the band cut into her wrists as she did so, she glanced around the airbag to see where she was.

Felt another rock. A bit of a slip with every little movement.
Saw the vast sea of nothingness in front of her.
And started to scream.

Climbing up a steep hill, slowing his truck as the road
veered right to the edge of the mountain, Mac approached
the curve up ahead with caution, not allowing himself to
imagine the terror that could take place in the location. Just
like he'd been doing all morning.

As he scanned the landscape his gut tensed, and he
breathed a sigh of relief as he saw nothing. No sign that
anyone had been out of a vehicle. No sign of a skirmish
or trouble.

But then, if a crime had taken place on the pavement,
how would he know?

A flash of red caught his eye just as he was about to
turn into the curve. A dot of color in a bushel of sagebrush.

He stopped. Put on his flashers. Pulled out his police
bubble and as he quickly exited, put the flashing light on
the top of his truck. Stopping at that point, a one-lane road
around a curve, was ludicrous. Anyone could come bar-
reling around the bend and...

He ran to the color. Two seconds was all he needed.

Probably just a piece of desert flower blown and caught
by the heartier plant...

It wasn't a flower.

It was a flare. The kind Stacy kept in her vehicle.

Reaching in, he pulled out the abandoned warning symbol.

And he knew.

Grew instantly cold.

And analytical.

The cap had been turned, but not far enough. As though someone had tried but couldn't complete the job.

Stacy.

On his radio, he put out the call. He needed another vehicle up on the road as soon as possible. They had to block the curve from both sides, where drivers would have a chance to pull off and stop safely. On one side, they could even turn around.

Backing his truck down, he blocked the road coming up the trail from Saguaro. Heard Miguel, a seasoned officer who had also grown up in Saguaro Bend, say he'd turned around and was five minutes out from blocking on the other side.

Miguel had gone to school with Stacy. One year ahead. He'd attended Stacy and Brett's wedding.

Thoughts surfaced. Facts only.

Nothing else.

Mac walked the area, his entire being a state of rock-hard ice, no feeling, thinking only about his next step as a cop on a case. Down to where Miguel would park.

Tire tracks.

He spotted them right as he heard his fellow officer, accompanied by Martha Mitchell, one of the oldest cops on the force, approach in their cruiser.

Pulled up against the mountainside on the opposite side of the road was a track identical to the one he'd seen in Stacy's yard. Snapping a photo, he opened it in his image and photo compare app, pulled up the one he'd taken early that morning, and confirmed what his gut already knew.

Standing straight, tall, he walked toward the curve, specifically to the place where something would go straight out and over the mile drop-off had it missed the turn.

He heard Miguel and Martha call out to him. Knew they were approaching.

He didn't respond. Just kept walking.

He would be the one. He'd do it.

For her.

Reaching the edge of the mountain drop-off, Mac forced himself to look over.

"Oh God, NOOOOO!" The sound tore out of him. Burned his throat. As, hands to forehead, burying his face in his arms, he dropped to his knees.

Chapter 4

Think, man.

The second his knees hit hard ground, Mac's mind went into high gear. So high up that there was no feeling.

Just numb determination. There was no mistaking Stacy's red SUV.

He had to get to the vehicle.

There was a chance it had gone over empty.

That someone had pushed it off the cliff to make them think that Stacy was gone.

That someone had her for information. Or other things that it didn't behoove him to think about.

That she still needed rescuing.

"It's wedged between two rocks," he heard Miguel say, and turned to see his fellow officer on the radio he wore on his belt.

"Fifty yards down," Mac said. "Sheer rock face." Clarity came as he worked, and he grabbed the radio. "Chief Benson, it's Mac," he said, waiting to hear the man acknowledge that he was on the channel.

"I'm here."

"We need Luke Dennison from Sierra's Web if we're going to save her, sir."

"That hotshot firefighter case we helped on?"

"Yes. He's an expert in mountain rescue. Tell him the vehicle is wedged, but only from just in front of the back tires. A move from the inside, in the wrong direction, will have it rolling down the mountain, front end first."

"I'm making the call now."

Mac handed the radio back to his fellow officer. Felt both of his peers watching him. And didn't make eye contact with either one of them.

"I'm going down," he said.

"Mac! No!" Martha spoke first.

"No way, man, you said it yourself, one tip of that SUV and…"

"I'm not going to touch the vehicle," he gritted out between clenched teeth. "If she's in there. And alive, she needs to know what she's up against. Not to move. To know that we're on it. And just to hold on."

She might not be in the SUV. He wanted to hope that she wasn't.

But why trash her vehicle if, ultimately, she wasn't going to die as well? Why destroy a vehicle if you didn't want people to think the person driving it was dead?

He *knew*.

There was no stopping him.

If there was any chance his partner was alive, he was going to keep her that way.

Or die trying.

Clarity returned slowly. And with it, came a stab of fear.

Feeling groggy—like the time she'd woken up in the dentist's chair after having her wisdom teeth pulled, only worse—Stacy tried to figure out what to do.

She had no phone.

Was afraid to move again. Scared about what could happen if the car rocked another time.

Looking out the windows on either side of her, she saw nothing but a lot of space between her and surrounding mountainside even on the farthest horizon. Same as she'd seen in the brief glimpse out front.

The rearview mirror was her only source of hope. Showing her she had solid rock at her back. Not just air. Keeping her gaze there as much as she could, she took comfort from the airbag she'd purposely left in place. Letting it cushion her chest, as though guarding her spirit, come what may.

And the odd calm came over her again. She was powerless. Had no more control. Whatever was going to happen was going to happen.

Mac wouldn't be missing her until shift time. He'd be heading to bed. Unlike her, when they worked night shifts, he liked to have his off time after work and before bed, getting up to go to work, where she went to bed shortly after shift, and took care of her personal life before heading in to work. His day was from six in the morning until sometime early afternoon. Hers was from early afternoon until nine when she had to get ready for work. Only when they were on night shift.

He came to work freshly showered. Always smelling like pine. She came to work hours after she'd showered, done her hair and makeup. No reason to have a fresh face to take on criminals. And her hair had to be pulled back when she worked.

The thought brought her back to a sense of self. Oh God. Was she going to die? She wasn't ready. Had too much to live for. She had to do something. *Think, woman, think!* Panic flared so sharply she felt dizzy with it.

And then just felt dizzy.

She had to face the fact that she was probably going to die. Her father would be devastated.

Mac would blame himself, though the fault was in no way his. She was the one who'd practically shamed him for being concerned.

And her? She sat there, the same woman she'd been when she'd pulled into her garage. Weirdly calm again. Shouldn't she be seeing angels or something?

Had Brett known, before he went, that it was coming? In that split second before the deadly right hook had caught him in the temple?

She'd have thought there'd be a connection with her deceased husband. Feel him reaching out for her. Coming to get her.

Comforting her at the very least.

All she felt was the hard thump of her heart pounding against her chest, a head that felt twice its size and full of pressure, and—as tears filled her eyes, slowly trickling down her cheeks—a longing for one more look at Mac's face.

He could slide down the rock face. It would be the quickest way. With the least chance of success. He wasn't going to do Stacy any good if he was dead.

To the left, on the driver's side of her vehicle, was a patch of rock and boulders, with some growth interspersed among them. A strip of land not washed smooth through the years—a strip the water didn't stream down when the snow melted.

Sitting on the edge of the cliff, with the two officers at his back—Martha asking him to reconsider, to at least wait until they could get a harness on him—he pushed off with his hands and lowered himself until his foot touched rock.

Steadied. Tested his weight. Finding the rock solid enough to hold him, he let go of the ledge.

"Radio for a harness for me," he called up. No point in being reckless. He could use the help climbing back to the surface. Most particularly if he had something to carry.

Any belongings Stacy might want from her car before it crashed into oblivion.

Unless the SUV was teetering, ready to go over, he wasn't going near it. Luke Dennison was the expert. If there was a chance of getting Stacy out safely, the hotshot firefighter would do it. And if there wasn't a chance—knowing Luke, he'd make one.

As he slowly lowered himself down, Mac kept the SUV in his peripheral vision, focusing on his own safety, and corralling his fears for Stacy's life so he could do his job effectively. He thought about the families Luke had saved from a small mountain town surrounded by fire a while back. Dennison had been the only one who'd been able to get into the town and had managed to have everyone lifted out safely.

Mac took another successful step. Rock to rock, testing every surface before putting any weight on it. Every stone, every boulder, could roll at any second. All he had to do was look down to see how many of them had already met that fate. Signs on the road above warned about falling rock.

As he had the thought, his right foot slid out from underneath him. Almost like he'd fated it to happen. He heard the rain of stones plunging down the hill even as he wrapped his arms around a boulder and held on.

"Come on, man," Miguel's voice called from above. "Wait for help."

He couldn't wait. If Stacy was hurt, on the brink of death... he had to be there. To let her know that help was coming.

To let her know she wasn't alone.

How he was going to get her attention if she was lying in the back of her vehicle, maybe even unconscious, was what he needed to be thinking about.

Not death.

Assuming she was even in the car. The hope that she wasn't presented again.

And if she wasn't down there, he was wasting time not finding out where she was.

It was possible that whoever had kidnapped her was still in the car with her. That the SUV over the cliff had been the result of traveling too fast to get away and missing the turn.

It was the tire tracks up above—like the ones in her yard—that told him otherwise. There'd been a getaway vehicle.

He slid again. Scraped his entire left forearm. Saw the raw skin, the bits of blood. Couldn't care less.

His gut knew what he was facing.

That SUV wedged on two boulders had not been the intent. Stacy was supposed to have hurtled, in her vehicle, more than a mile down to crash against the dry rock bed of what used to be a creek. Or maybe even a river, centuries before.

Someone had wanted her death assured.

But to have it look like an accident.

He had to save her first.

And to that end, started calling her name with every forward movement he made.

If she moved, the SUV was going to tumble down the mountain.

If she didn't, she'd starve to death. If she didn't die of dehydration, first.

She had a choice. Go quickly.

Or take it slow.

She could yell until she had no voice. No one would hear her.

And she didn't want to rock the unsteady vehicle.

Which meant she'd made her choice.

The last one available to her.

She wasn't going to go quickly.

Laying her head back against the headrest, she closed her eyes. Accepted that she was powerless to move, but that didn't mean she had to give up.

Or waste her last hours.

She could spend them reliving every good moment she'd had. Remembering all the good stuff.

With no earthly barriers left, no years ahead to protect, she could go imagining what it would be like to have sex with Jesse Macdonald.

Over and over and over again.

She could, so she did. And got so good at it, she even started to hear his voice, calling her name out every time they climaxed together.

He'd made it down as far as he could. A good ten yards to the left of the back of the vehicle, which was where he'd figured Stacy to be. Had radioed up that he was fine. Had heard back that Dennison was on his way. As were a couple of rescue helicopters.

As soon as Dennison got Stacy out of the vehicle, they'd be able to get her safely extracted from the mountain range and winging off to full medical care.

The plan was working.

If she was in the vehicle.

Made the most sense. Tie her up. Shove the car over the cliff.

Hands cupping his mouth, he'd given every ounce of himself into his repeated calls. "Stacy!"

Just her name. His voice.

Over and over.

"Stacy!" he called again, same urgency in his tone, uncaring of the rawness in his throat. He'd been hollering to her for more than half an hour.

There'd been no answer. He'd expected that. He just needed her to hear him. And to pay attention. It had to be enough to keep her hanging on.

So he stood there. Aching in every part of his being. Calling out to her.

And continued to do so, somewhat to keep his heart out of his throat, after Luke Dennison arrived, rappelled down, assessed and started calling up orders.

Stopping only when the man made his way over to Mac.

Because fear constricted his airway. He didn't want to know.

Wasn't ready to let go.

He had to keep hanging on to her.

"She's in there," the man said straight off. "Front seat."

Mac nodded. Appreciating the other man's no-nonsense approach. Luke had a reputation for being a man of few pleasantries. He was all about getting the job done.

Which was all Mac needed from him.

Front seat.

Whoever had taken her wanted it to look like an accident.

Or worse, a suicide.

"Airbag deployed."

And it hit him. "If she's still in the seat, she was belted."

"Right. Boulders holding her are solid, but the SUV is only slightly caught up."

Meaning it could go with any breeze. *Would* go soon. Mac had already figured that much. He nodded.

Was she breathing?

He didn't ask. It couldn't matter at the moment. They had to get her out of there before the vehicle went over.

"She's head back, eyes closed."

Jaw tight, swallowing with difficulty, he nodded again.

"I didn't detect blood."

Good. Good news. He kept staring at the SUV, was thankful for the sun glinting off the metal, even as he considered heat exhaustion.

January temperatures wouldn't reach more than seventy, but in a dark car, with no air, and Arizona sun, it could still happen.

They'd have her out before then.

One way or the other.

Dennison continued to talk to him in staccato bits and pieces, his eye on the scene in front of them at all times. The expert was waiting on equipment and manpower. He'd sent for members of his hotshot team. The plan was for a group of them to rappel down and do what they could to stabilize the SUV before lowering a claw to attach to the roof to pull the vehicle up and out.

Then suddenly, while they both watched, the red vehicle started to move. A forward slip. Just an inch or so, but Mac held his breath.

Steady. Steady. Steady.

Dennison rechecked the clasp on his harness. "I'm going over."

"I'm coming with you. You shore up one side, the other could give way." It didn't take an expert to see that much.

Pulling a second harness out of his backpack, Dennison tossed it to him, told him to put it on, while he unhitched a second rope coming down the mountain from his anchor system, separated it from his own and handed it to Mac.

"You ever rappel before?"

"A couple of times."

The man didn't look pleased. Mac didn't much care.

Following orders explicitly, he made it to the back left bumper of the vehicle, refusing to allow himself to glance toward the front. Seeing Stacy, in any form, would be a distraction he couldn't afford.

He continued to move as he was told, hold, lift, pull, settle, as he and Dennison got the SUV tires braced as well as they could until his team arrived.

After that, Mac stayed back, ready if his help was needed, but out of the way so that the trained professionals could do their jobs as quickly and efficiently as possible.

Jacks were produced, locked into the mountainside, and then up to the SUV, to steady it. And finally, after an agonizing hour, Dennison faced the mountain, his feet braced, leaned back into his harness and opened the car door.

Long seconds later, Mac heard, "She's alive."

And, staring at that open driver's door, swallowed as his eyes filled.

Chapter 5

Mac wasn't there.

"Stacy, can you hear me?" She heard the voice again but wasn't ready to answer. To open her eyes. She didn't want the dream to end.

"Officer Waltz."

She opened her eyes. Saw the concerned vivid blue eyes, short sandy blond hair and shoulders of an uber fit man leaning over her. "Luke Dennison?" Her throat hurt as she spoke. She couldn't cough.

The movement would kill her.

But why had the hotshot fireman she and Mac had helped the previous year suddenly appeared in her dreams?

She'd been happier hearing Mac's voice.

She blinked. And jerked upright. Or would have if not for the hand holding her upper chest gently in place. "We don't know what kind of injuries you've sustained," the man said.

"We?" Moving just her eyes, she glanced around her. Noticed harnessed bodies around the parts of her SUV she could see. "I'm being rescued?"

She couldn't comprehend…couldn't believe…until she heard the loud whirring of a helicopter moving closer and closer. A sound she recognized from car accident evacuations. Critical shooting victims. It was a care flight.

"I'm being rescued," she said then, tears filling her eyes. "Oh my God, I'm being rescued."

But Mac wasn't there.

He'd just been in her dreams.

Mac waited until the stretcher carrying Stacy was loaded into the helicopter. He heard it whirring away before getting himself back up the mountainside.

He had work to do.

"Make sure someone's there to meet the copter," speaking into his radio, he bit the words out. He paused, hanging off the mountainside, as another thought occurred to him. "Someone wants her dead. She needs round-the-clock protection."

"Chief's already on it, Mac." Martha's voice came over the radio. Followed by a chorus of others weaving in, one after another, congratulating him, as he finished the climb.

As though he'd had much of anything to do with the rescue.

He had been the one to find her, though.

He'd followed his gut and he'd found her.

Time to follow his gut and find her intended killer.

Several officers, most of them off duty, were at the top, waiting for him. Reaching to give him, and members of Dennison's team, a hand up.

He felt the pats on his back, heard the voices, but only had one real thought on his mind. Find the fiend, or fiends, and take them down.

He ended up at the closest hospital to Saguaro because the chief had insisted getting him checked out before he'd be cleared for duty.

And once there, he couldn't step away until he'd seen Stacy.

Just had to get a glimpse at the machines she'd be hooked up to, check out the steady heart rate, and be on his way.

Except that when he asked to see her and was shown into a cubicle much like the one he'd just come out of, she wasn't hooked up to any machines.

She was sitting up on the gurney, dressed in her uniform, minus the ponytail and gear, her phone in hand.

"Mac!" Was that joy he heard in her voice? He couldn't go there. He knew that. But deep down, he was glad.

"Way to go, Stace," he told her, assessing every inch of her, concentrating on the face that he'd grown to read better than his own. "Ruin a good night's sleep for me, why don't you?"

She grinned, the expression a little off. "Guess I shouldn't rub it in, then, that I managed to squeeze in a few hours."

She'd been drugged. He'd been filled in. Midazolam. It induced sleep. Lessened anxiety. And inhibited the ability to create new memories when one was fully under.

Also mild enough to be used in a dentist chair. And on animals.

A killer with a conscience?

He wanted to deliver a smart-ass remark and head out. When he looked at her, sitting there alone—as she'd been during the hours she'd been hanging on the brink of death— he just…kept looking.

"I heard that you were the one who found me, who asked for Luke Dennison to be called in," she said then.

He cocked his head. "Yeah, well, I knew you'd never let me live it down if I didn't."

Had she heard that he'd gone hoarse calling out to her, too? During the seemingly unending time he'd stood there, helpless, watching her teeter on the verge of death on those boulders? He didn't ask.

She didn't say, either.

"Yeah, well, I'm never going to let you live it down if you don't speak to the chief for me," she said. "He's telling me I have to take a mandatory week."

Mac had been hoping for longer than that. "Might not be a bad idea…"

She shook her head, and though those big brown eyes pierced him with the stare that criminals got when they were on the wrong side of the barrel of her gun, Mac stood his ground.

"Someone wants you dead, Stace. Until we know who… we can't let him get a second chance."

Chin raised, she slid off the gurney, came toward him. "Physically, I'm fine Mac. A little groggy still, but clear-headed in thought. My hands and ankles sting a bit from where I pulled at the ropes around them, and I've got some bruising around my rib cage from the airbag, but otherwise, I'm not hurt." She'd stopped moving. Was a few inches away, her face gazing up into his. "And who better to help you get him, but me?"

The challenge came through clearly. They'd long been deemed the partnership most likely to succeed. Which was why they were on call to police departments all over the state. It was why they'd been asked to help investigate when Luke Dennison had been left for dead in an arson case in the desert.

"I'm the one with the most details," she said then, not backing down an inch. "And while my memory of the incident is a bit sketchy, due to the drugs, you know as well as I do that as we get further into this, things could come back to me. Critical things that I might not otherwise ever remember."

She was good. One of the best. No argument there. And

she'd been at the scene of the crime. The entire time the kidnapping had taken place.

"I'm not going into hiding, Mac. I've already made up my mind on that one. It wouldn't be emotionally or mentally healthy for me to do so."

He nodded then. Not in agreement with any plan she'd come up with. But in acknowledgment of the truth in her words. Stacy didn't run. She fought. It was part of what made her who she was.

"He thinks you're dead. You're safe as long as he continues believing that."

"And you have a much more difficult time finding him without me. Which means, what, I stay in hiding for... ever?" She glared at him. "Right now, what do you have that's actually going to lead you to him?"

Tire marks, someone who hadn't wanted her to suffer unduly, a four-wheeler, a large male suspect from what he'd been told from her initial report...

"A large man with access to an off-road vehicle who likely has the capability to feel emotion, since he could have hurt you, made you suffer, and didn't. Maybe he thought sending you over the mountain would end things quickly without a lot of pain. And he's someone with some kind of connection to you."

"You've just described over half of the adult males in Saguaro Bend, and God knows how many everywhere else. With all the cases we've solved, the list gets longer. And if he's satisfied, goes away, we never find him. Like I just asked, you thinking I'd stay in hiding forever? Or even the months it could take to find him? We need him to know I'm alive, Mac. We have to draw this guy out."

He listened to every word. It was how they worked. Bounced thoughts of the case against each other. Pretty much every thought they had. As long as they were pertaining to the case.

And before he could think about what he was saying, he gave her the solution that made sense to him. "You're never alone," he told her. "My preference would be that I stay with you." They'd shared space before, with adjoining rooms. Several times. Out of town, working cases. "If I can clear it with the chief that we're assigned to this one twenty-four seven—and that's a big if—then we stay at your place, or mine, and if I have to be away, someone else is with you, period."

She was nodding and he held up his hand. "If at any time, for any reason, you fail to abide by this, I'm going straight to the chief and having you removed from the case. From the entire department if that's what it takes. I'll have your badge and gun stripped…"

With his reputation, he could probably do it. "At the very least, you and I never work together again," he said.

"You done?" she asked him, reaching for her clutch. Putting her phone inside it. Both things that had been retrieved from her SUV when they'd brought it up.

The vehicle was being processed. If they got exceedingly lucky, there'd be a fingerprint. A hair follicle. Something.

Stacy had said her abductor wore gloves, and she couldn't remember him having hair…

"I need more than a nod, Stacy."

With her clutch under her arm, she folded her hands in front of him, drawing his attention to the welts on her wrists, and looked up at him.

The welts almost made him take back his offer. The look in those eyes kept his mouth shut.

"I fully agree to your stipulations and more than that, I

thank you for them. For your concern on my behalf. And for working with me to catch this guy."

Her words were so different from what he'd expected, from anything she'd ever said to him before, that Mac stood there speechless as Stacy preceded him out of the room.

"Oh, and I think my place is best." Stacy continued talking to Mac as they walked through the emergency room out to the waiting area where she'd been told several officers, including their lieutenant, were waiting to see that she was fine. "That way he'll be sure to know I'm alive."

Thinking of being in her garage again made her shudder inside. But, as her grandfather had taught her, when you fell off a horse, you got right back on. She flashed back to her four-year-old self crying, not hurt just scared, being lifted back up on the new pony she'd slid off. She'd ended up riding rodeo in high school. Would still own a horse if she had the time to care for it.

She'd inherited her little home—and the bigger house as well as all the acreage—from her grandfather, her mother's dad. Bore his name, too, since her mother kept it when she married. Had spent many, many happy hours visiting with the man when she was growing up.

And had happy times on the property with Brett, too—both growing up and after they were married.

No way she was allowing some jerk to rob her of that joy. Of her home…

"Let me get the chief's approval and subsequent input first, before we start honing the plan," Mac was saying as they pushed through the doors—and conversation between them was halted by the crowd of cheering officers welcoming her back to the fold.

Which pleased her, but not as much as Mac's hand at

her back, his standing by her, and his reminder to everyone that she hadn't been to bed in nearly twenty-four hours.

The crowd of dark blue parted to allow her and Mac to
duck out to the waiting police van.

As of that moment, no one was supposed to know she
was alive.

The officers had all been waiting in a private room by
a back exit. No one else but the hospital staff who'd cared
for her knew she was there.

That was going to change, whether Chief Benson approved or not.

She'd waited at the hospital long enough for the effects
of the sedative to wear off. As long as anyone would wait
after coming out of surgery. She'd already talked to a mental health professional and would do so again. She'd suffered an incredible trauma. She wasn't ignoring that.

She just wasn't giving in to it. She wasn't going to let it
beat her. Or define her.

She was going to take it on, deal with it and continue
living life, albeit with a new appreciation for every minute, every day, she had.

Inside the van, strapped in a seat in the back with Mac
where there were no windows, Stacy started to sweat. She'd
been trapped in long enough. Unbuckled herself. Stood up.

And…maybe she was going to have some anxiety to
work through.

"Stacy!" Mac's call was little more than a whisper, but
she sat back down immediately. Buckled herself in.

And swarmed with a different kind of warmth. That
voice. Saying her name. It had been in her dreams there at
the end. Inappropriate and completely out of the blue—ha
ha, literally—in her sexy dreams about her work partner,

he'd been out of his work blues. Those dreams. They'd saved her sanity.

And now she had to wipe them out as if they'd never been.

"The chief arranged for us to have a cabin out on Westdale ranch for the night," Mac was saying, as though she hadn't just exhibited signs of being somewhat off the wall. "He's having toiletries and some clothes brought in for you. Mind you, he's still under the assumption that we're keeping you dead."

"So why are you going to be there?" she asked him, still reeling from the mental sexual replay with a man who'd run a dozen miles if he knew what she was imagining. Forcing herself to picture, instead, the popular tourist dude ranch half an hour from Saguaro.

"Because I was first on the scene," Mac said, "which means that, until I'm not, I'm the officer in charge and I have questions for you."

Right. Because, "It's not like you have any more conflicts of interest than anyone else on the force." And it wasn't like she didn't have her own very personal association with the case. Conflict of interest just didn't carry weight in light of getting the work done.

It was just that…she had to get them, in her mind, back on the professional ground that helped make them one of the best cop teams in the state. Had to make sure that he wasn't there because he'd been personally upset by her abduction, like she'd been personally comforted by thoughts of him throughout it.

Jesse Macdonald was just a cop on a case.

A case she'd be working with him. As his partner. Nothing else. They were after a killer. Not protecting a victim.

Regardless of what anyone else thought.

* * *

Saguaro PD was a small police force. Mac used that fact when he went to bat for his partner, set on getting her the positive response to her request that she needed.

He didn't kid himself, though. He needed the response just as badly.

"She's not going to stay in hiding, sir. You can fire her, but you can't cage her up." He didn't mention how clearly Stacy had made that point—her not being caged—in the van an hour before, when beads of sweat had appeared on her upper lip and she'd thrown off her seat belt.

"As long as you are in full agreement with this," the chief said, referring to Stacy's plan that Mac had just outlined for him, "you have my approval. Like you, I know full well she's going to be out there working on this anyway. She deserves our protection while she's doing so. And the two of you are who'd I'd call in if it was anyone else among us."

He'd been prepared for a battle when he'd met the chief on the lawn outside the cabin he and Stacy and Martha would be sharing for the night. Martha hadn't arrived yet— she was home sleeping so she'd be ready to take night duty while he and Stacy slept—and Mac was eager to get inside to Stacy.

Maybe because he needed time with them together more than she did. Something he was taking note of, keeping firmly to himself, and would deal with accordingly.

"Because this was such a blatant, destructive act against one of our own, I'm using private funds that the department has been given over the years for the benefit of the Saguaro PD, to hire Sierra's Web to assist with the investigation," Benson was saying. "Their tech and science experts will get you answers far more quickly than we'll be able to do here. Use them as much as you need."

Mac nodded. Feeling the load on his chest lighten some. "I appreciate that, sir," he said, itching to make his first call to them immediately. Some things couldn't wait until morning. Couldn't wait for sleep.

"You know they recommended, on the Dennison case, that Luke and the woman in danger with him go into hiding," Chief Benson said, with a raised brow.

"Yes, and I also know that they both agreed to do so." Stacy wasn't going to agree. "And in the end—"

Benson's nod cut him off. "I know."

Being in hiding hadn't been the best thing on the Dennison case, after all.

"She's in danger. We know that now," he said. "We can take measures to protect against it, while we go get this guy." He believed every word.

And hoped to all the fates that be that he wasn't going to be made to regret the decision to go with Stacy on this one.

She was alive. But it was only by a miracle of SUV meeting rock that she'd been saved the first time. Round two didn't sound at all palatable.

He just knew, without doubt, that he couldn't let her go fight her demons on her own.

Chapter 6

Stacy would have preferred her own stretch jeans and soft sweaters to the jeans and sweatshirt that came from the donated stash at the department, but she wasn't ungrateful for all the ways people were bending over backward to help her. She just desperately needed to regain her sense of self.

The unfamiliar clothes, along with the cabin and twin bed in a room much smaller than her own, just made her feel further away from achieving that goal.

She and Mac had agreed to stay up until a normal day shift bedtime—eleven for both of them—in order to get themselves back on track to hit the ground running in the morning. Or rather, Mac had said he was going to do so, encouraging Stacy to head to bed early—at which time she'd reminded him that she'd had some sleep during the ensuing hours after the abduction. He had not.

He'd made sloppy joes for her, and she'd almost teared up as she'd come out of the shower to find them on the table.

"I didn't know you knew how to make these," she said, pulling out her chair. Rich's diner made them. And she ordered them every time they went in together. Because anytime she and Mac were dining together, they were either on shift, or coming off one.

They didn't eat together otherwise. Work partners. Nothing else. The lines had been very clearly drawn, without words, from day one, by both of them.

"I learned to cook for myself when I was in elementary school," he told her, taking a seat perpendicular from her.

That was news. Taking a bite of her sandwich, finding it, amazingly, even better than Rich's, she said, "Your mother taught you?" The idea was interesting to her, especially since she'd been raised by a single dad and ate out a lot.

"*I* taught me," he told her. "My parents were going through an unfriendly divorce. Both of them had other love interests, and I found it more peaceful just to fend for myself. I'd offer, they'd be grateful, and it worked out all the way around."

He didn't sound bitter. Or even resentful. More like he was pleased he'd found a solution to a problem.

Stacy wanted him to know that he'd deserved so much more. But kept her mouth shut around the delicious food in it.

She was too busy searching for the woman she'd been on shift the night before. The one who'd known his parents were divorced—kind of a general piece of information since they each lived with their new spouses and had grown kids in town—but hadn't known that it had been an ugly one. Or that Mac had been caught in the middle of it.

Kind of explained why he didn't do Christmas morning with any of them, though. She'd always thought, when she'd upped herself for the shift every single year and he'd put himself on with her, that he'd just been feeling sorry for her. She'd explained that with her father overseas full-time, and then Brett dying, working on the holiday had just seemed logical to her. Leaving those with families to be with them. She hadn't wanted, or needed, pity.

Turned out he'd just been doing what she had. Being logical.

And to that point, "I didn't see the guy's face," she said. It was in her initial report. He'd have read it. But when they shared a meal on shift, they talked about work.

"What can you tell me about him?"

Also in the report, but she understood his question. Welcomed it. Something new could emerge. Most particularly with how comfortable she was talking to Mac.

"He wore cowboy boots," she told him. "At least an eleven. Brown. Worn. Nothing fancy, but not cheap. Real leather."

One glance had given her that? Mac had turned on his phone's recorder. Didn't seem to doubt her testimony. And thinking about her garage floor early that morning... "They were the same brand my grandfather used to wear. There's an engraved symbol on the toe."

She named the brand. Mac, holding up a hand, tapped his phone and lifted it to his ear. "Hudson? I've got a brand of cowboy boot." He relayed the information, hung up, and that's when he told her that Sierra's Web was on the case.

"That was Hudson Warner?" she asked, having heard the name a lot during the Dennison case.

At Mac's nod, she had to physically prevent herself from tearing up again. The department was going all out for her. Mac believed in her enough to be sitting there, risking his life, and bothering a partner in an elite, nationally renowned firm of experts, after hours.

What day was it?

Tuesday. They'd come off a Monday night shift Tuesday morning. Middle of January.

She didn't like that she'd had to think about it.

And wondered again about the cowboy boots. Was she

remembering right? Or had she only transposed her grandfather's boots on that same floor to the kidnappers?

Like she'd imagined Mac's voice calling her name during lovemaking?

Shaking her head, Stacy took another bite of the sandwich Mac had made. Wondering what else she didn't know about him.

Telling herself she didn't want to know.

But fearing that, deep inside, maybe she did.

She knew her captor was white. She'd seen a bit of wrist when he'd belted her into the driver's seat of her vehicle before pushing the SUV off the cliff.

"And there was a four-wheeler." Mac froze when he heard Stacy's words. Dinner had come and gone. Dishes done. And they were still sitting at the table, awaiting Martha's arrival before they turned in. He'd asked Stacy to close her eyes and just start talking. Any thoughts she'd had, pertinent to catching the would-be killer or not, could lead him to a clue that would.

But… "Have you read the case file?" he asked, his tone harsh, even to his own ears. "I apologize," he said before she had a chance to reply. "You weren't supposed to read the file until I finished interviewing you, and this isn't going to work if I can't trust you to follow the set protocol. You got what you wanted here…" He stopped when he saw what looked like real fear flit across Stacy's face.

"What?" he asked.

"You don't trust me?" The emotion in her tone…he'd have thought he'd been an unfaithful husband, hearing accusations from his wife. Or what he imagined it would be like, had he ever been married, or been unfaithful. The latter would never happen. He'd leave first. And the former wasn't an option he gave himself.

None of which had any bearing at all on Stacy's reaction.

He gave himself time to choose his response carefully. Then opened his mouth and heard the heartfelt truth come out. "Of course I trust you, Stace. I also know that you were abducted this morning and spent hours suspended over certain death with little to no hope of survival. No one could blame you, *I* don't blame you, if you're a little off. To the contrary, I'd worry if you weren't. But at the same time, your life is clearly in the balance here. We managed to get lucky once. I'm not relying on luck a second time."

Her gaze never left his. When he finished, those big brown eyes had cleared, and she nodded. "Fair enough."

She bit her lip. Straightened her shoulders. And he prepared himself to hear that she'd gone behind his back, understanding, just as he'd told her, that she wasn't herself.

"And to answer your question, no, of course I didn't look at the file. I'm struggling a bit here with finding my emotional equilibrium, but my brain is in full working order. I'm not eager to ever have a repeat of this morning. For myself. You. Or anyone else, for that matter."

Sitting forward, blood racing, he asked, "You saw a four-wheeler?"

"Yes, why?" Her frown comforted him. She really didn't know. He pushed back against the second of shame that hit him for doubting her, not once, but twice.

"Because I saw a tire track at the end of your driveway that indicated an off-road vehicle. And I found another track up on the mountain, just yards ahead of where your SUV went off."

"Did you run the images through your photo compare app?"

It wasn't an official departmental tool, but the two of them both believed in it because it had proven them right on several occasions. "Yes," he told her. "And they matched. But the tires could have been on any number of vehicles…"

"…and off-road vehicles are so prevalent in the area," she said, finishing his statement.

He waited for more. When nothing came, he said, "Close your eyes and just talk to me, Stace."

She nodded again. "Sorry, I'd forgotten about the four-wheeler, but now that I remember it, I'm trying to think if I know anyone who might own one like it."

Yes. Mac smiled. That was his partner. Jumping ahead to get the job done.

It was good to have her back.

And even better to know that they were still clicking.

By the time Martha arrived, and Stacy headed to bed, Stacy and Mac had made a list of items and winged them over to Hudson Warner's team. Techies would be working through the night to find out whatever they could about owners or renters of gray four-wheelers with extended chassis that had full windshields and black removable tops. The team was also running cowboy boot searches. Sierra's Web had also been given all surveillance camera coverage available to Saguaro PD, as well as a list of the cases Stacy and Mac had handled over the past five years, with emphasis on any situations where Stacy had made the actual arrests. Saguaro PD had already determined which of those cases corresponded with early jail releases and had been on the street since dinnertime, tracking down every single released inmate. So far, all they'd found had verifiable alibis.

It was a weeding out process to lead them to the one guy they couldn't find. Or who couldn't produce an alibi.

"It could all be over by morning," Mac said as Martha went outside to familiarize herself with the perimeter of their cabin—one of twenty set in a semicircle around a multiacre desert park area.

Stacy turned at her doorway, hardly thinking of the case. Instead, the sight of Mac's shoulders, so strong and real, distracted her, sending her tired mind back to noncase-related images from earlier that day. Ones that seemed so real to her she wanted to tell him about them.

Wanted to say, *I heard your voice saying my name.*

But knew she never could. If Mac knew she'd had sexual fantasies about him during her brush with death, they'd never be able to work together again.

Her job gave her life value and purpose. Her partnership with the eight years older cop made her happy.

"Get some rest," Mac said when she just stood there, not responding to his hopeful comment.

With a nod she went into her room, shut the door and stood there. It could all be over by morning in a bad way, too. Her killer could find her. Get the job done second time around. And she'd never know what it felt like, in real life, to be held by Jesse Macdonald.

Did she want to die that way?

Not knowing?

No! She couldn't think like that. Erotic thoughts involving Mac had never happened before that day, before she'd been perched on the verge of death. They were a result of the kidnapping. And she couldn't let that man, whoever he was, get away with stealing her from herself.

A killer had already robbed her of one life, the one she'd built with Brett. And while marriage to her husband hadn't turned out to be the paradise she'd thought it would be, she'd been happy enough. Content and secure. Ready to start a family and raise her children in Saguaro.

But then, she had no way of knowing if paradise even existed. Her father had spun such wonderful stories about the love he'd shared with her mother. Making love songs seem real. He'd certainly remembered himself deeply in love. To the point of never dating again after her mother died. He'd had his love, he'd always said, when she'd encouraged him to find companionship. No one was going to ever be to him what her mother had been. Not only did he not want to settle for second best, he'd never do that to another woman—never ask a woman to live as second best.

Stacy got ready for bed, slipping out to use the cabin's one bathroom, and then back to her room without even glancing in the direction of Mac's door. She saw a light on in the living area down the hall. And Martha's shadow as the veteran officer sat on the couch. But wouldn't let herself even check to see if a light still shone under Mac's door.

Whether the man was in there in the dark, was lying in bed, maybe without pants and shirt, was none of her business.

And she'd damn well make sure that she didn't make it her business. By thinking about Brett.

Lying in bed, she closed her eyes and forcibly ran through memories of her husband, one after another. The time Brett had hit a home run in the multicity baseball league he'd competed in. He'd been fourteen at the time and after touching his foot to home plate had run over to the stands to kiss her.

She'd been bowled over by the romantic move. As had everyone around them. It had been their first kiss. Her first kiss, ever. And she'd never looked at another boy after that. Not even after they'd started sleeping together and she never again felt the spark she'd felt that first day. She'd figured people overestimated the ecstasy of physical copulation. It was nice. Just nothing that reminded her of fireworks. Or mind-numbing pleasure.

And yet, in her moment of facing death, she was flying to the stars in a sexual dream? Involving a man she'd never even been on a date with? A man she'd never considered in a sexual way, at least, not consciously?

It must be the drug she'd been injected with. Nothing else made sense.

So thinking, she turned over, told herself to sleep.

And started thinking about the case, instead. Because it was a normal thing for her, because it felt good to be normal, she allowed the thoughts. Soon found them mingling with others she'd had that evening and sat straight up in bed.

Texting Mac, she asked him if he was still awake.

His response came immediately. Followed by a phone call.

"I have a suspect," she told him as soon as she connected to the call. "I can't believe I didn't think of it sooner…"

"Hold on…" Mac's voice came over the line, and then from outside her door, too. She heard the knock. Scrambled for the shirt she'd pulled off, to get her bra off, before lying down. Pulled it back on. "Come in," she said, sitting up in bed, the covers up over her breasts.

Since he'd had no time to dress, she had the answer to her earlier wondering about what he'd be wearing in bed in the room right next door to her that night. Jeans.

With the zipper closed, but the top button undone. And a tank style T-shirt. Thin. Ribbed.

She blinked. Told herself she hadn't been staring. And, too late, saw Mac's glance at the only chair in her room.

Where he might have taken a seat if not for the telling pair of jeans thrown across the arms.

"Just give me a name," he said, standing in the open doorway. Martha appeared then, gun out, surveying the room.

"We're good," Mac told the woman as Stacy hastened to say, "Landon Manning."

Both the other officers stared at her and then at each other and she blurted, "It fits." But she understood their skepticism. Even as she wondered how long it would be before the people in her world quit doubting her. She'd never given any of them any cause not to trust her. To the contrary, she worked hard to maintain that trust.

And now some fiend, in the space of a morning, had somehow lost it for her?

"The *rodeo* star?" Martha asked incredulously, standing in the doorway as Mac came farther into her room.

She nodded, suddenly dry mouthed, wishing so badly she had on those jeans taking up the one chair, not only so Mac would sit and quit towering over her, but also so she could get out of bed and take the conversation into the other room. Stacy realized she had every right to do just that. "Can we take this up out there?" she asked, pointing toward the door.

And seconds later was staring at her closed door. It was going to come out. Not even Chief Benson knew. She'd made a bargain with a killer, and she was about to break it.

But he'd broken it, first.

By coming after her.

Problem was, she hadn't made the deal for him. For him, she'd have turned it down. She'd made it for herself. Because she needed to come home and live a normal life.

Which she'd done.

Until that morning when the monster had come back into her life to ruin it a second time.

Pulling on her jeans, Stacy made one promise to herself. When they found the guy, she was going to do everything in her power to make certain that he never got his life back again.

Chapter 7

Mac was breathing again—out in the living room. Seeing Stacy in that bed…with those jeans where they were…on top of having almost lost her that day…he clearly needed some sleep.

And maybe a date, too. It had been a while, before the holidays, since he'd been out with anyone.

"You have any idea what she's talking about?" Martha asked, sitting in the room's only armchair. Leaving either end of the couch for him and Stacy.

"I do not," he said. Succinctly. He was not going to talk about his partner behind her back. Even if the concern he was reading in Martha's eyes mirrored some of his own thoughts.

He'd known it was too early for Stacy to be back at work. But in her defense, had he been in her position, physically unharmed, he'd have been just as adamant about finding whoever had tried to kill him. Department sanctioned or not.

Before Martha could say anything else, Stacy appeared, her hair pulled back into a ponytail instead of cascading down around her shoulders and over the covers as they'd been moments before.

An image he feared he'd be trying to forget for a long while.

There was a reason he and Stacy never saw each other outside of work, never even met for a meal on days off, or over holidays. As partners who faced life and death situations at work, they couldn't afford to be anything but 100 percent on the job. Couldn't allow anything to interfere with the determination to get the bad guy.

"I'm going to ask you both to consider, strongly, keeping what I'm about to say to yourselves." His heart sank further as Stacy started in. Drama was not her way. Ever. She wasn't meeting his gaze. Or even looking in his direction at all.

She always looked him in the eye when she was talking to him. He wanted to stop her—had they been alone he probably would have. But with Martha there, he knew he had to let the scene play out.

"You both know, I'm assuming, that Brett rode rodeo for a living." She glanced at him at that, then at Martha, gaining nods from both of them. And then just sat there. She rubbed at her wrist, and Mac couldn't look away. Hated the welts there.

Hated what the abduction was doing to her.

"He died riding." Martha's soft tone broke the tense silence. "At a rodeo in Colorado."

"No." Mac's gaze shot straight to Stacy's face when she uttered the word. He was shocked to find her staring right at him. She'd told him herself. Brett Bennet had been thrown from a bull, suffered blunt force trauma to the head. He was pretty sure the news had been in the local paper.

"Brett was killed behind a barn at that rodeo, breaking up an alcohol induced fight between a man and his wife. The woman had been talking to Brett about something—I suspect it was the way her husband was abusing her, but I have no proof of that. The man had seen the two of them together behind the barn and assumed the worst. He pulled them apart, though they weren't even touching, slapped his wife, and Brett intervened, to pull the guy off from her. I came around the corner in time to see the slap…and to see the guy throw the right hook that killed my husband."

She held his gaze the entire time. Showed no emotion. As if caught in the middle of some horror flick, Mac couldn't look away. Couldn't believe what he was hearing. Couldn't speak.

"I don't get it." Martha's tone was still soft. Caring.

Because she thought Stacy was remembering incorrectly? Mac knew better. Stacy was there. Just…changed.

And maybe, still under some effect from the drugs she'd been given? Was remembering something she'd dreamed?

"Why would everyone think that Brett died in the ring?"

"Because that's what I told my father, and what he told the local paper." She was looking straight at Mac again. As though trying to tell him something. If so, he wasn't getting it.

Any of it.

"Why would you lie to your father? If what you say is true, your husband died a hero. He grew up in this town. I know his folks were gone by then, but there are others here who've known him all his life, friends…they deserve to know the truth."

Sucking her lower lip—a move Mac recognized as meaning she was holding back emotion—Stacy nodded, and said, "I actually went to my in-laws' graves when I returned to town," she said. "I told them the truth."

As well as Mac could recall, Brett Bennet had been an only child, born to a man in his fifties and a woman in her late forties. The couple had been killed in a small plane accident shortly after Brett and Stacy were married.

He'd looked up the article about their deaths when he'd first heard that Stacy was being assigned to him in her second year as an officer, after her training and start with the Phoenix PD. A guy had to know who he was dealing with.

Yet there he was, five years into the partnership, finding out he hadn't known her at all?

"Why would you lie?" Martha asked, not seeming as appalled as Mac was.

No way the past five years had been a lie. Or did he need to get her to the hospital? They'd gotten the drug wrong. She was suffering aftereffects of a hallucinogen.

But when Stacy glanced down again, her chin to her chest, he had a flash of the first time she'd told him about her husband's death. They'd just finished telling a young wife her husband had died and Stacy had told the woman she'd been there and understood. She'd given the woman her card. Had told her to call, anytime day or night, if she needed help.

In their squad car afterward, he'd asked about Brett's death. It had seemed the human thing to do. And, her chin to her chest, she'd told him about the bull ride gone tragic.

She hadn't been looking him in the eye then.

But she was at that moment. Staring at him hard.

And he got it. She needed him to pay attention. To listen. To know. To trust their partnership.

"Landon Manning is the man who killed Brett."

Mac heard Martha's gasp even as a strange calm came over him. He waited.

"No way! The man just returned to the circuit six months ago after thinking he'd never get to ride again. That groin injury almost ruined his career."

"I wouldn't say almost." Stacy's tone was the same one Mac had heard her use when she knew a confession was imminent. She rattled off facts. "He's not winning. Not even coming close. He's too old. The riders are all younger than he is. Have been training full time for years. While he hasn't even been on a horse in more than five years."

Out of the corner of his eye, Mac saw Martha sit back in her chair. "Tell us," he said, and then added, "And I'll do everything I can to see that this goes no further than it needs to go."

He glanced at Martha and saw her nod.

Taking a noticeable deep breath, Stacy held his gaze steadily and started pouring out words as though she'd rehearsed them. "I held Manning, pinning him to the ground with his hands behind his back until police got to the scene. Everyone, including me, were frantic about Brett. He'd only been hit once, should have been fine. I'd expected him to roll over and get up and come after Manning again. Anyway, by the time anyone was questioned, Manning had had a good five minutes with his wife, holding her, talking quietly to her. Everyone just thought it was a simple fight between overcharged rodeo guys. Mrs. Manning testified that Brett had picked the fight. That Manning was only defending himself. I didn't know that, of course, and in my separate interview I said what I saw. In detail. Detectives went back to check Manning's wife for signs of his abuse, and while they did find it, including a fresh bruise right where I'd seen him slap her, she claimed that she'd fallen. I couldn't let it go. Wasn't going to let it go. Brett was dead for trying to save a woman from abuse. Detectives found a few more people to testify that they'd witnessed Manning get angry when he drank. Manning tested above the legal limit. Brett had only had one beer. It was still going to be a 'he said, she said' thing, but detectives determined they had enough to at least press charges. And when, the next day, the prosecutor's office agreed, Manning's attorney came forth with a proposed plea agreement. We'd all been under gag order until that point, because of the investigation still being open, and Manning being who he was. The agreement was that Manning would plead guilty to drunken disturbance, prosecutors would ask for a light sentence and Manning would go into counseling. We were looking at second degree murder at best. Maybe even manslaughter. And since so much of the evidence was either circumstantial or 'he said, she said,' we could have lost in court. The one caveat to the agreement was that the details of Brett's death had to be sealed. Manning didn't want to lose his reputation, and the future earnings it could bring him. I think that's why Manning didn't chance going to trial and winning. The details of Brett's death would have been all over the papers, and Manning's reputation would have died right along with my husband. So the story was drunk and disorderly charges with mitigators due to the fact that Brett died of blunt force trauma from a fall that was pursuant to the argument in the charges. And the judge, who had the right to impose a lengthier sentence than the plea agreement suggested, sentenced Manning to fifteen years in prison."

Her voice broke then. Maybe with a small hint of leftover victory, but not much. It had only been six or seven years. Manning had been back on the circuit, failing but there, for six months.

"Fast forward to today," Mac said then, pulling her out of the telling and back to the life she'd built. The one she thought this Manning guy was trying to steal from her.

She shook her head, shrugged. "Manning got out on a technicality. Something about the way the plea agreement was presented. He's lost his touch. Can't ride well enough to even place. And because he was egotistical enough to try, he's lost his reputation after all. If he'd just come out, gone with the groin injury story that hit the papers, retired, he still could have made a ton of money. Even if the criminal charges hit the papers, along with his prison term, a lot of his fans would have understood, explaining it away as a one-time thing due to frustration from the injury. At his heyday, he was the best of the best."

"He's lost everything, and you think he blames you," Martha said then, sounding completely cop-like.

Stacy looked at Mac. "Look and see what brand cowboy boots he wears. Look at the emblem on them."

He didn't have to look. He'd already placed it. They were Mannings. Named for Landon's father, who'd been a rodeo star before him.

"I can't believe I didn't get it this morning," she said then. "Or figure it out before now…"

"You were drugged." Martha's words, filled with anger now, said a lot.

But not enough. Not nearly enough.

Enough wouldn't happen until Landon Manning was back behind bars.

Mac got on the phone with Sierra's Web, and then, getting Heath Benson out of bed, Mac put an APB out on the fallen rodeo rider.

And strongly resisted his sudden urge to hug his partner.

Stacy was up and dressed in the uncomfortable clothes by six, undeterred by the blackness outside. She'd slept on and off, and the rest of the time had lain in bed fighting demons of one kind or another. Reliving her kidnapping and near death the day before. Looking for clues she might have missed. And trying to reason herself out of any sexual awareness she might have imagined for her partner as she sat at death's door.

Concocting the fantasy, she totally understood. Though she'd have thought she'd have imagined Brett in the male role. But having a body experiencing actual physical reactions now that she was back in her life—that was not cool. Or in any way acceptable.

Moving quietly, she tiptoed out to wave to Martha, who was sitting in the chair reading, and then went back down the hall to the bathroom.

A disposable razor and travel-sized can of shaving cream, and toothbrush and paste sat in one corner of the vanity. She'd carried her small toiletry bag in with her. Decided to wait until she got home to shower, not to get naked in a shower Mac could be using, and then, smelling bacon, headed out to help Martha with breakfast. Only to find that Mac was already there, fully dressed in police uniform, frying eggs.

"I've checked the perimeter, and the vehicles left for us outside," he said as he dished up plates of food. "As soon as we're done here, we can head out."

She should have put on her uniform—death stench or not.

Ignoring the sight of her partner in the kitchen, she sat across from Martha and ate. Was glad to have the other officer there. Made it like sitting in the break room at work. Except for Mac's cooking. The uniform helped put her back on track, though.

And once there, she intended to stay put. No more nonsense. She and Mac were going to be residing in the same place until her would be killer was caught. If the fates were on her side, it would be yet that day. And if not, she had to be able to stay on the job and off fantasies concocted on a death bed.

She could do it.

Her life was at stake. What better incentive could there be?

The thought straightened her backbone right up. A call to her father, as their little caravan drove away from the dude ranch, put the starch back in it. He'd been insisting on flying home until she told him that by the time he got a flight out and arrived home, they'd have her potential killer behind bars. And if not, no point in giving the kidnapper more chance to hurt her by kidnapping her father, too. She wanted him safely across the world until the danger was contained.

Martha and Mac both accompanied her home long enough for her to get a shower and into uniform. And to let anyone who might be watching her place see life there. With Mac patrolling outside and Martha in the house, she allowed herself to enjoy the warm water. Was actually starting to relax. And suddenly smelled a gaseous, rotten egg scent coming up in force from the drain.

Partially dried, dressed and out in the front room in less than a minute, she had her shoes, socks and gun in hand and already packed go-duffel with the rest of her gear over her shoulder, as she ordered Martha out of the house, telling her what was going on as they ran.

"Go!" she hollered to Mac outside, heading toward his truck. "I smelled gas." She told him what she'd relayed to Martha. The veteran officer was already in her patrol car, radioing for a bomb squad and Sierra Web's hazardous material response team.

Stacy didn't realize, until she was dripping all over Mac's front seat, that her hair was sopping wet. And other than what the water might be doing to his leather interior, she didn't much care.

"Did you get the soap out?" he asked, as she opened the window and tried to wring out the long strands, leaving them in the forty-degree winds to try to dry.

"Yeah. And I'm thinking that whatever he put in my pipes was backup in case he didn't get me in the garage," she continued, her mind racing. "I'm assuming the perimeter was all clear?"

"It was." Mac's expression flattened, as it generally did when focused deeply. His gaze was broad, taking in the road in front of him, the mirror views, and out the side windows, too, as he did when they were on patrol. The familiarity settled her. A lot.

"I hope the house doesn't explode." All her stuff...every piece of memorabilia from thirty years of life...

"At least you aren't in it." Mac's response, typically unemotional, came right back at her. Grounding her more.

"There's no reason for the guy to have gone to my house after pushing me over the side of a mountain," she said. "That has to have been from before."

"I agree, but I still want to check it out as soon as we get the all clear."

She nodded. In complete agreement. Tamping down her immediate need to buy a load of boxes to pack up all her stuff and hide it where no one would ever find it.

Or her.

Chapter 8

Stacy wasn't going to let her abductor get to her. He would not rob her of her mental and emotional stability.

"I just got off the phone with Hudson Warner before you and Martha ran out," Mac said, speeding down the two-lane road that led out of open desert land. "Manning isn't at his place in Colorado. His wife hasn't seen or heard from him since day before yesterday. Claims that he said he needed some solitude and time to think. That he's planning to retire from the rodeo. She also said that he dried out in prison and hasn't had so much as a sip of beer since he got out. She begged the investigator to just leave them alone."

Her gut tightened. "Do you believe that?"

He glanced at her. "You didn't say anything about smelling alcohol on your abductor's breath."

She shook her head. "He never spoke. For all I know, he never opened his mouth at all, but he didn't reek."

The stiff set of Mac's jaw told her he was worried. Which strengthened her resolve to stay focused and get the job done. She'd insisted she was capable of working the case. He'd given her the chance. She wasn't going to let him—or herself—down.

"His phone is off," her partner continued as he headed toward town. "Benson already got a warrant for a trace on

his credit cards and bank accounts. Sierra's Web is tracking surveillance cameras, and his internet accounts. We'll
find the murderer, Stace, but we have to keep you safe until
we do."

She frowned, tensing. "Why would he still be on the
run if he thinks I'm dead? And who was driving the four-
wheeler that followed us up the trail to drive him back
down?" The only theory that made sense.

"His wife says he's been spending time with the younger
brother of a guy he met in prison. Says the guy helped
him out on the inside and now he's trying to give the kid
a hand up whenever he can. Guy's name is Troy Duncan.
He's twenty-two and currently employed at a horse farm
north of Denver…"

"Let me guess, he didn't show up for work yesterday."

"And probably won't be there today, either," Mac told
her. Turning onto Main Street. "You all right with stopping
in at the station?" he asked, per usual.

He never just drove them someplace without actively
obtaining her consent. Something she'd taken for granted
until right then. And didn't like that she felt grateful for
the consideration all of a sudden. "Yeah," she said slowly.
Then, to save herself from further emotional turmoil that
served no good purpose, jumped right back to the conversation that gave her a sense of control. "If I'm clearly dead,
why are they on the run?" she asked.

The questions she and Mac asked each other provided
answers. Every time. It was who they were. What they did.

"Could have had a falling out," he said, pulling up in
front of the station, rather than heading to the officer parking lot around back.

"Or want to lay low until the dust settles," she offered,
opening the door, looking all around, with her hand on her

gun, before she left the protection of the metal frame. "He has to know that an officer gone missing, even if it's made to look like I might have just chucked it all and taken off on my own, is going to cause a fuss."

Mac was out of the vehicle, his body shielding her from the road, before she'd made it to the sidewalk. "He'd likely realize that we'd be watching your bank accounts to make sure you were okay."

"It's way too coincidental that he'd suddenly tell his wife he needed solitude to make a major life decision at the exact time I'm abducted and sent to my death." She had to say the words, to keep thinking them, to take away their power. She'd faced death.

And she'd survived.

She was not a victim. She was a survivor.

"Excuse me, Stacy?" The female voice behind them triggered instant response. Mac spun, ramming his backside against hers, as they both pulled their guns.

"Um, sorry, Officer Macdonald, I just… Stacy?"

Recognizing the voice, slowing down enough to let her brain process, Stacy dropped her gun to her side and turned around to stand beside Mac. "Kaylee," she addressed the city clerk, a woman three years younger than her that she'd tutored in history during high school. "I'm sorry, we're just…"

"I know, I heard," the pretty redhead said, her smile as sweet as always. "That's why I'm here, actually. I saw you guys pull up." She motioned toward the three-story brick building across the street that housed city offices. "I was going to come over this morning, anyway," she continued. "I thought maybe you should know that someone accessed your property records last week."

"Who?" Mac's response was gunshot sharp.

Kaylee shook her head. "That's just it. I have no idea. It wasn't current records. I was helping in the assessor's office, and I noticed a light on in the public records room. It houses everything that isn't digitized. When I went to turn off the light, I saw this paper on the floor. It was an old tax notice for your address. I opened the drawer where the file should be…"

"…and it was gone?" Mac interrupted, clearly needing the woman to get to the point at a more rapid pace.

Sending him a glance, Stacy looked back at Kaylee as the clerk frowned. "No, it was right where it was supposed to be. But I could tell that it had been gone through pretty thoroughly. Nothing was in the order in which we file it. I would have said something, but it's not all that unusual to have someone looking at old records. Especially during snowbird season when the gold panners are here. And, you know, they're public, so…"

"Surveillance tapes," Mac said. "Are there cameras in the room?"

"No." Kaylee almost seemed afraid of Mac, which wasn't at all uncommon when the man was on a hunt, but it struck Stacy differently that morning. More deeply. Not to have someone afraid of him, but to have him so fiercely ready to protect and serve.

It was the first time he'd been protecting her.

"As far as I know, they're only on the first floor," Kaylee was saying. "And only at the public entrance area where everyone goes through the metal detector."

"We need those tapes," Mac said. Kaylee nodded, as though she could reach in her purse and produce them on the spot. "I'll send someone over," he said then, his face softening. "And…thank you. You might have just helped us get Stacy's would-be killer off the streets."

Kaylee smiled, nodded, seemed a bit shy all of a sudden, and for the first time since she'd been partnered with Mac, Stacy felt superfluous standing there next to him.

Was Kaylee flirting with Mac? He was eleven years older than her. Not that age mattered so much, but...the clerk *was* his type. Pretty and with a soft spirit that gave the sense that she needed protection. The only kind of woman Mac ever dated.

Which left Stacy completely out in the cold in that arena.

And that was exactly where she wanted to be.

So why on earth would she be feeling jealous of her younger classmate of more than a decade ago?

He should never have come on so strongly with the city clerk. Mac tried to make amends as best he could with the younger woman but chafed at his uncharacteristic behavior. If she'd been a suspect, then, hell yes, he'd go at her. But someone who was only trying to help?

He needed to reel it in.

And maybe admit to himself that almost losing Stacy— seeing her in that car teetering on boulders that were going to let go with a good wind—had taken a toll on him. More than any other officer-down incident he'd encountered during his eighteen-year career.

Benson had designated the largest conference room in the building the Waltz case room, and Mac and Stacy set up there for the rest of the morning. They'd been through every case they'd handled together that coincided with a recent jail release. Had agreed on a couple of names for Sierra's Web to pay particular attention to.

Midmorning, they got word that her SUV had turned up nothing. Stacy's prints were the only ones present. The only hair they'd found had been hers. Both on the driver's seat and in the back.

Mac watched Stacy's face as the chief told her that the vehicle was totaled. She'd nodded. Hadn't flinched. But he knew how much she'd liked that vehicle. It had been the first one she'd purchased, on her own, with cash.

"Looks like we're going vehicle shopping, huh?" he asked, just to try to ease the pain she wouldn't show.

And was rewarded with a surprised smile sent in his direction as she said, "When this is over, you're on."

He'd been no part of the earlier purchase. Had no reason to be a part of the next one. And no acceptable explanation to himself as to why he'd offered.

The fact that she'd accepted didn't sit well, either.

What in the hell were they doing?

Shortly after that, Hudson Warner called in his morning report. While midazolam could be purchased at any drugstore with a prescription—and anyone could have easily used a portion of their own or someone else's prescription—it was also commonly used by veterinarians and others treating animals. That didn't even consider any illegal markets. Many prescription medications in the US were also legally available without prescriptions just over the border in Mexico and legally brought into the States after purchase. The firm wasn't going to give up on tracing down the substance used to drug Stacy. They were also looking at syringe purchases. It just wasn't going to be a quick task.

Hudson's team had found a couple of social media accounts that appeared to belong to Manning, in addition to the rodeo star's official accounts. One included a tirade against police and the entire legal system, stating that they ruin lives without ever considering circumstances. Ending with a statement that it had to change. It was posted after Manning's first rodeo humiliation coming out of prison.

Nothing had been posted since, but they were keeping an eye on both accounts, and still looking for others. That, too, could take days or even weeks, considering not only the plethora of internet social sites, but all the sites on the dark web.

Landon Manning's credit cards and bank accounts had still not been accessed.

Troy Duncan, the younger man Manning had been looking out for, didn't have credit in his name. Only a bank account with a small balance, set up with an address that led to a local grocery store. The account also hadn't been accessed.

After the Sierra's Web investigator had talked to Manning's wife, she'd headed to talk to the owner of horse farm where Duncan worked. The young man was a hard worker. Loved horses. Got paid in cash.

And had never before missed a day of work. No one knew where he lived. A couple of guys on the ranch thought he was renting a place. A few others thought he stayed with a friend but didn't know who. Duncan didn't own a vehicle. No one seemed to know for sure how he got to and from work.

A fact that brought dread to Mac's gut. They were looking for a somewhat famous man…and a ghost.

Hudson told him their investigator was looking for friends and associates of Wendall Duncan, Troy's older brother and Manning's eventual cellmate and friend, thinking they'd be looking out for the little brother, just as Manning had been doing.

Lots of leads, no arrests. Mac saw Stacy's shoulders droop as the call ended, and he felt her disappointment as though it was his own. Was reaching out a hand to squeeze her shoulder, when she stood and started pacing around the table. "I need to be out there, Mac, looking for this guy. Not sitting around waiting while everyone else does the work. I took him down before. I can do it again."

She had the best of the best working for her. And he didn't doubt her, either.

He also heard the desperation in her voice. "As soon as we hear that we're clear to head back to your place, we need to go over every inch of the property. You're the only one who will know if anything has been disturbed." He'd already told her he'd intended to do so. Had been picturing her safely in the house, but when he talked to her cop to cop, he knew that having her along made sense.

Just as her standing up to prevent him touching her did. Not that he was at all sure she'd stood when she had on purpose, or that she'd seen his hand coming toward her. But the messages were clear. Warnings being sent to him, by his psyche or some weird twist of fate, that they were on shaky ground at the moment, coming off from her near death.

They couldn't let a few moments out of time rattle who they were or the great work they did together.

"It sounds like Manning could be out for revenge, just as you thought. He lost years of his life, and potentially his career because a judge gave him a harsher sentence then he'd expected when he pled guilty." He told her what he'd been thinking. All strengthened by Hudson's report. "He might also be on a drinking binge, in spite of what his wife thinks. Unfortunately, as we've seen more than once, the wife is sometimes the last to know. He could also be on whatever substance he gave you, or something else entirely. He had a drinking problem. The addiction could have turned into some other substance during his time in prison."

"Both of which make him unpredictable," Stacy said, rejoining him at the table. "And more apt to make a mistake. Which is all the more reason to get me out there, Mac. To put me in his face, so to speak. We don't want him going into hiding."

"It also makes him that much more dangerous." The words came out. He knew she didn't need his reminder.

"That's right, it does," she said, meeting his gaze full on for the first time in a while. "We have to be smart about this, use backup everywhere we can, but if anyone can get this guy, it's you and me."

Meeting her eyes, seeing the strength in their depths, and the truth, Mac nodded.

And felt gutted, too.

She was just his work life.

But work was pretty much all he had.

What he was best at.

She knew that.

Was counting on him to help her bring this one home.

And, remembering how he'd felt, standing on that mountain, watching her vehicle rock and being unable to save her, he wasn't positive he could.

The one thing he was sure about, though, was that if he lost her on the job, he'd never forgive himself.

Stacy was energized by Mac's agreement to let her get out and show herself. To have her back, to be right by her side as she did so. It was risky.

But so was going to work every single day. They'd faced two shooters head-on the other night. Their work wasn't a walk in the park.

What bothered her was the strange look on his face. Like he'd just seen a dog get hit by a car or something. While

Mac wouldn't get a dog for himself, no matter how many times she'd told him he should, the man had a way with animals like no one else she'd ever known. He was sensitive to their pain in a way that touched her. He handled dead bodies with professionalism. The time they'd walked in on an illegal dogfighting ring at the end of a night of fighting, he'd had to turn around and walk out.

He'd made the arrest. But he'd called for another team to clear away the bodies.

"Property records in Arizona are public record," she said then, reminding herself that her job was to focus solely on the case. To work for her freedom from imminent personal danger. "In this county everything is on the internet. You just go to the assessor's office, click on parcel search and type in a name." Pulling the laptop they'd been using all morning toward her, she typed, clicked and typed, and turned the screen to him.

Her property address, acreage and tax information were all right there.

"So Manning does the current search, finds your address. Why risk coming to town, entering a public building, and getting caught looking at the records?"

She'd been wondering about that on and off all morning. "Because the property has two homes on it," she said. "Before my mom died having me, she and dad lived in what is considered the main house. It's a quarter mile down the road, around the curve. I actually go to that box to collect my mail—though anything of importance comes electronically now..." She stood again. Circled the table, feeding off her own energy, glad to have it back. "When my mom and dad got engaged, my grandfather had them move into the main house and built the house I'm living in now. Technically, it's a guesthouse on the property, not the single-family residence. He had the garage added later. After my mother died, Grandpa and Dad and I stayed in the house. Some of my dad's things are still there, though he moved into his parents' place in town when they passed. I didn't find out until my grandfather died that he'd willed the entire property to me." She stopped. Threw him a grin. "I live in my own guesthouse."

Mac didn't seem to find any humor in the statement. His gaze was sharp again. "We need to get to that main house. He might have hit that earlier, found it vacant..." He held her gaze. "He went to the city records office to physically look you up, to see any other properties that might come up..."

"He looks up property, finds out that it's more than the main house..."

Stacy sat back down. "And finds me."

"We need to get out to the house you don't live in."

They were no closer to finding Manning's current whereabouts. But they were doing their jobs. Putting pieces into place.

To find a killer.

Together.

Chapter 9

Being in the station, surrounded by memories of her own personal strength, working, Stacy felt more and more like herself as the morning wore on.

She and Mac were going to bounce back. They'd be just fine.

Or so she thought, until she came back from the restroom to see him out in a far corner of the squad room, speaking with the sheriff of Canal County.

The man who'd offered Jesse Macdonald a well-deserved, much higher paying position within the sheriff's department.

She'd forgotten all about the conversation they'd had just before she was kidnapped. They'd been on the phone after shift. Martha had told her just before they'd gone on shift that night that she'd heard Mac had been offered the position. She'd thought he'd told Stacy. That Stacy would know whether he was planning to take the job.

The phone conversation on the way home that night... she'd been distracted by the bright headlights in her mirror. And then the van she'd almost hit.

But... Mac had never said he wasn't leaving the Saguaro Police Department.

She'd asked.

And he'd turned the conversation on her. Asking her if *she* was ready to move on. As in, take on a new partnership. A younger officer she could help bring up.

Just like Mac had with her.

She remembered making it quite clear she'd let him know when she was ready. Thinking to herself that it would be never.

Had he been hoping for a different response?

Wanting her to be at a turning point because he was?

Taking one last glance at the two men conversing quietly in the corner, Stacy went back to the conference room in which she'd spent her morning. Stood in front of the whiteboard where most of the pertinent information was listed so that anyone working on aspects of the case could see where they were at.

She studied details as though Stacy Waltz was just a citizen she was serving.

If Mac wasn't planning to take the position the sheriff's office had put forth, or if he wasn't at least interested in discussing the possibility, he'd have sent an email. She knew from previous offers.

Instead, he was in conversation with the man who could potentially be his new boss.

Which was no business of hers unless he wanted to make it so. Not until she came to work one day to find herself partnered with someone else…

The idea had never been a pleasant one. But it was always a possibility. It wasn't like police partners were under any legally binding partnership. They didn't have to go through a divorce to separate. They just…moved on.

Those had been his words to her the other night.

He'd wanted to know if she was ready to move on.

Dread filled her, and a quiet fear that didn't strike out at her so much as it permeated her mood. Taking her down at a time when she was struggling to get up.

"Stace!" The sound of Mac's voice, saying her name in that urgent tone, rent through her, and for a second she wasn't sure if she was back in her dream or if he'd just come in the room. Until her eyes shot toward the door and saw the serious look on his face. "The sheriff just gave me an update on your place," he told her, grabbing his keys and holding out her clutch.

"Your address is Saguaro Bend, but the property is outside city limits. The sheriff's office insisted on being involved," he said as he led the way out of the station, forgoing his truck for their patrol car.

She'd liked being in his personal vehicle.

So the patrol car was definitely best.

She wasn't asking what the sheriff found. Wasn't sure she was ready to know how she might have died had she not been kidnappable two nights before.

She took a deep breath and thought about the fact that Mac had a legitimate reason to have been in conversation with the sheriff. But that didn't rule out job talk. Especially since whatever they had to say about the case, should have been said to her at the same time. Stacy mentally pulled on a pair of big girl panties and set her mind to work.

"Tell me," she said, as soon as they were buckled in and Mac had called their destination coordinates over the radio.

"Punctured canisters of methane had been dropped inside your septic tank," he told her. Natural gas had no odor. But when being produced for commercial distribution, something was added to produce a rotten egg smell, so consumers could be alerted to a leak.

"He knew how to kill me in a very insidious, and yet

painless, way. But he didn't know about the rotten egg smell?"

"Methane produces naturally in septic tanks. If you didn't get it cleaned out regularly, you'd end up with the smell anyway. I'm guessing he was banking on you thinking you needed the tank emptied."

"I just had it done a few months ago." But there was no way a man in Colorado would know that.

"There was enough gas being emitted to kill you overnight," Mac said. She appreciated his candor. Looked over at him, and so badly wanted to ask if he was taking the job with the sheriff's office but knew she couldn't.

She'd brought it up once. He'd prevaricated. If he wanted her to know, he'd tell her.

And as his work partner, she had to accept his right to handle things how he saw fit. She'd be fine. If not him, she'd be given another partner.

It was all part of the job, she reminded herself for what seemed the umpteenth time in the past fifteen minutes.

Maybe because she didn't want to think about going to sleep in her home, feeling safe and secure, only to never wake up again.

"Going to the cabin last night saved my life," she said then. "Good call."

"The tank has been emptied," Mac said, ignoring her praise, at least verbally. "Your house is being aerated. And yes—" he glanced her direction "—if you'd gone home last night, it would have been like someone who'd turned on a gas stove to commit suicide. You'd have probably started to feel slightly drunk. Might have worried what was happening to you as you drifted off to sleep."

She'd already seen that vision. Didn't need to dwell there anymore. "What's with this guy?" she asked then, filled with fear and frustration and a resurging sense of power-lessness that she absolutely abhorred. She was not a weak person. "He wants me dead, but doesn't want me in mas-sive physical pain first? He should do his research. A well-aimed gunshot would be the least fearful way…"

Even as she said the words, she knew. "He wants me to suffer emotionally," she said the words aloud. "He's inflict-ing mental anguish at the time of my death, just like he's suffering now at the death of his career."

"And probably as he suffered during the years he saw his rodeo life wasting away in prison." Mac's words came softly. But they were there.

Telling her that he was doing exactly as she'd asked. Treating her as he would on any other case. Any thoughts left unsaid could prevent them from finding the whole truth.

And without that, even if they were on the right path, they could be ambushed.

Or, after the arrest, the perpetrator could end up get-ting off.

Without a conviction, an arrest meant nothing.

"I'm assuming they checked the main house?" she asked Mac as he turned out of town toward the desert. "For gas, and other toxic materials, yes. I asked that they leave the physical inspection to us. I didn't want anything moved by one of our team until you had a chance to see if anything looked at all different from the way you remembered it."

As they'd discussed. He was doing just what he'd said he'd do. Because that was Mac. He might be leaving the Saguaro PD, but he was still Mac.

Exactly who he'd always been to her.

As long as he was her partner, she could trust him with her life, just as he could trust her.

And nothing else was on their table.

* * *

Mac parked in the drive of the house Stacy had grown up in, recognizing the home he'd passed hundreds of times. He'd just never known it was part of the same property on which she currently lived.

Five years they'd been together, and he'd never known that. The fact didn't bother him. They didn't share personal stuff unless it was pertinent to a job. But it felt odd, not knowing that she owned so much property. Or that she chose to live in a small home on the other side of that property, rather than in the one she'd shared with her father and, he was assuming, her husband.

"I was just here a few days ago," Stacy said, as they slowly made it through the mostly empty rooms of the sturdy two-story home. "I come in and flush toilets and run water in all the faucets at least once a month," she continued.

And he got another glimpse he'd never seen. A woman keeping up two homes, on several acres of desert property, all on her own. He wasn't surprised that Stacy could do it. Not in the least.

Just…the woman was changing before his eyes. Becoming more than he'd ever known before. That, on top of having just spent hours expecting to see her fall to her death, was messing with him. Making him want to grab her up, hold on and never let go.

He didn't ask, when they reached the upstairs, which of the empty bedrooms had been hers growing up. Or confirm whether she and her husband had shared what was clearly the master. The stuccoed home was old, yet had all the amenities, including a bath off the largest bedroom. Another bath between the other two bedrooms upstairs. And a full bath downstairs, as well as a fourth bedroom.

He didn't speak at all, needing her fully focused on every

inch of the interior of that home. Looking for any sign that someone had been there after her.

She opened every door and cupboard, checked corners, windowsills and behind every curtain, with him following right behind her.

Back in the living room, she turned to him. "Nothing's been tampered with," she said. "Even the dust bunnies are exactly as I noticed them when I was here. I made a mental note to get over here and clean…"

The two and a half car attached garage was completely empty. Swept clean. As impressive in its own way as the house.

And he just had to ask, "Why don't you live here?"

As soon as the question was out, the cop in him wanted to suck it back in. And slowly had to acknowledge that the man did not.

"After Brett died, it just didn't make sense for me to be wandering in all this space alone all the time…"

The words made perfect sense. And left a lot unsaid. Things he wanted to draw out of her.

But didn't. Couldn't.

"I keep thinking I'll rent it out," she answered one of his unspoken questions. "You know, next summer, or next fall, or next year." With a shrug she added, "Maybe I'll get on it as soon as we catch Manning."

Because she'd looked death in the eye and didn't want to keep putting off getting on with her life?

She was only thirty. Had lots of time to meet someone else, fall in love again, fill her big house with family. He didn't tell her so.

It wasn't his place.

Even if a part of him wanted it to be.

The greater part knew better.

* * *

Stacy was glad to be out of the big house. Every time she was over there, she struggled with the dreams she'd lost. All she'd wanted, growing up, was to find love as her parents had. To be with someone she'd known her whole life, who shared memories and values with her, so that they could be best friends and then forever partners, raising children in the house that had seemed so lonely her entire life.

First her grandfather, widowed young, living there alone as he'd raised Stacy's mother. And then her father, with her. She'd had such high hopes when she'd married Brett. Even after the sex hadn't turned out to be all that remarkable, and her heart had never lusted after him, she'd loved him. He'd truly been her best friend. And would have made a wonderful father...

"Stacy!" She heard her name called before she saw the older man heading up the front walk toward them as she locked up. "I saw ya over here and just wanted to say how glad I am that you're okay."

She'd known the tall man in jeans, a plaid flannel shirt, boots and cowboy hat her entire life.

"I'm fine, Tom, thank you," she said, trying not to sound as impatient as she felt. The last thing she needed at the moment was to have to smile and be polite. To be...normal.

Except in her relationship with Mac.

She wanted to feel in control like her normal self, but until her killer was found, her life was insular. Nothing mattered, not even neighborliness, until the man was caught.

"I couldn't believe it when I went into Rich's last night and heard what had happened..."

They'd wanted the word to get out that she'd survived. Confirmation that it had done so was welcome.

Introducing the neighboring miner to Mac, she continued slowly toward their car in the drive. Not so fast that she was turning her back on her visitor. He could walk along with them if he chose. She just hoped he wouldn't.

Which meant, of course, that he did.

"I…um…" He bit his lip. Not something she'd ever seen him do before. Or look the least bit unsure of himself. Which had her stopping in her tracks.

"What's up, Tom? Is everything okay with you and Mary?" The man's wife had been ill in the fall, but last Stacy had known she'd completely recovered.

"Mary's gone to stay with her sister for a while," Tom said. "She's fine, though. I came over to apologize to ya," he said then, glancing down, and meeting her gaze, his own eyes somewhat shaded by the wide brim of the hat she'd hardly seen him without. "The other night, I'd been in at the bar. Had my one beer and was headin' home…was on the phone with Mary, tryin' to get her to come home, and wasn't watchin' my speed. I came up on you a little too close, forgot I had my brights on and…"

"That was you?" she asked, feeling Mac stiffen and then relax beside her.

"Yeah." The man looked at Mac then. "My wife's not happy with my choice to continue workin'. Her illness last fall, she says it was a warnin' that it was time to get out and live life. She wants to travel. To cruise and spend time on the world's beaches like we always said we'd do. Problem is, I'm a miner. I run a business. It's all I've ever been or wanted to do. We went to the beach over the holiday and I 'bout lost my mind with nothin' to do and so much needin' doin' here. Still, I told her I'd give her one week every quarter, but it wasn't enough for her." Tom included Stacy in his glance as he said, "Anyway, after I heard what happened, and there I was, had to be just minutes beforehand, coming home myself. I probably scared ya, afraid I distracted ya. When I should have been noticin' whoever was out here, waitin' for ya."

Feeling oddly comforted, Stacy reached out to squeeze the older man's arm. "It's okay, Tom. As you can see, I'm fine."

Tom frowned then. "You got any idea who did this?" he asked. "Makes me kinda glad Mary's gone for now. And nervous, too, you know?" He looked back to Mac as he finished.

Like Stacy couldn't possibly know or understand. Tom was of the old regime, her father had always told her. Didn't mean Stacy had to like his chauvinistic way of talking "man to man" when she was standing right there, perfectly capable of understanding just as well as Mac did. Maybe even better, since she knew Tom and Mary.

"We have a lead," she told the man. Not just for his sake. Tom was a talker. And she should have cleared the move with Mac first.

Tom's eager nod showed his relief. "He from around here?"

"We don't think so." She answered quickly. If Manning got word they were on to him, all the better. She needed him desperate, making his move, or giving up and going home, where the Colorado police would arrest him on the out of state warrant that had already been issued to bring him in for questioning as a person of interest in an attempted murder investigation.

Straightening, Tom's relief was clear then. "Well, you just let me know if you need my help with anythin'," he said then. "I'm always here."

Telling the man she appreciated his offer, she made a beeline for their cruiser as Tom headed back toward the

SUV he'd left parked out by the road, headed toward his own drive.

What she appreciated far more than the offer was the reassurance that she hadn't called things wrong the other night.

She'd known the SUV wasn't following her. Or, rather, she'd been bothered at first, but had calmed down when the vehicle hadn't followed her turn.

But she'd let Mac's continued concern get to her.

Like she trusted him more than she trusted herself.

And that wasn't okay.

Chapter 10

Just as with the midazolam, the propane canisters pulled up out of Stacy's septic tank could have been purchased in hundreds of places all over the Phoenix valley alone, let alone anywhere between Colorado and Arizona. Sierra's Web was tracing serial numbers but had so far only narrowed a shipment down to a three-state radius.

Manning-endorsed cowboy boot sales were much harder to trace as no one knew how far back to look. Stacy had been certain the boots weren't new. They could be a decade or more old. Shops that sold them had come and gone. And thousands of pairs had been sold in that time. Beyond that, finding a pair that Landon Manning might have purchased wasn't likely. Since both he and his father before him endorsed the boots, he'd likely have whatever he wanted free of charge.

A team consisting of one city office employee and one Saguaro PD employee were going through the city building surveillance footage. So far, they had not turned up any likeness of Landon Manning. Or anyone else that they didn't recognize or couldn't trace to legitimate business in the building. There'd been one image, a tall person in a black hoodie whose face had never been visible to the camera, who'd been in the previous week. No one knew who it was. Or why he'd been there.

They'd sent the footage to Stacy via phone, and while she hadn't been able to identify Manning, she'd agreed that it could be him.

Mac and Stacy were just leaving her property, having found nothing suspicious, when he got another call from Hudson Warner. The firm of experts had found Manning on surveillance tape at a private airport in Denver the week before. There were no manifests with his name on them, but they were following other leads on the matter. When Manning's wife was asked about other absences, she admitted that her husband was gone a lot. For rodeos and just to work out his life, as she'd put it.

"If he's flying by private plane, he could be traveling between here and Denver daily," Stacy said, as she listened to the call over speakerphone as they sat in the cruiser outside her house.

"Exactly," Hudson's voice came over the wire. "We're checking flight manifests for Denver to Phoenix flights," he said. "We know his name isn't registered on any flights, but once we know which ones to track, we can get surveillance from the various airports, both private and commercial, in the valley, too."

"It's also possible that he drove," Mac pointed out. That would have been the more logical choice if the man was hoping to stay unnoticed. Almost an entire day had passed, Stacy had escaped death twice in the past thirty-six hours, and they still were no closer to an actual arrest.

To eliminating the imminent danger to his partner's life.

"We've got traffic cam footage between here and Denver," Hudson was saying, impressing Mac, if not easing his frustration any. "As many major and minor routes as we could find that had them, and we have people going through them one by one…"

"…but if he's not in his own vehicle, he'd be pretty impossible to trace." Stacy voiced what they all knew.

"We could also get lucky, get a glimpse of his face, and find out what he's driving," Hudson came back at once. "This isn't our first rodeo," the man said, adding, "No pun intended. We can do scans for facial likeness…"

"Have you had success with that before?" Mac had to ask. Had to know what they were up against.

"We have. Several times."

Good to know. He glanced at Stacy, who happened to be looking at him. Their eyes met. She was doing okay.

And his tension eased some.

Stacy wanted to be fine. She'd told Tom she was. If Mac or anyone else asked, she'd say the same. But having just spent two hours walking around her property, starting with the two houses and branching out from there, looking for anything out of place or that seemed unusual to her, she wasn't really fine.

Had she and Mac just been for a walk, then maybe. But canvassing her own property, her safe place, with guns out and covering each other's back, she felt…violated.

Not by Mac.

But by whoever had forced her to have to check her own land for criminal activity.

Landon Manning.

Again.

She'd thought, after testifying at his trial, that she could put the past to rest. Try to recover and move on.

Until the early hours of the morning before, she'd have sworn that she'd done so.

"I've been a bit on edge since I heard Manning was out of jail," she told Mac as they traveled back through town toward his gated community. The plan was for him to pack up some things and stay in her spare bedroom for the duration.

Or until the plan changed.

A couple of officers were being assigned to patrol her property, and the area around it, all night, every night, until Manning was caught.

"They had to notify me of his release, since I was the victim's family, and I've had this niggling feeling ever since. Like I had to be on constant watch."

"Why didn't you say something?" His question was probably natural, given the circumstances. She still felt affronted.

"Because there was no factual basis for it. It was just reaction from past personal trauma. And we agreed, Mac, from the very beginning. No personal talk. Look at us, a partnership known all over the state. Our boundaries work, Mac. We only let work occupy our working hours. And to do that we have to keep all personal life away from each other."

He nodded. Let it go.

When she'd wanted him to say something. To argue or discuss. Bring up another side to the story.

Instead of just confirming what, in her heart, she knew to be true. There were lines they couldn't cross, or they'd lose the best thing either of them had ever had.

She knew that to be the truth for her.

He'd said as much for himself in the past.

And she just couldn't stop herself from asking, "Are you taking the job?"

"What job?"

"With the sheriff's office. And don't prevaricate again, Mac. Not now. Don't try to put it off on me. I just need to know. After five years, if my work life is going to change..." She shrugged, and said, "I just need to know."

She'd almost said she had a right to know.

In reality, she didn't. Lieutenant Stahl could assign her to work with any other officer in the department at any time, without her prior consent or knowledge. When you signed on to serve, you turned those choices over to those who led.

"No."

He didn't elaborate.

And she didn't say any more either.

She was too busy fighting tears of relief.

And couldn't let that show.

Stacy had wanted to wait out in the cruiser while Mac ran in to collect his things, using his gated community as assurance that she'd be safe, but they both knew the fallacy of the remark. They'd worked cases where electronic gates had been compromised. He didn't call her on her weak argument, just looked at her and she'd followed him inside.

The incident in itself was a nonentity, except that it told Mac that Stacy hadn't wanted to enter his private abode.

Since he knew, by virtue of the fact that she'd strongly requested that he be the one to stay with her in her home, that she wasn't at all uncomfortable being alone in a private home with him. Which meant it had to be *his* home in particular that was getting to her.

And the guy in him took note of that with a small amount of pleasure.

Which, of course, couldn't please him.

She waited in the foyer. Had it been any other day, and them together for any other reason, he'd have teased her about it.

Had she been any other woman, he'd have taken pleasure in drawing out of her just why she didn't want to let herself get too far into his personal space, angling for an admission that he was having an effect on her.

Which would lead to a soft kiss.

And assurances that she was having an effect on him, too.

Well, any other woman who affected him as Stacy did. If there'd ever been another one who constantly challenged him. Keeping him on his toes all the time. Sparring with him. Making him think harder.

Just plain making him better.

At the job they shared.

With Stacy, it was always only at the job.

So thinking, he threw things in a duffel and got them both out of there in less than five minutes. They stopped for carryout chicken, to heat up and eat later, and then to exchange the cruiser for his truck. They were heading back to her place when her phone rang.

"It's Benson," she said, naming their chief, as she answered it on speakerphone.

"A couple of sheriff's deputies just found a white van matching your description, Stace. I'm sending you photos now…"

"Where?" Mac interrupted. He had to know location details. To have an idea of areas Manning had possibly been.

"Pushed over the side of a mountain off The Trail a mile east of Stacy's attempted murder. It's nose first, three-quarters of a mile down. Front end isn't visible in the photo. But we got a clear view of the back. It's been there less than a day. Helicopters flew over the area yesterday morning, looking for Stacy, and have footage of the area."

Too much of a coincidence not to see the connection.

"And the plates?" he asked, already knowing what was coming. Benson's tone of voice wasn't speaking victory.

"The vehicle was reported stolen a week ago."

"From?" he prompted, biting back impatience.

"Denver." Yep. That was the one.

"It's Manning," he declared. Appreciative of the confirmation. And uncomfortable with everyone's inability to find the fallen hero. They'd had the best of the best hunting him down for a full day, and they had nothing.

"Or his friend Troy," Stacy said.

Right. "He might be the easier of the two to find," Mac said, homing in again. "Find him, he'll lead us to Manning."

"Unless he's in that four-wheeler." Stacy's tone brought him straight back to her. He could almost hear the shudder within her. "The man had a pretty failproof plan. But it failed. We wanted to make him desperate. Maybe enough to not only get rid of the vehicle he used in the crime, but perhaps his driver, too. Like Mac just deduced, Troy would be the weak link. He's not going to leave that hanging around."

"This guy…he's making all attempts on your life look like accidents," Benson said, clearly to Stacy. "Late at night, after shift, you could have gone for a drive, missed that turn, gone over. The methane…a danger of septic tanks that haven't been cleaned out. If we hadn't been specifically aware, looking, we might not ever have found those tanks. They were small enough to sink if there'd been enough refuse down there. You were damned lucky you'd just had the tank cleaned. And now, with him trashing the van…we have to assume he's still here. We have to assume he's going to be escalating." Benson's tone had a definite warning to it.

One that Mac was already feeling to his core. He needed a different plan than hanging Stacy out as bait. A better one.

"Him escalating is exactly what we need." Stacy spoke strongly. Mac could feel her gaze boring into him. "I want this to end," she continued, "and end soon. We have to keep him worried."

"She told a neighbor, an older guy who dines at Rich's, that we have a suspect from out of town," Mac reported, feeling as though he was tattling on his partner, betraying her. Sent her an unapologetic look as he did so.

He was executing her plan with her. But he was going to cover all bases, everywhere he could. As long as she lived through the ordeal, she could hate him all she wanted.

"He should be getting the word around town right about now," she said, with a somewhat sheepish glance back at him.

Which meant what? She knew what she'd done. Had done it deliberately. Without talking to him first. He'd already known that much.

Had put it down to having spent hours trapped in a vehicle on the verge of death less than two full days before.

Had there been more to it than that?

What, she didn't trust him anymore? Not like she used to?

Shaking his head, he dismissed the thought immediately. Admonished himself for even having it. He wouldn't be there if she didn't trust him with her life.

And him not taking the promotion…that had mattered to her.

A lot.

The pleasure he took from that knowledge didn't bode well, however.

As he pulled into Stacy's drive, and then her garage, parking in her spot automatically, he made another very strong mental note to himself to put aside any over the top feelings that might be rolling around inside him where his partner was concerned. They had only emerged because he'd had to sit there waiting for help to come, knowing that any second he could be watching her plunge to her death.

That had to be it.

They'd been together too long, with no personal emotion issues between them, for there to be any other explanation.

A fact he reminded himself of once again as he entered her house.

Other than double-checking all possible entrance points, Mac didn't pay attention to the interior of Stacy's home as he dropped his bag in the room she'd indicated. He was glad to know he'd have his own bathroom—a hallway access, but fine—and as she warmed up the chicken and put a salad together, he got set up at the kitchen table for a night of work.

Hudson Warner had strongly recommended that Mac and Stacy go through Stacy's private life, talking through memories to see if anything stood out to either of them. To Mac, if not her. Just as Sierra's Web was still going through cases the two of them had handled, they wanted Mac and Stacy to do the same with her personal world. Looking for anything that could be a recent stressor for someone, case related or not, and all outside contacts that could point to Stacy in any way.

Because, as Hudson Warner had said, it was just plain foolish to only focus on one possibility. No matter how certain they were that they had their guy.

In the jobs Stacy and Mac did, assignments from detectives and higher-ups who ran investigations, they were always just on one trail.

Which was part of what made them so good at what they did. They were excellent investigators who followed one suspicion until it panned out or didn't.

And now they had to focus on all trails.

Mac had no doubt both of them were up to the task.

They'd both turned down multiple offers to move up to detective status. His discomfort lay in setting out to deliberately cross the line they'd swore they'd never cross. To break their cardinal rule. No personal life at work.

Manning had crossed the line when he'd tried to take Stacy's life. Both work and personal. One didn't exist without the other.

A fact that Mac was finding difficult coming to terms with.

Officers were already outside. Miguel, who was running the protection duty, was first up with his regular partner, Beth Parker. Another pair, deputies from the sheriff's office, would take over at midnight, and Martha and her partner would show up at six in the morning. All were volunteering for extra duty until Stacy's intended murderer was caught.

For everyone's sake, he had to get his instincts in full gear, be the cop he'd been born to be, and get the job done.

Once he was off duty, and away from Stacy Waltz, he could be a man with personal needs.

Chapter 11

She'd planted the seed with Tom on purpose. A move that, any other time, she and Mac would have discussed first. But she hadn't waited for him.

Because she'd thought Mac might be taking another job. Ending their partnership. Without even telling her.

He hadn't been.

She'd overreacted.

Responded personally, not professionally.

In five years as his partner, she'd never done that.

Which, in that moment, scared Stacy more than Landon Manning did.

But not quite as much as sitting down at her table with him, plates of food beside each of them, ready to go to work.

She'd stalled as long as she could. Had to look at her life as though she was just another person she and Mac were interviewing.

It wasn't personal.

Just like them delving into the intimate lives of their victims didn't mean any kind of relationship was starting between them. They were first responders doing their jobs.

Mac took a bite of food. She did as well. Searching her brain for a way to come out proving that she was in complete control and not the least bit emotionally involved in what was to come between them.

"Tell me about Tom Brandon." Mac seemed so relaxed, so ordinary. Like they were at Rich's sitting across from each other in a booth, rather than her kitchen table. He hadn't changed out of his uniform, which helped.

Neither had she.

She'd needed the barrier. For Mac.

And for herself. She was desperately searching for a return to the sense of safety the uniform had always given her. In uniform she was strong. Capable. Armed and ready.

She'd been abducted in her uniform. With all her gear on her. And hadn't been able to access any of it…

"What?" Mac's question brought her back to the table. He'd stopped eating, his fork halfway to his mouth.

Looking at her in that way he had of letting her know that he knew she'd gone somewhere, and he wasn't letting up until she'd told him where.

Because in the past, when she'd traveled off in her mind around him, it had always been case related.

Her personal fears were not so. And right then, when they were about to dive into her past to reassure themselves that there were no other possible murderers lurking there, she had to stay case related.

She blurted what came to mind. "My grandfather and Tom didn't see eye to eye," she told him. "Tom was younger, had all these ideas about making profits off the land, and my grandfather was this wickedly smart but extremely gentle man who cared about the land. And his animals."

"Brandon said he's a miner."

"Right. He owns the Layby mine. It butts up to his home property. He'd spent years up in the Clairs—" she used the term the locals did when referring to their mountains, the Clairvoyant Mountain Range "—searching for gold. He was the first person who ever told me the story about the

Superstition mine and spent his summers all through college trying to find it."

More than a century before, a German man had staked a claim and came out of the Clairvoyant Mountains with gold. Again and again. He mined alone, with a pickax and little else. And he died alone. Without ever telling anyone where the mine was located. People still flocked to Saguaro every year to head up into the mountains to try to find that gold.

"In later years, he made a lot of money hiring himself as a guide to visitors wanting to find the Superstition mine, or any other gold that hadn't been legally claimed yet."

"Layby mine?" Mac asked, frowning. "I thought that was a gold panning tourist trap for kids."

She shrugged. "In the front parking lot, it is. Like I said, Tom's all about using the land, and her legends, to make a buck, but he actually did find gold. Just not up in the Clairs. He found it not far from his property, bought the land, and staked the claim. He's got a crew. And they bring up enough gold to support them. Tom has always said that there's a main vein that his gold feeds off from and as soon as he gets to it, he'll be a millionaire. Mary's tired of waiting for him to strike it. And, frankly, I don't blame her. Still, she married him, knowing that his thirst for gold was as much a part of him as the blood in his veins. She used to tell me stories about some of his adventures in the mountains. He'd hit some coal and make enough money to support them for a year or two, and that just fed his lust."

As long as Mac would let her, she'd keep talking about her eccentric old neighbor.

"When he hit that small vein of gold, and started mining down here, that's when he and my grandfather started having problems. Until then, they'd share beers and stories on their porches. But once Tom started bringing in trucks and tearing up the land, once he built some of the processing operation, which my grandfather considered a huge eyesore, my grandfather started talking about moving. Instead, he gave the big house to Mom and Dad, and built this place. Since it's around the corner, and over the hill, the two of them were able to live compatibly enough…"

End of her story. And she still wasn't ready to begin.

"I'm not currently involved with anyone and have no exes, or exes of exes, no currents of exes…no one that we could look to as suspects," she finally told Mac, looking him right in the eye. There he had it. She wasn't drop dead gorgeous dating material. He wasn't the only one who didn't find her so. Yet, ironically, though she was pretty much invisible in the dating field, someone found her noteworthy enough to see that she dropped dead.

"Anyone who had a crush on you?" he asked, still holding her gaze.

"No." She shook her head. "Brett and I were inseparable from the time we were little. The segue between best friends and something more just kind of happened. Frankly later than I think everyone thought it had. Kids at school used to act like we were a couple, thinking we'd be attending junior high dances together as a couple, that sort of thing, long before we ever actually held hands. Or went on a date."

Because she'd already been getting everything she needed from him. His heart. His soul. And when he'd told her that he wanted more, that he'd fallen in love with her, that he wanted her to be his girlfriend, and eventually his wife, she'd been thrilled.

There'd never been anyone else who attracted her, either. Growing up an only child with only a father and grandfather to guide her, she'd been a bit of a tomboy. Not wanting to be a boy, just not knowing how to be girly, either.

Her relationship with Mac was a perfect example of the rest of her life, she could have told him. Great relationships with the opposite sex. Just…no sex.

"Miguel said once that if Brett hadn't already stolen you from the time you learned to walk, he'd have asked you out…"

"WHAT?" She stood as she hollered the word. Then, because she had to make it look like she'd meant to stand, started clearing their plates. "That makes no sense. When did he say that?"

Miguel Gomez was a happily married father of two adorable little girls.

"Years ago. When we first started working together. He'd wanted to make sure I knew that you'd lost your husband to violence…"

Mac didn't get up to help. Instead, he turned and glanced out the window behind him, as though checking the perimeter. In spite of the pitch-blackness.

And *Miguel?* She'd never known.

"My point is, if there's one Miguel, there could be more…"

"And out of the blue, a decade later, he decides I need to die because of it?" Just didn't make sense.

"Unless there's someone who's tried over the years." Mac's tone grew serious, and he was gazing at her again as, their plates in the dishwasher, she sat back down. "All I'm asking is that you think for a second, Stace. Open your mind to the possibility. Is there anyone who's been friendly with you over the years? Maybe off and on? Anyone who was even a little bit flirty? You'd probably have taken for granted that he was teasing. And maybe this someone just had a bad breakup. He might have told you about it. Could even be someone at work…"

Everything in her stilled as he said that. Not because she had anyone in mind. At all. But because he'd just taken away her last vestige of normalcy.

"We have to consider every possibility," Mac said then, his eyes looking solidly into hers. "This guy, he knew your schedule. Knew just how to time things to get in and get you out within a minute or two. If not for those boulders, his plan would have been near perfect. Even if we'd flown helicopters looking for a sign of you, there was every possibility that we'd never have seen your SUV if it had gone all the way down…"

He was scaring the hell out of her. And bringing her back to life, too. Keeping her sharp.

"Same with the methane. I'd have just gone to sleep and natural gas would have been the cause," she said then, nodding. Determined to do as Mac and Sierra's Web had asked. Look for any and all possibilities. Then look again. With a cop's view of her life.

They weren't taking any more chances.

Going back in her mind…grade school, a jump ahead to high school, college, police academy, her wedding, junior high, five years in the police department…just flashes. Faces. Moods. No real conversations. Just impressions.

And eventually, still looking at Mac, shook her head. "Other than Brett, I was pretty much an introvert. Lived in my own little world. I read a lot. And spent most of my free time with Brett and the horses. And after Brett… I joined the force. If there is someone else, I sure don't know it," she told him. Not sure if the pronouncement was all that great. Thirty years old and, other than Brett, she'd never raised any kind of intense passion in anyone.

Except the man she'd taken down, held down, after he'd killed her husband.

* * *

Relief flooded him. Sitting at Stacy's kitchen table, Mac couldn't stop the light flow of feeling, the lessening of tension in his muscles, as he listened to his partner talk.

He'd gone with Manning as their suspect—all clues led in that direction—but, like Hudson Warner, he'd needed to be sure he wasn't missing something right there in front of him.

He'd been dreading sitting there listening to a past filled with admirers. And others who'd been jealous of her. All potential suspects to rule out. Most particularly after he remembered Miguel mentioning once having had a crush on Stacy.

She hadn't known. Had been shocked.

All good stuff.

What wasn't good was an honest affirmation that a fair amount of his lightening mood had to do with the fact that Stacy wasn't romantically involved. And that there were no past loves she might still pine for.

There could be only one reason for that fact to bring him any pleasure at all.

Because he wanted her for himself.

Until the day before, when he'd been helplessly watching her teeter on the verge of death, he'd never even thought of Stacy in a personal sense.

Not because he didn't find her attractive. But because if he looked at her in that way, he couldn't work with her. And he valued his work life more than any other thing on earth.

Was it possible he valued Stacy more?

That she was part of the reason his work called to him, fulfilled him, as much as it did?

Or was he still just suffering the aftereffects of a traumatic experience?

Either way, he didn't doubt, for a second, his ability to give his life, and his full attention, to keeping his partner safe. No one cared more than he did, would give more than he would, to see her kidnapper caught.

But after that…

Unless he woke up to find his new awareness of the woman exorcized, he wasn't going to be able to continue partnering with her.

So he'd do whatever he had to do to exorcize the bizarre surge of inappropriate emotion.

"What about you?" Stacy, arms folded, pinned him with one of her "I'm not backing down" stares.

Had she read his damned mind?

In the second it took him to shake his head and get up to speed, she said, "We can only continue working together if we're on equal footing. We have a no personal information rule, which now has been revised in such a way that weights us unfairly."

"You want to know about my past relationships?"

"I want you to sit there and tell me who, in your past, could have it in for you. Or have unresolved issues that could result in some future shot across the bow."

Staring her down, determined to get her to look away first, Mac considered what she'd said. And what he'd just been thinking.

His partnership with her meant more to him than anything else.

Including his own privacy. Or pride.

Without looking away, not needing to lose that battle to give her what she required, he said, "I've never been in a serious relationship. I'm always exclusive when I date a woman, but it's clear, up front, that it's not going anywhere permanent. No moving in. No plans for the future. If, at any time, I get an inkling that she's starting to want more, I end things immediately. So, perhaps I have a woman or two out there who's not happy with me."

Stacy's chin jutted like it did when she was accepting information she hadn't yet processed. Information she intended to process.

He liked knowing that. Wanted to goad her about it. But wasn't sure if he should.

Which, in itself, was uncharacteristic of their relationship.

"Saguaro is all about family," she said then, surprising him. Her tone was conversational. Maybe a bit challenging, but only marginally so.

The Stacy he knew and loved working with.

"So." He shrugged, still looking her right in the eye.

They'd once eye wrestled, as she'd put it, for half an hour at Rich's diner. A more challenging form of arm wrestling, she'd told him. She'd won that round. But only because he'd allowed himself to get bothered by those coming and going, people they worked with, noticing them sitting there staring at each other like lovers.

At least, he'd been afraid others might see it that way.

"You grew up here." Her tone remained completely uninvolved. "More to the point, you stayed. How, then, could you not want the life?"

He blinked. Blinking was allowed. Closing out sights, otherwise known as a long blink, was not. Mac kept his gaze steady on hers. Fending off the near glitch.

"I have the life I grew up in," he told her, comfortable with his truth. With choices deliberately made years before. Ones that suited him. "The latter part, where I was happy. And no risk of the former, where I was not."

"You didn't grow up alone."

He hadn't dug deeper into her revelations. Was considering calling a foul on her. But, that hint of challenge in her tone, he didn't want her to think she was making him sweat.

"My early years were filled with arguing, then fighting, then tense silences, and finally bitterness and attempts to win at all costs. When my parents remarried and had children with their spouses, I had loving families. Two of them. Those years were spent living week by week, back and forth between two homes, two sets of rules, two sets of siblings. I loved. And was loved. But was never fully a part of either family. My experience with love and loyalty, with security, is living on the edges of it. Not all in. It's what I know. What I'm good with. I get the good without risking the arguing, then fighting, love turning to hate thing."

Stacy's gaze changed. Slowly. Challenge drained away, leaving…warmth.

Compassion.

And Mac looked away.

Chapter 12

They were living in a bizarre no-man's-land. Being full time on one case wasn't unusual for her and Mac. Even staying in the same lodgings with separate rooms, same.

Eating food that one or the other of them prepared, in a private kitchen—never.

Having no time off—just didn't happen. Police work was hard. All encompassing. They needed down time to keep themselves sharp.

But death wasn't going to wait around for any of them to get rested before it struck again. And since it was knocking at Stacy's door, she couldn't very well pass the job on to someone else while she took a moment to rejuvenate.

When she woke Thursday morning to find Mac already in full uniform in the kitchen, with coffee made, she tried to get him to at least take a breather. Just the day, if that's all he wanted, to return before dark.

"That's what you'd do if it was my life on the line?" he asked.

Hell no. She didn't speak the words aloud.

"And why not?" he asked anyway.

"Because living it every minute, you take in every detail as it happens, every piece of information as it comes in, and the accumulation is what often brings the break in the case." He'd taught her that.

"We retired to our rooms early last night," he said then. "Just like when we're on the road and have done all we can do for the day."

He was right, of course.

She just…needed more space from him. To get over the insidious dreams that continued to come even now that she was off the drug and out of the SUV casket.

Made worse by her new visions of a younger Mac, a kid Mac, being passed back and forth between families without ever belonging fully…anywhere.

She'd never had a mother. He'd had two.

She'd only had one father. He'd had two.

And yet, she'd always been wholly part of a solid family unit that drove her to want exactly that for her future. A husband, children.

The big house filled with squeals and laughter, with challenge and obstacles, too. But always with the security that set you free.

Things Mac not only didn't value, but things he didn't even understand.

Which was fine.

He wasn't the man in her mental scenario. He couldn't be.

She didn't even want him to be. No way she wanted to trade her days with Mac for days without him.

She just…needed some space.

She badly needed time apart from him to recover from her recent emotional trauma.

And just as much, she wanted him there. Doing what he did best. There was no one she trusted more to get the job done.

They'd just finished a working breakfast. Going over reports from the night officers watching her place, checking in with Martha. They were determining that they'd start the day back in the conference room at the department head-quarters when Hudson Warner called.

Thinking it would just be his morning report, updates with no immediately actionable news, Stacy tended to her tattering nerves by clearing the dishes from the table as Mac answered on speakerphone.

"We've got a lead," the expert tech boss said. "Manning flew into a small private airport about fifteen miles east of you last week. The runway is part of a gated community. Owners park their planes at their estates, some in hangars, some not. There's parking for a few nonresident planes as well, but you have to know someone who knows someone to get landing permission."

"Someone there knows him?" Stacy asked, dirty bowls—empty of the oatmeal and bananas that had been in them—in hand. "His name came up?"

"Not that much of a lead." Hudson's reply showed no emotional response at all. "We got him on a homeowner's security system. I'm sending the image to you, but not only is it pretty obviously him, we've run it through software as well. We can send someone out to the neighborhood to question people if you'd like."

"No." Mac spoke before Stacy could. "We'll go. This is the part we do best…"

And just like that, they were back to work. Their real work.

Stacy and Mac.

Police partners.

With an assignment.

Adrenaline surged through Stacy. Leaving the dishes in the sink, she grabbed her gear and followed Mac out the door.

Telling herself that by nightfall, life would be normal again.

And she and Mac would go back to being who they'd always been.

Mac opted to take his private vehicle to the south valley. Not only did he want to get right on the road, hoping to catch at least some of the homeowners before they left for the day—he also wanted to be free to go wherever the wind took them from there.

Like he and Stacy always did when they were on assignment outside Saguaro PD.

He didn't say so, but he also hoped that Stacy would be a little less conspicuous in a truck that looked like so many other vehicles on the road. While he understood the reason for making it known that she hadn't died as intended, potentially putting a target on her back, he wasn't going to dangle her in front of Manning with a light shining on her.

He'd driven about a mile or so up her road, approaching the area's largest gold mine that had been closed a century before due to flooding. It had since been turned into a ghost town tourist stop. Suddenly, Stacy yelled, "Stop!"

He pulled off into a dirt circle in front of a small gold panning venture and local ore and rock shop, which also had a restaurant known for its biscuits and gravy.

Hand on his gun, instincts on full alert, he was reaching with his other hand to push her head down out of shooting range, when she pointed. "That van, Mac. The white one..."

She was getting out, her hand on her gun. Stood behind the opened passenger door. "I recognize it," she told him, glancing into the truck. "That's the van I almost hit the other night. I don't know what's down the mountain, but that van right there was pulling out just as I came around the corner."

He slid over to her side of the vehicle, and then down, behind her.

The van was a full-size, seven passenger model, and from what he could tell it was American made, newer. And looked to him like any number of others they saw on the road every day. In the Arizona heat, white was one of the most popular vehicle colors.

But he didn't doubt his partner. Stacy, even on her worst days, wasn't prone to drama.

"That sticker on the windshield. It just hit me. It's what I saw when I swerved," she said. "My headlights caught it. It's fuchsia and yellow. They don't really go together…"

"That was right before you pulled into your drive," Mac said, all senses on alert. "Maybe he'd been waiting for you to pass so he could follow you, let his passenger out in the dark to duck into your garage as you pulled in…"

Adrenaline flowing, he assessed the situation.

"If at all possible, we need to wait until he comes out," Stacy said. "Least chance of civilians getting hurt."

Mac, having reached the same conclusion, said, "Get back in. I'll pull up and park nose to nose with the van." She did. And he did.

"It's a Parker Lake sticker," Stacy said without a hint of fear in her tone.

And Mac, glancing over at her, thankful that she was alive, replied, "Get down." And then, "Please. We're here. We've got him. There's no point in alerting him with your face shining right at him. Or giving him an easy chance to get you."

"If it doesn't go down quick and smooth, I'm coming out to help," she warned him.

"I know."

Which was why he had to focus and get it right.

He took in the parking lot, the people coming and going from the restaurant, the distance between the van and the cars parked next to it, a window in the distance behind the van. He figured his best chance to take Manning down without anyone else getting hurt was to wait until he was reaching for the door of his van.

If he wasn't alone, Mac was going to have to involve Stacy.

Either way, they'd have their doors for cover and show their guns before Manning had a chance to reach for his—assuming he was carrying.

He'd order the craphead to the ground, and enjoy putting a foot to the man's back as he cuffed him.

"If he's not alone…"

"…already on it, Stace. You'll take your door, I'll take mine."

She nodded. Glanced up at him. "I hate pink."

"I remember. The nightclub in Globe. Pink walls. Waiting for the coroner." They'd had three dead bodies.

"Yeah, that was a tough one."

But they got the shooter. Stopped him from taking another ten lives.

Two minutes of silence seemed like hours. "Maybe you should go inside. Make sure he doesn't go out the back…"

He'd been thinking the same. Didn't like it, though. He'd need her backup. Which could put her right in Manning's line of fire. If the guy was escalating—a ruined life, with no hope, set on revenge—he wouldn't likely care who he hurt in the process.

"There are a lot of kids in there," he said. He'd been watching three of them, elementary school age, sharing a doughnut as they walked behind their parents in the parking lot. Two of the three had chocolate on their faces, reminding him of his dad's kids when they were little. Innocent. Probably on vacation since they were getting along so well.

The closer they drew to his truck, the tenser he grew. He needed them in their car and gone before Manning appeared.

They didn't veer off. Instead, they just kept coming at him. Mom, Dad and three kids. Walking right into the path of potential danger.

Until...they stopped at the van.

And climbed inside.

"We know the van I almost hit visited Parker Lake at some point." Stacy told herself not to feel stupid for her overreaction, but she did anyway. Mac had called Sierra's Web, to have them get any surveillance cameras they could from the lake's public parking, and also to see if the van trashed down the mountain had the same sticker.

"Parker Lake's between here and Colorado," he said. "We know Manning flew into the valley once, prior to this week, but he could have driven this time. Or other times, too."

She'd been ready to tell him not to humor her—mostly because she was feeling a distinct rush of letdown—when his phone rang.

Hudson Warner again. Mac answered on his truck's audio system.

"I had one of my experts trace times on the east valley private plane neighborhood security footage and compare it to the footage from the city building. Same day. Manning isn't wearing the hoodie in the east valley tape, but he's got a duffel on his shoulder that obviously contained something."

"Why not a hoodie?" Mac asked, smiling over at Stacy.

She knew that smile. They were getting close, and he was eager to bring the guy down.

"We should have the Parker Lake footage within the hour," Hudson reported then. "I've got my team looking for Troy Duncan, too. Could be Manning flew but had the kid drive."

And just like that, Stacy felt validated again. Something that should have been happening from the very beginning. Mac didn't doubt her ability to do her job.

Hudson Warner certainly didn't appear to. Had she not recognized the sticker, had that flash of memory, they'd never have known to look at Parker Lake.

Or to check the van they found for the Parker Lake sticker. An actual identifier. Mac had already called the chief to have all patrol officers on the alert for any other white vans with Parker Lake stickers as well. Just in case.

The only one who was doubting her was her.

Just then on the job—and before that, with the bizarre dreams about Mac.

And that was just going to stop. Period.

Manning had already robbed her of one life—her life with Brett.

He was not going to take her ability to do police work, her life with Mac, away from her, too.

Manning had flown into town within an hour of the black hooded likeness of him appearing at the Saguaro city building. They were closing in on him, one step at a time.

Doing their jobs.

Getting closer.

And Stacy was still with him.

Doing hers.

As he pulled into the east valley gated community, stopping first at the house where the security cameras had caught images of Manning—the owners of which had given them the access code to enter—he and Stacy made their rounds all over the neighborhood. One house at a time. Walking door to door. Looking for anyone who knew Landon Manning personally.

Needing to find the one who'd given him permission to land on the private runway.

And in the end, found out that a private company leased a couple of small-plane parking lanes from the homeowners association to bring celebrities in and out of Phoenix anonymously.

Apparently, Manning still qualified as a celebrity in some circles.

Or knew someone who'd pulled strings for him.

The company was refusing to give any further information without a court order. Their entire business was built around the promise of confidentiality.

And as yet, there was no solid proof that Landon Manning was a kidnapper and attempted murderer.

He glanced at Stacy as they walked back to his truck. "Feel like some lun…" Mac's heart lurched, his gut turned to rock as he dove for his partner, tackling and rolling with her in the pebbled desert landscaping of the yard they'd been passing.

He'd moved on instinct. A sense of immediate danger, not conscious thought.

Keeping his body over hers, tucking his face in her hair, he put his hands over his head and felt her breathing beneath him. Felt her softness…

A boom rang out. Leaving his ears ringing, encased in

cotton. Still, he lay there. Waiting. His body pressing into Stacy's knee to knee, groin to butt, chest to back.

Seconds passed. He heard running. "You guys okay?" a voice called out.

"I've called 911," another said.

Nine-one-one. First responders. The police. He and Stacy, in full uniform, *were* the police.

And Mac didn't want to get up. He wanted to stay right where he was, feeling Stacy's body beneath him. Her body breathing.

Her head lifting brought him back to reality. Slowly rolling her, he waited for her to turn over, waiting to see her expression. And saw the blood on her wrists, instead.

Scrapes. And a spot on her sleeve that was wet with blood.

She was staring at the remains of an explosive on the sidewalk. "How...what..." Open-mouthed, she looked up at him as if they were the only two people there. Seemingly completely oblivious of the crowd that was gathering.

"It seemed like a bird," he said, looking up at the sky. Thanking the fates that some part of him had realized in time...

"Wow, man, I saw it from my window," a young man, maybe eighteen, said, coming up to them in jeans, a sweatshirt and flip-flops. "I'm into drones, but you know, with the airstrip, we have to be really careful. But this one, it came in quick, dropped its load and left just as quickly."

"A drone?" Stacy was staring from Mac to the kid, to the sky, and back to Mac. Paying no attention at all to the blood dripping down her forearm. A woman came up, pressing a tissue to the gash, and Stacy took the white substance from her, holding it as she walked with Mac to the explosive.

"It had one of those new hooks on it," the kid said, keeping up with them. "You can get 'em now for really small drones and with the cameras on good ones, you can hit your target within half an inch…"

With his ears still ringing Mac pulled out his phone. Called the chief.

And reported that there'd been another attempt on Stacy's life.

If Mac hadn't noticed the "bird" flying low above, the drone would have dropped its load right on Stacy's head.

Chapter 13

If Manning was trying to put her in mental hell, because he himself was in one, he was doing a fair job of it. Stacy wouldn't say she was paranoid as she and Mac headed back to their part of town, but she was most definitely jumpy.

Uncomfortable.

Constantly watching from all directions.

"It's not too late to get you to a safe house," Mac said, watching all his mirrors as he drove. His attention, like hers, was all around them. Guarding against what could come next from any direction.

When it must have become obvious she wasn't going to validate the comment with a response, he added, "Manning clearly knows you're still alive. We can make it harder for him to find you."

"And then what? He implodes on someone else? His wife, maybe? I'm a cop, Mac. Sworn to protect others. Not to run and protect myself. We need this guy off the streets. As soon as possible. Let me do my job."

Fear wasn't going to stop her. It was going to make her better. More aware.

Hudson Warner, who lived with his wife and newly discovered daughter in the east valley, had come to the scene to take the remainder of the explosive, and surveillance footage into custody. Glen Thomas, Sierra's Web science expert, had people in the lab waiting for the explosive, and Hudson's team would put the morning's footage on priority status.

She and Mac were the feet on the street.

"I fully understand if you'd rather not partner with me on this one," she told him. As badly as she wanted him with her, a part of her didn't want him there at all.

Not after that morning's episode. He'd saved her life.

And could so easily have lost his right along with her.

"When it was just me he was after, that was one thing. But if he's escalating, not caring who gets hurt in the process of taking me down, then—"

"You need law enforcement to help you stop him," Mac said, cutting her off, his tone stern. He was watching all mirrors, almost frantically, as though they were in a war zone.

And while most of the vehicles sharing the rush hour road with them were driven by good citizens on their way to living another normal day, there was an enemy out there.

A war of one.

"I don't want to lose you." As soon as the words were out, she wanted to pull them back. Held her breath.

Until he said, "I don't want to lose you, either."

His words seemed to settle something in her, put them on equal footing, and she let her lapse into personal emotions fade off into the ether. They had much bigger problems at the moment.

"We need to minimize his target area," she said then, suddenly finding a sense of power. A way to be in charge. "He's coming after me, Mac. We don't have to chase him."

The morning's drone, in addition to the methane and the midazolam, made it clear that Manning was smart—and had access to pretty much anything he wanted. With his fame, it was possible that he had people who'd help him with whatever he asked, without needing to know why he'd asked.

There was no way of predicting what he'd come up with next.

Or protecting against it.

But… "We choose where it goes down, Mac," she said. "We limit his access to us and have eyes all around us. On the ground and in the air. We set the parameters of where he gets to try and come after me. And when he does, we have our own traps set and get him."

It was all kind of esoteric now…

"Good. Okay. We've got the plan. Let me focus on getting us back to the station in one piece and then we'll work on it."

It wasn't a smiling morning. Or even a happy moment.

But as she kept watch on their backs, sides and fronts, right along with Mac, Stacy felt a little bit like smiling.

In spite of everything, she and Mac, as a working partnership, were still going strong.

Mac had a bad feeling in his gut. Infiltrating a cop's garage, a perfect injection of prescription medication, the getaway. Methane in a septic tank. And a drone? All accomplished like clockwork without leaving any traceable clue.

As he took the highway exit to cross the patch of desert that led into Saguaro, thoughts of the case infiltrated his focus on his surroundings. Theirs was the only vehicle on the road. No others to protect against any potential attempt to kill.

And wide open desert was much easier to surveil than building after building, possibly hiding or camouflaging who knew what attack.

He had no doubt that Stacy's help would bring the agonizing hours or days before them to a close sooner.

And no doubt that knowingly walking her into further danger, exposing her in any way to a perpetrator whose only goal was to kill her, was going against his every instinct.

His only comfort was that if he kept her close, he could exchange his life for hers if need be. He'd have the chance to jump in front of whatever death knell came ringing in her direction.

"We've got a problem," he told Stacy.

Keeping her head below the top of the headrest, she was leaning back, studying side mirrors.

"I don't see anything," she said after long seconds.

"Not imminent," he told her, realizing how ominous his words had sounded. "Overall."

"What?"

"We've got a guy who's escalating his attempts to see you dead, and crimes that are executed in minute detail with extreme precision."

She nodded, as though she'd been silently traveling in the same direction. "Doesn't fit, does it?"

"Manning's here. Or he's been here, we know that. But what if he's not who we're chasing? He could have gone to some mountain retreat for the week, as his wife intimated, to wait to hear that the job is done. This guy, he somehow knew where we were, and was prepared to drop the bomb no matter where it was."

"He hired a professional."

"Or a team of them. This is all happening so quickly. There were backup plans already in place before they began. The methane, in case the garage heist had to be forfeited. The drone…you don't just go buy one and fly it that perfectly. With Manning having been in prison for the past several years, I'm guessing he's not up on that technology enough to pull off something like that."

"Troy Duncan could be the drone guy."

Mac allowed the possibility. "Still, this is all clearly thought out, planned."

Stacy didn't take her eyes off the area around them as she said, "Manning could have been working on it for years. Who knows how many plan Bs he has stacked up, ready to go into action? He could be escalating and just executing preplanned, even preprepared, actions."

"This guy's got money. And plenty of connections to criminals, after living with them for years. He'd know who to hire."

Jaw tight, Stacy's expression was grim as she continued to keep watch. He'd been doing what they did, discussing the case aloud. He hadn't been out to scare her.

But if it worked...and she'd agree to go into hiding...

"Whoever is executing the plan clearly knows your truck, Mac. It was a given, eventually. We'll need different transportation."

They were staying-to-fight words.

And Mac accepted the inevitable.

Stacy was going to be by his side until the end.

"I'll ask the chief to figure that out while we get to work on building our fort," he told her.

And hoped her case wasn't the last one they worked together.

"Get down!" Stacy's scream rent the truck and she braced herself. Mac turned the wheel to get them off the road, slamming on the brake and throwing the truck in park, then ducked.

Stacy, her head between the seat and metal frame of the

truck, kept her view on the paloverde tree. She'd seen a tell-tale glint.

The kind that came from the front end of a gun when the sun hit it. Almost blinding.

She'd been up against them enough to know.

As soon as she had the shot, she pushed the button to lower her window and pulled her trigger.

Mac, who'd positioned himself with dash protection without losing visibility said, "No body fell."

"Or jumped down," she told him. She'd aimed for the trunk. There'd been no shots fired in their direction. And no way to verify if a loaded gun was pointed at them.

Could have been a hunter, out for illegal game.

She knew it wasn't.

She wanted to get out of the truck. To take on the demon haunting her and get it done. To find footprints at the base of that tree, anything to prove that someone had been up in those branches.

But if he was still up there, no matter how much bra-vado she mustered, he'd shoot her dead before she took her first step toward him.

Mac was on the phone, asking someone to approach the area on foot, from the opposite side. They were on the lookout for a possible shooter as, keeping low, he shifted the truck into drive and sped down the road.

"If Manning's doing this all himself, he had time to get from the east valley back out here and set up in the tree," she said.

"And if he isn't, positioning someone on the only road into town was a smart, calculated move just the same," Mac told her.

She looked over at him for the first time since they'd

left the gated airstrip community. "You believe I saw what I saw."

"I believe you saw something and took appropriate action."

Or had she overreacted?

Again?

If so, he wasn't calling her on it.

She didn't want to be mollycoddled. And didn't want to make any bigger deal of the incident, either way, so took him at face value.

And told herself, even if she hadn't seen the glint—which she was still certain she'd seen—she hadn't endangered anyone with her zealousness.

Unless, coupled with her sighting of the white van that morning, she was slowly losing Mac's confidence.

If that happened, then whether Manning killed her or not, he'd win.

Mac had to consider the possibility that Stacy was not capable of doing her job. He didn't blame her. Didn't even think less of her.

He just had to determine what he was going to do about it.

If, indeed, that was the case.

Twice in one morning, she'd called out danger with few results.

But then, she'd done so the morning before as well, with the methane, and that had saved her life, and possibly Martha's as well.

If anyone had lit a match, the whole place could have gone up.

The van that morning…she'd recognized a sticker.

A good lead.

And a way to weed out thousands of other white vans rolling around the Phoenix valley.

One shot to a tree in the middle of acres of uninhabited desert…it couldn't hurt.

While she might be a bit quick to jump, her police work was still on track. She'd followed protocol.

His deciding factor, though, was that if he didn't keep her with him, he wasn't going to get her to stop hunting Manning. She'd just do it without help.

Without any kind of protection other than what she could offer herself.

That last realization gave him some doubt to his own culpability in the overreaction zone. Or nonprofessional arena, at least.

As a cop, he never let emotion rule his choices.

And yet, he'd just done so.

His emotional need to keep Stacy safe at all costs had made a critical decision for him.

It was up to him to make certain that neither one of them paid for that with their life.

Back at the station, he had Stacy fill the chief in on their new battle plan. He called Sierra's Web to ask for the experts' input on possible locations for him and Stacy to set up to draw out Manning, and best practice, unseen safety measures that would protect them while they brought the man down.

Alive, if at all possible.

Mac and Stacy each shared their theory that they might be dealing with a professional, or even a group of them, which would highly impact any safety measures put in place.

And then they got to work. Bouncing ideas off each other. Listening to input from others as it came in.

Wherever they ended up, they needed Manning to be

able to find them. To know where they were. Without being too overt about doing so.

"Clearly he's got tracking measures in place," Stacy pointed out to a table of officers, as well as the chief, Lieutenant Stahl and Hudson Warner. "He found us in the east valley within an hour of us arriving. Maybe we just get to wherever we're going, as carefully as we would if we didn't want him finding us, and trust that he'll get there, too. If he doesn't, we find a way to lead him to us."

Pride in Stacy got in Mac's way for a second as he watched everyone at the table nod. She had a way of getting to the inside of a situation and working her way out that generally led to great police work. He'd seen it again and again over the years. Her ability to evaluate all sides and come up with something that made sense.

She was still on.

He wanted to celebrate that victory with her. Not in a condescending manner, not like wow, she wasn't losing it, but in a you-are-one-hell-of-a-person-and-I'm-honored-to-know-you kind of way.

Instead, he focused on the professionals around the table, there to work the case, Stacy included.

Chapter 14

"If we're going to proceed as expected, we get you two to a safe house," Chief Benson said, looking between Stacy and Mac who were seated together on one side of the table. "You can work your magic from there."

Stacy saw Mac's nod. Clearly, he liked the idea.

It would put her where he'd wanted her from the beginning, but sending him in with her, to work with her when Manning hit. It still let her get her man.

And in the controlled environment she'd suggested.

Except that her gut told her Manning wouldn't breach police boundaries. The man knew what would happen to him if he got caught.

Which was why all his attempts to kill her had been so carefully planned.

"We could use a county safe house instead of a city one," Stahl offered.

Hudson Warner, the Sierra's Web expert, wasn't nodding. Neither was Stacy. They were the only two.

"What do you think?" she asked the one non-law enforcement body in the room.

"I think outside the box," the dark-haired man said, his brown eyes meeting up with all those around the table.

"Which is what I think we need here," Stacy said. "We believe his plans have all been put in place already. They're just awaiting execution. He won't be prepared to breach drawn police lines. Even at my place, he didn't come near when Mac and I were inside and we had patrols outside. We need him to think we're out looking for my intended killer. Landon Manning knows me. He'd likely see through any safe house attempt. He might still try to get to me. More likely, he'd head back to Colorado, and as his failure feeds his burning anger and frustration, he'd hurt someone else. Could be his wife. Or, God forbid, his little girl. He knows I don't give in to bullying and that I don't give up. Which is what ended up getting him into prison for second-degree murder. Without my refusal to quit fighting my fight, he'd have had a manslaughter charge at best, but most likely would have walked away with no charges at all."

She glanced Mac's way, and he didn't make any attempt to discourage her conversation. He met her gaze openly.

Five years of trusting in "them" didn't just evaporate.

She wondered if he knew how badly she'd needed that validation.

"Manning needs to believe that I'm hunting him down," she continued, "while I'm in whatever kind of controlled environment we can create."

"I agree." Mac didn't sound happy about that. But she took a lot of strength from his honesty.

"Warner?" Heath Benson didn't look happy as he turned to the expert.

"We had a case not long ago. A schoolteacher who'd happened upon a crime, talked to the police and ended up on the wrong side of some powerfully bad people. Her father had trained her in outdoor survival skills, and she got herself to a small cave. She wasn't there long. We were able to ping her phone and help our client get to her while we did what he'd hired us to do, but what's key here is what she did in the meantime." The man's delivery was compelling. Mac found himself open to considering possibilities, even while he wanted Stacy in the safe house. With perimeters already set and protocols ready to go.

"The woman used all natural items to build a booby trap around herself. Digging a trench around the cave for instance, filling it with twigs, and then covering the entire thing with desert dirt and pebbles so that anyone approaching would walk through it. At which time, she'd hear a loud crunch and know that her perimeter had been breached."

Mac seemed impressed, though she got no sense at all that he was buying into being a part of such a plan. He'd be giving his own input if he was onboard.

"I like it," Stacy said anyway, glancing at Mac again, quickly, but then right back to Hudson Warner. "It makes perfect sense. We just have to find the right cave—it's not like we have a shortage of them here at the base of the Clairvoyants—then get our traps set. And figure out a reason for Mac and I to be trapped out there. Maybe we're hiking and I twist my ankle and can't walk. We try to radio for help, but there's no service…"

"I'd simply pick you up and carry you out." Mac's words stopped her.

He wasn't on her side.

Which meant she had a choice to make.

Try to push through what looked to be an entire department of negativity or give.in and do it their way.

"So we figure out a different reason," she said. She'd just told them all…she didn't give in. "Or I go in by myself."

In a million years she'd never have seen herself for the person laying a gauntlet down to the chief.

Or to Mac.

"Hold on a second here." Chief Benson sat forward, his tone commanding.

And Mac rapped his thumb on the table. "Stacy's making a good point here," he said. "A valid one that could mean the difference between getting this guy or getting someone else hurt."

She had to blink. Fast. More than once.

No way in hell she could sit at that table and let her eyes fill with tears.

"I agree," Benson said. "The point is valid. But, hear me out. I saw Tom Brandon, your neighbor—" the chief nodded toward Stacy "—at Rich's this morning. He wanted to know if we were any closer to getting this guy. The old man is clearly worried about you. He couldn't understand why we weren't getting you to a safe house, in spite of how hardheaded—his words not mine—you could be at times. He said your grandad must be turning over in his grave."

Stacy felt every eye at the table on her. Withstood the contact without getting the least bit warm under her skin.

Chief Benson continued to hold court. "Listening to everything here, it's made me think…since Manning is proving to be as astute as he is, and has backup plans to prove it, he'd have one for a safe house. Because if someone like Tom Brandon can't believe you aren't in one, most everyone else would expect it as well. Including Manning. If his first plan failed, and you lived, he'd expect you to be in a safe house."

"Right, and doing it now, after this morning's attempt, plays into what you were saying, too, Stacy," Mac said, his tone growing in ownership of the discussion as he sat forward. "You've refused to go, you think you can get him, and he's showing you, you can't. He's winning, which will fuel his need to succeed even more. He'd have to figure that no one would send you out alone to take on this guy," Mac continued. "He knows you'd be outvoted if you still, in his opinion, were lacking in intelligence enough to take him on, and he would probably take pleasure in having made that, the outvoting, happen."

Mac was making too much sense, dammit. Thinking like a man of Manning's caliber might, in terms of underestimating her intelligence.

"We just need to be predictable," Mac continued. "Shift changes have to be at regular hours, protocol has to be exactly as it's already set. He needs to feel confident that he's got us figured out and will show us just how stupid we were to think Stacy would be protected in a safe house."

"Which means we have to be prepared for an abnormal breach," Stacy said, not happy, but not altogether against the plan.

It was better than heading out on the case of her life—literally—without Mac. She might be hardheaded, but she wasn't a fool.

"I'll get my team on a nationwide search of ways safe houses have been breached in the past," Hudson said. "A smart man would do the same research."

From there a house was chosen. Set out in the desert down the road from an old church. Martha went out to Stacy's house to collect a list of her things. Miguel set out for Mac's place to do the same.

And all that was left was for Mac and Stacy to learn all the ways the house could be breached and be prepared to counteract every one of them.

Oddly enough, she wasn't very worried about that. When it came to the job, she and Mac always found a way.

What was giving her the jitters was knowing that until Manning was caught or a week had passed, she and Mac would be holed up alone in a tiny two-bedroom stone building, with a very small kitchen and only one bathroom. She'd been picturing less intimate quarters.

She could hold her own against Manning. Now that she knew he was out there gunning for her.

She wasn't nearly as confident that she could control her new and wholly inappropriate awareness of Mac. The man.

Mac and Stacy were in the safe house by late afternoon. They'd driven a department-owned unmarked tan sedan with a private vehicle escort in front of and behind them.

Mac took the front bedroom, wanting to be between the only entrance and Stacy. He tested all four of the window locks, making certain that, if necessary, he and Stacy could exit through them. And tested the electric wire around the casings that would alert them if anyone tried to breach the openings, making sure all of them were on and working properly.

He didn't unpack.

Stacy had set up a portable whiteboard. Was filling it in based on a picture of the original she'd shot with her phone before leaving the conference room.

Right after they'd had confirmation that there were signs of someone having been up in the paloverde tree Stacy had shot at late that morning. Not only had officers found her bullet wedged lower in the trunk, there'd also been broken twigs right where she'd said she'd seen the glint. And a partial toe print in a clod of loose dirt on the hard, rock-strewn desert ground at the base of the tree.

Didn't mean it was Manning, or anyone working for him. But it did validate her response.

They'd heard on the drive out to the house that the white van had been pulled up the mountain. The entire front end had been smashed like a pancake to the back seat, making any kind of sticker discovery in the strewn shards of glass like looking for a needle in a haystack. There'd been no sign of a body inside. No blood. And no discernible fingerprints. It was being sent to the Sierra's Web lab for further testing.

The drone hadn't been caught on any radar, or security cameras—which wasn't a surprise. But Mac had hoped they'd be able to at least figure out its launch site. Something to give them a starting place. He wasn't about to just sit around and wait for Manning to come to them—though he agreed that it was a good backup plan.

The Sierra's Web forensics team had been able to narrow down the methane canisters to having been sold in two-packs by a chain of national stores. Sierra's Web was in the process of contacting the store's East Coast headquarters to get hundreds of stores with surveillance footage.

Baby steps. He needed leaps and bounds.

As he came out to join Stacy in what they'd set up as their conference room—by moving the kitchen table into the middle of the living space and shoving couch and chairs up against walls—he noticed her cupping her forearm as she brought it down from the board.

"You should have let them stitch you up," he told her. Other than the first glimpse, he hadn't seen the wound she'd sustained that morning. She'd been tended to by paramedics called to the scene of the drone-induced explosion, and by the time she'd been back in the vehicle with him, she'd had her stained uniform sleeve back down to her wrist.

"It's butterflied," she told him. "I wasn't going all the way to the hospital for two stitches."

The gash wasn't deep, he'd been told by the paramedic. Just enough loose skin that it would have been better suited tied together for less scarring.

She'd switched out her uniform shirt since then.

"Let me know if you need help changing the bandage," he said then, knowing he had to let it go. She wasn't his to worry over. Not if it wasn't life or death.

Dropping his legal pad to the table, along with his phone, Mac grabbed a bottle of water, wishing it was beer, and pulled out one of the two wooden chairs just as his phone rang.

Stacy turned, glancing at the screen: *Sierra's Web Hudson Warner*.

They were waiting on the safe house breach report.

He answered on speakerphone.

"I'm sending over what we have so far of the breach report," the technical expert said. "Our preliminary assessment shows the biggest threat to be by air. You're in a brick building with a tile roof so there's no burn threat, but there could, of course, be an explosion."

"Thank goodness for Arizona's tile roofs," Stacy said, half beneath her breath. But Mac heard. And smiled. For no explainable reason.

"We're setting up aerial surveillance," Hudson continued. "Will have someone watching the airspace within three acres of you twenty-four seven. If a drone enters the airspace, it will be brought down."

He didn't ask how. Didn't need to know what he didn't need to know.

"Of more interest to you, and concern to me, is what my team found. You're both going to want to hear this," Hudson said then. Mac saw Stacy stiffen across from him, and he sat forward.

"Stacy and I are sitting right here."

"We've found a motherlode of posts on private sites on the dark web. Various screen names, but they all eventually lead back to various servers in Colorado. All of which have also been frequently used by the verified Landon Manning accounts on popular social media sites."

Mac automatically glanced at Stacy, met her gaze and nodded. Finally. They could be getting somewhere.

"Millions of people use the same servers," Stacy pointed out.

"Yes, but these posts all coincide, within minutes, of the public Manning posts. Always right after them. And from the same server with the same sign in."

"He was in a minimum-security prison," Stacy said. "But he wasn't supposed to have internet access." Mac glanced at her again. Noticing an almost auburn light in her brown eyes.

Finding it familiar.

And completely brand-new.

At a time when her life was at stake?

At any time?

Being locked in with her in such a small space was already getting to him. Why had he ever thought the safe house a good idea?

"Clearly he had a publicity campaign going to keep his name out there. We know he had email access to approved addresses…" Hudson's voice filled the room.

Mac shook his head. "He's Landon Manning, serving in a prison in his home state." He heard the frustration in his tone. Felt it even more fiercely. "It's likely that he got special privileges—even if they weren't officially granted. I'm guessing he had whatever computer access he wanted. Routed however it had to be routed to not come back on him. Let's hear the posts." Pent-up energy raced through him. He needed to work. Not sit.

"They're all rants, and I mean rants—as in they go and

on, but never really get anyplace—about women in the police force, in general. Women who don't know their place and think they need to get involved in their husband's business. Women who can't leave well enough alone. And then about wives who like coming to their husband's defense so much that they decide to be cops and beat up on men for the rest of their lives. Ruining the lives of great men. In several of them he mentions brown hair and brown eyes. Saying the brown hair needs to burn."

Mac froze. Tuned in. All senses on high alert.

Brown hair burning.

A small, relatively harmless explosion—meant for Stacy's head. It would likely have killed her. Or at least left her with permanent injuries.

And it would have set her hair on fire, too.

Glancing at Stacy, seeing the realization dawn in her eyes—and the there-and-gone flash of raw fear—Mac knew he was going to do everything in his power, no matter how much it angered her, to keep her in his sight, to trade his life for hers if that's what it took. To bring Landon Manning down for good.

Chapter 15

"The biggest problem is the unpredictability." Stacy paced the small living area, stopping in front of the whiteboard. "If we had any idea where he was…"

She stared at the board, feeling like bugs were crawling under her skin. Nerves on edge, ready to start popping.

Until Mac came walking in from the kitchen, handing her a cup of the herbal tea she loved. "I asked Martha to pick some up," he told her.

And then she just wanted to cry.

She sipped tea instead. "I asked for it, too," she told him. And had told their fellow officer to make sure that the coffee was dark roast and strong.

Because that was how Mac had to have it.

"Which explains why there's so much of it," he said, standing there with his own cup. He glanced at her over the top of it. "There's an ample supply of coffee, too."

She nodded. Didn't admit aloud what they both knew. They'd put in orders for each other.

It didn't mean anything.

Only that with all the meals they'd shared on shift, all the times they'd heard each other order, they knew preferences.

"This case sucks," she said then, feeling like it had been forever since she and Mac had been coming off a normal shift.

She'd thought that their last night as just two cops working their jobs—the three shootings—had been tough.

Seemed like a cakewalk at the moment.

And she couldn't find her footing. She wanted to. Swore she would. Was doing all she could. Had no intention whatsoever of stopping until Manning was either captured, or he got her. She couldn't stop. Not and live with herself.

But… "I'm not myself." She had to be as honest with Mac as she was being with herself. He was putting his life on the line, and while she had to accept that she might die, she couldn't be responsible for him losing his life.

Not ever.

She'd put herself in front of the bullet first. Every time.

Frowning, Mac set his coffee cup on the table and moved closer to her.

A move that made her situation worse. Plopping down on the wooden chair she'd deemed hers for the duration, she glanced up at him. Took a deep breath. And said, "I'm… unusually emotional."

Truth. Just not explicit.

Did it need to be to save his life?

Pulling his seat around the table next to hers, Mac sat, rested his elbows on his knees as he leaned toward her, and met her gaze. "Do you need to pull off the case?" he asked. And then said, "I'll understand completely, Stace, and no one, no one," he reiterated with a strong nod of his head, "will blame you. In fact, I think everyone would prefer it."

She withstood his stare. And returned a stronger one of her own. "I'm not going to sit back and wait while others put their lives on the line for me, Mac. How could you even think that I would?"

Mac, of all people.

Didn't he know her at all?

The swell of hurt that swamped her for a second was testimony to her earlier statement. But it was no reason for her to run and hide.

To the contrary.

"Wishful thinking is more like it." He sat back with a bit of a wry grin. "Because to be honest with you, I'm finding a bit of…unusual emotion…showing up in some of my reactions as well."

Another swell. More tamping down inappropriate feelings. "You want me to partner with someone else?" Why did she keep coming back to that?

Was she really so afraid of the two of them breaking up?

And if so, was that a reason for them to do so?

"No, Stace. I don't want to lose *you*. I can't get the picture out of my head of your red SUV against those boulders, seeing it rock…" He swallowed, his chin wavering.

Something she couldn't ever remember seeing before. Not in five years worth of dealing with hard stuff.

Her hand lifted, on its way to take his, until she got ahold of herself and laid her palm on the table instead. Making a decision she might regret for the rest of her life. But knowing inside that it was the right thing to do.

They couldn't do their jobs if they were hiding from each other.

"I was in and out that whole time," she told him, forcing herself to look back. To remember. It was life and death on the side of that mountain.

But it was still life and death.

"From the time I was dumped in the back of my car… I'd be dreaming about times when I was a kid, and then I was awake, aware, planning my moves in various eventualities. Biding my time. Fading out again…"

She shook her head. Glanced at him. Met an incredibly

potent look in those brown eyes and had to look away. To draw a deep breath.

He didn't move. Didn't speak.

It was just like Mac, to know that he didn't need to push or pull. If he gave her time, she'd get it out.

He never pressured her. She hadn't consciously realized that until just that moment.

She thought about the seconds when she'd known her vehicle was going over the side of the mountain. When she'd been certain death was seconds, a minute or two at most, away.

And the last memory she'd grabbed, held tight, so that her last feeling was a good one...

He didn't need to know that much.

"I was actually out again when my SUV hit the boulders. The impact jerked me awake. And that whole time, it's hard to believe it was only hours...looking back on it, it seems like it was days..."

She was procrastinating. Had to just get it out there.

If he left, it was for the best.

But if he could live with where she'd gone, if they could get past it as the team she knew they were...

"I tried to plan," she said slowly. Her memories of that part vague. "Thought about climbing to the back...but mostly, I...dreamed."

She looked at him then. Had to if she wasn't going to hide. "They were...hugely inappropriate dreams about you, Mac. I swear to you, I've never had them before, or even entertained thoughts of that nature."

He had to know that. To believe it.

He was looking at her. Nodded. But he didn't seem like Mac.

She didn't blame him. But didn't regret telling him, either. She'd been remiss in not telling him before they'd gotten to the point of being locked up alone in a safe house.

"I kept hearing you call out to me," she continued, moving forward. Giving him all the ammunition he needed to feel justified in walking out. "It was so weird," she remembered. "It was always just my name. No other words. But it's like I had you in there with me..."

She swallowed. And hurried with the rest, focusing on the darker ring around his iris, rather than any expression there. "You'd be touching me. Doing all kinds of things that sent me straight to heaven and I clung to you, wanted more... I'd hear your voice say my name and I'd be right back there, feeling you, wanting more."

He didn't need to hear that she'd been riding him. Or he her.

She was done. He still wasn't talking. Nor had he looked away from her.

"It's okay, Mac. I'm prepared for you to get up and walk out." As prepared as she'd ever be. But she knew, with every fiber of her being, that it was what she truly, deep down wanted, if he felt it was best that he go.

The weaker part of herself would take a bit longer to get there, but she would.

"You heard my voice." When he finally spoke, Mac's throat sounded dry.

"Yes," she told him, nodding. Needing to be strong. For him. But for her, too. Was actually surprised how much more capable she suddenly felt for having told him.

For speaking her truth, rather than living with potentially shameful secrets, knowing that, no matter how difficult, she'd be able to live with the consequences.

"No, I'm telling you, Stace. You really did hear my voice." Frowning, she blinked, and looked right back at him.

"What?" Where was he going with that? Trying to tell her there was some telepathic communication between them?

"For hours. I stood just yards away...unable to get to you. I kept hollering your name. Over and over. Needing you to know that you weren't alone. That you had to hang on because help was coming."

Stacy's mouth fell open. She closed it.

Then she pushed back her chair, jumped up and walked away.

There wasn't anywhere for her to go. But Mac understood Stacy's need to escape. Had such a conversation ever even hinted at something like this between them in the past, it would have been after shift, and she'd simply have exited their shared vehicle, entered her own and headed off to her private life.

At least, that was the way he was seeing her departure as Stacy walked down the hall to her room. She'd shut the door. As effective a move as she could make to leave the workday—including him—and enter her personal life for the night.

Her exit was for the best.

There was no justification for him to ignore the message. To walk down the hall and knock on that firmly closed door.

He did it anyway.

Not to start anything.

To save something.

"Stacy, please. I don't want to lose our partnership. And we will, if we don't work through this together."

He heard movement and backed away from the door. When he heard it open, he turned before he could see her, see inside a room he'd inspected an hour before. Headed back to their shared workspace.

Mac didn't want to sit. Or stand. He didn't want to be still. The house was too small for him by himself, let alone two people.

Just knowing he couldn't head out for a walk, a drive, a beer, made him need those things all the more. He could cook.

Feed them. They had to eat.

Pulling his chair back around to his side of the table, he sat. He'd called the meeting.

"I can't do this, Mac," Stacy said as she sat down across from him. Taking the meeting out of his control before he'd begun. "I can't lose you, lose us. I mean, of course, I can. And I will, if it comes to that, but I don't want to. I love my job. I'll be a cop, no matter what, but I actually get up kind of excited, anticipating the day ahead, when I know we're going to be working together. It's been that way since our first year together and me feeling that way has never screwed us up. So let's not make a big deal of this…little issue…okay? Because give me a break. As far as I knew I was in my last minutes, or maybe even seconds, on earth, and I subconsciously chose to go with pleasure rather than fear. That's all this is…"

She looked him in eye. On and off.

On when she'd been talking about them working together. On when she'd been designating her last minutes. Off, when she'd referred to the issue as little. And off when she'd said, "that's all this is."

"If it's in your subconscious, Stace, it doesn't make it less valid. It just means that you're refusing to acknowledge it."

Why?

Why was he making it worse?

"Yeah, well, why were you standing on a cliff calling my name for hours?"

Her honesty, coupled with his deep respect for her, called for truth. His instincts pushed for a comeback as defensive as hers had been. An attack. A fight.

He might win. Shut it all down.

And...

Be where?

Accomplishing...what?

"Because I couldn't bear the thought of losing you." There'd been no other thought. Just that. For hours.

She nodded. Then said, "Well, I'm sorry I perverted your call, Mac. I swear to you, I've never, ever had a sexual dream about you before. I don't sit around and ogle your body or entertain inappropriate thoughts about you."

Not what a guy really wanted to hear.

And exactly what the cop in him needed.

He wanted to just nod. Accept what she'd said. Let it go.

"I don't *entertain* those thoughts about you, either," he told her. "Anytime they've presented in the past, I simply divert my thoughts and move on." And there was the rub.

A king-size, in his face, disturbing truth.

Her nod seemed...easier. If he wasn't mistaken, he'd seen a flash of relief in her eyes. And a hint of something more...gratification, maybe.

If she made something of it...

"So...since we're both aware of the situation and have proven completely capable of keeping our personal lives out of our professional relationship when we're together, we're good to go."

She'd made a statement. It felt like a question.

Because he had to answer it.

"We've proven capable of keeping our humanness out of things because we didn't acknowledge that it was there.

It wasn't permitted to enter our space. And from the sound of things, your awareness is brand-new."

He wasn't sure how he felt about that. Other than to know he couldn't feel anything long term. Not and keep her in his life forever.

"I've never let myself think about you that way." Stacy's gaze was straightforward. Her expression troubled.

So what was she saying? That she'd been attracted and, like him, had redirected every single thought any time it presented?

Or now that she'd had conscious awareness of her feelings, she was finding him attractive?

Why did it matter? Either way, they had to get a handle on things. Fast.

He was going to get hard, just thinking of her having dreams about him, if he wasn't damned careful. As in having to think of her hanging on those boulders, think of life and death, to keep himself on track.

Because those moments had changed him.

And it couldn't mean anything.

"I don't ever want marriage, or any kind of committed relationship, Stace," he said then. And, when her eyes immediately lit with fire and she opened her mouth, he held up a hand. "I'm not, for one second, assuming you'd ever want one with me. I'm just explaining why it's so critical for us to get this out and done," he told her. "My struggle is twofold."

Again, what was he doing? He, who never admitted personal struggles to anyone…

"Personally, I'm just not that guy. No matter how much I loved a woman, maybe even the more I loved a woman, I'd be adamant against any kind of long-term coupling."

She frowned. "That makes no sense, Mac," she said, her

tone easy. Argumentative as it would have been talking about a case. "If you loved a woman, why on earth would you subject yourself to that kind of heartache?"

"To prevent the worse one."

"Which is?"

"The passage of time. Watching the love erode and turn into hate so gradually you don't even know it has until one day, there it is, staring you in the face."

She could shake her head all she wanted. He'd been there. She hadn't.

"Real love doesn't do that," she told him. "I'm not saying I'm at all in love with you, by the way. Only acknowledging the attraction here. And a deep caring, professionally, for the man with whom I entrust my life every day. But real love, it stands that test of time, Mac."

In that moment, she seemed…young…to him. "How would you know that?" he challenged her.

"My parents were married almost twenty years before they were able to conceive me. And I witnessed that love every day of my life, watching my father live without her." The conviction in her tone grabbed his attention, if not his buy-in. "My dad's a great man. One who suffered huge loss but still brings joy to those who are suffering in any way he can. And he does it through the very real love he holds in his heart. In memory of my mother. My grandfather, the same. And Brett and I… I might not have been head over heels in love with my husband, in a man-woman sense, but I loved him deeply. For almost twenty years, from the time we were kids. Until the night he died. I risked my life to save his, without any training other than the self-defense classes my father had me take in high school. Our love changed. It grew in some ways, faded in others, but at its core, it was there. It's still there. Strengthening me as I head out to get the man who took Brett's life from him."

Like strikes of lightning in a violent storm, her words hit him. He tried to blink them away, close his eyes and ignore the thunder. He didn't want to be in that particular storm. Didn't want to see what the lightning could reflect. He'd chosen to live a life without storms that were out of his area of control.

To live his life fighting the bad that could be stopped.

And there she was, the woman he trusted above all, raining upon him. Not for her own sake. His choice to forgo love didn't affect her personally. But there was a passion there that bothered him, just the same.

He wanted to defend his position. To challenge her. To debate.

He had to step aside from it. At least until they got Manning.

"This is all kind of irrelevant to the topic at hand," he told her. "Right now, we're talking about you and me. This... awareness between us. The way I see it, we have a choice to make. We either give in to it, see where it leads, take what it gives us, or we continue working together."

"Which do you want?" she asked him. And he shook his head.

"No matter what I say, by merely speaking it I could persuade you to feel the same way. As I suspect your choice would persuade me. If I knew you wanted to be working partners more than sexual partners, I'd likely opt that way myself," he said.

"So, what...we just...leave the elephant here between us?"

"No." He pulled his legal pad over, flipped to the blank pages in the back, ripped two out and handed her one.

"Write your answer, and a justification for it. I'll do

the same. And then we switch. Only one caveat," he said. "Total honesty."

Desperation might have driven him. A need to get out of the conversation that was overpowering him. He'd acted like a schoolboy. Passing notes.

To get the question settled.

Mac, decorated cop and grown man that he was, hadn't stopped to think.

Stacy hadn't called him on his ridiculousness.

Her pen moved across the page with confidence.

She wrote several lines. Then put the pen down, folded the page and set it in the middle of the table.

After which she went into the adjoining kitchen, and he heard a pan land on a burner. The refrigerator open and close.

Water running.

Apparently, she was making dinner.

For both of them?

Would they be eating together? Catching Manning together?

Mac sat there with a blank piece of paper, having forced himself into a corner, and started to write.

Chapter 16

Stacy saw the paper land in the middle of the table. She'd started the stir-fry for something to do, not because she was hungry. The sandwiches they'd had at the conference table hours ago were still sitting heavy on her stomach.

More so once the folded yellow square landed on the wood of the table.

She'd tried not to look. Standing at the stove, she had the living area constantly in her peripheral vision. Movement catching her attention couldn't be avoided.

It made it hard for her to breathe.

Was that really going to be it? Her entire life at a crossroads, and a few written lines were going to decide her entire future?

No.

She had to talk to Mac.

Find another way.

Maybe if they just had sex, were really bad at it, or at least unremarkable enough, they could put the whole situation to rest.

And be fired, if anyone found out.

No fraternizing between officers on the job.

No exceptions.

Not even if death was imminent.

Of course, if one was going to die, being fired wouldn't be a huge concern.

She wasn't planning to die.

Putting a lid on the thawing food, she turned the heat down to low and walked to the table. Mac wasn't there.

Both sheets of paper were.

His bedroom door was open. The bathroom one wasn't.

Sitting down, she waited for him to return. Took deep breaths. One after another. Deep in. Slow out. In through the nose, out through the mouth.

Whatever would be would be.

Their fates were sealed.

They'd each spoken their truths.

And no matter what they were, if they didn't mesh, she and Mac would be breaking up. If their truths didn't mesh, she *wanted* to break up with him. Anything less would be a sacrilege.

She did not want their truths to be at odds. She didn't want to die, either, but with possible—and according to the day's theory, likely—professional killers after her, she might.

She heard the bathroom door. Watched the six-foot tall, gorgeously fit, blond shaggy-haired man walk down the hall toward her. And held his gaze the entire way.

There was no game playing going on. No hiding. She was, in a very real sense, fighting for her life in those seconds, as much as she had been the night she'd been kidnapped.

With much the same helplessness.

Mac pulled out his chair. Sat. Glanced at her, and looking her in the eye, nodded toward the two folded sheets between them.

They reached at the same time.

And all eye contact ceased.

With shaking fingers, Stacy opened the page. Recognized Mac's handwriting straight off. Had the inane thought that he'd written less than she had. Felt a slice of worry, of fear, that his lack of verbosity meant they were through.

And then, as if pulled magnetically, her gaze went to the words he'd penned for her.

Working together. Sexual attraction can be found elsewhere. You cannot. Five years together proves we fit. I would rather spend most of my days with you, than risk trying something else, having it fail, and being left with no you.

She'd written a bit more.

It was a good thing he hadn't.

With the tears blurring her eyes, she'd never have made it to the end.

I choose to continue being your work partner. Whatever I'm feeling, whether it's a form of love, grows into love, was always love, will never be love, will be. It will be. And I will be happy as long as you are in my life. The only guarantee of that, for as long as we live and choose our employment, is for us to remain partners. As your partner, I do my best work. We hear over and over, from departments all over the state, about the lives we help save. As your partner I get to spend hours with you every day—more hours than I spend with anyone else—making the world a safer place. Doing meaningful work. As your partner, I look forward to every day.

As to the rest... I hope we can continue to be hon-

*est with each other. To talk if necessary. To find so-
lutions. Just as we do with every single challenge
we face at work and do better than most. Maybe, at
some point, we end up with a one-nighter. Off duty
and apart from work. We see, as I did with Brett,
that the actual event is nice, but nothing to lose sleep
over. Maybe, after we retire, or a promotion comes
that can't be passed up, we want to reassess. Maybe
we're both happily married by then. Maybe at some
point...is the point. The future will be waiting for us
when we get there.*

For now, I choose us just as we are. Flaws and all.

She'd written a damned book. The closest thing to a love
letter he'd ever had.

And all Mac could home in on was *the actual event
is nice, but nothing to lose sleep over.* He had to bite his
tongue not to debate with her on that.

Before his mouth talked her into letting him show her
just how much sleep they'd both want to lose if they got
started with the *actual event.*

Instead, he gave himself time to calm down by reading the note a second time. And allowing that part of his
adrenaline surge, sexual as it was, came from the fact that
they'd made the same choice.

And he had no next step. It felt like a celebratory moment. Did you tip a glass of champagne when you decided
not to pursue a personal relationship?

If you had champagne.

A hug felt in order.

Which would be like taking a starving man to food and
telling him not to eat.

He heard her restlessness across from him. A sigh. Her

pen bouncing lightly against the tabletop, and he knew his time was up.

"We need tomorrow's plan," Stacy said.

Calling his attention right where he'd not been ready to take it. Her face. Her body. Only to find that she was staring at the whiteboard.

Not him.

"Obviously, we aren't just going to sit inside this house. Waiting."

He'd hoped they would. But knew they wouldn't. It wasn't Stacy's way. Or his either.

"It's not that I don't very much want to sleep with you, Stace," he told her. "Because I do."

She swallowed. Looked over at him. And smiled. The sexiest, nonsexy grin he'd ever seen. "Yeah, it's kind of a relief, knowing that I'm not the only one. Now I can lust after you all I want and not feel guilty."

Right. They couldn't act on it.

"It's a get out of jail free card," she added. "No impropriety because we aren't acting on it, and no harassment because we've talked about it, both know the other has the wants, and, in full disclosure, have decided we still want to be work partners."

Yeah. Because she had no idea what she was missing. What they were missing.

He might not ever want a full-time woman in his personal life, but he liked sex enough to lose sleep for it. As did the women he had it with.

Who would not be Stacy. But maybe, at some point, he could encourage her to try again, with someone else.

At some point, her letter had said. *At some point...*

Their futures would be waiting for them.

In the moment, they'd removed their so-called elephant.

And had the most important job of their careers to complete.

"What would we do if this was any other case?" Mac came at Stacy with an energy she hadn't seen in him since the day of her kidnapping—when they'd been taking down shooters.

She welcomed its return with a surge of relief. Of gratitude.

And affection, too.

A feeling she didn't have to fight. That in itself was a load off.

"We'd be out there looking for Manning. Physically drawing him out," she repeated what she'd already fought for at the conference table.

He nodded. "So how do we do that from here?"

His gaze was head-on. Open. Drawing her response. "What matters to him right now? In his current situation? He's angry to the point of probable irrationality due to his lost reputation, his lost career. So that's where we hit him. He's all over social media. We can sit right here and attack him there."

Mac picked up his phone. Dialed and set it on the table. In seconds she heard Hudson Warner pick up. And within twenty minutes, she and Mac had their own secure, untraceable accounts on several of the social media sites where Manning had the most active followers and posted regularly. Both dark web and not.

They spent the next several hours posting from their phones. Checking back at each site every fifteen minutes, in between eating, doing dishes and scheduling future posts.

At shift change, the officers joining them came in to say

hello, to go over protocols, followed by the officers leaving coming in to report no suspicious activity and wish them a good night.

No one seemed to blink at the idea of her and Mac sharing the little cabin by themselves all night. Not even Chief Benson.

A week ago, she wouldn't have either.

She couldn't give it any more thought. She was lusting after the man. Could go ahead and dream about him all night if that's what came to be.

Without breaking any rules or risking the end of a life that she loved.

Without guilt.

As she yawned and stood up, excusing herself to bed, she realized their talk that night had made things much better. Because now she knew that Mac found her attractive, too, and she didn't feel so pathetic coming to terms with her newfound subconscious truths.

All was good until she got to the door of her room, opened it and heard Mac's voice come at her from the living room.

"Sweet dreams!" he called.

And she shut her door with a decidedly unamused click.

By noon the next day, Mac could almost convince himself that the job was going to go like clockwork. He and Stacy would continue to ramp up the tension on social media, which would inflame Manning. He'd charge out to kill Stacy himself, making a mistake, doing something foolish or just plain getting caught by those who were trained to catch men like him.

Or the kidnapper and murderer would send professionals to do it for him.

Either way, they were all ready. Chief of police. County sheriff. Sierra's Web. Officers and deputies pulled from surrounding areas as needed. And him and Stacy, the proven partnership.

"There's been zero response," Stacy said, as they sat at the table, both surfing their phones and eating peanut butter and jelly sandwiches. "Even on the dark web."

"He's beyond being able to get any satisfaction vicariously," Mac told her. "The internet isn't doing it for him anymore. He's here somewhere, getting ready to issue a planned response."

She bit. Chewed. Swallowed. Nodded.

And his mouth watered.

But only for a second.

The lack of attack from Manning had him on edge. He was hoping the tension was just because it left them with little to do, and he and Stacy were just not the sit and wait type of officers.

Unless they were sitting on a house. Then they could be still, shoot the breeze, for hours. To be ready for two minutes of action on a second's notice.

She took another bite.

The man in him noticed.

He had no doubt Stacy would be cover model material in a swimsuit with that long dark hair arranged around her.

And he'd rather have her in uniform with her hair in a ponytail. He got to spend his days with the real woman.

She put down her phone. "We've been here almost twenty-four hours and there hasn't been so much as a pack of coyotes getting our attention, let alone a real threat. What if he's already back in Colorado?"

"Sierra's Web checked in with his wife this morning.

She hasn't seen or heard from him." Which Stacy already knew. "And they're watching all airports," he reminded her.

Officers were also watching Stacy's house and property.

Mac wasn't comfortable with the lack of action, either. Something big was coming. He could feel it. And would take it on. He didn't like being a sitting duck not knowing what was coming.

"We're usually the ones on the offensive," Stacy said then. "We're the hunters."

He met her gaze. Nodded.

"We need to get back out there, Mac. Do what we do best."

His gut agreed.

His emotions greatly overwhelmed his response. Rendering him...immobile. Even while he knew that Stacy wasn't going to just sit at a table for much longer. Not without a specific job to do. Without a plan of action.

So they had to find one. Getting lost in fear for her life was exactly what a cop couldn't do. That was the sort of thing that could ultimately have Mac costing Stacy her life.

The realization hit home hard. "You still think Warner's mountain cave suggestion has merit?" he asked her.

And with a long glance, Stacy handed him her phone. She had it all there. The area. The natural traps—a ditch similar to what Hudson had described. Filled with twigs and just enough ground cover to conceal them. One step and they'd be alerted to anyone encroaching on their space. Tree limb camouflages over their enclosure. Mouse traps barely covered with dirt. The list went on and on.

"Take your pick of them," she told him. "We aren't out to kill him, unless he attacks first. We want our chance to bring him in alive. Personally, I don't want him put out of his misery."

On the surface, the idea had merit. But he had questions. "How do you propose getting safely to this cave? Getting it set up? Getting him to follow you? How is being trapped in a cave any different than being trapped here?"

"First, I was thinking Sierra's Web would scope out the exact cave. And set the traps, whatever we choose. Second, we quit hiding. He had no trouble finding us when we were out doing our job. We head back to the station, and then, later in the day, as if we're on a call, we drive out to the base of the mountain. And we have each other's back as we get to the cave. Just like we always do. The cave will need to be accessible and close, and we'll have predetermined natural shields, a route through tall brush, for instance, to get us there. Or maybe Hudson Warner watching a drone camera to alert us to any danger. Third, no patrol around us. We do this you and me. Like always. As long as we stay in the cave until he appears, we're safer than we are here. And the key is, we need a reason for being there. We can radio in that we've got something, that we're checking it out, one of us could even shoot a bullet to make it seem as though we're under attack, and I can slide down a ravine and appear as though I hurt myself. You get me to the cave. You can jump in any time here, Mac. I'm open to any tweaks this idea needs."

He nodded. Cop to cop, she had every angle covered. And while the idea was a wild one, under the circumstances, the overall plan made sense.

"It's either we take a chance to bring him to us, or I live my life as a prisoner, live in constant fear of attack. He could go underground for weeks, or months. Sometimes fugitives manage to elude the law for decades. How do I have any kind of life, knowing that at any time he could strike out at me. Or worse, at those I love?"

Love. There was that word again.

She'd used it in her note.

Mac shook his head against a thought that didn't serve the moment, and said, "I'll call Sierra's Web." And in the meantime, he could hope to all the fates that be, that Manning made a move, was in custody, before the mountain plan became action.

Chapter 17

The plan made Stacy nervous, but not as much as sitting around with nothing happening. They could be giving Manning, or his professionals, time to wipe out the safe house somehow. Considering the small explosive dropped by a drone meant for her scalp, methane gas released into her home's plumbing system, being kidnapped in her own garage and being shoved over a mountain... Manning wasn't fighting in any ways they were used to.

His only signature seemed to be expertly planned unpredictability.

From what she'd seen of the man during her times in court, fighting him, he'd be enjoying the cat and mouse game he was playing with her. Not as much as he'd have enjoyed having her simply disappear off the face of the earth as originally planned...but the man seemed to get off on showing her he was the superior one of the two after all.

If she let him make her cower, she'd risk being a mouse for the rest of her life. And not just with Manning. He'd have won a mental battle inflicting wounds from which she might not ever recover.

She would be strong for those she loved. As her father had been. Her grandfather. Brett. And Mac, too.

Just admitting that her partner mattered, being able to

think about him with her heart and not feel guilty, gave her strength. Fantasizing about his body to get through tough moments…well, that was a delightful bonus.

Did she want more? Of course. But then, she'd have liked to have grown up with a mother. To have a father who found his life's calling a little closer to home. And not to have buried Brett, too.

She was almost excited when, a couple of hours after lunch, Mac's phone rang. With an entire mountain at their backs, she and Mac had the best chance of bringing the case of her life to a successful conclusion.

Expecting the caller to be Sierra's Web, she was surprised to see the chief's 911 come up on Mac's screen as he tapped for speaker call and set the phone between them.

"Mac, Stacy, we've got a missing and endangered. Jimmy Southerland's four-year-old daughter."

"Mariah?" Mac stood abruptly. "Where? How long ago?"

"He called it in five minutes ago. We need all hands on deck. You guys stay there, but I need to pull your protection detail…"

"No way we're staying here." Stacy stood, too, watching Mac. He'd gone to high school with Jimmy. Sometimes stopped at the pub after shift to have a beer with him.

With a quick glance at her, he nodded.

"Jimmy was walking with her out to his car. He got hit from behind. When he came to, the car and the girl were gone. We've since found it broken down out on Granada Road."

A road that led to a popular tourist hiking trail. Stacy's stomach sank.

"Give us a grid," Mac said then, as she reached for her clutch and gear.

He'd already grabbed his and picked up his phone as

they headed out the door. They'd both been ready to run in an instant from the moment they got up.

She'd just never thought…little Mariah. Stacy didn't know Jimmy and his wife, or their only child, personally. But she'd seen the parents around town her entire life.

"It could be a good thing, him taking her to the mountain," she said, after a glance at Mac's tight chin. "He's keeping her close. With Jimmy's money, there should be a ransom call coming…"

"He doesn't have money," Mac told her, topping their car with a bubble and speeding through the first red light they'd come to. They'd been in the desert, but Granada Road felt like it was on the other side of time. "He inherited his folk's mansion, but the money went to charity. His old man wanted Jimmy to have to work, to earn. Said giving him everything would make him lazy."

As shocked as Stacy was to hear that the Southerlands weren't rich as she'd always thought, she was way more focused on the next hour. "I've lived here my whole life and I didn't know that. I'm guessing the kidnapper doesn't, either."

So there'd be a ransom call. "We'll come up with the money," she told Mac. "Saguaro takes care of her own."

"Let's just hope we get that chance…"

With a sharp turn, he squealed out in front of a car that had slowed for them and took backroads through town at a faster clip than she'd have done.

"As soon as we're out of the car, you head up the mountain," Mac told her as they quickly neared the site they'd been given. "I'm right behind you. Every step of the way."

They'd have to split up to cover their territory. But with him behind her, even just to the west of her, they'd be within hearing distance of each other the entire time. Five years of working together, they had their search protocols down pat.

For a split second, as Mac turned the last corner, Stacy was consumed by a stab of fear so sharp it took her breath. "What if this is some ruse to get us out here?" She asked the question aloud, on the verge of paranoia.

Glancing her way, Mac said, "I had the same thought. I put it down to being cooped up in that damned house for twenty-four hours," he told her. "Manning's a master manipulator, coming at us in ways we'd least suspect, making us paranoid, but taking a four-year-old child? It doesn't fit. He's got a young daughter of his own. From what his wife said, he's a great father."

Mac pulled into a turnout, concealing the car as best he could. Her fear gone, Stacy checked her weapon and went to work. Filled with the drive that got her out of bed every morning. To do her best to rid the world around her of any evil that lurked within their midst.

She had one goal. Find Mariah alive.

Every sense, every nerve ending on high alert, Mac watched Stacy head up the mountain, and then took off in his own direction. Combing the ground for any sign of human inhabitation. Listening for the slightest sniffle.

He assumed whoever took the child had her mouth covered, but he'd have to leave her nose free for her to breathe. And scared kids cried.

Before he'd gone far, he put in a call to Jimmy, Mariah's father, just to reassure the man that the entire department was on the case and would find his daughter. And to get any pointers in terms of where she might hide if she got free.

Jimmy had been so distraught he'd barely responded. So

Mac had promised him they'd find her alive. Something he knew better than to do.

But he believed it—assuming they found her soon.

The guy wasn't going to kill Mariah. Not right off, at any rate. He'd need to give proof of life to get any ransom money. And if he'd taken the girl for any other reason, he'd have headed out of town. Not to the mountain.

Until he'd been told differently, Mac wasn't allowing any other scenario to enter his mind. His job was to find the girl, and visualizing finding her alive was the way to do his best work. To have every ounce of his adrenaline focused on a good outcome.

And while he listened for any minute sound a child might make, he'd pick up any other unusual sound as well. Including all signals his partner might send.

Beyond that, he had to trust Stacy to do her job. She was the best cop he'd ever worked with. Partially because while she was aggressive in all her pursuits, she had an eye on all risks always.

But neither of them would put their own safety above that of a four-year-old child.

He grew more and more uneasy as he slowly traveled farther up the mountain, noticing all the little caverns and boulder formations that could hide a person being silenced while searchers walked right by.

It wasn't his first mountain search, by far. Nor his first child abduction.

But it was the first time in his career the two had coincided with each other.

He was sweating in his long sleeves as he pushed through some brush to look around and pulled back as he sustained a sharp prick from a cactus needle on the other side. Cactus needles had been on Stacy's list of a weaponized nature for their upcoming cave maneuver.

The plan had been to give them an excuse to be alone in the mountains...

Mac rubbed his arm and pressed on. He couldn't allow himself to be slowed down by thoughts of his partner's own danger. While the midday January sunshine was warming the valley, it would be cold farther up in the mountain. And when darkness fell...

They had to find Mariah before that happened. Searchers would be called back in for the night.

An hour into the search, Mac heard the muffled tones of the recall siren. Like the town's tornado warning, the sound meant the child had been found.

Thank God. Sending good thoughts for her well-being and unharmed condition, his thoughts immediately went to getting his partner back under protection.

Turning, he gave a whistle that used to get him in trouble when he was a kid. The sound was shrill and carried long distances.

It was a call to his partner for a location check. Stacy's response wouldn't be nearly as piercing as his, but as close as their designated paths had been, he'd be able to hear her.

He'd turned as soon as he'd heard the siren. Was heading toward Stacy's assigned east-west coordinates, and, thinking she might have been checking out any of the innumerable caves in the Arizona mountains, he whistled a second time.

Heard nothing in return.

And, heart pounding, started to run. Downhill. Sliding. Righting himself. Heading east. And calling for all he was worth.

"Stacy!"

Over and over.

A sickening replay.

Had Manning actually been behind the kidnapping after all? An elaborate ruse to get Stacy alone? He and Stace had both had the thought.

Stacy. She had feelings for him.

And he'd finally admitted his for her. To himself. To her.

Did Manning have her? Or maybe she was just out of earshot…maybe she was already heading down to join their peers in celebration of a quick and successful rescue.

But Stacy wouldn't vacate their grid without him. Not ever. They didn't leave each other behind.

And she wasn't answering, dammit. He slid. Reached out with his hand. Took a palmful of cactus needles, and just kept going. If Manning had her…

Mariah's speedy rescue gave weight to his fears. The kidnapper had only held the child long enough to…

It couldn't be. His imagination was in overdrive.

He ran. He slid and scraped.

He called.

With no response.

And for the first time in his adult life, Mac knew what a shattering heart felt like.

She heard the siren.

And Mac's whistle.

Heard him calling her name.

Heard the sound grow more distant.

Heard it all with a growing panic that she fought to contain. Tears squeezed through lids shut to contain them. Even as prey to her captor, she wouldn't let him see the extent of his victory.

He could hurt her body. End her life.

But he wasn't going to take her heart and soul away from her.

She hoped.

Eyeing her gun on a patch of open dirt, yards in front of her, she listened as Manning came down the mountain. She had no way of knowing if she was in his sights.

Could have a bullet in the head at any second.

But as long as there was the possibility of saving herself, of taking him down, she'd be there. Fighting.

She'd seen him behind her shortly after she'd set out on her own. Had hoped if he didn't realize she knew he was there, she could lead him to a cave, duck inside, distract him until searchers could find Mariah. Or she could get a shot off before he noticed, if that was the only way.

Instead, from just feet behind her, he'd called out to her. Telling her to stop. She couldn't see the gun pointing at her back, but she felt it's excruciating weight in the middle of her spine.

So she'd ducked and run. Planning to circle around, to get behind him. Had managed to lose him for a while. Only to see that he'd climbed straight up. With a vantage point that would allow him to see her farther down the mountain. That's when she'd seen the ledge. The drop-off.

Five feet or so.

A jump and roll had happened automatically. Training taking over when thought threatened to freeze her.

It wasn't until she was safely under an overhang of the mountainside that she'd realized her gun, which she'd shoved into her holster for the jump, had come loose during the roll. And she'd been holding her breath, almost literally, ever since.

Waiting for the demon to appear.

Or her life to end.

Her Taser, her Mace…none of it was going to help her against a man with revenge in his veins and a gun in his hand.

She didn't dare move. Or make a sound.

Instead, she listened to Mac calling her name. Taking comfort even as his fading voice told her he was getting farther away. With Manning's superior vantage point, chances were he'd see Mac, take him down, before Mac even knew he was there.

She couldn't let the fiend take down another man she loved.

The thought trickled through her panic. Heightening her senses. Making her aware of the sounds coming from above her and the small rocks trickling over the ledge. Manning was directly above her. Approaching the ledge from which she'd jumped. If she was calculating right, as soon as he left the drop-off, to wind around the mountain to the side of it, she could have a small window of chance to roll for her gun and get back without him seeing her.

A millisecond…

And…go!

She rolled, grabbed, rolled back.

Held her breath.

And heard, "Drop the gun."

Chapter 18

Not finding Stacy, Mac raced far enough out of the interior of the mountain for his radio to have range. Calling into the chief on a private channel, he heard, first, that Mariah was back with Jimmy and her mother, unharmed.

Relief flooded him, even while he stood in a pool of fear. Knowing the four-year-old was okay lightened his load some. If she'd been part of an elaborate ruse, at least whoever had taken her, Manning or a hired man, had some humanity.

"Is Stacy back?" he bit the words out.

"No."

The expected response put him right back in hell. Asking for any available officers to move toward Stacy's assigned coordinates, he turned and ran, clipping his radio back in place as he took rocks and hills at top speed.

It was a bold move, taking a child to get a veteran officer out of hiding. An even bolder one to attack her with officers combing the area. Manning had to know that they'd get to her quickly.

Unless he figured on everyone being out of radio range. And looking for Mariah much longer than it took to find her.

His mind sped as he slid down an incline and clawed his

way right back up again. He'd managed to pull the cactus needles out of his hand as he'd headed down the mountain, but one had broken. Was embedded.

He welcomed the pain. It kept him grounded in the moment. Aware. Distracted him from the agony exploding deep inside him.

He'd known.

And he'd told himself he was overreacting because of his newly admitted feelings for Stacy. Afraid of being overprotective to the point of unprofessional, he'd erred in the other direction. He'd failed to listen to the instincts that made him a decorated cop.

No way he should have agreed to stay partnered with Stacy. Not even for an hour. Not after she'd made her revelation.

And he'd been honest with himself, and Stacy, regarding his own attraction to her. While he'd been under the impression that she just saw him as an older guy, a veteran cop and partner, he'd been able to keep himself under wraps.

But once he'd known that she wanted him, too…

The department's no fraternization rule was in place for solid reasons. In their jobs, conflict of interest, conflict of emotion, of split-second choice, got people killed.

With sweat dripping down his face, soaking the T-shirt covering his back beneath his uniform, Mac kept up his pace, watching his compass to keep him on Stacy's coordinates.

If Manning had her, he could have taken her anywhere.

And he had to believe his partner would have left some sign for him. Given him some way to find her. She wouldn't just leave him.

Not if she could help it.

He wasn't leaving her, either. If he was out on the mountain all night, in the dark alone with the animals, then he'd be there. He didn't go home without her.

Period.

The thoughts continued to tumble as he climbed. Others would be covering the mountain as well. Helicopters had already been on their way to look for Mariah. Mac figured the chief would have radioed to have them keep on coming.

But with all the interior hills and valleys, cliffs and deep gullies, any of them could be right on top of her and not find her.

The chief would call Sierra's Web. Bring Luke Dennison back. With search and rescue dogs. He knew the ropes.

And knew, too, that in all likelihood, if it got to that point, Stacy would already be gone.

They weren't going to get lucky boulders a second time.

He should never have left her.

He'd known…

Was that a voice? Or the wind in a gulley? Playing with his mind.

Stopping, Mac listened. Was certain he heard voices.

Went toward them.

And jerked back, his gut slamming, as the unmistakable sound of a gunshot rang out. Echoing all around him.

Stacy jerked, her body feeling the pushback impact as the warning gunshot rang out. With her head still protected by the overhang, and her back to a mountain wall, she stood, gun in hand, facing Landon Manning for the second time in her life. He'd lowered his gun. She had not.

Because he hadn't dropped the weapon as she'd told him to.

He'd just stood there talking.

A man who looked like Manning, but not one she recognized as anything like the egotistical excuse for a man who'd killed her husband.

"I'm telling you," he said, repeating himself for at least the eighth time. "There's someone out there, gunning for you. It's not me."

She didn't believe him. Wasn't going to be played the fool and have his fiendish smile, his laughter, be the last thing she saw and heard.

She had to outsmart him. Outlast him.

There was no doubt in her mind that if she fired her gun at him, rather than up in the air, the gunslinging rodeo rider would have seen her finger pressure on the trigger and have his own gun up and fired before he went down.

He'd take her with him.

She'd rather that than have him get away.

But if she just hung on, they could get him.

"You're out here all alone," he was saying. "The search has been called off. Everyone's gone. It's a perfect scenario for whoever is after you. He kills you, dumps you in some ravine out here where the animals will get you and they'll never find the evidence."

She swallowed, chin up. He was telling her his plan. She got that. Wasn't going to give him the satisfaction of showing fear.

When she didn't show up down below, the chief would send people back up. Mac would be back, but with help. All she had to do was hang on.

There'd likely be a helicopter at some point. They flew anytime anyone was reported missing in the mountains. She knew the ropes.

Just had to keep herself focused. And show no fear.

She wasn't going to leave the earth without giving Mac

a chance to do his job. Wasn't taking any chances on missing seeing his face one more time.

And if she got out of her current situation alive, if she survived this one, she was going to beg the man to kiss her. To devour her.

She didn't want to die without knowing him completely. She wanted reality to take with her, not to die on a fantasy.

Her arms, her shoulders, ached. Her fingers had mostly lost feeling. They still worked, though. She'd pushed flesh against metal enough to know that much.

"I don't know what else to do to convince you I'm telling the truth."

"Put your gun down."

"And have you shoot me? And throw *me* over the cliff? You think I don't know that's what you'd love to do? Like I said, I get it. I don't blame you. I also don't want to die. I have a wife and daughter who've stood by me, who, for whatever reason, still love me…"

Love. He'd told her all about being a changed man. About having gotten sober in prison. And realizing that he'd been given a second chance. With his wife. His little girl. How he'd come to Arizona to see her. To apologize to her. He'd realized that until he could do so, he wasn't the man he needed to be. He'd chickened out the first time he'd seen her in uniform. Naming the date of the private flight into the east valley. Half afraid she'd arrest him for some bogus infraction. But he'd come back because he needed her to know that, while he couldn't give back the husband he'd taken from her, he was going to live the rest of his days honoring Brett's life. When he came back, he'd heard on the news about the attempt on her life. Had figured in some weird way fate had given him a chance to redeem himself. He could keep an eye on her. Maybe even help save her.

Not in exchange for the life he'd taken. But to do what Brett would have done had he been alive.

She'd heard it all. More than once. Including him saying that he'd been tuned into the local police band radio for the couple of days he'd been there. Had heard the all-points bulletin go out regarding Mariah Southerland. Had figured she'd respond. And had waited for her to arrive. Intending to have her back.

She just didn't believe any of it. She'd heard the man spin his tales in court, too.

Was he so full of himself that he didn't know to change the black hoodie he'd worn on his trip to the city building to look her up? She'd recognized it the second she'd seen him.

He'd lowered his gun the second she'd told him to. And though she'd been waiting, hadn't raised it again.

She could kill him. There wouldn't likely be anyone who'd blame her or make trouble over it. But it wouldn't be a good shot.

And she didn't want to die a bad cop.

Didn't want to leave Mac with doubts about her...

"Drop the gun or I put a bullet in your head."

She heard the voice. Saw the face behind the man she'd held at standoff until her entire body ached.

And though his words hadn't been directed at her, she dropped her gun to her side.

Then, her chin trembling, she watched Jesse Macdonald take Landon Manning into custody.

She was free.

They had him. All the way down the mountain, pushing an insistent ex-rodeo star every step of the way, Mac heard all the garbage Manning had been feeding Stacy up on the mountain.

Trying to break her. To get her to trust him, Mac reasoned silently. Making his final victory that much sweeter.

Other than the part where Manning was lying, Mac heard it all from Manning himself. Stacy stayed one step behind them, ready, he knew, in case Manning tried to make a run for it. She hadn't said a word.

While he hadn't done more than a visual check, Mac felt confident that Manning hadn't touched her. She had met his gaze, and at his silent question in a raised eyebrow, had shook her head. And other than sweat and grime from her climb, there were no visible changes to her since he'd last laid eyes on that beautiful form. Her shirt was buttoned and tucked just as she always wore it. Second to the last button above her belt buckle.

So the buttons and buckle didn't rub, he knew, after having teased her about it a few years before.

"I swear to you, man, I've done nothing wrong. I was trying to help her."

Yeah, yeah, yeah.

Mac didn't bother to respond.

He didn't trust himself to follow protocol if he opened his mouth any more than to read the man his rights, and issue directions when necessary.

As soon as they were able to get a radio signal, Stacy called in.

And Mac smiled as the suddenly vibrant device, exploding with cheers from the various law enforcement personnel on the channel. Just from hearing her voice.

He wasn't the only one who valued Stacy Waltz.

When she reported that they had Manning in custody and were bringing him in, the chief responded, saying he was sending backup to escort them the rest of the way down. No one was taking any chances with the man.

Landon Manning would be lucky if he ever experienced a moment of freedom again.

With Sierra's Web gathering evidence, and Mac and Stacy testifying, the man was going away for a very long time.

And Mac was going to be heading out as well. His pre-occupation with his own emotions had nearly cost his partner her life.

He'd rather be dead himself.

Stacy had to watch the interrogation. Several people, including the chief, had told her to go home and get some rest. She couldn't be done until it was done.

Mac stood with her, watching through the glass, listening over the speaker, as Manning continued the smooth talk. The man was good. Knew his story so well, he never missed a beat.

"This is exactly how it was five years ago," she told Mac. "If I hadn't been there myself, if I hadn't seen what happened, I'd have believed him. If not for me there, being a witness, he'd have walked away without any charges at all. He'd have gotten away with murder."

"At least now he's admitted to what he did," Mac told her. "He's given you some vindication."

"Only because he's trying to get something for himself," she told him. "If you start to believe he's sincere, you fall prey to his manipulation. I sat with his wife. Saw a bruise to the right of her eye that I know he gave her, and she wouldn't speak up. Not even with me there taking the stand."

Manning had told her that afternoon that he'd only raised a hand to his wife once. The same night he'd hit Brett. The actions had put him in jail, but he'd said that hadn't been his wake-up call. It had been the look on his wife's face after he'd flung out his hand in frustration and caught the side of her face. He hadn't had a sip of alcohol since.

At the time, he'd told the arresting officer that he'd bumped into his wife. And that Brett had come at him, that he'd only been pushing Brett away and that Brett had tripped and hit his head.

Manning had finally fallen silent. And Lieutenant Stahl, sitting across from him, pushed sheets across the table in front of him. Photos of posts from his dark web sites.

"You have a story prepared for these, too?" Stahl asked.

Manning appeared to read, taking his time, going from page to page. Until he suddenly stopped and pushed the whole lot of them back across the table. "I've never seen these before in my life," he said, looking straight at the lieutenant.

"He looks right at you as he lies," Stacy said. "It messes with your head."

It was messing with hers. She saw her kidnapper, the murderer, her stalker in custody, and still didn't feel like it was over.

"He's fighting for his life," Mac said. "People without conscience can say whatever they have to say."

He'd been acting odd, ever since they'd come down the mountain. Distant. And yet…not. He was right there by her side, making sure people gave her space, watching over her. Had already said he'd be the one driving her home.

But he wasn't looking her in the eye. At all.

It had been a rough day. But a hugely successful one. There would be celebration time.

But at the moment, she wasn't feeling at all open to socialization, either. She needed time to process.

"I swear to you, I didn't write any of that…" Manning

was still denying his culpability. And it hit her…the reason she couldn't seem to believe it was actually over.

Because she knew what the man was capable of doing. The weeks and months ahead, the trial…the entire time she'd be worrying that he'd find a way to get away with it all. He'd come so close the first time around…

"…but I think I know who did." Manning's words grabbed her attention. She glanced at Mac. Jaw tight, his eyes seemed to be trying to bore holes into the glass in front of him.

"This kid, Troy Duncan. He's the kid brother of one of my cellmates. Grew up idolizing me. He wanted to help me out, so I told him to run my social media accounts. Who better to keep my memory alive? Since I've been out, I've been watching out for him some. Seemed like a good guy. Has a job. Does good at it." Manning flicked a hand at the pages again, throwing a disgusted glance in their direction. "This stuff… I had no idea. But he's the only one who'd have had access to my accounts…"

Stacy's heart dropped another notch. "See I told you, he has an answer, an explanation, for everything you throw at him."

With knots in her stomach, she glanced up at Mac. Tugged on his shirtsleeve until he looked at her. Really saw her. "I swear to you," she said, holding his gaze. "I saw him kill my husband."

In the end, it had been her word against his. She'd been believed.

"I know, Stace." Mac's nod, his expression, was completely open. "I've never doubted that for a second. And now we have proof."

Heart pumping harder, from his look, his trust…and his last statement, too. "We do? Where?"

Had she missed something big while she'd been up on that mountain?

"You weren't a cop back then. Didn't have access to records. But they're here now, if you want to see them. Manning had apparently filed for an appeal. The DA hired a pathologist to go over all the evidence one more time. The report proves, medically, that Brett was hit in the head with an object that matches, exactly, an imprint from Manning's fist."

Staring, hearing roaring in her ears, she stepped back. "Why wasn't I ever told?"

"That's the question I asked an hour ago. Because the appeal was denied, there was no reason to notify family. You were young, grieving. You knew the truth because you'd been there..."

She got it. One of the hardest parts of being a cop was dealing with family members. Knowing how best to serve them. What to say, or show, what to spare them of.

"We need that kind of proof now, Mac," she said, staring at the man. Vowing to herself that the truth would win again.

She was going to be free of Landon Manning once and for all.

Physically, but mentally, too.

They had him in custody. The rest would come.

So why was she still afraid? Feeling hunted?

Why wasn't she feeling like celebrating?

Chapter 19

Mac felt more uneasy than he'd have liked as he and Stacy left the station after dark that night. Manning had denied seeing Troy Duncan in Arizona. He knew nothing about a stolen van. Had never owned or even played with a drone. He'd admitted to being at the east valley airport. Claimed that he'd never been at the city building.

And he'd never been in Stacy's garage or even on her property.

Could Duncan somehow be behind the attacks on Stacy's life? Maybe the man he idolized had changed, seemingly because of Stacy, no longer able to win in the rodeo ring, and dedicating his life to making amends for killing a man. If, by any chance, any of what Manning was saying was true…was it feasible that the younger man had decided to kill the person responsible for bringing down his hero?

The dark web rants made it a possibility.

And even if Manning was just doing as he'd done last time, lying through his teeth, he still would have had to have a getaway driver after putting Stacy's red SUV in neutral and pushing it over the cliff. There had to have been a second perp.

He'd mentioned as much to the chief before he'd left. And had been there when the chief had called Sierra's Web, too, to start a photo recognition search on the younger man, on the internet, in the system, anyplace they could search. Mac had screwed up once trying to keep Stacy safe. He wasn't going to take any chances a second time.

"What were you and Benson talking about back there?" Stacy asked as they turned off Main Street, heading out to her place.

He had to tell her. Knowing Stacy, she was already entertaining her own thoughts on the matter. He just wanted her to have some time to breathe.

And that wasn't his call. For the moment, they were still partners. And when they no longer were, it still would never be his right to do her thinking for her. Or make choices as to what she should or should not know. Not when it came to her life.

"We're looking harder at Troy Duncan. If there's any chance at all that Manning isn't lying about everything…"

"His reaction to the dark web rants," she said then, looking over at him. He saw the movement out of the corner of his eye.

Mac kept his gaze on the road. "It's not quite over yet."

"With Manning down, the biggest part of it is. The midazolam. It's a common drug used by veterinarians. There are plenty of those on the rodeo circuit. You notice he didn't deny having access to it."

Their bosses had mentioned that in the brief meeting they'd had after Manning's interrogation. He hoped they were all right. Figured she was hoping, too.

And then he was pulling into her drive. With no intention of leaving her there alone. Proper cop behavior or not.

Even if it meant hanging out in his truck for the rest of the night.

"I've got the jitters, Mac. Like something's not right.

Maybe it's just residual. Probably the Troy Duncan piece. But it doesn't seem smart for me to stay here alone tonight. Most particularly with no transportation."

There'd been no chance to do car shopping. He mentally added it to the next day's agenda. The chief had told them both to take a couple of days off as they'd left the station that evening.

"I'd already planned on staying," he told her, as honest as always. Maybe, when everything was over, the fear was gone, and he'd moved on to another department, another job, he and Stacy would be friends. "But I was half figuring I'd be sleeping in my truck. This makes it easier. I've got my bag from the safe house, and I already know which room is mine." He grinned at her.

And when she smiled back, he finally let himself soak in the relief of knowing that they'd ended Manning's reign of terror.

There were loose ends to tie up, but Stacy was free from the monster.

The whole Manning thing would slowly sink in. She just had to give it time. Seeing the man again…spending those last moments in a standoff with him on the mountain…was still surreal. A nightmare come to life.

Hearing his voice again had ripped her at her core.

"I don't think I'm going to be able to relax until Manning is sentenced and in prison—hopefully not in this state," she told Mac as they entered her home. Hoping she could find the relief that normally came at the close of a case.

It felt good to be in her own space. And to have him there.

Even if he was acting oddly.

Ordinarily she would have gone in and changed the second she got home. But with him there…

"You want a beer?" she asked as he came back into the great room after dropping his bag in his room. Still in uniform as well. She'd already pulled a bottle of hometown brew out for herself.

And was glad when he took the one she held out to him.

They'd had beers together before. But only in a group. For an office gig. Never just the two of them.

She looked in her refrigerator for something for dinner. After they ate, they'd have to find something else to occupy their time until sleep. The thought of watching some television with Jesse Macdonald just seemed…weird.

She had no idea what kind of shows he liked. And that felt off, too. As much time as they spent together, as close as they were—as much as she cared—she felt bereft, robbed, not knowing such a simple thing about his normal life.

He wasn't talking. Was just standing there. "What's wrong?"

He didn't answer.

"Mac?" she asked, her stomach filling with dread. "What aren't you telling me?"

Manning was going to go free. They didn't have enough solid evidence to hold him. She'd known it. They could hold him for forty-eight hours, and then he'd be out. Able to strike again.

Unless Sierra's Web, or their own detectives, or she and Mac, were able to find irrefutable proof that he'd been the man in her garage the night of the kidnapping. That he'd taken her. Or had hired someone else to do so. Troy Duncan could be found, might turn on him for a deal.

She couldn't rely on that.

But with Manning in custody, law enforcement could

get access to his finances. Sierra's Web had already offered their finance expert to do a deep dive on them.

Something that could happen in less than forty-eight hours, she reminded herself. Took a sip of beer. And looked at Mac.

He'd emptied half his bottle. Was looking down at it. Her chest tightened.

"Mac? You're scaring me." He wasn't looking at her, but she couldn't look away.

"When this is through... I'm changing my mind, Stace." She heard the words. They made no sense. Changing his mind about believing what she'd seen Manning do to Brett?

She shook her head. That made no sense, either.

His gaze, when he finally pinned her with it, held something she'd never seen before. Resolution. Like...he was giving up?

She didn't get it. Frowning, she tried to figure out what was going on, to find a way to be a part of the conversation.

Seeing what she thought was a pained expression on his face, her fear rose to panic level. Was Mac sick? Hurting?

When he pulled a chair out from the table, away from her, sat down in it and took a long swig of beer, she wasn't sure she wanted to hear any more.

Not yet. Not until Troy Duncan was found and Landon Manning was charged and locked up.

At the very least...

"We almost lost you out there today because I wasn't doing my job."

Mac's words brought her up short. She shook her head. "What?"

Had she missed something?

"I was so wrapped up in being just a cop so that nothing else got in the way, shutting out all sensation, relying only on thought, that I stifled the instincts that make me good at the job. I knew you weren't safe out there. Not with a killer on the loose."

Oh. Heady with the relief that had been eluding her ever since she'd seen Manning in handcuffs, she almost smiled. "I knew it, too, Mac. I'm sure everyone knew there was a possibility Manning could find me out there, but, in the first place, that was the plan all along, right? To draw him out?"

He glanced up at her from a lowered brow. Tossed up a hand. She wasn't sure if he was acknowledging her point, or just motioning that he had no response.

"Mariah Southerland's life was at stake. What cop wouldn't put their own life on the line in those circumstances?"

He looked at her then. Hard.

Officers had found the child sitting on a boulder not far off the tourist path. She'd been crying, scared, but otherwise unharmed. Detectives and FBI were working the case but had very few answers. All the child had said was that "he" had told her to sit on the rock and not move or she'd be in big trouble. Anytime anyone, including her parents, asked who'd taken her mommy and daddy's car, who'd left her on the rock, she just kept crying for her daddy. The thought was that the trauma of being trapped in her car seat while someone drove her away from her father had been too much for her. And so, for the time being, they'd quit asking.

"Apart from any of that, I'm an adult, Mac. I made my choice. And that was my right. No matter who you are, my partner, my boss, a stranger on the street...you weren't going to stop me."

His eyes glistened. Not with tears. But she saw the emotion there with a strong reminder of their conversation, their notes, the night before.

"You were worried about me," she said softly, her gaze daring him to look away.

He did not. "To the point of not thinking straight."

"Who found me? Who took down my kidnapper?" He pursed his lips. Held his beer in both hands. As though needing to keep them occupied.

"We care," she said then. "As do a lot of partners, most that I know, who've worked together for a long time. Just because I have the hots for your body all of a sudden, and you might have noticed mine—though I find that harder to believe since I'm not your type—doesn't mean we can't do our jobs. If we're doing it in the back seat of the cruiser while a robbery goes down...then we need to worry."

She'd spent a good part of the night thinking it all through. The lines between fraternization and being human.

"We're all human, Mac. Every single cop out there..."

When she saw his face relax, Stacy wanted to reach out and touch it. To touch him. Place a soft kiss against his lips. Instead, she stood and asked him if he wanted homemade vegetable soup for dinner. She had some in the freezer.

And when he answered in the affirmative, helping himself to a second beer, and searching out saltine crackers and bowls, she went to work with a smile.

Mariah had been found. Landon Manning was in custody. And Mac was there.

All in all, a very good day.

She didn't believe she turned him on. In all that had gone down that day—a little girl's abduction, the capture of a murderer turned kidnapper—the one thought that completely dominated his thoughts as he lay in bed down the hall from his partner was that one. She didn't believe she turned him on.

She wasn't his type.

Showed how little she knew. Problem was, a strong confident woman, a woman who knew exactly what she wanted, didn't generally want to waste time on a guy like him. Someone who had no interest of ever being more than a casual date.

Lying there in desperate need of a cold shower, not wanting to wake her by having one—or to risk her figuring out why he was taking one—Mac almost laughed at the irony in his pain.

Perhaps some of the lighter heart he was feeling that night had to do with the fact that he'd been lucky enough to be given the perfect partner. For him, at any rate.

He and Stacy hadn't had to have some long, drawn-out agonizing heart-to-heart talk to deal with what had, at the time, seemed to him to be an irreparable problem with devastating results. With the awareness between them of personal feelings, those feelings seemed to procreate by leaps and bounds, which had made it seem impossible for them to continue as partners.

With a few simple words, she'd made the impossible possible again.

All cops are human. They all feel. And as long as he and Stacy weren't hooking up—in the back of the car or otherwise—they'd be fine.

Thankful that he hadn't had a chance to call the sheriff yet, to accept the position he'd been offered—something he'd thought he'd had to do as soon as he got Stacy to safety—Mac rolled over. Closed his eyes.

And smelled…smoke?

Flying out of bed, Mac screamed Stacy's name as he pulled on the clean uniform and skivvies he'd laid out the night before—a habit he'd formed after his first emergency call—and rushed out his door. Just as Stacy, also in uniform, though not fully buttoned up, raced toward him.

As they ran through the living area, he saw the brightness of flames out front, and, hearing a telltale rumble, rushed toward the house door leading to the garage. Smoke was already billowing up beneath the automatic garage door.

"There's no flame out back yet," Stacy yelled through a cloth she'd grabbed from the kitchen. The back wall of the garage had no exit. Holding the towel she'd thrown to him, he nodded toward the truck and she ran. Before either of them were fully inside, he pushed the button on the ignition. Yelled at her to buckle up, and, throwing the truck into gear, pushed the accelerator all the way to the floor.

Cracking wood, splintering glass, the sounds of crashing all around them hurt her ears as they burst through the garage wall and out into the night. He spared a quick glance at his partner. Saw her eyes open, no visible blood anywhere, and sped with bumps that sent their heads to the ceiling, as they crossed her desert property and out to an access road to neighboring land.

He couldn't slow down. Tried to think, to assess. Knew only that they had to get out of there, get away, as quickly as possible. He was pretty sure he'd broken a chassis on the truck. But didn't smell gas. The windshield was intact. The broken glass had to have been something in her garage. Maybe head light glass, too.

"You okay?" he hollered as he sped out the service road to the long stretch of highway that would take them farther north. Toward a secluded mountain community for people far richer than he was.

"I got a text," she told him, her voice raised to be heard

over the rumble of noise his truck was making against rough road.

A text? Had he heard her right? Couldn't take his eyes away from his driving that second. Was almost at the road when it hit him that if anyone was watching for an escape, they'd have the road covered. Switching course, keeping his headlights off, he threw the truck into four-wheel drive and careened them toward miles of desert land.

"From Sierra's Web," Stacy said. "It woke me up. It told me to get a burner phone and call a number. Not the one we've been using. It told me not to trust anyone."

Her voice was shaking. His breathing was rickety, too. But he kept his shoulders straight and his head up as he acknowledged what she'd said.

An explosion sounded in the distance. With lead in his gut and pain in his heart, he knew Stacy had just lost her home and everything inside it.

Figured, by the tears in her eyes, that she knew, too.

"We're alive," he told her.

And vowed that one way or another he was going to keep her that way.

Chapter 20

She didn't want to keep traveling across the desert. She had no idea what they were driving into. What lay ahead.

And she didn't want to stop, either, to be a helpless body lying in wait to have a trap sprung upon her.

So when Mac pulled over in the desert behind an eight-foot retaining wall surrounding Golden Gulley, the upscale community built at the base of the Clairvoyant Mountains almost twenty miles west of Saguaro, she looked at him slightly wild-eyed.

"What are we doing?"

"Talking at the moment," he told her. And she nodded. Good. Talking was necessary. They had decisions to make.

"I left my phone at the house," she told him, nervous as hell as she glanced around them. Coming up against a pitch-black darkness that comforted her in the cover it gave them,, and scared her to death, too. Who was out there?

Were they being watched?

Glancing frantically around, she did her best to have their backs. To protect Mac, if she could, from whatever nightmare she couldn't seem to get out of.

"No one followed us." His words were soft. Kind.

Her glance shot back to him, wide-eyed and seeking. "How can you be sure?"

"It's me, Stace."

Just those words. Right. Mac knew how to detect a tail—and how to lose one—better than anyone she'd ever known. Even better than her.

And she jumped back to what she'd wanted to tell him. "I figured, since Hudson told me to get a burner phone, that mine had been compromised."

Mac had pulled out his phone while she was talking, and she stared at it as though it was loaded. And aimed right at her.

"You need to get rid of that. They'll find us." She heard the panic in her tone. And just…couldn't step away from the fear. The godawful paralyzing sense that she just was not going to win.

Or ever be safe again.

"I have a text from Warner, too," he told her. Relief flooded her. She wasn't alone. They'd included Mac. A fresh flood of mind-numbing fright followed right behind. "Turn off your phone! Crush it. Something."

He turned it off. His expression grim as he looked at her. "My text only said that they'd found Troy Duncan. He's been in jail in northern Colorado. Was picked up for drunk driving. He'd been using a fake ID, so wasn't there under his own name. Sierra's Web tracked him down with photo recognition software, running it against Arizona and Colorado mug shots for the past week."

But…she shook her head. That didn't make sense. If Troy hadn't just started the fire at her house and Manning…

"He got out of jail?" That didn't make sense either. *Nothing* was making any sense. Unless. "That's why Sierra's Web told me not to trust anyone? They're trying to tell me someone, one of *us*, is dirty and let Manning go?"

That didn't add up, either.

"I don't know what they're saying, but, Stace, I'm one of them."

He was looking her in the eye, like he was imparting some serious message. She couldn't slow down enough to get it.

"They texted you not to trust anyone. They did not text me the same message, and I'm the lead on the case. Think, Stace."

She nodded. Got where he was going. And couldn't believe he'd even...

"If you want to go, do it," she said to him. And then just kept spewing. "But if you think, for one second, I'm going to let anyone make me doubt you, then you can just stick it where the sun don't shine, buster." The phrase she'd heard her grandfather say growing up just came up out of her.

Slowing down, she met his gaze, the glints of his eyes, in the darkness. "If I can't trust you, Mac, then I just don't care anymore. About running. Or even dying. If I can't trust you, I can't trust me, either, because my heart and soul tell me that you're true blue."

He touched her face. Palm to cheek. Something he'd never done before. And she cradled his palm between her cheek and shoulder. Took a breath.

And began to find her strength.

They had to get down to business. Agreeing with Stacy that it was best to ditch his cell phone, Mac ran it over with the truck several times, and then buried it in the desert.

"We need to lose the truck, too," he told her. "And get to some kind of hiding place before it gets light outside."

"We have to get a burner phone, Mac. To call Sierra's Web and find out what we're up against."

He agreed. And taking the cash he kept in the truck's

glove box, along with the registration and license plate, he grabbed his emergency bag out of the back, which had extra bullets among other things, and started to walk. They both had their guns. Stacy had what cash she'd had in her bedroom. And her Taser and Mace.

"We're both in fresh uniforms. We have our badges," he said, thinking out loud. "I think we need to risk stopping in Golden Gulley for a phone and a few supplies, and then head up into the mountain. At least until we have more information. It'll give us time to come up with a plan."

She kept pace with him easily. Pushed by the devil at her back. And energized by a strange gratitude to be alive with Mac.

"From now on, we don't split up," he told her. "Not even in a separate room in the same building. Not until this is done."

She nodded. Wasn't sure she could pee in front of him, but wasn't going to worry about it, either.

It wasn't likely that they'd have the convenience of a bathroom in any event.

"You think Manning is out?" she asked as they walked. As much to shut up the thoughts in her head as to get an answer. Anything he said at that point would be the same as her—only a guess.

"I think that I hope he's out," he told her, bringing her mind back into clearer focus. He hadn't just guessed. She might be keeping pace physically, but he was steps ahead of her mentally.

And she quickly caught up. "Because with Duncan in jail, if it isn't Manning, and anyone he would have hired would have hightailed it upon his arrest, we have a much bigger problem."

"And not one single suspect." He delivered the grim

news she'd just arrived at herself. As her mind slowed, she heard a replay of the loud bang they'd heard while driving.

Could hardly begin to contemplate the fact that her home was likely the source. That there'd been an explosion. And focused on what she could process. "If we're lucky, everyone will think we blew up with the house," she said.

"I'm guessing that was the plan," Mac agreed, his voice soft on the cool night air. She shivered and he moved closer to her. Put an arm around her shoulders.

Like a pal. Or a parent, she told herself.

But let herself lean on him, anyway. Just for a minute or two.

"They made a mistake then," she said next, as though she and Mac had walked with their bodies tucked together... ever. "Because just like there'd be no evidence left behind, they also have no proof that we died."

His chuckle, so...out of place...had her looking up at him. "What?"

"So you, Stace, to find the bright side. Even in this."

She might have elbowed him—if she'd wanted to lose contact with his side against hers long enough to do so. And if she hadn't heard the admiration in his tone.

"We're going to get through this," she said instead. Conviction lacing her tone. Born of hope, or some natural instinct, she didn't know. Didn't care.

She just had to keep believing.

Until a time came that she couldn't.

The sun was coming up as they neared the town. While most of the thousand or so homes were in gated communities, the main strip was open to public traffic. Mac had been to the area a few times, and could never get over how completely different Golden Gulley looked, just feet away from rough barren desert and succulent mountain that housed mountain lions, rattlesnakes, brown recluse spiders and numerous other potentially deadly prey.

But once you left the dirt road leading up to the small municipality and entered the walls surrounding it, roads were perfectly paved blacktop, with garden dividers separating the lanes. Even at dawn, the overabundance of color from the plethora of flowers hit him. And the fruit trees lining the sidewalk sides of the road were all perfectly groomed, all the same size, sporting luscious looking fruit. Lemons, grapefruit, oranges.

It was the type of place where Stacy deserved to live. Her spirit should be surrounded by beauty.

But even as he had the thought, he knew better. Stacy would shrivel and die if she wasn't charging out to do good.

And she'd suffocate without her open space.

The thought brought him upright as, silently, they headed toward the only place that looked open for business. The first business heading into town. A gas station and store combination.

Stacy had lost her home. But… "I know it's too early to be thinking ahead, but…you've got the big house, Stace. Insurance will probably help rebuild, and there could be other funds once this all gets solved, but in the meantime, you still have your property. And a home."

She nodded. Then said, "I can't really think about that right now."

And he wished he'd kept his mouth shut. But figured he'd made the right choice to remain a working partner, rather than risking anything more. If he hadn't, he wouldn't be there with her. Wouldn't have been at her place when the fire started.

Until she said, "I could always stay with you, if need be."

And then, when he stumbled, she elbowed his side, stepped away and reached for the handle to open the store's front door.

Had she been serious?

Did he want her to have been?

While the thoughts were a distraction they couldn't afford, at the same time, they kept him focused on a future where the danger in front of them had been conquered.

And it dawned on him that's what she'd been doing all along. Holding on to something that felt good, even if only in fantasy, to keep her from giving up.

He was an intelligent man. Knew a lot. Sometimes Stacy knew more.

They made a great team.

He moved quickly through the store, grabbing what he thought they'd need, while she did her own shopping. Mac allowed the possibility that they'd find a way, at the end of the current ordeal, to continue partnering with each other. The thought lifted him.

Gave him a surge of the optimism Stacy generally seemed to have in abundance.

They both bought phones. The clerk didn't ask why two uniformed officers needed them. Just rang them up, bagged them and handed them over with the other supplies, mostly food, they'd picked up. He'd grabbed some extra batteries to add to the one in his emergency bag.

She'd picked up an extra first aid kit. And some pain relievers.

If not for the fact that they'd almost been burned to death in their sleep, and had no transportation, they could have been heading out on an adventure. A part of him chose to pretend for a few seconds that that was the case.

Right until someone else came in the door, and he was

all cop. Ready to defend with his life. The woman was middle-aged. Picking up premade breakfast sandwiches and juice boxes.

He still kept his eye on her. And the small blue sedan she'd parked out front.

Until they were out of the store, and the parking lot was no longer in sight. They immediately headed back out of town, into the desert, toward the mountain. Finding a cove to huddle in together while they activated their phones, taking turns keeping watch.

And then, gun in hand, he crouched, hidden behind shrubbery, and watched the desert, glistening with a near blinding morning sun, while Stacy called the number she'd memorized.

"Thank God you called."

Mac recognized Hudson Warner's voice on speakerphone, even with the volume down so low. It had occurred to him, the cop, that he'd never seen the text. Had only Stacy's word that it had come at all, let alone that it had been from the verified number. And while he hadn't doubted her, at all, at the moment his mind was all over the planet in terms of foul play. The kidnapper could have sent the text.

"Where are you?"

"In hiding," was all Stacy said. They'd talked about hearing Warner out before giving away any personal information or asking for possible assistance.

The text she'd received had told her not to trust anyone. They had to know why. Had to know if Manning was still in custody.

"When Benson called to say there was a fire at your place, I was afraid we hadn't been in time…"

"I got out." She didn't say how. But described the blast. She got out because Sierra's Web's text had woken her.

Mac didn't like the coincidence of that. Every attack against Stacy had been so carefully planned. So perfectly timed.

And yet, if they'd texted to warn her...

"Landon Manning isn't your guy." Every instinct Mac had went on high alert. Keeping his back to Stacy, standing up right in front of her, his head barely visible above the desert plants, he listened carefully.

"We've had a team on his financials since he was arrested. Everything adds up to a T. The man is an IRS dream. We've got his phone, too. Everything is clean. His phone's location is kept on. I can see where he's been, see money spent. I see funds in and funds out. We've already been deep diving for foreign accounts and made a thorough pass last evening. There's nothing."

As he listened, Mac watched a bobcat slink along slowly in the distance, hunting. He'd never have known it was there if not for the movement. And the sun shining on the golden coat.

The fact that it was still hunting past dawn was a bit odd. Could be rabid.

Hudson's voice continued. "His wife moved out of their big house when he was sent to prison. She's been working, too. He's still getting sponsorship monies and they're all accounted for. In addition, we used his phone to trace him to a ranch in Colorado during the time we saw the black hoodie at the city building. There was no surveillance footage at the ranch, but we caught him on a traffic cam in the area. Following his phone's location, he was here when we saw him on camera in the east valley. We also have him in Arizona this week, but at a campsite an hour south of here. Security cameras show him on-site. Credit card usage supports this as well. He ate at the same diner every meal, including breakfast and lunch the day of the drone strike. Hard as it is to accept, we believe he's telling the truth."

"Is he still in custody?" Stacy asked. He'd left it up to her to tell Sierra's Web that Mac was with her. Until she indicated that she wanted to do so, he was remaining silent.

"Yes. I'm reporting only to you at least until later this morning. It's a corporate decision. I've run it by my partners. If need be, we'll sever our employment with the Saguaro Police Department and take you on pro bono."

Mac turned, met the look of fright in Stacy's wide-eyed glance up at him, and put his finger to his lips.

Something was definitely off. Way off. Life-ending off.

Until they knew what, they had to gain information, not give it.

And in the meantime, he had to be better at everything he did.

He had a feeling he was about to enter a battle that would mean more to him than anything he'd ever done. Or ever would do.

He was not going to let Stacy Waltz die.

His heart would die with her.

Chapter 21

Stacy didn't like hiding at Mac's feet.

She didn't want to cower in front of anyone.

Wished she could bury her head in her knees, close her eyes and sleep. She wasn't so much physically tired as her heart and soul just needed respite.

With each word that Hudson Warner spoke, she felt her chance of inner peace slipping further away. If Mac hadn't been standing there, exuding his warmth all over her, she'd have had to dig impossibly deep to find the strength to hold the phone.

Manning wasn't their guy?

If Warner had talked to him, was making his assertions based on anything Landon Manning had told him, she'd have been able to refute his words. But with the hard proof they'd been seeking for long days and nights right there, she couldn't argue.

As much as her heart needed her to be able to do so.

Weighing her down even more was where that proof led them next.

If not Manning, then who? She didn't even want to think the question, let alone ask it.

But if she wanted to stay alive, she had to know. She couldn't take down a mystery man. Or fight a mirage. And now that Mac was with her...

He'd almost died in her home that night. Because of her. No one else knew he'd been there.

The case had seemingly been over. He'd been going to drop her off—the chief had offered her department transportation of her own for the night, but since he'd told them to take a few days off in the next breath she hadn't wanted to have to return the vehicle in the morning—and then head home.

Two off-duty officers shacking up together would raise eyebrows, if nothing else.

Her thoughts weaved in and out of Warner's proof that Troy Duncan also hadn't been involved in any part of the attempts on Stacy's life. Once they'd found the younger man sitting in a jail cell, and had access to his phone and financials, they were quickly able to rule him out.

"He's still being held," Warner said. "He made the dark web rants under Manning's name, but that's for the FBI to sort out." Rants that Sierra's Web had uncovered. And would be reporting.

Warner had been speaking quickly. Like a machine, clicking off each pertinent piece of evidence.

"I spent precious time filling you in on Manning so that you don't get yourself killed still thinking it's him."

Stacy stood. She couldn't keep hiding. "Who's after me?"

"We don't know yet," Warner said. "But we know he's local. And he could be in your department."

No. Oh, God, no. She felt the blood drain from her face. Her fingers went cold. Mac was the lead on the case, and Warner had only texted him about Duncan's whereabouts.

If Warner was about to tell her Mac wanted her dead, he'd lose all credibility with her. And then what? How were she and Mac, on the lam, going to find out anything?

They would. They had to.

"I'll make this as quick as I can, but you need to know details to understand. And maybe fill in some pieces. The city building access of your files. We've checked every single signature sign in against the surveillance photos in and out of that building during the time your file was accessed. They all check out except for one. We have an illegible signature—a straight line—and a Saguaro Police Department general key card going through the restricted access lane. There are no cameras there."

"There are a couple of those cards," Stacy said. "They're generally kept with reception."

"Fine, we'll check on that. Next. We got parking sticker records from Parker Lake and ran it against owners of white vans in the area. Two names came up. One is a college student who's had his van in Tucson with him since he went back to college after Christmas. The second is owned by the grandson of your chief of police."

Her stomach lurched and her hands started to shake. "The white van that crashed over the mountain…the stolen van…wasn't the one I almost hit."

Stacy glanced up at Mac who just shook his head. But the look in his eyes, he was all there with her. Ready to go to work.

He wasn't leaving her.

She might run from him. Maim him a little if she had to, to get away. He'd almost died in her home. She was not going to let him get himself killed for her.

The chief? She just couldn't believe it.

It made no sense.

And just because the van had been on the road she'd taken home that night didn't mean that it was at all involved in her kidnapping. It had just been something she'd seen minutes before. Something worth checking out. Most particularly since one like it had been stolen and ditched the very next day.

It was as though Mac's voice was in her head talking to her. Giving her facts. Keeping her on track.

She'd been a little off-kilter that night. Had almost run into the van. Could have been her fault.

It had been heading from a pullout.

The kid could have been parking with his girlfriend.

"The four-wheeler at the end of Stacy's drive, and at the crime scene…your description matches department four-wheelers. As well any number ones owned privately by members of the force. And who better to know your schedule. And one of our techies was able to enhance security camera footage to determine the brand of drone used by the airstrip." Warner just kept talking. "It's the same kind the Saguaro Police Department just requisitioned and received."

Her glance met Mac's and held. She hadn't even known the department was looking at drones. Had he?

His eyes didn't talk to her. Didn't tell her either way.

Even if the drones were the same brand, it didn't mean they were the same make or model. Or that one was missing.

"I intended to get the drone information to Jesse Macdonald, as soon as it was reported to me, but you all were already out on the Amber Alert."

Wait. He'd still been reporting to Mac before Mariah's disappearance, but hadn't texted him that night…

She was still having the thought, not even beginning to process yet, when Hudson Warner said, "As to yesterday's supposed kidnapping…"

Supposed?

"Kelly Chase, our expert psychiatrist and a child specialist, did an interview with Mariah Southerland late yesterday afternoon. Her mother asked Chief Benson to have her interviewed by a child specialist. He called me and I set it up. I wasn't in the interview, but I've heard tapes from it, and have been in consultation with Kelly. She's convinced that the child wasn't kidnapped. She was left on that boulder by her father. He threatened her that if she moved, she'd be in big trouble. The reason the little girl just cried for her daddy every time anyone asked anything was because she was answering their question. Who took you? Daddy. Who left you there? Daddy."

"So what are you telling me?" Jimmy Southerland had made up a kidnapping to get the entire police force out looking for her? Made no sense.

"Did you know that Jesse Macdonald called Southerland once the two of you were split up on the mountain yesterday, looking for the child?"

Stacy's skin crawled. Her throat clogged. Her chest so tight she couldn't draw air.

She shook her head.

Dropped down to the ground, the phone still clutched in her fingers. The entire world had gone mad.

She gasped for air and a question came out. "Why?" She wasn't sure who she was talking to. God, maybe.

"We don't know yet." Warner's voice just kept coming. She needed to hang up. Couldn't move enough to make it happen. "We have no motive. Not for any of the people involved."

"It makes no sense," she said then. Talking because when she did, her body did the natural thing and took a breath. "What good did it do to get us all out on the mountain? If it wasn't something Manning had done to occupy every member of the force and get me alone?"

Mac had already had her alone. That one was a no-brainer.

But if someone was trying to frame him?

Or just plain kill her one heartbeat at a time...

Making her think Mac had betrayed her.

It still made no sense. Drawing them all out to the mountain.

Except that Manning had said he'd seen someone, hadn't he? That he'd been there to keep her safe?

Or was she just imagining things?

"Talk to Landon Manning," she said then. "He rambled so much yesterday and I had to tune it all out. I knew he was trying to manipulate me. But I think he said something about coming to town to talk to me. Heard the fuss, came out to the mountain, knowing I would be there. He wanted to help search since, you know, he's living the rest of his life in honor of Brett..." Her voice broke. She made herself breathe and started again. "He said that he thought someone was following me..."

Mac would be the logical suspect on that one. He'd waited for her to set off and then had headed to his own coordinates.

She couldn't help what conclusions others might draw. She knew it wasn't him.

As the shock filtered from her brain, the sense that someone was trying to make her doubt her own heart, was trying to manipulate her into giving up control of her mind took hold, and she shook her head.

Started to think. To talk. "The kidnapper could have seen Manning, knew he'd been seen, cut bait, put Mariah on that boulder, told her to always just answer 'Daddy' to any question and no one would hurt her family..."

"Great. We'll talk to Manning..."

"And Mr. Warner, please don't waste any time or resources looking into Mac. I can vouch for him over and over...he's the one who saved me from the drone. And found me over the mountain, who called for help and saved my life."

"Have you ever heard of the hero complex?"

Of course she had. She was a cop. Had a degree in criminal justice. "You think Mac is deliberately causing all these near deaths just so he can save me?"

He'd met her in the hallway of her home that morning, before she'd been able to get to him, to wake him to warn him. Had rushed her out of the home. Known where to drive to keep them away from the flames.

He'd ended her standoff with Landon Manning the day before.

Everything inside Stacy stilled. Just her and stillness.

She'd recently told Jesse Macdonald that she had the hots for him. Had intimated that she loved him in her note that night at the safe house.

What more could he possibly want?

It took every ounce of self-control Mac had to just stand there. To hear what was being said about him, from a source he'd been trusting with Stacy's life, and do...nothing.

He needed to grab the phone and crush it beneath his shoe. To hit a rock so hard with his fist he'd know nothing but the physical pain.

He *knew* he wasn't the one who'd been trying to kill Stacy Waltz. But if everyone thought he was...the real killer would get her. He couldn't just walk away.

No matter what she thought. What she believed.

You think Mac is deliberately causing all these near deaths just so he can save me?

He heard her words again, and while a logical voice in his brain could see how she'd been so thoroughly played she couldn't be blamed for doubting him, another part, a very small, barely acknowledged part, shriveled up and died.

Or started to, until she said, "Every second you spend looking at Mac, you're giving my intended killer the chance to succeed." He heard the words. The strength behind them.

And went weak. Every sinew. Every muscle. Defensive energy drained out of him.

A surge of warmth hit him, one he'd never ever felt with such impact in his life, and in the next second, he started to fill up again. With the cold anger it was going to take to kill a killer. If that's what it took.

"Jesse Macdonald is standing right here, Mr. Warner," she said then, with no warning to Mac. "He was with me in my home last night when the fire started. Asleep in bed. I'm thinking even someone with a major hero complex wouldn't kill himself in the process of trying to look good."

My home. Asleep in bed. Hearing her say the words, admitting something that could hurt her reputation with the department, brought another surge of warmth. He let the distraction pass through him. Focused on finding whoever was after Stacy.

The other end of the line had fallen completely silent. "We need a motive," Mac said then. "Why would someone from the department want her dead? What does Stacy have that anyone would want? Or anyone in town for that matter? We've been over her life, you've been over her life. What did we miss?"

He shot the questions like the professional he was. With a good dose of personal fire beneath them. No one was going to hurt the woman who'd just heard evidence against him, and had chosen to listen to her heart, to believe in him, instead.

He'd never personally witnessed such a show of…the love she'd talked about. The kind that lasted through anything. Even death.

"Ms. Waltz, please take me off speakerphone."

Stacy glanced at Mac. He nodded. She pressed to end the open call.

After a few seconds Mac heard her say, "Elizabeth." Verifying her middle name? Or had Warner told her to say her middle name if she was in trouble?

She'd turned so he couldn't see her expression. But he heard the conviction in her, "Yes… With my life, yes… I'm positive. I've been riding with Jesse Macdonald for five years. Look at our cases. There's no sign of hero complex. If anything, he's unassuming. Doesn't take the credit he's offered. He just turned down a major job offer with the sheriff's department that would have made him look like a real savior. And I've got one more piece of information for you. I just this past week told Mac that I'm interested in him, personally, and he chose for us to remain work partners. That's not a guy trying to impress me. If you want to assign someone to verify everything, all but that last, which you'll have to take on my word, you do that. Go verify. But we need help out here, and since it's us against the world at the moment, we're trusting you to be it."

She was silent for another moment, and then Mac heard her say, "Yes, I will."

At which time, she tapped her phone and said, "Go ahead."

Hudson Warner came back on the line. The man didn't apologize. There was no need. He'd been doing the job Mac had been asking him to do.

They discussed, the three of them, Sierra's Web coming to get them. To meet them somewhere. But they determined that if they could stay gone for at least a few hours, it would give Warner and his teams, including forensic experts, the chance to spend the time at the latest crime scene. And not draw any attention to the Golden Gulch area.

At the moment, whoever wanted Stacy dead could assume she'd burned up in the fire. An official report might say there were no signs of human remains in the debris. But not yet. Not with the explosion. There'd be too much to comb through to know for certain.

And Mac was expected to be taking a few days off. No one would be looking for him.

Not unless they wanted him involved in the investigation now that it looked to be closer to home. He expected "they" wouldn't. Sierra's Web would be watching for calls to his line, and have someone watching his home, just in case.

His truck abandoned in the desert was a concern. He and Stacy gave as much of a description of its location as they could. Hudson Warner said he'd take care of getting it out of there and into a scrapyard as soon as possible.

And he and Stacy agreed to call in to the same secure number every two hours until further notice.

In the meantime, they had to climb. To find a cave.

And to set their boundaries.

Just like Stacy had wanted to do two days before.

Mac was beginning to realize that his partner was far wiser than he'd even thought. Scales ahead of him. In matters of life, as well as work.

What he did with the information, he had no idea.

And couldn't think about it, either. Until he knew they had her someplace safe.

Chapter 22

They hiked for a couple of hours. Up, and over, too. Circling around a mountain range that was so large it would take days to get to the other side. And yet, they'd already made it to the top of two small peaks.

They didn't stand there long. From the first peak, she'd made a call to Sierra's Web. The two-hour check in. As far as Sierra's Web could tell, it was believed that Stacy had perished with her house. The department appeared to be in a state of shock and grief. Warner reported that Benson had told him Mac had a few days off and he wasn't planning to call him back. There was nothing Mac could do to help Stacy, and he needed the time. Benson swore that the department would pay Sierra's Web whatever it took to help their detectives find whoever had done this to her. Then Warner had told Benson about the van registration with the lake sticker. Heard that Benson's eighteen-year-old grandson was not at home and his phone appeared to be off. No one knew where he was. Or they were denying knowing, at any rate.

It was feasible that Benson didn't know that—the young man, who was well known and liked around the station, had driven to the lake, and possible that the young man had gotten ahold of a courthouse secure access card, used it and returned it. But why?

Same with finding a way to access the department drones. He'd likely have heard his grandfather speak of them. Had known they were there. Not yet in service. His grandfather trusted him. She could see it happening.

What on earth would the kid have against Stacy?

"He has to be working for someone," Stacy told Mac after they'd hung up. And then, at his instruction, had destroyed her new phone.

He was already scoping out the landscape. "It's a burner. They can't trace the number, but…"

"…he department could put a trace on all towers from which a phone call had come, giving them our approximate location," Stacy finished his statement for him.

Mac started back down the peak. Something they'd already determined they were going to do after the call. The trek up had been for phone service only. "Assuming that the killer has the number to the secure line Warner gave you," he said, lifting a hand up to her.

Without thinking, she took it, held on and jumped down to level ground next to him, before they half slid down the next patch directly in front of them.

It was only when he'd let go of her hand that she realized what they'd done. Holding hands. Him offering to help. Her accepting.

A definite variation from their protocol. More like a couple, than partners.

Working partners. Police partners.

Shaking off the tingling of warmth his grip had left behind, she continued the rest of the way down to the small gulley they were planning to follow west, keeping enough distance between them that neither made any other natural moves that included them touching.

And staying close enough that they could both duck behind the same rock face if necessary. Two hours later, planning to use Mac's burner to make the second call to Sierra's Web, they stood at the top of the peak they'd just climbed, but were so far into the mountain range that they had no service.

Stacy looked at Mac. "Our job is to stay hidden," she told him, hardly believing that she was saying the words.

From the beginning she'd refused to let the fiend force her into hiding. Had been fighting what had turned out to be the inevitable ever since. She'd been so certain she wouldn't hide, and yet there they were, further into the Clairvoyants than she'd ever thought she'd be, than she'd ever wanted to be. Hiding.

Was her death inevitable, too?

"Right," Mac said, frowning at her as they stood looking out over lower peaks and valleys, and up at higher ones. "Where are you going with that?"

"I think it's time to make the choice to stay out here for the night. We've got the provisions. We definitely know how to prepare safe lodging. The ditch perimeter, all the things Hudson talked about, those warnings of someone getting close will work for mountain lions and anything or anyone else who might happen upon us. But we need time to prepare. We can't just keep hiking farther into nowhere, waiting to make a call in the hopes of getting the all-clear to come home. Darkness will fall and we'll be unprepared to meet it…"

She was rambling. Heard the panic starting to taint her tone. But stood completely by what she said. She was afraid. And still thinking clearly. Whatever game anyone was trying to play with her mind…she wasn't going to let them win that one.

Life or death.

Mac looked around them. "I agree," he said, but didn't

seem at all happy about the plan. He seemed to be studying the entire Clairvoyant landscape. And then pointed.
"There."

It took her a few tries, him pointing out landmarks that
she could find to get to what he'd seen. And once her gaze
arrived, she knew he'd found the perfect spot. A cave set
back far enough from the edge of a cliff to be private—and
to give ample warning if anyone got at all close.

They could live there for years and never be invaded.

The idea—her and Mac staying lost for years—wasn't
nearly as unwelcome as she'd have thought, even a day earlier. Another couple of hours passed as they made their way
to the cave he'd spotted, keeping an eye on their coordinates
so they'd know how to get back out again. They spent another few hours getting the place set up for the night, and
Stacy continued to entertain herself with the fantasy. She
and Mac, alone in the wilderness, like the settlers of old,
or the Native Americans who really had lived for centuries
in those very mountains. Setting up house.

Securing the cave, first, with a flashlight check of even
the smallest crannies, they used the branch of a pine tree
as a broom. And then stripping paloverde branches of their
leaves, mixing them with other small brush to make sleeping pallets. From there they concentrated on their perimeter.

It was good to be working toward something other than
running. The only conversation they had pertained to the
tasks at hand. Ideas for making them safest. Which plants
and desert ground cover to use to make the loudest sound
if stepped upon. They tested some out.

Laughed a little.

And all the while, they were watching over their shoulders. Making certain that if they got close to the cliff edge,
they were down low so they wouldn't be seen.

On constant look out for drones—though as far in as they were, the chances of one finding them were minimal. Unless their want-to-be captor was close.

Which was possible.

So they remained on constant vigil.

They'd eaten semicold breakfast sandwiches purchased from the convenience store, followed by the banana and orange Stacy had picked up. Had consumed four granola bars. Peanut butter on bread was on the docket for dinner. They had one loaf. And then a box of crackers to put the high protein spread on as well.

Mac had had a wearable water pack in his emergency bag. She'd been lucky enough to find a second in the store. They'd filled them and had been wearing them, drinking from the straws that were always accessible with a turn of their heads, throughout the day. He'd packed a couple of gallons more water at the base of the emergency bag he'd strapped to his back with elastic cords as they'd set out. He'd strapped his go-duffel to her back, and it had smaller water bottles in it as well as other supplies.

Thank God for Mac's truck, and the preparedness their daily grind had instilled in them.

If they hadn't been on the run, hiding for their lives, she might have found the adventure fun. Because it was with Mac.

One thing she knew for sure—if they survived, she was going to remember the experience for the rest of her life.

Keeping a handle on her imagination, fighting the panic, was easier when she was physically exerting herself. But then they were done.

Dusk was falling.

Mac did a last check of their area, keeping the beam of

his flashlight low to the ground so it couldn't be seen from above or below them, making them potential sitting ducks.

Then, turning off the big light, he ducked his tall, athletic body into the cave and sat down on his roughly hewn mat. Right beside hers.

They'd been up since before dawn. Needed to sleep. It had been a physically grueling day.

She handed him a peanut butter sandwich.

"How long do you think it will be before Sierra's Web sends someone looking for us?" she asked him. They'd failed to find cell service to make any other calls.

He shrugged. "If they've got the killer, I'd think they're already looking. If not…" He took another bite, chewed, swallowed as though he didn't have a care in the world.

The peanut butter was sticking in her throat. She didn't want to waste water washing down every bite.

Mac spoke again. "Knowing our plan, I'm counting on them figuring that we're out of service. If they want to find us, chances are they will. They've got Luke Dennison, his team, and search and rescue dogs at their disposal. If you're still considered dead, they're not going to want to do anything to make anyone think otherwise. Instead, their investigation will be just what Warner described from his call with Benson—instead of finding the killer to save a life, they're finding him so he can be prosecuted for murder."

And another option, one he didn't mention… Sierra's Web could have a mole.

Fear struck anew.

She'd been trying not to doubt Hudson Warner or any of the Sierra's Web team members. She'd certainly done nothing to make any of them want her dead. But she'd have trusted her child's life to Chief Benson, too. If she'd had a child.

"We're screwed, aren't we?" The words were so unlike her, even she was shocked by them. Mac's snap of the head in her direction made his reaction clear. She couldn't read his expression, but she knew him well enough to fill in the blanks.

"Anything could or might find us, Stace, but we're well armed and we have the mountain at our back. Our odds are good."

"As long as no one gets close enough to throw something in here…"

The cave had already begun closing in on her. She'd been gassed and burned out of her home. Had an explosive drop out of the sky and nearly hit her head. What was next, a fireball from a mountainside perch? Landing on their pallets made out of flammable brush?

Mac's shoulder rammed into hers. "You aren't going to quit on me now, are you?" he asked, his tone teasing.

But with a note she didn't recognize.

"You're worried, too." She said the words out loud. Because of the surreal circumstances. The darkness.

They had no ability to run through a mountain range in the dark. No transportation. No way to make a phone call, even.

"I don't like not knowing," he told her then.

She shivered. The night's cold would come. They had shelter, but no blankets. Just the long, leaf-filled branches they'd brought in to cover themselves.

And many hours to get through before the light came again.

Mac would have liked to try a night hike. Or sit out under the stars. Both would be preferable to being caged in. And it would be poor police work. Putting them at risk. Not only from whatever human or humans were out to get Stacy, but from all the other predators that hunted for dinner every night.

Stacy talked about television, of all things. Wanting to know what shows he watched.

Not many. He wasn't a big sitter.

What shows he'd watched as a kid.

He'd been more interested in the gaming console hooked up to the television in one house and forced to listen to kiddie shows in the other.

When that conversation soon petered out, she dragged him into a conversation about cop shows. Those he'd seen. Both in the past, and more recently as well.

Eventually, Stacy produced a small pack of disposable disinfecting hand wipes, taking one for herself, giving him one and they took turns heading to a pre-dug hole to relieve themselves, him last so he could fill the hole with dirt. And they laid back.

He waited for the deep, even breathing that should tell him she was asleep. After long minutes of feeling her restlessness, he began to pray for that breathing.

For her. And himself, too.

Instead, he lay there and listened. Catching every coyote howl. Every owl hoot. And myriad other sounds he didn't recognize.

Feeling Stacy's body heat, even as the night's chill seeped into his bones. She was smaller, so she had to be feeling the cold even more than he was. But hadn't yet pulled her branches over herself for cover.

Should he do it for her? In case she was asleep and just restless about it? For all he knew, she fidgeted and sighed every night when she was out.

In the cave the temperature shouldn't drop as low as freezing. Was a bit of chill worth risking waking her?

Her hand moved, ever so slightly. He wasn't sure if it was a sleeping twitch or deliberate movement, but the append-age was moving again. Touching the back of his fingers.

Then…nothing.

Did she need the comfort of human touch?

Closing his eyes again, trying to will himself to keep them that way and give his body some chance at sleep, he had to admit the warmth of Stacy's hand resting there was…nice.

He heard another sigh. He was really going to have to look up the possibility of people emitting what sounded like such deliberate gusts of air in their sleep. Opening his eyes, he turned his head to look at her, and thought he saw the glints of opened eyes staring back at him.

For no good reason, Mac turned his hand over. Felt her palm fall against his. Gave her time to snatch it away. When she didn't, he threaded his fingers through hers. Holding on.

When her fingers gave an answering grip, pleasure shot through him, pooling in his groin.

"I can't help thinking…" Her voice sounded thick in the darkness. Could just be that the air in the cave lacked cir-culation. He didn't think so. But he wanted that to be the reason for the odd tone as he laid there, failing to respond. To draw her out.

"What if this is the last night of my life?"

No. He wasn't going to let her give up. How he'd prevent it, he had no idea. But he had to keep her alive. No matter what the morning brought to them.

Or, at the very least, give up his life for her, trying to save her. Die before her. Because he sure as hell didn't want to live without her.

The thought stuck there. Stunning him into complete silence.

"I don't want to spend my last hours on earth lying in fear." She just wasn't stopping. He held tight to her hand.

He knew what she wanted.

He just couldn't give it to her.

Well…technically he could. The bulge beneath the zipper in his uniform pants was proof of that. It wasn't something she could see in the dark.

He had to be the strong one of the two of them. Because they were going to get out of there alive. The reign of terror would end, with guilty parties locked up for the rest of their lives. Or damned close to it.

And he and Stacy would need to be able to continue on.

He couldn't lose her.

Agonizing minutes passed. Her hand slowly left his.

And Mac swallowed a lump of regret that nearly choked him.

Chapter 23

Stacy had one clear thought.

He wasn't telling her no.

Mac wouldn't roll over and kiss her. He'd never initiate anything between them. If she knew him at all, she knew that much.

And she did know him. Sometimes better than he knew himself.

Just like he did with her.

It was the type of knowing that came from complete trust.

And for her, true love. The kind that, once there never died.

That existed without condition.

Maybe she was living in fantasyland. Creating a fairy tale in her mind as a result of experiencing more trauma than she could bear.

She didn't really care.

Not anymore.

Truth was, life could end at any moment, for anyone.

And she didn't want to go out lying in a bed of panic.

Moving her freed hand slowly downward, she heard his low hungry moan and lifted her palm against the side of Mac's upper thigh. Lightly grazing its entire length. After scaling to the top, she just kept going. Across the plain of flat stomach he'd risen to meet her and on to the next peak.

She knew it would be there.

Didn't take a partner who knew you well to figure that one out. The way his body had stiffened the second her hand had touched his had clued her in on that one.

Her knuckles got there first, but her palm was right behind them, sliding over the jutting mountain on Mac's belly. And resting there.

Not moving. Just cupping him.

Giving him a chance to roll over. A long chance.

Had his interest started to abate, she'd have rolled over. Instead, she felt the manly muscle moving against her palm. A jerk. A spasm. Nothing overt. Just Mac's desire letting her know it was there.

She laid there, on fire, pools of sweetness swirling in her lower body, her nipples tingling. And…laid there.

Unsure of what to do next.

She was a great cop. A great friend. She was sure some great other things, too. She was no femme fatale.

"I've…uh…actually never initiated…things before," she told the walls of the cave. Hoping Mac would hear.

"You're doing a fine job of it." The voice…it was Mac's… and something completely new, too. A depth, a timbre that ignited her all over again. With more force than ever before. Even in her wildest dream of him.

Still, he laid there. Mostly still beneath her.

Figuring she'd had all the permission she needed, Stacy forgot about where she was, or why. Her mind filled with Mac.

All Mac.

Rolling, sliding one of her legs between his, she rested her breasts over his upper arm and chest, letting her nipples feel the pressure of her weight against him, and dropped her mouth to his.

* * *

Mac gave her all the time he could to change her mind. To figure out that she didn't really want what her imagination had conjured up to keep her alive during her time on the boulders, waiting to be rescued.

Even after those sweet lips—the most delicious ever—touched his, he held back. Letting her experiment.

Problem was, she didn't quit. Her lips explored his, causing his penis to feel like it was coming out of his skin. He opened his mouth just enough to make it easier for her to see what was there and be done, and then she was moaning. Pushing her tongue into his mouth.

"You sure you want this?" he practically growled then.

Her eyes were open, pointed right at him. He yearned to see into them. Didn't dare turn on the flashlight. "Positive." He heard the hunger in her voice.

Reminded himself she'd been married for nearly five years—she knew what she was starting—he rolled her over, grinding his aching penis into her thigh just long enough to give him a second of relief, and then kissed her fully. His lips devouring hers. His tongue dueling and dancing with his partner's. Treating her to things he never should have shared with her.

Things he'd been wanting to show her ever since she'd admitted that sex wasn't all it was cracked up to be.

And once he'd broken all the rules, there was no holding him back. Sitting up, he started in on her buttons. "I need to see beneath the uniform," he told her. "I want the woman."

He'd admitted it. He wanted her.

Real bad.

And got the shock of his life. For all her strength and lack of girliness, his partner liked extremely...girly...underthings.

"Stacy Waltz, please tell me you haven't been wearing these to work every day for the past five years."

"Can't," she said breathlessly, squirming and pushing sheer, lace covered breasts into his hands. "I've always had a thing for underwear that makes me feel like a woman…"

Undies. He could hardly stop himself from heading straight down there. Ripping the pants off her and seeing what the bottom half of her intimate decor did for her.

The thought of how quickly things would end stopped him.

They had a good ten hours until dawn.

And he was going to fill as many of them as he could with ecstasy.

Him and Stace.

How had he not known it would be that mind-blowingly incredible?

And he hadn't even been inside of her yet.

If she was going to die, she wanted it to be right there in that cave. With Jesse Macdonald's body inside of hers.

Thirty years of living and she finally knew that sex really could elevate you to another planet. One where only sensation and the highest joys existed. There were no thoughts other than finding more pleasure. No awareness of anything around them. Just a need for as much as she could get as long as she could get it.

Mac traveled with condoms in his wallet, of course. And the wallet always went to bed in the next day's uniform pants, so he was ready to jump and go at a moments' notice.

She'd once teased him about that, when she'd asked how he'd gotten ready so quickly on one of their out-of-town emergencies, but that night, she was overjoyed to have them there.

Though, she wasn't the one who'd thought of them. She'd been whirling on ahead without any thought of precaution.

When the last condom was used, he stayed inside her as long as he could. And then held her until she slept.

It was a good sleep. Deep. Peaceful. The best she'd had in…she didn't know when.

So much so that when she awoke, just as dawn was breaking, she didn't want to. She just wanted to stay right there in her Stacy-in-wonderland cave forever.

Opening her eyes, she glanced toward Mac…only to find empty space where he should have been.

Sitting up, she quickly dressed, was just pulling up her pants when he burst into the cave. "Grab everything you can," he said, his voice almost harsh. "We have to go."

Heart thudding, her brain still yearning for the land of foggy happiness, Stacy shoved her feet into her shoes as she stuffed the couple of things she'd left out of her bag back in and turned for Mac to strap it to her body. While he fixed his own pack, she strapped on the rest of her gear, helped him clip his pack, and they were out.

"Grab your pallet," Mac said as she exited, bending to get his own. "Throw it over the cliff."

He wanted no sign of them having spent the night there.

Which could only mean one thing. Something had spooked him into thinking that someone was after them.

"It's not Sierra's Web?" she asked, as soon as they were heading around the side of the mountain to go…somewhere.

"I don't know." His words were sharp. "There are two of them. Together. About the same height. Maybe half an hour's climb down, across the gulley. I saw the sun glint off binocular lenses, I think. I'm not sure if they caught me or not."

But the lenses had been pointed in their direction. She got that much.

And just because someone was in the mountains with a pair of binoculars didn't mean they'd been searching for Stacy.

She and Mac weren't going to wait around to find out.

"Give me your phone," she told Mac. Took it from him when he immediately pulled it out of his pocket and handed it over. "I'll keep an eye on it to see when we get service," she told him. Turning it on, and then, as soon as no bars showed, back off again. "We can figure out between now and then whether or not we call in."

It had to be all business. She got that. Wanted it.

If they were being hunted, an unforeseen bullet could come flying at any moment.

But she missed him.

Missed *them*.

And had a feeling that they were never going to be *them* again.

Mac hadn't even looked at her when he'd come into the cave. Nor when they'd headed back outside again.

The harshness in his voice—it was as new as the passion had been the night before.

And she figured she knew why.

She'd pushed him into a corner—Jesse Macdonald didn't believe in forever, and never kept his lovers in his life for long. She'd left him no choice.

And she had to pay the price.

She'd had the night she wanted.

But in the process, she'd lost the man she loved.

Mac had one thought. Keep Stacy safe. He didn't give a damn if she was a cop and fully trained and capable of protecting herself in her own right. If Stacy's kidnapper was in the mountains, death could come any second.

All the little caves and indentures, the overhangs, boulders and natural growth that he used to keep them unseen, would also hide a killer.

Stacy was staying close, watching for phone service. He was purposely guiding them to a high point of the mountain to get just that.

She'd provided granola bars. An energy bar. He wondered, but didn't ask, if the food was sticking in her throat as it was his.

They'd split their last banana.

While he led the way.

The interior was safest, but they had to know their enemy. If Stacy's kidnapper had been caught, and Sierra's Web was out there looking for them, there was no need to take risks climbing deeper into a world where they had little chance of survival once their supplies ran out.

If Sierra's Web was in the mountains to find whoever was after her, he had to know that, too. To have some indication of who might be friendly. To get Stacy to a safe place and guard her while the others found the wanted man.

"I'm scared to death that we'll come upon one of our own," Stacy said, walking closely beside him as they slowed to flatten their stomachs against a cliffside and sidestep to what he believed was a ledge that would give them service. "Do we shoot first, so we aren't killed? Or trust that they're out here to help us?"

He didn't have an answer to that, so said nothing. He couldn't borrow trouble. He had enough of it in every step he was taking.

Stacy turned on the phone as soon as they were on more solid ground. Full battery. No service. For the next hour, it was more of the same. They'd seen no sign of another human out there with them. Which worried him. If the two people he'd seen were on their side, they'd be trying to be visible to them.

And his quest for phone service was sending them farther and farther out of the mountain range. He didn't like that, either.

"Got it!" Stacy's low cry of victory came just as they reached the top of the peak on the outer edge of the mountain. Standing in the middle of a patch of six-foot plant growth, they could see, but not be seen.

He hoped.

She dialed. He gritted his teeth together as he kept watch. And listened.

One ring…

"Warner here, are you okay?"

"Yes," Stacy answered. "Someone's out here."

"We know. We're there, too. Dennison and his team headed out at first light. They're all in beige pants and orange shirts. They'll have on orange wristbands with Dennison's unit number on them. Trust no one else."

The words were delivered ominously. Every syllable succinct.

"We can't stay on here long enough to be traced," Warner continued. "We've closed in on your kidnappers. There are least three of them. Can't verify if police are involved or not. Benson's grandson is. No time for a full report. Just watch your backs. Every second. And watch for the orange wristbands."

With Dennison's unit number. Mac noticed that the tech expert didn't designate the number. Warner knew that Mac and Stacy knew it. Authorities had used it to designate the Dennison case the previous year.

"We need another cave, Mac. We've got to let the mountain have our backs."

"But if we're seen, they could shoot from another mountaintop and obliterate us. They could shoot an explosive in…" She knew it as well as he did.

Was she giving up? Just wanting to curl up in his arms so that if she went, she died feeling good? She'd said something similar the night before. Speaking again of the dreams she'd had while her SUV had been balanced on the edge of death.

"Our best bet is to keep moving. It's hardest to hit a moving target." He wasn't letting her plan her death. They weren't giving up.

He got it. So many days of being strong against constant fear. Existing with death on her shoulder every second. It would wear on anyone.

And blurted the one thing he believed would keep her looking toward the future. "You know, Stacy, all those times last night, and not pulling out right away. There's a chance something slipped through. You could be in the process, right now of…well…you know."

He couldn't say it. Couldn't even think the words that would complete that sentence.

But she obviously did. He saw the most beautiful expression flash over her face…

Then the sharp blast of a gunshot in the canyon obliterated the moment.

He dove. Fell to the ground on top of her, his body gouged by the various things in the duffel he'd strapped to her back. No way a bullet would make it through his pack, his body and her stuff to her heart. Slowly, he scooted them up to the wall of a small peak.

Another shot fired. Echoing through the small valley to the left of them.

"It's not coming in our direction." He felt Stacy's body move beneath him as she spoke, and slowly rolled himself off her.

She was right. One shot had come from the north. The other from the south.

Just one of each.

"Could be Dennison's team found them," she continued.

Or "they" found Dennison's team, Mac knew, but didn't say out loud. He was trying to keep her positive.

He owed it to her after five years of her optimism keeping his head above water.

Keeping Stacy believing in a future was the purpose he clung to as they started to slowly climb again, moving back to the interior of the mountain, toward a smaller, higher peak, where, hopefully, they'd have a view of those looking for them down below.

They'd had a head start.

And, other than scrapes and bruises, were in great physical condition.

They had plenty of ammunition and were both steady shots. Both hit the bull's-eye every time they went to the shooting range.

Besides...if there was the slightest chance that something *had* slipped through the night before, a chance that Stacy could have what she most wanted, a child of her own, a little family in her big house, then he had even more reason to make sure she stayed alive.

For her. And for any possible new life that might be forming.

He didn't let himself figure into the picture.

He clung to the vision for her.

And pressed onward.

Chapter 24

She knew there was no baby. Nothing had leaked. Mac had been overly careful about that. But the fact that he'd dug so deep to try to give her strength...

Even if he hadn't been able to finish the sentence...

She clung to the thought, a little smile inside, as she quaked with fright. Fearing with every step she took that it could be her last.

Would she hear the bullet before it hit her? Or would she just be there one second, and then not?

Or worse, would she hear the bullet and see Mac fall?

Shaking her head, knowing full well that she had to focus all her mental abilities on keeping watch, looking for any sign of movement, Stacy trekked on.

For hours.

Shots rang out a second time. Closer to them. Heart pounding, she moved up to Mac's side. Ducking with him into a little cavern. Her hand touching his.

He didn't pull away.

"What do you want to do?" she asked him softly. And then continued, "Because I'm tired of being hunted."

"You want to hunt."

"Don't you?"

He didn't answer.

"You do, don't you?"

They were both perusing the entire horizon within view, each with their free hand on their gun, as they spoke.

"It's our way," he finally said, sounding more like the man she'd been trusting with her life for the past five years.

"Then let's get to it," she told him, finding her own core steady as they finally came face-to-face with what could be their last major choice as partners. Their last one on earth.

"We don't know our enemy," he said, his tone firm, though almost at a whisper.

Reminding her that their hunters, their prey, could be moving closer to them. Could already have them in their sights.

Maybe not their physical bodies—shots would have fired at them already if that was the case—but the killers could be closing in on their location.

"We know Benson's grandson," she shot back, just as softly. And fiercely. Linking her fingers with his. "We have to assume we're equally matched," she added. The kid had long expressed the desire to become a cop. Had been training at the shooting range since he turned eighteen. And he had others working with him. Possibly cops. Possibly Jimmy Southerland.

"We can't hope to reason with them," Mac said then. "If we had any idea of a motive, or how high up this goes, then maybe, but right now…we'd come off as desperate."

She agreed. "Which means we have to take them down before they get us."

As he wrapped his grip around the fingers touching his, Mac's other hand pulled his gun out of its holster. "We're outnumbered. Warner said there were at least three of them."

Looking her in the eye, he continued. "If we have to shoot first, we do."

She nodded. Understood what he was telling her. They weren't going to play this one according to protocol.

She jerked, her heart pounding.

"What?" Mac's whisper was right in her ear.

More with her eyes than her head, she nodded to the right. And then down. Several yards below, heading up toward the cavern in which they hid, were two men. Wearing jeans. No orange shirts. No wristbands. Neither of them Benson's grandson. Nor were they Saguaro cops. She'd seen them before, though.

"They're miners," she whispered back. "They work for Tom Brandon."

Mac's elbow pushed against hers. "I've seen Jimmy at the bar, playing pool with one of them."

Her heart sank, and for a split second, she and Mac held gazes. Sierra's Web had told them the kidnapping had been faked...

The men split up. Veered off on either side of them.

As though they knew exactly where they were.

And it hit her.

They weren't going to get the chance to hunt.

They'd already been prey in a trap before they'd started the conversation.

Mac's gut was speaking to him. Urgently. "We have to jump them." He made the pronouncement. Didn't allow another thought. "It's our only shot."

When Stacy nodded, the walls around his heart shored up.

He squeezed her hand. Felt her fingers on his, as though saying goodbye.

And maybe they were.

But they'd go out fighting for their lives.

Not die as sitting ducks holding hands.

He'd promised himself he'd save her. His mouth filled with bitter bile as he nodded for her to head off to the right while he broke left. She knew how to keep herself covered.

As did he.

The next minutes needed his full focus. If he got to one attacker soon enough he could...

Hearing a branch crack directly below him, he had no more thought.

Holstering his gun, he jumped. Landed on heavy flesh. Rolled.

Heard the gun go off. Felt the blow against him. Blood pooling against his hand.

And landed a fist in the face inches away from his— one that was staring at him with blank eyes, wide open.

What the hell?

Jumping up, watching the rugged, bearded man flop to the ground, Mac still felt no pain. Saw the blood on his hands.

Saw the blood pooling on the ground from beneath the other man's body.

And, pulling his gun from his holster, backed to the mountainside, pointed in a circular direction all around him.

Where had the shot come from?

And why hadn't another followed it, killing him?

Without waiting to find out, Mac scaled around the edge of the drop-off, and, keeping behind boulders, made his way higher up on the mountain.

Listening.

Looking for Stacy.

Had she shot his man?

Made no sense.

That would have left her back open to the guy's accomplice…

Stark cold fear struck him.

If she'd given her life to save his…

He slid, he clawed and he ran. Stepping as silently as possible, going from boulder to boulder up the mountain, taking it on an angle, bringing him closer to his partner's direction.

At least the one she'd started off in.

I might need to call in a dead body. He threw the thought away. Along with the fact that he had no way to contact anyone. No matter the state in which he might find Stacy's body.

He'd long since passed the cavern where he'd last touched his partner. Squeezed her hand. Was sweating, feeling the blood pounding through his veins.

Stopped behind a boulder to assess his location.

And heard, "Mac!" A harsh whisper.

One he knew.

Turning, he saw Stacy, fully intact, crawling down an incline toward him.

Throat tight, he ran toward her, hauling her behind the boulder with him. Pulling her into his arms and squeezing with every ounce of energy in him.

She was alive.

"Mac… I can't breathe." Stacy whispered the words against her lover's neck. She was holding on as tightly as he was. Didn't ever want to let go…

Or to feel his arms drop away from her.

Which they did.

"My man's dead," he said then, studying her gaze intently. And she nodded. Blinking away tears that she refused to let fall.

He was there. Standing in front of her.

Perfectly okay.

"I know."

"You do it?" The three words were all that came, like he could barely get them out. He thought she'd shot the man? As soon as she'd seen him, she'd assumed he had.

She shook her head. "I don't know who," she said. "I had my guy in sight. Was ready to jump when I heard the shot. The guy I was after stopped, and then took off in the opposite direction."

"In my direction?"

"No, that's what was so weird. He took off down the mountain. Was out of sight before I could get a good shot off."

"So who shot Jimmy's friend?" he asked, nodding toward the ground he'd left behind him.

"No idea." But… "Sierra's Web?" She desperately wanted to think so.

Mac didn't seem convinced either way. He just kept perusing the landscape visible from both sides of their boulder. "Whoever it was, either they are an excellent marksman, or they missed their guy," he said. "I'd already jumped him. We were rolling on the ground when the bullet hit." He showed her his hands. Small streaks of smeared blood were left, and it looked like he'd tried to wipe off a whole lot of it.

Reaching into her pack, she pulled out her wipes. She couldn't help it. She had to do something. Had to get the stain of a killer's blood off Mac's hands.

She didn't know what it said to her that he let her do so.

He was as freaked out as she was? Nearing the end of a tether that felt as though it was tightening around her throat, too?

She'd find her strength, and then, in a low moment, or when the adrenaline dropped off, the fear would be there. Waiting insidiously, an accomplice to those who wanted her dead. A product of their campaign to kill her.

But Mac…he'd always been so calm. So…not looking at her as though she was a pot of gold. Which he currently seemed to be doing. She tried to hold the gaze, to soak in it, but his head just kept on moving. Taking in their surroundings.

"We have to keep going," he said. "We risk being seen, but if we just sit, we have less chance of finding these guys. And more chance of being ambushed."

He wanted to stay on the interior of the mountain for another hour or so, and then move up and outward before nightfall. At least to make a phone call.

She agreed. Was ready to get moving. To try to wipe her mind of the fact that they were leaving a dead body behind them.

Incredibly thankful that it wasn't Mac's.

When she'd heard that gunshot…in the direction she knew he'd gone…

"I love you, Mac."

He'd stepped around the edge of the mountain wall behind their boulder. Stopped. Didn't turn around. And then started out again.

She was right behind him. Watching one side of them while he watched the other, the mountain hugging their sides.

"When I heard that last shot…"

He climbed up a boulder. She followed. "I can't die without telling you."

"You aren't going to die." His voice was gruff. He kept moving.

And she kept up with him every step of the way.

Chapter 25

Mac had a real bad feeling about that shot. If it had been meant for him, because he was reaching for his gun, why wasn't he dead?

His first thought—that he'd been shot, since he knew he hadn't fired his own gun—had slowed him down. There'd been a couple of opportunities for the shooter to get off another round. To get Mac on the second try.

And he hadn't done so.

If it was Sierra's Web, they'd have come to get him.

Unless they'd seen imminent danger in the area.

Which meant he and Stacy could be walking into a minefield at any second.

Stacy.

Loved him.

Had put it right out there.

He couldn't deal with it.

Had to stay focused.

"We need to go up and out now," he said, changing course as he spoke. "They know we're here. Climbing out puts us in more danger of being seen, which is what makes it something they won't expect us to do."

"You think it's possible these guys are turning on each other?" Stacy asked from behind him, indicating to him that she was once again on the same mental path he'd been taking.

His partner.

"I don't know. Either that or someone knows why they want you dead, and they want to be the one to kill you."

He didn't mince words.

They were fighting demons they didn't know, trying to avoid bullets from areas they couldn't possibly pinpoint. They couldn't predict their killer because they didn't have any idea what drove him. Had no inkling of a motive.

He was no longer certain he could keep her alive.

Their time was running out.

They were halfway up the tallest peak inside the mountain range. They planned to get over it and start heading down as they worked their way out over smaller peaks to the edge of the range. They'd be exiting on the Saguaro side of the Clairvoyants—if they made it that far.

They'd eaten more bread and peanut butter. Had had to refill their water packs. Stopping only long enough to prepare and pour, consuming as they traveled.

She was growing slowly numb inside. Figured it was partially a product of fatigue. Physical, yeah, but more psychological.

Who hated her so much?

A dead man lay over the mountain peaks behind them. A life lost because of that hate.

It made no sense to her.

Mac's abrupt stop in front of her shocked her out of her thoughts. He held up a hand, pointing over the cliff they'd been traveling along because of the taller, fuller trees that gave them cover.

Reaching his side, she tucked up against him, to see

what he had to show her, and felt his arm come down out of the point and rest around her.

It took a moment to see what had caught his attention. The movement was slight. There and then gone. But as her gaze adjusted, she predicted the next move. And the next.

A man was moving stealthily among the cacti, desert trees and brush that grew lower on the mountain. Every few steps he stopped, gazing upward. She had him about one hundred yards below them. But one thing was clear. There was no way they could head over the mountain as planned without him seeing them.

And worse… "He's got an assault rifle," she whispered.

And no orange or beige at all.

Where was Sierra's Web? Why weren't they on the trail of those following Mac and Stacy?

Doubts crept in again. Was anyone on their side?

How could an entire police force and nationally renowned firm of experts all be against her? Want her dead?

They'd come far enough out of the mountain, were high enough above other peaks, that she had cell service. Had had it for the past twenty minutes.

Still wasn't sure she wanted to tell Mac.

Maybe they shouldn't call out.

They couldn't live in the mountain for much longer.

She had to trust someone.

Starting with her partner.

"We've got cell service. You want to call out?" she asked him.

He shook his head. Just as she saw another body move. Tall, but slighter, not far behind the rifleman.

"Could just be a couple of guys out doing some illegal hunting," she said then. The disgusting problem wasn't uncommon. Sportsman wanting mountain lions to stuff and hang.

"You might be right, but we can't take the chance," Mac told her.

That's when she heard a tumble of small rocks behind them. Turning, she caught the top of a head before it disappeared. Drawing her gun, she saw Mac do the same, and he motioned for her to move slowly along the mountain wall to a fairly large gouge in the rock face that would have to serve as cover. If the head continued up and around the mountain, they'd have a chance to take the guy down before he could get them.

Unless…before there'd been two of them. One on each side…

She turned, gun in front of her, and saw Mac lunge at the man who'd just rounded a corner, gun pointed. Mac landed before the gun went off. Deflected the bullet. She kept her gun aimed and ready looking for a shot as the men scuffled. And kept an eye behind her, too. Preparing to rapidly fire two shots in opposite directions.

Mac had knocked his assailant's gun away, but the man was fighting hard. Landing blows. Moving Mac and himself toward the fallen weapon, while pounding her partner's gun hand against the ground. Mac kneed the guy, maintained hold of the gun, until…

She swung around as she heard a foreign sound from behind her. A scuffle.

And saw Benson's grandson round the curve of the mountain, a pistol pointed right at her. She'd been a second too late.

"NO!" Mac heard Stacy's scream. Saw her fly through the air as he wrestled for control of his gun. He was filled with an inhuman anger, propelling his arm upward, going for the jugular. He let his gun go, using both arms to pull tight against his assailant's neck, just as he heard a shot.

"Stacy!" he called out automatically. Calling to her as she might lay dying. He felt his prey go limp in his arms and jumped up, grabbing his gun. Running over to the bodies in the dirt. Stacy on top of Benson's grandson, her knee shoved up between the young man's legs and her forearm across his throat.

He didn't see blood. But he heard a sound behind him. Turned to see the man he'd strangled, eyes open, still lying on the ground, but reaching for his own gun.

"Stacy!" he hollered again, his voice filled with agony, and warning, throwing himself on top of her. And felt blood splatter hit him on the cheek.

"Mac!" Stacy screamed.

He glanced behind him, saw the shooter dead on the ground, his gun still clutched in his hand.

"Tell him…" His gaze swung to the body on the ground, seeing the wound just below the left collarbone. Blood pouring out of it.

He shoved his fist on it, applying pressure as hard as he could. Was aware of Stacy throwing off her bag. Heard a zipper.

"Hold on," he said then. Only starting to realize what had just taken place.

Benson's grandson had shot the man Mac had already subdued. And that man had come back enough to shoot him back?

Or had he been aiming at Stacy?

The young man groaned, and Mac pressed harder, fearing, from the amount of blood, that a major artery had been hit. "Hold on," he said again. "We've got you."

"Tell him I took them down," Scott Benson said. "I didn't know. I swear I didn't know."

Stacy was back, kneeling down with gauze and her supply of wet cloths. "Shh," she said, helping Mac get the gauze packed into the wound, as he continued to apply pressure. "You can tell him yourself as soon as we get you down from here."

"I didn't know," Scott said again, his look urgent as, with wide open eyes, he held Mac's gaze. "He said I was helping him to protect his land. To guard it. They'd found gold, and I was going to get a percent for guarding the land…"

Half thinking that the kid was hallucinating, Mac nodded anyway. "I'll tell him," he said.

"I didn't know."

"Know what?" Stacy asked.

"That I was…keeping…watch…so they could kill you."

Mac saw her hand shake as she wiped at Scott's face, and reached for the phone. He heard her swear, assumed there was no service.

"I took the drone." Scott's eyes were clear again as they focused on Mac. "From the station." His story came in patches. Scott's voice growing weaker with every one. "Wanted to check it out… Broke it… Bruce said he'd fix it… They used it… I found it… Said I was already in too deep." Scott lifted his head, as though he was trying to sit up. With pressure still hard on the young man's chest, Mac held him down. Held his head while it lay back against the hard dirt.

"Said I'd take the fall for all of them." Scott's words were disjointed. His eyes closed. "My grandpa too, if I talked…" Scott's voice drifted off. His eyes closed.

Mac almost hoped they stayed that way. That the young man could remain unconscious until they got a helicopter up to rescue him, but a part of him knew that wasn't likely to happen. So when Scott's eyes popped open again, Mac said, "Is there anything else you want me to tell him?"

Getting his last words to his grandfather seemed to be keeping the guy alive. He'd dig deep for any words he could think of to pull from him.

"I'm going farther up," Stacy said. "I have to get service."

"No!" Mac couldn't risk it. Not again.

Scott's mouth moved. He gurgled a little. Then said, "Two more."

"There are two more out here?" Mac asked. Scott didn't respond.

Then, very softly, eyes closed, mouth hardly moving, Scott said, "Tell him I got him." His head fell to the right.

"He's still got a pulse," Mac told Stacy. "Let's get some branches, make a stretcher," but even as he said the words, he knew his plans were hopeless. He and Stacy couldn't carry a stretcher out between them. The terrain was too rough.

They not only risked doing further damage to Scott Benson, they risked getting themselves killed as well.

Grabbing a heavy enough rock to suffice, he placed it over the gauze, using it to keep pressure on the wound in place of his hand. "Let's get to cell service," he said.

And was glad when Stacy took his hand as they headed around the mountain wall once again.

They were alive. Stacy couldn't let herself think about anything else for the first minutes after she and Mac set off. They were both on guard, watching, careful as always, fully aware that though she'd survived once again, she was still not out of danger.

Maybe she never would be.

"I don't get it," she told Mac. "They found more gold? That's what's behind all of this? So what? My grandfather was the one who complained about the mining, the trucks, the noise, the pollution, destroying the earth. He filed complaints, but nothing ever came of them. Tom Brandon owns the land. He's allowed to harvest his own minerals. My grandfather built the other house, moved, and the two of them tolerated each other just fine after that."

A whirring sound interrupted whatever response he might have made. Both of them looked up at the same time. Saw the helicopter. Waved their hands and ran back toward Scott Benson.

She worried that the chopper wouldn't have enough room to land, but the pilot had a much better view than she did and found a flat piece of ground just over a small hill from the ledge where they'd almost lost their lives yet again.

In minutes a paramedic was tending to Scott. But she knew, even before she saw the woman shake her head, that the young man was gone.

All he'd ever wanted to be was a cop. He'd been too young to attend the academy. To join up. So he'd been offering private protection service to a friend.

And then had gone full metal in the mountain to try to prevent his consorts from killing Stacy. That was how Chief Benson was going to hear the story.

Scott might have let greed get the better of him. He shouldn't have stolen the drone from the department. They'd probably never know what else he'd done, knowingly or not, to help those who were after Stacy. But in the end, he'd risked his life to protect Stacy and Mac.

He'd gotten himself killed attempting to save them.

"I wonder if he was the one who shot Jimmy's friend?" Stacy said to Mac as they stood together, as partners, with a foot of desert ground between them, and watched para-medics load Scott's body onto a stretcher. Strapping it down for a secure ride.

"I'm going to say yes," Mac told her, his face grim.

"We still have two more out there," she said then. Did they stay to get them? Or ride back in the helicopter and hide out somewhere else?

She had no home. No possessions, other than the uni-form on her back.

Mac met her gaze. Held on. Looked like he was about to say something when the helicopter pilot approached from over the hill. Heading straight to them.

"I'm supposed to tell you both to climb aboard," he said. "Sierra's Web took down the remaining suspects. It's all done. We're here to take you home."

Stacy took a step back. Didn't want to go.

She didn't know the guy. How did she know if he was telling her the truth?

It was done?

The horror was over?

"Hudson Warner and Chief Benson are waiting for you at the hospital," the man told them. Stacy still didn't move.

The pilot pulled out his phone, showed them a photo of the chief and Warner. Sent as proof. Just in case.

And she stood immobile. Couldn't make her muscles work.

Not until she felt Mac's hand in the middle of her back. A light touch. The touch of a stranger. Guiding her over the hill.

It was over.

Mac saw Stacy to a seat right behind the pilot. She strapped in, expecting him to sit across from her, but he moved to a seat in the back. On one side of the stretcher.

It was truly over.

All of it.

For a second there, as tears filled her eyes, she wished she and Mac were back in their cave.

Thought of the night before.

And prayed that the memory would be enough to help her start her life over one more time.

Chapter 26

Stacy was safe. His job was done. Mac kept repeating the words to himself as he was checked over in the emergency room, and was just as quickly released.

Benson and Warner were both talking to Stacy, who'd also been checked, as he came out. Even in her dirty, well-used uniform, ponytail awry, she looked beautiful to him.

And more than he'd ever be able to handle.

She was safe. His job was done. He heard the words as a rhythm, right along with the tires of the chief's unmarked, high end police sedan on the highway as they headed back out to Saguaro Bend. Stacy was up front with the boss, Warner in the back with him. Mac figured it worked well that way. His partner hadn't looked him in the eye since they'd been brought down from the mountain.

Not that he'd given her much of a chance.

Back at the station, they were met with a line of cheers as he and Stacy walked down the hallway together to the conference room for their debriefing.

From there, he'd be free to head home.

He'd need transportation.

Stacy needed that plus a home.

Random thoughts hit him as he walked along the floor of the station that had been more of a home to him than any other he'd ever known. He accepted a couple of pats on the back. Nodded. But held back, too, letting Stacy collect most of the love from their pseudo family. She'd go far in the Saguaro Police Department. He'd be shocked if she wasn't offered a promotion. Lieutenant at least. Maybe assistant chief. The woman had a way with people that many cops lacked.

Lieutenant Stahl was a great cop. A great leader of cops. But he didn't deal with the public in any way that could be deemed a success.

Cheers and voices faded as they entered the conference room. Leaving a deafening silence as Warner and Benson came in behind them, closing the door.

Stacy sat in the chair she'd been using throughout the case.

He took his next to her because it was about the case.

Benson started in, stopped, teared up and started in again. He thanked them for trying to save his grandson. For making his last moments as comfortable as possible.

Then he apologized to them. "I knew he was heading for trouble," Heath Benson said. "His parents didn't marry and he never really knew his dad. He got in with some bad kids in the east valley. Older guys. I tried to tell my daughter, but she just kept saying she could handle things…and I stepped too far back. The van… I didn't put that together. When the one showed up at the bottom of the mountain… it seemed so obvious that it was connected. I blame myself fully on that one. The van that went over is now evidence for the Denver police in a case involving a ring of vehicle thefts. But back to us…when I heard that the drone used in the east valley was the same as the ones we'd requisitioned… I knew."

The man looked down. Shook his head.

"You should be proud of him, sir." Mac spoke with heart. With soul. He'd watched a young man die. Had heard his last words. And spent the next five minutes repeating them, verbatim, to his grieving boss.

When his voice faded, Stacy's picked up. "He died with honor, sir. Doing the job of a cop even without a badge. He saved Mac's life out there."

The dead man they'd left on the bluff. Jimmy Southerland's friend.

"About that," Warner said, looking at the chief, who nodded. "Southerland was in on it all along," he told the two of them. "It was his four-wheeler at Stacy's house that night. And that she saw just before she went over the mountainside."

"Tom Brandon is in custody as well," Benson said, with a shake of his head. "His wife's agreed to testify against him. He was the ringleader of it all."

"And are we ever going to hear just what *it* was?" Stacy's voice sounded odd. Fed up. Angry. And lost.

It was the lost part that Mac had to fight off. But just until Hudson Warner started talking. Then Mac just sat in shock.

"Brandon and his son Bruce hit a new vein of gold where they've been mining for years. It led to what turned out to be a much larger, much less polluted vein that covered enough land to turn them all into millionaires."

"On their land?" Mac asked.

"Yes," Benson said. "But not originally. It was on the land he bought from Stacy's grandfather."

Then Warner started to talk again. "We kept coming back to those records of Stacy's being messed with. Why would someone be looking at her property records? If it wasn't Manning…everyone else in the area either knows the history of the land or could ask dozens of others who knew. So we did a deeper dive."

"What kind of deeper dive do you do on land owner-ship?" Stacy asked, frowning,

But Mac had a strong idea he knew what was coming. And said, "Mineral rights." He should have guessed.

And when Warner nodded, Mac sat back. Way back. Scooting his chair away from the table. So much for Stacy getting a promotion.

Chances were, she wouldn't be working another day in her life.

"Mineral rights?" She sounded confused. "They go with the land."

Hudson Warner shook his head, looking straight at Stacy. "Your grandfather sold Brandon that land decades ago, but, because he knew Brandon was a miner, and hated the min-ing, he kept the mineral rights, which automatically pass on to any heir he has left, before they can revert to the land owner."

Mac seemed to feel Stacy's intake of breath, as much as he heard it. She stood up, glaring at Hudson Warner, as though the man could somehow take back what he'd said. "Are you telling me I almost died, Mac almost died for some damned rights? Why didn't he just ask me for them? Or offer to share them with me?"

Mac could answer that one. "He couldn't risk you hold-ing your grandfather's views and shutting off any possibil-ity of him getting that gold."

Nodding abruptly, over and over, she stood there. And then said, "I own a gold mine worth millions?" as though that part was just sinking in.

Warner's face was deadpan as he nodded.

Until Stacy fell back into her chair. Then, the technical expert smiled and said, "Congratulations."

At which time Stacy broke into tears.

Floods of them.

And Mac quietly let himself out to find a change of clothes.

She was a millionaire? Owned a gold mine? Stacy could hardly comprehend the information. She'd had a shower at the station, leaving the conference room almost as soon as Mac had. She'd called her father, who hadn't picked up, and left a message for him to call her. She had a new burner phone, given to her until she could get herself a new cell of her own.

She'd been told she was being put up by the department at a lovely hotel not far from Saguaro, at least for a night or two. Longer if she wanted.

And they were providing her with an unmarked department vehicle until she could purchase a new one of her own.

Mac had been given the same—the car portion, that was.

They'd walked out to the parking lot together. She'd felt nothing at all like herself as she'd told everyone she'd be fine and headed out as soon as she'd seen Mac getting ready to go.

"It's wild, huh?" she said, to break the unbearably awkward silence between them.

She'd known she'd lost him. That once they returned home, if they did, nothing would be the same between them.

A pile of money wasn't going to help that.

"No one deserves it more than you do, Stace." His tone was… Mac from the mountain. And for a second her heart soared. Could miracles happen?

And make fairy tales come to life?

Complete with a happy-ever-after?

No sooner had she had the thought than Mac nodded at her, pulling out his keys, said, "Take care," and headed across to the car he'd been assigned.

Hers was right in front of her. He'd walked her to her car.

And then left.

Take care?

For a second Stacy started after him. Angry. Filled with fight.

And just as quickly as the will to go after him had come, it dwindled. Jesse Macdonald had written it all down for her.

At her request.

He'd told her what he did and didn't want. What he could and couldn't do.

He'd made his choices.

And they were right for him.

With that thought, she got into her car, pulled behind Mac into traffic, and as soon as she could, turned to head to the closest box store.

She had some shopping to do.

Possessions to replace.

Before she could check into a hotel where she knew no one, to eat by herself, and try to figure out what she was going to do with the rest of her life.

Mac drove around Saguaro, every street, past his parents' houses, the people he'd known all his life. And eventually ended up at home. He typed in his passcode at the gate of the community. Something he'd have to do until he got a new truck, and then a new bar code sticker for the windshield.

He pulled up to his place.

Stacy was safe.

And while she'd lost memorabilia that she'd never be able to replace, she had the means to go wherever she wanted.

Buy whatever she desired.

Be whomever she chose.

He couldn't have scripted a better ending.

For her.

And for him, too.

He was getting exactly what he wanted.

Stacy was safe.

And he was home. Alone. Just as he'd ordained.

Exactly what he wanted.

Except that…he didn't.

His house, the thought of a new truck, the flattering offer from the sheriff's office that he'd just called to accept… none of it gave him any pleasure at all.

The things that he used to value most didn't matter to him.

He drove around the block. Looked at his house again. Thought of another long shower, some sweat shorts and a T-shirt. Ordering delivery from three different places and eating parts of all of them in bed.

Didn't matter.

Second time around, he headed back out the gate. Drove to Stacy's hotel. Took an elevator up to the room he'd heard the chief mention when he'd given her the key.

And knocked.

He heard her approach the door. Waited for the pause as she checked the peephole. Stacy was Stacy. She'd always check the peephole.

Even before…

When she opened the door, still wearing her uniform, a glorious smile on her face, he shook his head.

"How do you do it?" he asked.

Still grinning from ear to ear she replied, "Do what?"

"I just broke your heart and you're still glad to see me."

"I will always be glad to see you, Jesse Macdonald. I love you. The person you are. Not who I need you to be for me."

He didn't walk into the room.

Didn't trust himself to be alone in there with her and a bed and nobody looking for either one of them.

"I'm not sure I'd be good at…any of what you want. Having kids…the idea isn't horrible. But then we're both stressed and tired. Our careers are pulling at us. The two-year-old is having fits and the baby is teething and…"

She put a finger to his mouth. Her digit was shaking. "I just poured a glass of wine," she told him, sounding relatively steady. "You mind if we take this inside, because I really need a gulp or two."

When she put it like that…and the residual reaction of her uncertain soft touch still throbbing against his lips…

Hands in his pockets, giving himself a firm command to keep them there, he followed slowly behind her. More of a meander. Like him being there with her was no big deal.

Just partners, coming down from days of running for their lives.

They needed a private debrief, was all.

She uncapped a bottle of beer. Handed it to him.

And one hand came out of his pocket.

He drank an eighth of the bottle. Pulled it away.

"I just… I don't want the love to turn to hate," he said then. "I can't bear the thought of ever hating you. But I figured out something that's even worse."

She'd taken a seat at the dining section of the room. Lifted her black police shoes to the table, crossing her ankles.

"What's that?"

Did she have any idea how sexy she looked?

Was she doing it on purpose?

"Not loving at all."

Her feet fell down to the carpet with enough force to have been heard in the room below.

"Excuse me?" Her chin was wavering. Her eyes shooting warmth, and suddenly moist, too.

"Not feeling a deep love for one person is one thing. But to feel it…and waste it…" He shrugged. Held his beer with one hand. Kept the other trapped.

Just not at all sure what he was hoping to accomplish.

"Are you saying you love me, Mac?"

With a sideways cock of his head, he said, "I'd have thought that much was obvious. The problem is…how do we…"

He didn't get the words out. Stacy flew at him. Knocking the bottle out of his hand to pour out on the carpet, as she wrapped her arms around his neck and covered his mouth.

His arms came around her. No permission. They just did.

When she finally pulled back, he started to talk, and she shook her head. "Just let me…okay?"

He nodded.

"This isn't a case, Mac. The only plan we're going to have going in is to promise to remember this…right now… this minute. How we feel. And the time on the mountain, the best and worst…any time life starts to get the better of us, we come back to what our deepest hearts have learned."

She made it sound so…possible. And the way she'd greeted him at the door…knowing him…happy with whatever he could give her…

Mac gave up. Then and there.

Just quit.

Stopped fighting the one battle he suddenly realized he'd been meant to lose. "I love you, Stacy Waltz."

"And I love you, Jesse Macdonald," she told him. "My Mac," kissing him even as she led him to the bed.

They fell together. Got out of their uniforms with much more finesse than they'd used the night before, fell to the quickly exposed sheets and touched each other in ways they'd already discovered. And in new ways, too.

Right up until Mac hovered above her spread legs, and she closed them. "Condom," she said. "I'm guessing you didn't manage to refill your wallet sometime today?"

He opened her legs again. "You want to fill that big house of yours with babies, right?"

Her eyes glistened. "Yes, but not until you're ready…"

He looked her straight in the eye as he plunged into her. Kept hold of her gaze as they moved together, moaned together.

And came together.

Figuring that if the fates had any more bounty left in store for them, they'd just made their first baby.

Epilogue

Mac took a bite of chocolate-covered strawberry and fed the rest to Stacy. Juice dripped over her chin and down to her chest.

He licked it off.

Then sat back in the limousine, sliding his hand up beneath her slim-fitting, long white dress just a little, enjoying the darkness with her.

"My parents handled themselves well," he said. Purposely bringing up family to calm himself down enough to wait until they were in the honeymoon suite the men and women in the department had rented for them at one of Phoenix's five-star resorts. A wedding present for their new, very lovely and very determined assistant chief.

A position that would have Stacy's brain receiving all information, and giving suggestions as she saw fit, on all major cases, without actually being out on the streets. Unless it was to attend a police or community function.

"I think my dad's actually going to stay in town this time," she said, sounding happier than he'd ever heard her. And in the three months since they'd come down off the mountain, Mac had heard a lot of happiness from her. More than he'd ever thought possible.

He'd expounded a fair amount of his own, too. Something he was growing used to. And liked even more for the fact that the emotion wasn't completely new. He and Stacy had been happy together for five years.

And he'd figured out that as time passed, trust in what lasted grew.

His trust in her as a cop.

A loyal partner.

A lover.

And a lifetime.

"I told him about the baby," she said then.

And Mac smiled. He'd known she would. They'd only found out for sure the day before. Had decided to wait to announce until after the wedding. But… Adam Sorenson was a man you just wanted to share your news with.

"And?"

"He talked about selling his place in town and building a small place on that driveway that's left on our land."

Her driveway.

They'd had the land cleared. Small nubs of new growth were already beginning to show through the ash and dirt.

They'd shopped for all new furniture for the big house, too. She hadn't wanted to live anywhere else, despite her newfound wealth. And he didn't, either. She'd bought the Brandon property. Had the house taken down. The mine closed.

And was in the process of getting the mining operation going where Tom had struck gold. Out of sight and sound of any residence. She was creating much-needed jobs for Saguaro, and was giving the city 50 percent of the profits, too.

The rest, she'd signed over to a company the two of them owned together.

There might be a time when Stacy "got over" the trauma she'd been through. When she quit waking up in the night in cold sweats, reaching for Mac. And falling back asleep in his arms. A day could come when she quit missing the things she'd lost—all the keepsakes from her former years that kept memories of other times alive. The day could come. He didn't think so.

But he understood that she was still going to be okay. That she *was* okay. That they'd always be okay.

Because love didn't burn up in fire or get shot. It didn't die.

It just kept growing.

And building.

As long as those who'd felt its power took care to remember it was there.

* * * * *

Don't miss the stories in this mini series!

SIERRA'S WEB

MILLS & BOON

Undercover Cowboy Protector

Kacy Cross

MILLS & BOON

Kacy Cross writes romance novels starring swoonworthy heroes and smart heroines. She lives in Texas, where she's seen bobcats and beavers near her house but sadly not one cowboy. She's raising two mini-ninjas alongside the love of her life, who cooks while she writes, which is her definition of a true hero. Come for the romance, stay for the happily-ever-after. She promises her books "will make you laugh, cry and swoon—cross my heart."

Visit the Author Profile page
at millsandboon.com.au for more titles.

Dear Reader,

I'm so happy to be writing to you again with the publication of my second book for Harlequin Romantic Suspense, *Undercover Cowboy Protector*. It's the first book in a new series that takes place in a real Texas town called Gun Barrel City. I have long thought it was a great name to use in a book, and you are finally holding it in your hands!

As you read, you'll be whisked away to the intriguing world of Hidden Creek Ranch, where danger and romance intertwine as a treasure hunt heats up. Our hero is Ace Madden, a former SEAL turned private security agent, whose unwavering dedication makes him the perfect guy to go undercover to ensure his employer stays safe after a break-in. Sophia Lang, who recently inherited the ranch, is thrust into a web of secrets and danger that threatens everything she holds dear. Soon she's falling for her cowboy protector, but what will happen when she finds out he's not the ranch hand she thinks he is?

I loved writing this book and dropping the seeds for the other two Lang sisters' stories too. I learned a lot about Maya artifacts (yes, it's *Maya*, not *Mayan*—the things you discover while researching a romance novel...), so I hope you learn some things as well while reading about the treasures from Pakal the Great's tomb. Happy reading!

PS: I love to connect with readers. Find me at kacycross.com.

Kacy

DEDICATION

To the hero of my own story, Mr. Cross, because you don't think it's a burden to do all the housework while I write. I am truly blessed.

Chapter 1

Sophia could feel the new ranch hand watching her again. And not in the I'd-like-to-buy-you-a-drink kind of way she was used to.

That, she knew how to handle. In two languages. She could send a midlevel exec in a suit packing before he'd even rounded the bar with that expectant, hopeful expression on his face.

This ranch hand business was something else. Something she needed to figure out how to handle. Stat. Especially since this was the third time and he'd just started yesterday.

Plus, she was technically his boss. As soon as she figured out how to boss cowboys, she'd be the bossiest boss in East Texas.

As she walked toward the barn, the back of her neck heated, then the warmth spread right down between her shoulder blades. Jeez. Had this guy come equipped with lasers instead of eyes? The skin on her arms prickled and all her senses blipped into high alert.

Whipping around, she let her gaze flit along the scarlet siding that made up the barn, searching for the now-familiar battered hat the color of beach sand. Sure enough, the cowboy her ranch manager had called Ace leaned against the split-rail fence, casually looping a rope with gloved hands.

His eyes stayed locked on his task. This guy was good. But he was faking it, plain and simple, because she *knew* he'd been staring at her five seconds before, while she'd skimmed the report her accountant had emailed her.

The fact that she could never catch him in the act made not one bit of difference. He had a lot of practice hiding his avid interest in his boss, that was for sure. Why he chose to study her on the sly—that was the million-dollar question.

Maybe he was quietly plotting whether to use an ax or his bare hands to murder her. He had that hard, dangerous look about him. As if he'd seen things people didn't talk about in polite company. Perhaps he'd done some of those things too.

Or, more likely, he was just a regular ranch hand trying to reason out why a woman wearing a designer dress was running a place like Hidden Creek Ranch. For the record, because she didn't have any other type of clothes to wear while running this ranch. *Run* being a generous term, especially if you didn't look too carefully behind the curtain.

If she'd known the nebulous verb called *ranching* would be so difficult, she might have reconsidered this cocka-mamie idea of turning Grandpa's property into a luxury dude ranch. Folks who paid a lot of money to hang out for a rustic weekend expected horses to be a part of their experience. Horses meant ranch hands.

Ergo, Sophia now employed ten or twelve of them. She'd lost count, but the number was part of a long list of details that woke her up in a cold sweat at night.

She couldn't do it all. That was what she kept telling

herself, even as she continued to spread herself thinner as the clock crept toward midnight, then turned over to a new day. A day where she still didn't have anyone she could lean on when it all got to be too much.

That's fine. It was fine. She could handle this and anything else life wanted to throw at her.

"Jonas," she called as she caught sight of the ranch manager and double-timed it across the hard-packed earth that led to the barn's south entrance. "How highly recommended did that new ranch hand come?"

Jonas's face resembled a statue 90 percent of the time, and the other 10 percent didn't count because you couldn't tell what he was thinking anyway. The man never registered a blessed thing in his expression, a trick Sophia would like to learn. So, if he thought the question was weird, she'd never know.

Jonas spat on the ground, but she refused to jump as she assumed he meant for her to. It was no secret that her ranch manager didn't truly consider himself her employee. He let her act like the boss and accepted the paycheck that her accountant issued, but that was the extent of his concession toward the illusion that Sophia was in charge of Hidden Creek Ranch—a name she was still testing out in her head but liked.

"Didn't come recommended at all," Jonas finally said after an eternity of silence that she suspected was meant to scare her off.

Except she didn't scare easily. If she could shoulder the probing stare of Ace, the Ranch Hand Who Had Zero Recommendations, she could handle Jonas.

"Curious why you hired him, then." She crossed her arms in a show of stubbornness—the same flaw that had gotten her into this situation in the first place. "I thought I made it clear that you could only hire experienced ranch hands."

"You didn't ask about his qualifications. You asked if he came with a recommendation."

They stared at each other for an entire sixty seconds. Which she knew because she counted. It was a trick she'd learned at a corporate retreat, where you use the rhythm of counting to soothe yourself before you blew up at an employee.

It didn't work.

She caved first. She had to. The to-do app on her phone beckoned, the one she never closed because she was always doing something on the list while rushing to get to the next item down. When cell service worked. Which wasn't always.

"I don't have time for semantics," she informed Jonas frostily, wondering yet again if that was his first name or last. "That guy bothers me."

Unlike Ace, the ranch manager had come recommended by her housekeeper, who knew everyone in Gun Barrel City. Sophia had hired Jonas on the spot, too pressed for staff to be choosy. So far, he'd done a stellar job getting the rest of the personnel lined up.

Ace notwithstanding. And the irony didn't escape her that she'd yet to learn the name of any of the other ranch hands. The rest of the nondescript guys in cowboy hats roaming the place barely registered with her.

The back of her neck prickled again but she refused to glance over at the sandy-colored hat or the face underneath it.

"If he's bothering you, I'll fire him," Jonas said blandly as if it didn't matter to him one way or the other.

Guilt. Okay, that was her least favorite emotion and it tasted sour in her throat. Jonas made it sound like Ace had cornered her in the barn and made inappropriate comments. In the corporate world, yes, that was grounds for termination. And probably on a ranch too.

But that wasn't the situation. You couldn't fire an employee because you had a feeling that he'd checked you out a couple of times. Could you? Besides, what if he had a family he was trying to feed with this job? She'd be taking food out of a baby's mouth all because a ranch hand had her spooked.

"No, it's fine," she ground out through clenched teeth. "He hasn't spoken to me. It's just...keep an eye on him for me. I don't trust him."

To be fair, she didn't trust anyone. But Jonas didn't have to know that Sophia was a recovering control freak who had burned out as an ad executive and then grasped the lifeline of this inherited ranch, determined to remake herself into a luxury destination resort owner. Along with that, she planned to be Zen all the time and forget how to spell the word *stress*.

Obviously, that was going well.

Jonas tipped his Stetson in her direction and waltzed away in his funny one-two step that she'd decided meant he'd spent a lot of time on the back of a horse. He was exactly the kind of person she needed running this ranch. She'd do well to remember that delegation was her friend before she questioned him again about his hiring decisions.

Sophia turned on her heel and strode back toward the Victorian-style house that she still thought of as Grandpa's but really belonged to her, legally and everything. Out of the corner of her eye, she noted Ace's head swivel in her direction, his gaze no longer on his rope. She ignored him.

Maybe he was attracted to high-strung women working on their second career before the age of thirty-two. It wasn't a crime and she had too much else to worry about to pay much attention to the hard-edged cowboy who didn't know how to talk to a girl.

When she hit the paved part of the sidewalk that curved around toward the back entrance of the house, it occurred to her that she'd completely forgotten her original reason for heading down to the barn. Dang it. Distracting ranch hands would be the death of her.

What she needed to do was inspect the new riding equipment that she'd noted on Becky's accounting report—that's why she'd been on her way to the barn. The saddles and other horse-related paraphernalia had cost her over $25,000, according to the line item. Naturally, she'd wanted to see the stuff herself because surely it had been handcrafted out of solid gold, then encrusted with diamonds to warrant that kind of price tag.

Just as she started to turn around again, she noticed the back door leading to the kitchen wasn't closed. Huh. Had she really been *that* distracted on her way out a few minutes ago?

Sure, part of the appeal of Hidden Creek lay in the fact that folks swore you didn't have to lock your doors in this part of East Texas. A born-and-bred city girl like Sophia needed more than a few days to be cool with reversing a lifelong habit, but the door was *open*, not just unlocked, and she'd have sworn she'd pulled it to.

Maybe someone else had left it open. Except her housekeeper had gone to the grocery store, her blue four-door still conspicuously missing from the circular drive in front of the main house where she always parked. Everyone else lived in the bunkhouse down at the other end of the paver stone walkway or, in Jonas's case, in the manager's quarters.

Something heavy settled in her stomach.

She shook it off with a laugh. First, she got riled over a ranch hand checking her out and then panicked over an open door. It might have a faulty latch for all she knew. She'd only been living at Grandpa's ranch for less than a week.

She'd never been this paranoid in Dallas, and while she'd lived in a pretty upscale part of the city, crime wasn't unusual. Generally, if you kept your head down and didn't go out after 10:00 p.m., nothing bad happened, though.

Nothing bad was happening here, either. Sophia herself had left the door open on her way to the barn. Plain and simple. The stress was really getting to her.

But when she reached out a hand to grab the doorknob, intending to pull it shut for real this time before heading back down to the barn—*again*—she saw the faint scratches on either side of the keyhole. As if someone had inserted instruments of the long, thin variety into the slot and then jiggled them around to spring the lock.

Sophia's pulse leaped higher than a frog introduced to firecrackers for the first time.

Someone had broken in.

Someone was inside who wasn't supposed to be there.

Someone who probably thought she'd be away from the house for a bit longer.

This someone had vastly underestimated Sophia Lang

and her tolerance for people taking things that didn't belong to them. This ranch had been left to *her*.

Without hesitation, she flung the door open and called out, "I know you're in here. Come out and play nice, and I'll handle this situation civilly. Otherwise, I'll start dialing the cops."

That's when the sheer distance to the main road wormed through her adrenaline-laced brain. It took eight minutes to drive to the edge of Grandpa's land, for crying out loud. How long would it take a police car to arrive from town? A vague idea formulated that maybe they didn't even have a proper police department in Gun Barrel City—it might be more like a sheriff's office.

So she'd be handling this situation herself.

She needed a weapon. She glanced around for anything that would do in a pinch. Umbrella? No. Something heavier would be better.

The housekeeper, Jenny, had a line of cookbooks set up on the kitchen counter, held in place by an iron bookend shaped like a pineapple. That would do.

She hefted the iron weight to shoulder height and crept past the island where the housekeeper had left a giant bowl covered in a dish towel. Good, Jenny would obviously be back soon. Sophia would feel much better with a wing-woman.

Man, she needed to get back to the gym. This weight was *heavy*.

The door to her office stood ajar. No way would she have been distracted enough to skip closing it. She liked her privacy and liked to maintain the fantasy that she had her ducks in a row. The chaos of her office told a different story, one that starred a tornado wrapped in a hurricane, which frankly described her life over the last two months. Since she didn't want everyone to clue in that her ducks were more like squirrels in a mosh pit, she kept the door closed. Always.

The thief must be in her office.

A thin film of wrath turned her vision red for a moment.

No one touched her stuff. Of course, Grandpa had left the whole ranch to Sophia in his will, so technically everything on this side of the office door belonged to her too, but the things inside she'd brought from her corner office in the Hathaway Building. It was all she had left of her previous life, all she had to remind her that she'd conquered the Dallas advertising space. Promoting a luxury destination resort should therefore be a piece of cake.

The office was like a giant motivational poster. No one got to invade her sanctuary.

Peeking through the opening where the hinges met the frame, she spied a man in dark clothes rifling through her desk.

"What do you think you're doing?" she screeched as she flew into her office, bookend raised.

The man glanced up, clearly not feeling all that threatened, his expression growing hard and focused as his gaze landed on her. A stranger. She'd have remembered if Jonas had hired this guy. Faces, she committed to memory, even if she didn't always remember names.

The guy dropped the notebook he had in his hand as if it had burned him, then skirted the desk. Toward her. With intent. Fast. As if he meant to tackle her.

She didn't think. She reacted, swinging the bookend toward the intruder.

She missed. He hit her shoulder with the brunt of his weight, knocking her against the wall.

Pain exploded across her clavicle and down her arm. The thief twisted her bookend-wielding arm up over her head, shaking it. No, pushing it down in the direction of her face.

He was trying to force her to hit herself with the book-end! She fought back, screeching a litany of nonsensical words, but her brain wasn't exactly functioning at top speed. His fingernails bit into her shoulder as he pushed her back against the wall.

All at once, the pressure on her arms vanished. So did the guy, in a whirl of dark colors and a blur of motion.

Someone had pulled the intruder away from her, and the two men grappled with each other for a few heart-rending seconds. Then her attacker broke away to race out of the door, her rescuer hot on his heels.

Ace. She'd recognized him instantly. The ranch hand's hat hadn't even been knocked askew. Her lungs certainly had. She couldn't catch her breath.

She was still standing there in that same spot when Ace returned, his expression taut and searching as he met her gaze for the first time. Unflinchingly. Yeah, this was not a guy who was afraid to talk to a woman.

Holy cow. His eyes were gorgeous, the color of the ocean in a storm when it couldn't decide what color it wanted to be, and all of them were fascinating.

"Are you okay, Ms. Lang?" he drawled, his voice honey as it flowed through her, coating all the bruised places inside. Even the righteous indignation of being victimized.

"I think so." Dropping the bookend, she stretched out her arm, rolling the shoulder that had hit the wall. "The

more important question is, are you? Don't women in movies put a steak or something on the guy's hand who punches
their attacker?"

The ranch hand's mouth twisted up into a half smile so
unexpected that it dazzled her for one crazy moment. Why
had she never noticed his dimples and magazine-worthy
cheekbones? The eyes she could be excused for missing,
given his avoidance issues, but the rest? She needed her
vision checked if she'd missed how hot he actually was.

He bobbed his head. "I'm fine, thank you. I'm not one
to waste a woman's offer of a steak on my hand."

Okay, she absolutely should not be so charmed by someone she'd labeled untrustworthy not too long ago, but she
got a pass given the circumstances. Anyone who played
the part of a white knight had earned the right to a second
first impression.

"I guess I don't have to ask how you knew I was in
trouble," she said ruefully, figuring it was better to call a
spade a spade. As closely as he'd paid attention to her all
day, it was no mystery.

The ranch hand raised an eyebrow. "I heard you yelling all the way down at the barn. I figured it was my civic
duty to investigate. Just to make sure you were all right."

Dulcet tones she did not have, a fact that she readily acknowledged. But really? That's how he wanted to play it?
As if she'd made up the whole idea that he'd become her
number one fan and he just happened to be there, ready
and willing to jump into a fray that included an intruder
who had attacked her.

She quirked a brow right back at him. In this case, it
had worked in her favor to have earned his interest and

obviously he'd saved her instead of being the one to come after her with his bare hands.

But neither did he actually appear to be as reticent as she'd first thought. What was his story, then?

"Well, I appreciate the assistance regardless. You're a real hero."

Ace scrubbed the back of his neck where his skin had turned a mottled color that had nothing to do with the sun he worked under for hours on end. She'd embarrassed him. Adorable.

"Well," he drawled with a faint accent she couldn't place. "He got away. Maybe save the praise for next time."

"Oh, goodness, let's don't assume there will be a next time, okay?" She shuddered, suddenly aware that he had a valid point.

The guy had escaped. *Without* whatever he'd been searching for, presumably, since she'd interrupted him. Why wouldn't he come back? Maybe at night when alert ranch hands would be asleep.

"I don't assume anything," he said grimly. "What do you think he was looking for?"

She threw up her hands. "I have no idea. I've barely been living here a week and there's so much I don't know about this place."

"If you're okay, I'll contact the local sheriff's office." He jerked his head toward the door. "I'll give them my statement about this situation. Ask for them to send a regular patrol around, just to be safe."

Heroic and thorough. If this guy kept exceeding her expectations, she'd have to figure out how to keep from switching places with him—and then she'd be the one checking him out on the sly. The hard edges she'd noted certainly weren't imagined and translated into a whole lot of very well-defined muscle.

After spending several long minutes in his company, she had the impression the drool-worthy cowboy hid behind that edge deliberately. What else was he hiding?

Chapter 2

The law enforcement in this backwater place left a lot to be desired, but Ace Madden didn't usually take no for an answer, and today wasn't looking like the day he'd start.

"Madden," he repeated into his phone, glancing behind him to make sure Sophia Lang hadn't materialized two feet away, as she'd been prone to do lately. "Look, I'm authorized to make this call by the property owner. I need you to send a squad car by so we can reassure her that the cops will keep the intruder away."

It was rare that Ace missed Afghanistan, but no one there ever questioned whether he had the authority to take care of business when the need called for it. On the plus side, he could opt to spare lives in his current profession and did. That was the important thing. He clung to that while repeating to the dispatcher once again that he'd happened upon his employer being attacked and pulled the intruder off her.

No one had to know that he'd learned that particular technique strictly so he didn't have to kill anyone. Deep inside, it felt like a gutless move, but that was the real problem, wasn't it? He had talent for violence, but he didn't particularly like having to get violent with anyone. And even if he was going after bad actors who posed a threat to innocent people, it was a paradox that had driven him from the navy into private security work.

At least he liked the cowboy hat. It was better than eighty pounds of gear and a HALO drop out of a helicopter over the Persian Gulf. In the dark.

Finally, the dispatcher agreed to send the sheriff to check out Ace's story in person.

"Thank you, ma'am, I appreciate that," he told her sincerely and hung up, shuffling back out of view before someone noticed him.

Jonas had too much going on to pay much attention to Ace, but some of the other hands were the good sort who liked to be friendly to newcomers, prone to chatting him up about the weather or throwing out a "How 'bout them Cowboys?", which he'd quickly learned meant the football team, not the ranch hands. Who were also cowboys, but paid considerably less, and no one wanted to talk about them.

Such was the enormous learning curve for being an undercover security operative tasked with keeping Sophia Lang safe without alerting her to his hired-gun status, as dictated by his employer.

Of course, he didn't even know who had hired him. A minor detail he cared not one whit about given the number of zeros tacked onto the end of the paycheck deposited into his business account. It hadn't covered all his sister's medical bills, but the second half, payable in one month, would nearly clear the deck.

While waiting for the sheriff, he texted the other ex-SEALs who made up the staff of the security company he'd formed, telling them simply that the job had just gotten interesting.

While there hadn't been any call thus far for McKay and Pierce to join him on the ranch, Ace had been on the premises for less than twenty-four hours, and he'd already scared off an intruder who may have been after Ms. Lang. This might quickly turn into a three-person job.

The sheriff rolled onto Hidden Creek property with his lights flashing. Ace's eyes drifted shut in disbelief. And maybe in hopes of some fortification.

Obviously, he should have told the dispatcher to instruct the sheriff to come in a little less hot. Of course, he'd have to explain the presence of a squad car to someone eventually no matter what, but it would have been nice to do so with a little less fanfare.

Nothing to do for it now. Ace strode forward to clasp the sheriff's hand, introduced himself and flashed all his fancy new civilian identification. In the end, the sheriff just nodded at the dog tags peeking out from the V of Ace's shirt.

"I'm a vet too." The sheriff tipped his Stetson to the back of his head. "What branch?"

Finally, something was going Ace's way. "Navy. Served in Afghanistan mostly. You?"

"Army. Saw a lot of Gulf War action but that was way before your time," the sheriff acknowledged with a belly laugh.

Ace smiled, relieved that he'd managed to score an in with the sheriff his first week on the job without even trying. That couldn't be a coincidence and he took a moment to thank his lucky stars.

"Not that much more before my time," he countered lightly as a courtesy toward the older man, who did seem to be graying at the temples and carried a lot more weight than he likely had when he'd been active duty. "About my intruder…"

The sheriff took his statement, nodding absently when Ace brought up the idea of sending around regular patrols in case the intruder made a repeat appearance.

"We're a small department," the sheriff explained without sounding apologetic at all. "We'll come by as we can."

Ace checked his eye roll. Obviously, whoever had hired him knew the local cops weren't going to be much use. Fine. He'd keep Ms. Lang from being attacked again. That's what he got paid for, but it would have been great to keep doing it on the down-low while the police did the heavy lifting.

The sheriff went up to the main house to have a word with Sophia Lang, whose statement wouldn't sound much different than his, no doubt.

When he turned around, Jonas was leaning against a fence post, chewing on his tobacco with a laziness that didn't fool Ace for a moment. "What was that all about?"

Couldn't a guy get even a second to conjure up a plausible cover story?

"Oh." Ace ducked his head, shrinking himself down as much as possible in a likely futile attempt to blend into the background. "Nothing major. Helping out Ms. Lang."

Maybe if he left it at that, Jonas would too.

The ranch manager nodded, if you could call that slight head tip a nod. "Uh-huh. That fence on the back pasture fixed?"

"Will be," he promised and hightailed it out before Jonas could ask any more questions.

Unfortunately, the back pasture's proximity lay out of sight of the main house. In the last twenty-four hours, he'd followed his initial plan of lying low and getting a feel for the environment, but that strategy wasn't going to work anymore now that a very real threat had made its presence known.

Therein lay the difficulty of this job. He didn't quite know what to expect since the assignment had few details. All he knew was that Ms. Lang had inherited the ranch and someone wanted to ensure her safety. From what, he'd had no clue until today. That guy would be back, no question. And the intruder might have friends lurking in the shadows of the trees ringing the ranch property.

Once Ace had the fence repaired, he took a long walk around the perimeter of the tree line, just to familiarize himself with the layout in case the knowledge came in handy in the near future. It also couldn't hurt to look for places someone might hide out with the intent to spy on Ms. Lang or any of the other ranch personnel.

Truthfully, it wouldn't be difficult to infiltrate the population of the ranch. He'd done it, almost without trying, and no one had looked twice at his made-up résumé that swore up and down that he'd worked on a ranch before. He hadn't.

But this seemed to be a pretty chaotic period in the life of this ranch. Lucky for him. If things settled down, there might be more scrutiny over his lack of cowboying skills.

A flash of dark against the lighter-colored ground caught his eye.

The color and shape didn't belong. But he couldn't tell what it was from here.

Fading into the trees, he circled around behind the area. No need to open himself up for his own surprise attack.

Ace shimmied up one of the taller trees without breaking a sweat, even though his cowboy boots worked as well at gripping bark as oil would help him hold on to an eel. He was used to less-than-stellar conditions and assignments that pushed his creative and physical limits, though. Cowboying was child's play in comparison.

Silently, he surveyed the remote spot, noting it had a good view of the ranch goings-on but didn't seem to be visible from the barn. Hard to tell from here.

Quick surveillance revealed no one was hiding in the trees. The dark thing was a tarp, stretched out over the ground, ready for someone with binoculars to spread out on. Unless he missed his guess, that's exactly what Ms. Lang's attacker must have done.

But alone or did he have a partner?

Well, he wouldn't be letting his guard down either way. And he realized he'd been away from Ms. Lang too long. After giving the area a quick but thorough search, he headed to the main buildings.

When he got back to the barn, he scouted around for another task to keep his hands busy and settled on helping Rory Montgomery feed the horses. A never-ending job, but Ace didn't mind it too much. It had a good view of the house, and since his primary objective was keeping an eye on Sophia Lang, he'd gladly feed horses all day long if they'd let him.

Except the joke was on him. Ms. Lang wasn't at the house. She'd stepped out the door and started down the long path on a straight line right toward him.

He put his head down, praying it did actually give him a less noticeable vibe, but at six-two, it was hard not to be one of the tallest guys around.

"There you are," she said brightly, her voice carrying across the open expanse. "I've been looking for you."

He bit back the urge to shush her. First the sheriff and then Ms. Lang seemed bound and determined to point a bunch of arrows at his face. This was his first undercover gig and might be his last, based on his inability to keep a low profile thus far.

Montgomery, who had that look about him as if he'd been born and bred in East Texas, let a slow grin spill over his face. "Madden, did you get crossways with the boss already?"

Not likely, but given what she'd most certainly sought him out for—a recap on his meeting with the sheriff—he'd prefer a dressing-down due to some ranch duty infraction.

"Not at all," she corrected, tucking a long strand of dark hair behind her ear, one of many that had escaped her tight hairdo. The real mystery lay in why she bothered to put it up.

"Could you excuse us for a minute?" he mumbled in Montgomery's direction.

Ace gave the dude credit for flicking his gaze in his boss's direction and waiting for her to nod before heading off. At least most of these boys had manners drilled into them at some point.

"I wanted to thank you," Ms. Lang said. "For earlier. I didn't get a chance to tell you how grateful I am that you came to my rescue."

Normally, Ace was a fan of grateful women. Especially one who looked like Ms. Lang. This was not the time to segue the touch of "my hero" shining from her bright gaze into a little more of a mutually satisfying thank-you.

"No problem." He lifted his hat, edging backward a bit to give her the impression he had to get back to work. "Anyone would have done the same."

"No one else was paying attention," she said wryly. "Only you. I have to admit, it came across as a little questionable at first, but in retrospect, I'm pretty happy to have been the subject of your interest."

Dang, she'd noticed him watching her? Here he thought he'd been a lot more subtle than that. Damage control time. Better to err on the side of looking like a flirt than a one-man surveillance crew. "You caught me. Sorry about that. My mama really did teach me better, but in all honesty, I think she'd agree you're pretty pleasing on the eyes."

"Well, I wasn't expecting you to come clean," she said, her eyes wide and her smile warming up things nicely.

So she'd not only taken the bait, the idea of him finding her attractive didn't seem to be too unwelcome. And that part wasn't a lie, thankfully. Sophia Lang might be one of the prettiest women he'd ever seen, but he'd never expected to admit that out loud—in fact, he'd have laid odds on keeping that fact all to himself.

Distractions of the female variety, he did not need. Especially one who had The Job slapped all over her. Distance between them worked better.

On the flip side, it was nice to be able to speak the truth for once. The number of lies required to maintain his undercover status bothered him. It was so much easier in a lot of ways to drop into a firefight wearing fatigues and black paint on his face, fingers curled around an M4A1. Everyone who saw him knew what he'd come there for.

No one knew what he'd come to the ranch for, and he needed to keep it that way.

"I'm an open book, Ms. Lang," he told her with a dose of false cheer.

If only he'd met her under different circumstances, and he had the latitude to flirt with her for real.

She wrinkled her nose. "Call me Sophia, please. Listen, when you talked to the sheriff, did he say anything about sending out more officers to do an investigation?"

"He didn't mention it."

In the sheriff's mind, the hard work was done—he'd taken their statements. What more was there to do? Such was the mentality of many small-town law enforcement departments.

The tarp in the woods lay fresh on Ace's mind, though. That signaled intent and planning on the part of the man who'd gotten away. And worse, it meant the threat still loomed.

He couldn't tell Sophia any of this.

Worry sprang into her eyes. Wouldn't it also be nice if he could reassure her, let her know that he was on the job and he wouldn't let anything happen to her?

"Figures." She hmphed. "I asked him about it, and he brushed me off. He could have at least dusted for fingerprints or something, to see if the guy has a record. That's what they always do on *CSI*."

He grinned. "Want me to call him back and mention that?"

"No. I'm sure he's doing what he's supposed to."

That made one of them. Just because the sheriff and Ace had the armed forces in common didn't mean they were both competent at their post-service professions.

All at once, he realized that his current plan of keeping Sophia at a distance wasn't going to work. Surveillance only made sense if you were searching for an active threat. He'd found one.

Time for a new strategy. Especially one that set her mind at ease. "If you like, I can make it a point to keep an eye on things. Circle the house a few times during the night. Set up some floodlights around the doors and windows."

Curiously, she eyed him. "You'd go without sleep on my behalf? You really are a white knight."

He ducked his head, a reflex that had become more common than he was used to, but the number of times he'd been put in the spotlight lately had become alarming. And slightly embarrassing. "No, far from it. You're my boss and anything you need done is part of my job."

"What if I needed a sounding board?" she suggested with raised eyebrows. "Someone who clearly has keen hearing, eyesight and a secret ability to scare people off without blood or flashy weapons."

"You mean me?"

Her smile broadened. "Yes, you. That guy was looking for something. What? I don't know anything about running a ranch or horses or even cowboys for that matter, but I do enjoy your 'aw, shucks, ma'am' routine. More than I thought I would. So maybe your paycheck could extend to helping me figure out what was so interesting in my office."

He stared at her for a moment. Never in a million years would he have expected Ms. Lang herself to come up with his next move—and for it to be such a perfect way to keep close to her without raising suspicion. "You bet. Anything you need."

"That was easy. I'll clear it with Jonas."

That got a hearty *yes, please* from him.

"It's not a routine, by the way." Which wasn't at all important to clarify in the grand scheme of things but he felt compelled to mention for some reason. "I'm just a guy who has a healthy respect for women, especially if they are the ones signing my paycheck."

"Stop, you had me at 'pleasing on the eyes,'" she told him with a laugh. "I've never been called that before and let's just say it's my new favorite compliment."

So, Ms. Lang had a bit of her own flirting game going on. He couldn't rightly say he objected. "You're welcome, then."

"Come by the house in about ten minutes after I've had a chance to explain your new duties to Jonas."

She sauntered off, leaving him a bit dumbfounded. And trying to sort through the distinct feeling that Sophia had asked him to help her not because she really needed another set of eyes. But because the attacker had spooked her, and she didn't want to be alone.

If so, why hadn't she just come out and said she'd like to repurpose him as her temporary bodyguard?

Chapter 3

Sophia risked another sidelong glance at her companion because *hello*.

Ace Madden—last name now known thanks to the other cowboy—was very easy on the eyes. *How* had she missed that before? And his voice. That was the secret star of the show. It was the kind of voice made for close quarters with low light and no other people.

This time, he caught her mid-perusal, but he just smiled. "Wondering what a guy like me is doing in a place like this?"

She had to laugh. He didn't exactly fit into her ergonomic desk chair. In fact, most of him spilled over the edges and into the surrounding area.

Okay, maybe not physically, but he had this presence that she found both affecting and oddly comforting, despite knowing very little about him. What she did know counted though—he missed nothing, with a sharp-eyed gaze rivaling a bird of prey and an alertness that said nothing would get past him.

If someone had told her back in Dallas that she'd suddenly find alertness attractive, she'd call it ridiculous. But after nearly being brained by her own bookend courtesy of this unknown assailant, she'd quickly revised her understanding of basically everything. Especially the mysterious circumstances around her inheritance, which she'd been ignoring thus far in favor of her enormous to-do list.

It was time to change that.

"Maybe you should be asking me that question," she advised him and picked through the contents of the second desk drawer.

Ace lifted his brows as he glanced up from his own drawer on the left-hand side. "What is a girl like you doing in a place like this?"

Touching her nose, she leafed through the papers Grandpa had left behind. "That's the one."

"To be followed by the more pointed question—if you don't know anything about running a ranch, why are you here?" he asked. "Assuming you don't mind me asking since you brought it up."

Yeah, she had. It hadn't occurred to her that admitting such a thing to one of her ranch employees might not be the best way to instill confidence in her ownership of Hidden Creek. All she'd been thinking at the time was how to get a desperately needed second set of eyes, preferably ones used to evaluating ranch-type details.

And maybe she wanted to spend a few more minutes in the company of the man she'd stumbled over in her backyard. It wasn't hurting anything.

"The ranch was supposed to be a family venture," she said, struck by how bitter it tasted in her throat to say so. "My sisters and I were each left one-third ownership, but they both bailed on me. I can't afford to buy them out, not yet, so they basically gave me a year to get this place profitable or they want me to sell and split the proceeds."

"That's rough," Ace said with what felt like genuine sympathy. "No pressure or anything. The original owners were your parents?"

Somehow, she'd assumed Ace Madden hailed from Gun Barrel City and thus would know the ranch's history. It was interesting to learn that he wasn't a local in this roundabout way. "No, my grandpa. Billy Lang. He ran a stud farm that was pretty well known for producing quality horses, but my dad wasn't interested in following in his footsteps. As my grandpa got older, he had to let the business go."

All delivered with an even voice that belied none of the horribleness that had represented her childhood. Two sentences to encapsulate a decade and a half of listening to her parents fight about moving to the ranch. Sophia's dad cared nothing for horses, never had. He cared about one thing and one thing only: treasure. Rumors of treasure, stories about treasure, searching for treasure…anything and everything that even hinted that something valuable might be there for the finding.

And he'd finally left his family over it.

She hadn't seen her father in over fifteen years. Last she'd heard, he'd been headed to Bolivia with his partner in search of some obscure Incan artifact rumored to be buried in a tomb near Lake Titicaca. As far as she was concerned, David Lang didn't exist.

But Hidden Creek Ranch did, and she had a more than fair share of indignation at her dad for abandoning not only his wife and daughters, but his father, and the legacy left behind.

Ace glanced at her. "Pardon me for saying so, but it seems like a tall order to get a breeding program up and running in a year. You know, because the horses have to have time to breed and such."

"That would be a fair statement if I planned to resurrect the stud farm. I'm opening a luxury destination resort instead," she told him and swallowed back the sheer panic that rose up as she contemplated all the work left to do and the very small amount of time to do it in. "You know, like a dude ranch? With trail rides and cabins along the creek."

"That sounds like a fine idea," he said immediately, earning major points by not listing all the reasons it wouldn't work, like her mother had done.

"Really?" she squeaked out before she could stop herself, but she'd become desperate for validation and apparently not very picky where she got it from. "You don't think it's a dumb idea? The smartest thing to do would be to resurrect the breeding program by contacting my grandpa's old clients. The records are all here somewhere."

Ace's mouth curved up and she didn't mind at all that he noticed she'd stopped rifling through the papers in favor of watching him.

"Smartest things and decisions of the heart are rarely the same," he said simply and lifted his hands in a lazy shrug. "I always figure it's better to be happy than it is to do what might seem to make the most sense."

Boy, if that wasn't the solid truth. If she'd intended to do the smartest thing, she'd have stayed in Dallas and gone to therapy to work through her burnout, then kept on climbing the ladder in the advertising industry. Instead, she grasped the lifeline of this inheritance, plunking it down as the path to a happier, healthier life.

"Thanks for that," she said sincerely. "I needed to hear

that someone doesn't think it's silly to completely convert a stud farm into a resort."

Though, she had just met this someone. And he was an employee. Who until recently, she'd mistrusted. Had she jumped the gun on reversing her opinion of him for no other reason than because he'd come to her rescue? After all, he could theoretically be in cahoots with her attacker in a good cop, bad cop routine.

But she didn't think so. Up close, Ace had this warm vibe that made her comfortable, not edgy. Sure, he still had that hardened exterior that he presented to the world, but that's what had saved her bacon earlier. The man knew how to command a tense situation, had obviously used his skills before, many times.

Honestly, that dichotomy intrigued her. *He* intrigued her as a whole. Plus, she had extra incentive to keep him talking. She had a feeling she'd be hearing his voice in her sleep tonight.

"So, you think maybe there's some valuable information about your grandpa's breeding business in here?" Ace asked as he resumed glancing through the papers she'd pointed him toward.

Sophia sat back in her borrowed kitchen chair, the slats hard against her spine. She'd given Ace the larger padded chair behind the desk out of courtesy—she was a head shorter than him and never until this day considered whether she'd fit into a chair or not. Ace clearly had to worry about that often.

"I mean, I guess that makes the most sense," she said slowly, trying to recall how the breeding logistics worked from the many conversations she'd overheard as a kid. "I do know that the baby horse is less valuable without the lineage paperwork."

"I think they're called foals," Ace said with a tiny smile that wasn't the least bit patronizing despite the correction.

"See, this is why you're here. I need someone who knows the lingo and understands what they are looking at. Otherwise, I might not know that I've found what the attacker was searching for."

Task solidified, they worked side by side for another hour, carefully paging through her grandpa's old files. Her mother had pushed to have this all cleaned out after the will had been read, but Sophia had resisted, largely because she had a mile-long list of things to do to get the ranch ready for guests. Paperwork had been the last thing on her mind.

"I found a list of all the stallions my grandfather owned." Sophia held it up, reading off the first few. "Franklin, Kennedy, Reagan, Lincoln. He named them after presidents."

"Keep that," Ace said decisively. "That could be useful later. I have a stack of vet bills. I can't imagine that would be helpful, but just in case, hand me a paper clip and we'll be sure to keep them all together."

Sophia did as asked, and frowned at the envelope she'd just uncovered simply labeled "David." Her father's name. Probably something her grandfather had intended to give his son, but since no one knew where he'd gone, never had the chance.

She reached toward the trash, intending to throw it away—after all, her father hadn't even bothered to come home for the funeral—but at the last second, slid it back into the drawer. Just in case. A stupid, ridiculous notion that one day, her father might show up so she could give it to him. Vain hope.

She pushed that whole subject out of her mind. Or tried to anyway.

Jenny, the housekeeper, finally back from the store, kept making excuses to walk by the office, obviously curious about the cowboy Sophia had brought into the house, as if she'd rehomed a feral cat and let it make a nest in the corner.

Okay, yes it might be a bit unorthodox to have one of the hands sprawled across her desk chair, but this was Sophia's house, wasn't it? She could do whatever she wanted to do.

But after ten minutes of second-guessing herself, she'd finally had enough. "I think this is a lost cause."

Ace glanced up from his sheaf of papers, his lashes low in an affecting way that put butterflies in her stomach. Oh, man. This was not good. She had no latitude to be thinking about him in any way other than as an employee. It was unprofessional. Besides, she needed him to be doing cowboy things to help prepare Hidden Creek Ranch to become a tourist destination. Period. That was the only thing she should be focusing on right now.

She stood, determined to put an end to whatever this interlude was.

"We didn't find anything," Ace reminded her.

"We might not ever, either. We have no idea what that guy wanted. For all we know, he might have been a random thief who hoped to find jewelry or money in my desk. I'm probably making too big of a deal out of this."

In a flash, the hardened side of Ace appeared, his expression becoming one she'd bet scared a lot of people into doing whatever he said in no time flat. She stared back at him, curious what had flipped that switch.

"I don't think we can make a big enough deal out of it,"

he finally said, his arms crossed. "No random guy breaks into a house with ten ranch hands a stone's throw from the back door. A run-of-the-mill thief would start in the bedroom. That's where people keep jewelry. He targeted this room specifically. I'd like to know why."

"This is why the sheriff should be the one doing the investigating," she said wryly. "How do you know so much about what a thief would and wouldn't do?"

"It's not because I have a history of running on the wrong side of the law," he said, his mouth tugging up into a half smile. "It's common sense."

"Well, be that as it may, I have some pressing things on my agenda, so I'll let you get back to your day."

Ace didn't move from his sprawl. "Why do I feel like I'm being dismissed?"

"Because you are?" she said with raised brows and crossed her arms in kind to match his, hating that he probably saw it as the barrier that she'd meant it to be.

But she didn't know how to trust him all at once and that wasn't his fault. She had issues with all men, thanks to her father. And yes, she was quite aware of how silly that sounded, thanks. Knowing about her mental blocks and removing them were two different things.

Besides, it was better to depend on Sophia Lang only. Then she never had to worry about whether an unexpectedly sexy cowboy had her best interests at heart or was the type to be eyeing the door behind her back.

Well. She didn't have to worry about that anyway. She was his boss. Nothing else.

Maybe the one she really didn't trust was herself.

"I should stick close to you," he argued, clearly not pick-

ing up on her skittish vibe. "In case that guy comes back.
Or has friends."

"Plural? I might have to worry about more than one other
guy out there who's planning to break into my house?"

His expression softened all at once and something inside her chest did too. Against her will.

"You don't have to worry about it at all, Ms. Lang," he
said. "That's my hope anyway. Let me be the eyes in the
back of your head and you do your boss stuff. I promise I
won't let anything happen to you."

"You can't promise that," she countered, wishing that
he could, wishing she could melt into that promise and roll
around it in, safe from harm.

The problem was that while he might keep her safe from
another attacker, who was going to keep her safe from Ace
himself? Obviously, he excelled at rolling right through
her man-shield.

"Try me." His voice had pure steel running through it.

That's when he stood, towering over her with his trade-
mark combo of authority, command of every situation and
extremely cut body.

What, exactly, he was challenging her to try got lost in
the shuffle as she stared up at him. Hard-edged cowboys
with warm, gooey centers were not her type, and everything inside was demanding to know why.

"I'll go," he murmured. "Since obviously I've done
something to make you uncomfortable. But I'll be on the
other side of that door, making sure nothing comes through
it besides folks you choose."

Including himself. He'd solved her problem in one fell
swoop. He wouldn't come inside unless she invited him.

Even though he'd already clearly expressed his attraction to her as a woman.

That spoke volumes to her. This was a principled man who had readily volunteered to watch out for danger without her having to ask him. Without forcing her to admit she was scared. Without pressing his advantage, which he easily could do while they were alone here in her office.

Before she could figure out which direction she planned to waffle, a deafening crash reverberated outside.

"What in the world was that?" she said.

Ace didn't blink, even as people started yelling. "Sounds like it came from the direction of the barn. You should stay here."

"Not on your life. This is my property."

The wall of man in front of her didn't move. "There are a lot of people employed on this ranch, most of them new. Any of them could be a threat. It would be safer for you to stay in the house."

Impasse. And she had a feeling he wouldn't budge until she did. "Fine, I get it. But I need to see what's going on."

"Look from the window. But stay to the side."

What, like someone might take a shot at her as she peeked through the blinds? Ridiculous. Right? But anxiety and the sheer stress of the day had taken its toll on her will to argue. Besides, she'd be a fool not to heed the advice of someone who clearly knew a thing or two about dangerous situations.

She dashed to the east wall of the house and louvered the plantation blind open so she could survey the barn area.

It was chaos. Half of the back section of the building had collapsed on itself in a pile of scarlet siding and dark roof tiles. Men scrambled like ants. Hand to her mouth,

she watched as Jonas and some of his cowboys heaved together to move the debris in erratic motions.

Her barn. It was half-gone. The other half wobbled un-
steadily like it might come down any second.

Ace materialized at her back, silently taking in the scene
from over her shoulder.

"Is someone…trapped under there?" she asked, pulse
hammering in her throat. "Is that why they're so frenzied
to get that pile of siding moved?"

She glanced back at Ace, who jerked his head in grim
acknowledgment, his lips flat. "It's likely."

"You should go help," she decided instantly.

That was one of her employees under the heavy beams
and wood walls that had once held her barn together. They
would need all the strong backs available.

"I should stay here," he corrected. "Because the odds
of that having been an accident are low. It was meant as a
diversion. Fortunately, I wasn't outside when it happened,
so you're not left here alone. Which I am pretty certain
was the intent."

Sophia's stomach squelched as she processed what Ace
had just thrown down between them. He was saying the
barn collapse wasn't an *accident*? Someone had done that
on purpose? Surely not. He was making way too big a
deal out of this.

She crossed her arms. Tight. "I'm not going to be a prisoner in my own home."

By way of answer, he pulled her out from in front of the
window and positioned her well away from it, his hands on
her shoulders. "Until we know what we are dealing with,
you should consider all of your activities risky."

"Ace, I'm in the middle of renovating this property to

be a dude ranch," she burst out. "I don't have time to play a nervous woman afraid of her own shadow."

And then it hit her that the barn had just collapsed. One of her employees might be hurt or worse. The expense and the time alone would be a prohibitive blocker to opening on time, but the potential loss of one of her people—that weighed heavily on her heart.

Because it was her fault. Either way. Someone had done it deliberately to get to her. Or it was an accident, due to faulty construction of a building she owned.

Someone banged on the back door.

Sophia's whole body jerked in involuntary fear. Her heart hammered painfully against her rib cage.

Ace put one finger to his lips. *Shh.*

Sure, like she intended to yell out, *Here I am, come and get me.* Besides, his other hand still lay on her shoulder, holding her in place. Comforting her, even.

Ace Madden was here, and he was more than willing—and capable—of standing between her and whatever threats might be about to spill through that door.

She'd just about reached the point where she saw the wisdom in letting him.

Chapter 4

Somehow, Ace got Ms. Lang—Sophia—to agree to stay in her office with the door locked while he did a sloppy recon job to figure out who stood outside the house trying to get in.

Sloppy only because he didn't know the house that well and he was used to having a lot more tools at his disposal, like a SOCOM satellite feeding him an on-the-ground livestream of the enemy's position. But he'd get this job done despite the less-than-stellar circumstances because that's how he did things—efficiently and thoroughly, even if he had to improvise.

Stealthily, he maneuvered to the window near the door and peered outside. Jonas. It was the ranch manager standing on the back doormat. Ace breathed a little easier. As far as he knew, Jonas was on the up and up, a solid guy who worked hard and expected the same of others.

But when he swung the door open to face the man who might have fifty pounds on him, Ace realized that he'd put himself in a tenuous position as Jonas swept him with a look.

"What're you doing answering Ms. Lang's door?" Jonas asked, his gruff voice laced with suspicion that didn't bode well for the rest of this conversation.

He ducked his head but making himself smaller wouldn't take the spotlight off him. "I was helping her out with some files in her office. She said she cleared it with you."

The expression on the other man's face spoke volumes. "There's a big difference between helping a lady move boxes and answering her door like you got privileges."

Ah, dang. That was a wrinkle he hadn't expected.

Ace met Jonas's stare head-on, refusing to back down or respond to the implied slight. It was no one else's business if Sophia had invited him into the house to go through papers, bake a soufflé or strip him naked and have her wicked way with him. Though it was obvious Jonas had the idea that Ace might have been the one taking liberties.

As if he'd even remotely consider seducing his boss to gain favor above the other staff.

"Did you need something?" Ace asked coolly. Because right now, he was the one with privileges, namely the right to protect Sophia from all harm, and until he determined the state of things, she was staying in her office.

"There's been an accident. Ms. Lang needs to know what's going on." Jonas glanced behind Ace as if he hoped to spot her hovering in the background, maybe wearing a filmy robe that would lend credence to the idea that the manager had interrupted something illicit.

"We saw. What's the status?"

Jonas shifted from foot to foot. "I'd rather talk directly to Ms. Lang, if you don't mind."

"I do." Ace crossed his arms. He wasn't ducking his head now and Jonas had to look up to him to meet his gaze. Not an accident. "She can catch up with you later. For now, tell me the status. Did you call in the fire department? They should have contacts who can bring in some cranes."

Nodding, Jonas appeared to at least accept the status quo whether he agreed with it or not. "Yeah. They'll be here. Lost half the barn. We pulled Hanes out from under a beam. Broke leg, looks like, but he's breathing, so that's something. They're sending an ambulance. Horses were all out to pasture. Mostly all the tack is okay on account of it being stored in the standing half."

It sounded like the best possible outcome, but he'd let Sophia be the judge of that. Since Ace had stood in the open door for a good three minutes now with no issues, he'd downgraded the situation from critical to serious. But he wasn't the target. Anyone could take a shot at Sophia as she stood here listening to the manager give the rundown. That might have been the end goal for whoever set up the barn to collapse.

"Deliberate?" he asked Jonas, curious if the man would even have the slightest clue where to start that determination. And if he did, would he be up-front with Ace about it?

Jonas jerked his head. "Couple of the support posts were sawed through. Hanes noticed it right before the roof came down. What do you know about it?"

"It was a guess." An educated one. "Barns don't just fall over."

"True enough." That seemed to be all Jonas had to say, to him at least. "Tell Ms. Lang I need to see her."

"Noted."

Jonas stalked off, and Ace watched him go, his gaze casing the perimeter by habit, but all activity on the grounds seemed centered on the barn. He took a half second to look for sunlight glinting off long-range surveillance equipment, but the woods around the place seemed clear as well.

He knocked on the office door. "Ms. Lang, it's me."

She immediately opened it as if she'd been on the other side waiting on him. "What's going on? I heard Jonas's voice."

Deep strain marks edged her eyes, the kind that would age a woman who wasn't as delicately beautiful as Sophia. As it was, seeing them just made him want to smooth them away with the pads of his thumbs. Or something else that would be more boss-employee appropriate. Which didn't exist.

He stuck his hands in his pockets. "Yeah, that was him at the door. Barn's a loss, which I'm sure you expected. One of the hands broke his leg. Ambulance is on the way."

"You're hedging." Her gaze flitted over his with shrewd attention. "What are you not telling me?"

"It wasn't an accident."

"That's confirmed?" When he nodded once, she let out a long breath. "And you think it was meant to be a diversion. So the intruder could finish what he started."

Not to put too fine a point on it. But whether the intruder had meant to harm Sophia or had merely intended to draw her out of the house, he wasn't sure. He didn't like being unsure, not when he had a job to do. Two jobs.

"We need to talk about how to handle security around here," he told her flatly. "Jonas was a little too keen to get a handle on what my presence at your door meant. I'm going to apologize in advance for not thinking that through when I insisted you stay out of sight."

"What?" She bristled, hands on her hips. "What are you saying, that he insinuated I'd lured you into my clutches so I could oil you up and chain you in my basement?"

Well. Someone had a vivid imagination. He filed that information away for later. Much later. Like when he needed a laugh. It would never be appropriate to think about Sophia with a bottle of oil in her hand in any way, shape or form.

Too late.

Annoyed with his lack of control, he flushed the entire slew of provocative images out of his mind. It took a lot more effort than he'd like. "I think it might have been more the other way around."

Her brows rose. "He pegged you for the one to be chaining up women in the basement? He has met you, right?"

This bizarre conversation actually put a spark of heat in his cheeks. "No one is being accused of activities involving oil or chains. But the point is that my presence around you will raise questions. I don't want you subject to that kind of scrutiny. It might be best if I handled it a little more discreetly."

"Why don't we just tell everyone that we're dating. Isn't that what they do in the movies?"

When she crossed her arms and leaned on the doorframe, he had the distinct impression this whole scene amused her. Which made one of them. "I'm not cut out for fake dating. Sorry."

Fake cowboying seemed to be his hard limit. And there was enough half-truth and playacting that went along with that to have him second-guessing why he'd ever thought that was a good idea.

He couldn't even imagine how difficult it would be to fake date a woman as beautiful as Sophia Lang.

"You could ask me out for real. Then it wouldn't be fake."

The challenge hung there between them, the space heat-ing with the spark she'd set. One he needed to put out quickly. But that die seemed to have been cast.

Since he'd already admitted to her that he found her attractive, he had to tread carefully here. "That sounds like the worst idea I've ever heard."

Okay, so he wasn't going to be known for his smooth moves around Sophia Lang. Noted. Fortunately, she laughed.

"Just what every woman wants to hear from a hot cowboy," she said with a flat expression he couldn't read. "I didn't mean actually go on the date. I just meant…you know what? Never mind. It is a terrible idea."

Great. That comment certainly fixed the awkwardness and inability for him to get his wits about him. No less than he deserved, though, after telling her she was pleasing on the eyes and setting all of this up to be one big flirt match.

"I'm sorry," he said and then shook his head to jar loose some words that worked in his favor. "Maybe we could stick to business for the time being. You need someone to keep you safe and we also need to keep all of this on the down-low so no one else suspects there's anything going on."

She clapped her hands like a little girl at a birthday party with ponies. "Ooh, I love secrets when I'm the one keeping them. But why all the cloak-and-dagger stuff? The more people who are aware that Intruder Man might come back, the more eyes we have to alert us."

The way she dropped *we* into that sentence shouldn't have warmed him as dangerously fast as it did. But he clung to it for a brief moment. It was as much of this woman as he could allow himself to take.

She didn't know him. What he was capable of. If he told

her, she'd run very fast in the other direction. Which he couldn't afford at the moment, given his assignment. Neither could he stomach romancing a woman under false pretenses. She thought he was a cowboy. A simple guy from a good family who could sweep her off her feet with pretty phrases and still have energy left over to take out bad guys.

At least it seemed as if she'd moved on from the cover story that had apparently cast him in the role of the romantic bodyguard hero. He wasn't who she thought, nor was he capable of romance. Better to let all these sparks die out and leave the ashes on the floor.

"Intruder Man might be working with someone on the property," he explained, adopting her term because he liked it. "Easier to keep everyone on the suspect list than to try and weed out the bad apple. Plus, you're hiring people left and right. We can't trust your existing guys not to do their amiable cowboy routine and accidentally tell the wrong person we've got surveillance going on."

Sophia's gaze zeroed in on him a little too closely. "You've worked in law enforcement before. Is that why you talk like that?"

This was where he should be aw shucks-ing and ducking his head, but it was starting to hurt his neck. Maybe it was better to just be as much of himself as he could be. No one had ever told him he couldn't be truthful about his background, and it wasn't like he'd intended to keep it a secret.

"Former military. It's in the blood."

Or in his case, the thirst for excellence had been in his blood since the beginning. He'd gotten very good at being a weapon for the United States Navy and they'd pulled him out of their toolbox often.

By the time he'd quit, the blood he had spilled made up most of his résumé.

Dawning understanding lit up her features as she swept him with an appreciative once-over. "That explains a lot."

Hopefully it explained why she needed to listen to him and stop dropping hints that she found him attractive right back. "So, are we agreed that I'll keep an eye on things, you'll keep this between us and neither of us are going to talk about dating?"

She made a face that didn't hold any real heat. "Fine. I have too much to do to argue."

Now he was just being reckless for the sake of being reckless. "Well, if you wanted to argue with me about whether we should date, I have a few minutes."

Also known as not letting the sparks die. Idiot.

Laughing, she shook her head. "No, you were right about that. Business only between us. I meant arguing about keeping quiet. Silence is not one of my skills."

"You don't say," he muttered, which also got a grin out of her.

Points in his favor, though. At least she wasn't still upset about the intruder and the worry lines were gone from her face. Looked like he'd managed to soothe them away, after all.

"So how is this going to work?" she asked. "Are you going to follow me around?"

Actually, it would work a lot like it had been already, where he watched her from afar, except this time he had the benefit of her being aware of his attention. And he could speak to her when necessary.

That part was key. Because he needed the distance from Sophia—Ms. Lang. Fast. "Why don't you let me worry about how it works, and you do what you do best. Run the ranch."

She rolled her eyes and pulled out a phone from the pocket of her off-white dress and handed it to him. "As long as one of us thinks that, I'll take it. My to-do list is beckoning. Enter your number so I can text you if I need to."

Dutifully he did so, understanding the wisdom. But it felt more intimate than it should. As if he really did have those privileges Jonas mentioned.

She called him and hung up, so he'd have her number in his missed calls.

"I best get back to work," he told her and exited the house as fast as possible.

He made a mental note to find his phone and keep it on him. Maybe get an industrial-strength case to protect it from ranch life. He'd never gotten used to carrying one in the first place since he never took a phone on a mission and cowboying didn't lend itself to something solid in his back pocket.

But for Sophia's sake, he'd work it out if it made her feel safer. Ms. Lang. Dang if he didn't need to tattoo that to his hand so he'd remember she was his boss, not a woman he could pursue, no matter how much he liked her. This was a job and he needed to figure out how to do it without compromising the whole thing.

Quickest way to do that would be to make good on his sudden strong desire to text her something inappropriate and non-work-related.

The first thing he did when he found his phone was save Ms. Lang's contact information with the label Limpet. It was a particularly nasty magnetic mine he'd used a time or two to take out al-Qaeda destroyers. And every time he saw the name come up on his phone, he'd be reminded what would happen if he ever told Ms. Lang the truth—any warm feelings she had toward him would die in a fiery explosion.

Chapter 5

The designs the contractor had emailed Sophia for the pool were all wrong.

She fired back a bullet point list of the nine missing elements she'd requested and the fifteen—scratch that—sixteen blatant errors in the details, willing away a monster headache. How hard was it to take notes during their conversations? For that matter, how hard was it to look at a CAD drawing and see that the spa feature sat off-center?

Like everything else she'd had to touch around Grandpa's ranch, Sophia was about to become an expert in pool design. As if she totally had time to do other people's jobs, especially when she was paying the company six figures for the pool and cabana that would overlook the back pasture.

Okay, mentally blocking the headache wasn't working and now her arm hurt from being propped up over the keyboard since it still hadn't healed from when Intruder Man twisted it. Sophia poured out two ibuprofen pills from the bottle that seemed to have made a permanent home in the corner of her desk and popped them into her mouth, swallowing with the glass of water next to it.

Could you manifest a new stomach lining? Because she

might need one by the time the ranch renovations were completed.

Creak.

She jerked her head, breath stalling in her lungs. What was that?

After several seconds of tense silence, she finally exhaled shakily when no dark shape appeared at her office door to finish the job Intruder Man had started yesterday.

Rubbing her arm, she tried to focus on the paperwork in front of her. But man. Her nerves were shot. Where was her nicely built cowboy who had promised to keep her safe? She could use a distraction with great biceps.

He'd earned her trust the old-fashioned way, by showing up, keeping his word—and she couldn't stress this one enough—not taking advantage of her offer to get cozy while playing the part of her bodyguard.

Ace had made it clear that he was not interested in anything fake.

That idea had been born out of sheer lunacy. A brain scramble that was part terror and part curiosity. And he'd shut it down while making her feel good about it. That took some skill. The whole scene had done nothing more than intrigue her further. Ace was obviously a complex guy and she wanted to peel back another layer in the worst way.

But true to his word, Ace had been doing his surveillance things from the split-rail fence surrounding the barn. Not that she'd scoped out the situation a time or twelve, peering through the slats of the blinds in the kitchen like a woman scared of her own shadow.

The scenery was nice. Anyone would agree that having a man who looked like Ace in easy viewing distance didn't suck. But the reason for it—that was what had kept her up all night long, imagining she saw Intruder Man's face at the window over and over.

And if she'd spent some time dreaming about Ace's hands on her shoulders as he impressed upon her the importance of staying clear of the window, no one had to know.

Her phone buzzed, rattling against the teak desktop.

Ace. No. Jeez. What was wrong with her? He could walk fifty feet and knock on the door if he wanted to talk to her. He wouldn't call her unannounced, like a heathen. Only one person did that.

"Hey, Charli," she said dryly, opting not to mention yet again that prearranging a time to call before hitting the button wasn't that hard.

Honestly, she appreciated the interruption. For once.

"What's wrong?" her sister demanded, sirens wailing in the background.

Sophia did not miss city noises one little bit. She settled back in her chair, absently tapping a pen against her paper notebook where she kept a written to-do list of "maybe" tasks that she transferred to her phone as they became real jobs. "Is that the standard greeting you kids are using these days?"

"Ha, ha. Wait until I pull out some real slang, O ancient one. You'll be lost."

"Doubtful."

Charli was only three years younger than Sophia but it felt like ten sometimes. Her sister spent twenty-four/ seven putting the "free" in free spirit, mostly because her bank account found new and exciting ways to register a zero balance. That's why it was so baffling that Charli wouldn't want to start fresh at the ranch, working alongside Sophia. It was a sure thing, a solid, guaranteed job. They'd be partners.

But neither of her sisters had jumped on the offer. Sore spot. For all three of them.

"Seriously," Charli said, sounding as if she might be getting comfortable on a couch, possibly even in her own apartment, though that wasn't a given. "You sound like you could use a spa day. Meet me at Solange this weekend and we'll splurge."

Oh, man. What did it say about the state of everything that Sophia actually thought about it for a moment? Even though she knew it was ploy to get her to pay, it was still tempting. "You know I can't. If you loved me at all, you'd be here at the ranch picking up half my to-do list so I could make time for a spa day."

Sophia could hear the face her sister was making. Unexpressive, Charli was not.

"That's what I was waiting for," her sister said with a laugh. "When you didn't start on me immediately, I was concerned. Glad to hear everything is normal."

"I don't ride you about your decision." Very much. "You don't want to work at the ranch. I get it. It's a tough job, far from the city. That's what makes it great, though."

"Hard work. No fun. Nothing but dusty, dirty ranch people. And you wonder why I said no." Charli and sarcasm were old friends.

But Sophia did wonder.

Because it felt like a betrayal, even as much as she really did get it. This wasn't the life Charli or their baby sister, Veronica, wanted and sometimes, Sophia had just enough energy to wonder why it mattered so much to *her*. Especially after Intruder Man had broken the quiet sanctuary she'd been building here.

What had he been looking for anyway?

Since Charli had been the one to call, Sophia figured it was a sign she should at least work the angle to see if her sister knew anything.

"Do you remember Grandpa at all?" she asked her sister.

"A little, sure. Is it weird being at the ranch without him there?"

Sophia had to pause for a minute to check in with herself on that since she hadn't actually thought about it. "No, not really. It might be different if we'd spent a lot of time here as kids. But now, it mostly just feels like a home."

That part, she had thought about. A lot. This place felt right, as if it had been here waiting for her to show up and settle into turning the ranch into something new and different. Something luxurious, yet down-to-earth, sustainable, a large employer for the area. Lofty goals, sure. But if anyone could check off a to-do list in record time, it was Sophia Lang.

As long as she didn't keep flinching at harmless creaks and groans. Ace would be here in a heartbeat if something happened. She had total faith. She did. It was just... She was used to being in control of her own destiny, not feeling like this freaked-out, shuddery version of herself.

"Well, that's good, I guess. I can barely recall what the grounds look like. You should send more pictures," Charli said with a laugh.

"Really? You've never seemed all that interested." And maybe Sophia had censored her texts to her sister out of hurt. If Charli didn't want to do this ranch project with her, there was no reason to share any of the high points or even low points.

But maybe that was a petty way to look at it.

"I'll send you some. The dusty people you've turned your nose up at are basically cowboys and there's not a lot there to hate."

"Ooooh," her sister squealed, making Sophia immediately sorry she'd opened her mouth. "Are they hot? They're hot, aren't they? If you tell me there's even one as tragically beautiful on a horse as Kasey Dutton, I will be on the next plane."

"This is not *Yellowstone*," Sophia commented wryly. "No one is tragically beautiful. There are just a lot of guys in hats and boots doing physical labor within sight of my kitchen window. You can draw your own conclusions as to why that might be of interest to a red-blooded woman."

Honestly, she'd put Ace Madden in a sexy cowboy contest with the actor who played Kasey in a heartbeat, and she was pretty sure Ace would win. Not that she was biased or anything, but that other guy was playing a cowboy. Ace was one. There was a huge difference between walking the walk and spending hours in wardrobe to shoot a three-minute scene, then strolling back to your trailer for an espresso.

She had a feeling Ace would do a lot of non-job-related things with his unique blend of intense precision and authoritative capableness. Things she should definitely not be thinking about as his boss, particularly after he had made it so clear that it should be business only between them.

The problem was that knowing she should steer clear wasn't the same as being able to unring the bell now that she'd imagined what a thorough kisser Ace must be.

Sophia fanned her face. Well, she'd wished for a distraction. She'd found one. And it wasn't her sister.

"That sounds oddly specific," Charli mused. "Are you watching one in particular, by chance? Is this an announcement that you've met someone?"

"Of course not. Don't be ridiculous. We're talking eye candy only. They're my employees." It was almost like Charli could read her very unprofessional thoughts.

"What's that got to do with the price of tea? Like, forty-five percent of all relationships are made up of couples who met at work. Do you have a no-fraternization rule at the ranch or something?"

That set Sophia back a bit. It had never occurred to her that she could make up the rules. That was not one she wanted to put in place all of a sudden for reasons she'd rather not examine. "Totally not the point. I'm not the type of woman who can handle being the boss of someone I'm seeing. Maybe other people can but keeping things on a professional level is something that makes sense to both of us."

The slip had already left her mouth before she realized her mistake. Charli pounced on it.

"Aha! I knew there was someone. And this someone is important enough that you've already had a conversation about the rules. Tell me everything."

The way Charli emphasized "the rules" put a hitch in Sophia's throat. Was that what had happened? Ace had laid down the rules and planned to stick to them?

That was fine. Totally fine. Great. Exactly what should have happened. The last thing Sophia needed was a hot cowboy taking up all her head space while she desperately tried to focus.

"There's nothing to tell," Sophia muttered. "Besides, that's not what I wanted to talk about. I found a bunch of Grandpa's papers, ones from the breeding program. Did you ever talk to Mom about that? Or Dad?"

She threw it out casually as if they talked about their father all the time when in fact, this was the first time she'd brought him up in years.

"Why would I talk to Dad about anything?" Charli's tone dripped venom.

"I don't know. I was just asking. The paperwork is... odd," she threw out lamely, cognizant of the fact that she wouldn't do herself any favors if she flat out told Charli about Intruder Man.

Not if she had any hope of her sisters eventually changing their minds about partnering with her on this place. No one would be swayed if they thought the place was dangerous. Plus, if she told Charli that someone had broken in, word would get back to Mom and then Sophia would be spending umpteen hours arguing with an upset woman about whether the ranch was in fact safe for her daughter.

"My advice—throw all the paperwork away. No one needs it any longer, least of all you."

Sophia frowned. That wasn't a bad point, as much as she hated the idea of throwing away something that might be a clue. But if she cleaned out the office and made a big show of putting all the papers into boxes at the curb for bulk pickup, maybe that would get back to Intruder Man. He wouldn't have any reason to come around again.

"I might do that," she said and glanced at the clock mounted to the wall above the fireplace that didn't work, nearly yelping out loud at the time. "I have to get back to work. I have an appointment with the decorator in a few minutes."

"Sounds delightful," Charli said with heavy sarcasm. "I still want to hear about this mystery guy. But I'll give you a pass for now. At least until you figure out why you're so set on throwing down the boss card. It sounds like an excuse to me. Before I let you go, tell me that you're happy out there in the boondocks."

"I'm happy," she responded immediately, gratified to feel the truth of it in her bones.

The other truth Charli had forced her to reconcile—that being Ace's boss felt like an excuse—wasn't sitting so well with her. Because she wasn't the one who had thrown that card down. He was.

Chapter 6

Ace found excuses to hang out near the split-rail fence with the best view of the house for as long as he could get away with. It wasn't the best angle, but someone had seen to clipping back the shrubbery ringing the wide porch, so no one was getting past his eagle eye.

Not even Sophia. He'd hoped to catch a glimpse of her this morning, even from afar. But she hadn't left the house. For the best. He couldn't keep an eye out if she took off somewhere.

His luck ran out at midday when Jonas strolled by with that look in his eye that meant Ace was about to be set on a job no one else wanted to do.

"Madden."

It was as close to a pleasant greeting as he would get. "Fine day, Jonas."

"Ain't seen you lift a finger on that barn yet." The ranch manager set his hat back on his head, which was what he did when he expected a fight.

Since a skirmish was the last thing he had the time for, Ace shrugged. "Seemed like there was plenty of folks already on that. I didn't want to get in the way."

"Sent Pokney and Thomas over to the south pasture.

Seems like there was something going on over there." Jonas spat on the ground, a nasty habit that was definitely Ace's least favorite thing about cowboys.

"Yeah?" he said noncommittally because he still wasn't sure where Jonas was going with this.

"Fire. Looked like someone built it while camping on the property overnight. Least ways whoever it was put it out."

Fortunate, yes, but not unexpected, given that Ace had his suspicions about who the squatter might have been. If he was right, burning the place down didn't suit Intruder Man's goal.

Ace didn't like the way Jonas was eyeing him. "One of the hands sneak out there last night?"

"Well, I don't rightly know. That's the thing I'm looking to find out. You know anything about it?"

Ah, so *he* was the cowboy currently under suspicion. Whatever Jonas thought was going on between Ace and Sophia—Ms. Lang, and he'd do well to remember to think of her formally—had crawled up his backside and sat there, festering. Ace didn't mind extra scrutiny most of the time. Live your life right and you never had to answer for anything.

But this wasn't the military, and he wasn't following Jonas's orders, as much as the man might like to think Ace was. Extra scrutiny wouldn't help that situation.

"Don't know a thing about your fire," Ace told him, which didn't really count as a half-truth since he didn't know for sure if Intruder Man might have been the one hanging around. But it was a safe bet. "You want me to check it out?"

It would work out handily if Jonas would assign him

to that task, but he had a feeling that the ranch manager might not be letting Ace out of his sight much.

"Nah, that's what I sent those two boys to do. Asked 'em to check around and see if they could figure out if we have a trespasser or something else going on. Meanwhile, need you at the barn. Clear away that back section where the hay bales were stored and see what you can salvage."

Grunt work. No less than he'd expected. Ace nodded and kept his thoughts on the matter to himself. It wasn't too far off the main path to the house, so his view would only be partially blocked. If Jonas would mosey off to do something else, Ace could still stroll by the house occasionally to make up for the decreased visibility.

The collapsed barn was still a mess. Earlier today, they'd gone on and knocked down the rest with a tractor, using the front loader like a battering ram. The cranes hadn't made it yet, probably being shipped from Dallas or Houston, so they'd only worked on the parts that could be more easily managed with a strong back.

Except it was hot. And Ace hadn't done this kind of heavy lifting in a while, not since leaving the navy and his brutal workout routine behind. If it wasn't for his inconvenient principles, he'd be inside the house, lounging on a sofa or something while Sophia—Ms. Lang—worked.

Idiot. That's what he got for throttling back the dating idea she'd cooked up. Couldn't he have faked being her boyfriend for a week or two while making sure he had ready access to anyone who tried to get through him to her?

Obviously not. Instead, here he was lifting splintered boards out of busted bales of hay in hopes of salvaging some of it. He got it. Hay was expensive and any little bit they could save meant something to Sophia. So he'd do it and complain in his head.

"What's up, Madden?" Rory Montgomery strolled into view, pulling on his work gloves. "Looks like we both got the short end of the stick."

"You here to help?"

Montgomery nodded and dived right in, bless him. Ace had a fine appreciation for solitary work, but he'd been part of a team for too long to sneeze at an extra hand.

"Jonas is sore because I broke a pair of wire cutters trying to use 'em to fix a hinge on the back gate," he admitted cheerfully and grabbed a long board on top of the pile, trucking it by hand over to the dumpster that had appeared earlier this morning. After heaving it into the dead center, he dusted off his gloves. "This is supposed to learn me to use the proper tool for the job."

Well, Ace couldn't argue with that as a great life lesson. But that would mean admitting he was wasting his own skill doing menial labor when he could be acting like a proper bodyguard for Sophia.

But that would mean admitting he couldn't stop thinking about her. He'd always had a thing for dark hair on a woman and Sophia's was amazing. Plus, she had this birthmark high on her cheekbone that changed positions depending on how she smiled. He did like being the one to shift it.

Taking her up on her fake-boyfriend offer would mean having to temper his attraction to her while in the same room with her, and he needed his faculties about him. The job—the real job—mattered more than his intense desire to curl up with Sophia near that fireplace in her office and tease that wry humor out of her over and over again.

And maybe see whether she kissed with as much fire as she spoke.

"Don't you think so?" Montgomery asked, jerking him out of that fantasy at the worst time.

Best time. *Best.* He had to stop indulging in that kind of thing or he'd miss more than whatever his barn-clearing mate had been jabbering on about.

"Sure, I guess," he hedged, hoping he hadn't just agreed to partner with Montgomery at the next hot-dog-eating contest or greased-pig-wrangling event.

"Oh, come on. Even a straight arrow like you wouldn't sneeze at that much money."

Montgomery pulled a pretty good-sized bale from the pile that hadn't lost too much of its hay and set it aside, taking his sweet time to get to the rest of his point. Which now had Ace's full attention since it included an assessment of his personality.

So much for lying low.

"I like money as much as the next person," he commented mildly. "It buys stuff that keeps you from starving."

And paid medical bills. Eventually maybe Stephanie would be able to handle them on her own, but for now, he was happy to help.

"Well, whatever this treasure is worth, I can pretty much guarantee it'll do more than buy some groceries."

Casually, Ace pulled another board out of the pile, wiping the back of his neck with his bandanna as if it didn't matter to him one way or the other, but was meant to keep his mate talking. "That sounds like some treasure."

"Most folks in town say it's just a story, but there's so much land out here, it's not hard to imagine someone could've buried a treasure somewhere and no one would ever know." Montgomery eyed one of the splintered boards he'd yanked from the pile. "You don't think it was in the barn, do you?"

"The treasure?" Ace shrugged, doing his level best not to react to the huge possible clue Montgomery had just dropped to Intruder Man's presence here. "Seems like that would be too obvious. If you're going to hide something, it would be someplace that never has a lot of people around."

"That's true," Montgomery mused thoughtfully, as if he might solve the mystery right then and there. "Where would you hide it?"

Apparently, Ace wasn't going to have to do a whole lot to keep Montgomery talking. "Depends on how valuable it is. Are we talking pirate treasure or Knights Templar treasure?"

The look Montgomery shot him told Ace that the other man didn't read a whole lot. "Knights hid treasures in a temple?"

Ace flashed a brief smile. "Something like that. I'm asking if it's supposed to be like a chest full of gold pieces or a room full of gold statues. Big difference in where it might be hidden and how valuable it might be."

"Oh." Montgomery frowned. "I think it's both? Mr. Lang's son chased after it for years down in Mexico. Supposed to be some kind of famous emperor of the Mayans who had a bunch of stuff in one of those pyramids."

Mr. Lang? As in the former owner of the property? Montgomery must be talking about Sophia's grandfather, and possibly her father. Did she know about these rumors?

He shot a glance in the direction of the house, wondering if clues about the location of this mythical treasure might be what Intruder Man had been after in Sophia's office. Not horse records. A treasure map.

"This is legit? The treasure?" he asked, hoping he didn't sound too interested, but Montgomery seemed like the type who would readily talk someone's ear off without any encouragement.

The other ranch hand shrugged. "I don't know, man. Everyone talks it about. Has for years. Seems like Mr. Lang would have been driving a Ferrari or something if it really existed, but maybe he never found it. Wouldn't it be sweet to stumble over something worth a lot of money while doing nothing more than pulling pieces of barn from a pile?"

Indeed it would, but only because it might help him do his job. His real job. "Anything we found would belong to Ms. Lang."

"Sure, yeah, of course anything valuable would belong to the owner of the ranch," Montgomery agreed readily.

Sophia. He had to mention this to her. Possibly she'd already heard of the treasure and may even know if it had already been found. Or never existed in the first place. This might be a red herring.

But he didn't think so.

The same gut instinct that had kept him alive deep behind enemy lines kicked in. And he knew this treasure Montgomery had so casually mentioned played some kind of part in the presence of shadowy figures here at the ranch.

The big question in Ace's mind was why now? Had the death of Sophia's grandfather set something new in motion? Introduced some new players to the treasure hunt game?

Ace let the conversation drift, an easy thing with a guy

like Montgomery. So far, he'd learned his new friend grew up in Gun Barrel City, Montgomery knew everyone in town since there weren't that many residents, and that the town motto was "We shoot straight with you."

Sounded like a place Ace could appreciate.

After twenty minutes, Ace started scouting around for some earplugs. Man, could this guy jabber on about nothing and everything. They'd only cleared about 20 percent of what could be moved by humans, which lent further credence to the fact that Jonas had stuck his least favorite people on the job.

"I'm going to get some water," Ace finally broke in during the middle of a story about a tornado that had touched down in Ellis County, which, as best he could tell, was about an hour away. So it wasn't entirely clear why the tornado was of interest, but to be fair, he'd lost the thread of the story long ago.

"Bring me a bottle, would ya?" Montgomery took his hat off and wiped his face with his shirt.

Without his hat, he looked young enough to be carded at the beer store, but most of the hands did. With age, some of the romanticized parts about being a cowboy must wear off.

Ace strode across the packed earth, ducking into one of the buildings where the ranch hands lived so he could text Sophia without anyone noticing.

Need to talk. Let me in the front door in three minutes.

The answering text came immediately.

Limpet: Okay

Jeez. He tried not to read anything into it. She was obviously the type to carry her phone around in her hand. It wasn't like she'd been sitting there, waiting for him to text her, smiling as she saw his name pop up on her screen.

Though it was a nice little fantasy to imagine exactly that.

He didn't have time to waste answering her back with something else she'd have to reply to, just so he could watch her name pop up on *his* screen. It wasn't her name anyway. It was Limpet. On purpose. He should add an explosion emoji or something.

Circling the house via the woods so he could enter from the front where none of the hands—or Jonas—could see him took longer than he'd expected thanks to a squirrel who had forced him to freeze for an eternity behind a wide oak tree. He'd half hoped it would be Intruder Man, but it was better that it wasn't.

Sophia was waiting on him.

Literally, as it turned out. She swung the door wide before he'd even mounted the first step to the wraparound porch, then she stood there, one hip kicked out, framed by the eggshell-white doorframe, her dark hair escaping from the severe knot at her crown. A pink dress poured down over her curves, fitting her to a T both in style and cut.

She was stunning and he forgot to breathe.

He had a terrible, wonderful moment where he wished she'd thrown open the door to greet him at the end of a long day. As if she belonged to him and this place with her was his life that he'd earned.

Not in the cards for a guy like him. He swallowed against the catch in his throat.

Besides, Sophia Lang might be gorgeous, but she had

high maintenance written all over her. Not his type. And even if he thought for a moment he could make an exception, all of the other stuff that stood between them wasn't so easily dismissed.

"You rang?" she murmured with just enough irony to tease a reluctant smile out of him.

"I heard about something. A treasure," he said without preamble because this wasn't a social visit, no matter how much he might wish otherwise.

Her brows shot up. "Do tell."

That didn't sound like a woman who knew what he was talking about. "One of the hands mentioned it. Said it's common knowledge that Mr. Lang's son buried something on the property. You ever hear anything about that?"

The expression on Sophia's face went so utterly blank that he worried for a second that something had happened to her. He'd already taken a step toward her, hand outstretched to check for a pulse or gauge her pupil response, when she shook her head.

"My grandpa's son was a deadbeat. If David Lang ever found anything of value, you can guarantee he either lost it or sold it to fund his expeditions. He definitely never sent any of the money back to his family."

Her voice rang with enough certainty and grief that he didn't have to ask if they were talking about her father. "So you've never heard any rumors of a treasure? The ranch hand grew up here. He says the local folks have talked about it for years."

Sophia's expression never changed. "There's no treasure."

The alarm bells in his gut went off. He couldn't put a finger on what had tripped them. Something in her tone or her ramrod-stiff stance hinted at a fragility that contradicted the outward appearance of strength.

If there was anyone who understood putting on appearances so no one else could tell that a body was a mess on the inside, it was Ace. "Are you saying that because you're sure there's not one? Or because the alternative is unacceptable?"

That's when her face crumpled.

Chapter 7

Crying in front of Ace was not happening.

Except Sophia's eyes seemed to have received a different memo and welled up at the same time her throat closed.

"Hey," he murmured, suddenly a lot closer to her than he had been, his hand warm on her shoulder as he peered down at her with equal parts compassion and confidence, as if he had every right to be the one right here when she fell apart.

"I'm fine," she said, the lie rattling in her aching throat. "I don't talk about my dad often. For a reason."

"I get it." He nodded but didn't move his hand and she hated how steadying it was.

Oh, she liked him touching her. That part wasn't in question. Her greedy insides had gobbled up the heat instantly and started sniffing around for more. But the fact that she needed someone to steady her—that was a problem.

She'd asked Charli about their father. That had gone fine. Mostly because Sophia took her responsibility for being the oldest sister—and therefore the one who managed everything—seriously.

This was one time she didn't have to have it all together, but it was fine. She could lean on someone else for a change. It was…nice.

She should step back. Her legs didn't obey her. Most of the rest of her seemed to think it was a fine time to sway forward, in fact. Closer to him. Where it smelled like man and grit and evoked thoughts of unspeakable things that were not on her to-do list.

But she very much wanted to do them.

Worst idea ever.

A man like Ace would be a shock to her system—wild, untamed and a little bit dangerous. None of which sounded like a cautionary tale all at once.

Too bad he wasn't interested in her. He couldn't have been clearer that there would be far more business between them than pleasure. As in a 100/0 split.

That was enough to dry up the emotion clogging her throat. "I'm sorry, I'm not normally this much of a mess."

His lips turned up. "If this is you being a mess, you should teach a class."

Dang, he wasn't supposed to be both kind and funny. She dabbed at her wet lashes, likely making her raccoon eyes worse. "I'm actually pretty capable and can handle myself. I promise. What you've seen so far is not at all representative of who I am as a person."

The light that came into his expression transfixed her for a moment as he cocked his head, evaluating her curiously. "But capable is exactly how you come across. As someone who makes no bones about being in charge. Who knows her own mind and speaks it. None of those things have anything to do with being broadsided by a memory that digs into places that don't have calluses. It's not something you should apologize for."

Her insides went liquid as she stared at him. "Are you

sure you can't ditch the cowboy stuff and follow me around all the time? You can be my motivational coach."

"Sure," he said with a shrug and another of those small smiles. "Since it was my fault you got upset in the first place. That sounds like a great plan. I stick my foot in my mouth and then figure out a way to take it back."

Good gravy this man could not be for real. Principled, hot *and* able to admit he was wrong without wincing. It was like winning the lottery and then misplacing your ticket. She couldn't have him and the sooner she got that message through to her brain, the better.

"Maybe we should start over," she suggested with an answering smile. "Hi, Ace, nice to see you. How was your day?"

"So far, so good," he said, instantly falling into the rhythm she'd set into place, as if they'd done this a million times. "I heard about this treasure from one of the guys and thought we could discuss it. Does that fit into your schedule?"

"Everything on my agenda has just been canceled. Would you like to come inside?"

She'd offered before thinking through how much more of Ace would be accessible behind closed doors, away from potential prying eyes. Or how he would fill the foyer as he swept past her on a wave of solid male.

"We can sit in my office," she said briskly because, come on. She wasn't a simpering sixteen-year-old at her first dance, for crying out loud.

Ace was just a man. Who was here because he'd heard something of note that he thought she needed to consider. Given that she'd been attacked in her own home and then someone had sabotaged her barn, she'd do well to remember that the only reason she had any interaction with Ace was because he'd agreed to keep watch for threats. That's it.

She crossed her arms and stood in the doorway as he sprawled in one of the chairs on the guest side of the desk. Which she appreciated. Last time, she'd let him have her chair and he could have taken that as permission to always sit there, as if he had some sway in her life. But he hadn't taken any liberties whatsoever.

A shame. She had a sincere desire to figure out what would set Ace Madden on simmer. Did he even let himself near a fire long enough to feel the heat?

Shaking her head, she dived into the matter at hand. "About this treasure. I don't think it exists."

"Oh, actually that's not true," a voice said from the hall.

Sophia spun to find the housekeeper, Jenny, standing behind her with a stack of folded towels in her hands. The elder woman paused in her mission to put the laundry away, clearly interested in the reason this subject had come up.

"You know something about a treasure?" Sophia asked cautiously, not sure she should be having a conversation like this in front of Ace. Not that she wouldn't immediately spill every detail to him later, but it didn't seem like the best plan to clue in other staff members that he had her confidence in what some might consider a private matter.

Jenny didn't seem overly bothered by the presence of the cowboy in Sophia's office, though. She nodded, her eyes brightening the way they did when she talked smack about other people in town, especially if the gossip was particularly juicy. "You better believe it. Everyone knows about the treasure. Your grandpa never told you he found a Maya coin in the flower bed? About five years ago, seems like."

Five years ago, Sophia would have been twenty-seven.

The exact age she'd been the last time she'd had any contact with her grandpa. He'd invited her to the ranch out of the blue, no reason given. But she'd been too busy climbing the corporate ladder in a sad cliché. Especially given that Grandpa had left the ranch to her after all, even though she hadn't made any time for him while he'd been alive.

What would he have said to her if she had come?

Shamed all at once, she bowed her head. Turning this place into a luxury dude ranch was her tribute to a man who had entrusted her with the property, and she *would* succeed at this thing she'd set out to do. Selling it to someone else sat wrong with her.

And so did dismissing this treasure that she'd never heard about. Until today.

"I'm sensing I should have asked you about this much sooner," she told Jenny wryly as she recalled that the housekeeper had come with the property, having been employed by her grandpa for many years. "I didn't know anything about the Mayan coin he found. What happened to it? Did he still have it when he died?"

Oh, goodness. Had he left it to Sophia in his will? Wouldn't that be a slick move, to discount the idea of a treasure, only to find out she owned a piece of it unwittingly.

"It's Maya, by the way. Your grandpa taught me that after he did some research. Mayan is only used to mean the language they spoke." Jenny shook her head, then. "To answer your question, no, he didn't still have the coin. He sold it. Always planned to use the money to start his breeding program back up again, but he got sick before he could. I think a lot of the proceeds went to medical bills. Your grandpa didn't have health insurance after he quit the horse business, so it was a lucky break he had that extra cash handy."

Lucky? Or something else? "He never found any more coins? One Maya gold piece doesn't sound like much of a treasure to me."

"I don't guess he ever mentioned finding more," Jenny mused. "But I always had the idea he thought that there was more. He just didn't quite know where to look for it. Seems like Mr. David wasn't too chatty about where he'd buried it."

Dumbfounded, Sophia stared at the housekeeper. This whole time, she'd had no idea any of this was a thing and her father had been the one smack in the middle of it. "That's where the treasure came from? My father? David Lang?"

And if she tacked one more question mark on this situation, it still wouldn't be enough.

Because of course that's what all of this would come down to. A legacy of pain perpetuated by Sophia's father, who couldn't be bothered to act like one, but could certainly find the energy to tromp through sweltering jungles for a couple of decades in search of almighty gold.

Jenny shrugged. "That's what your grandpa said, at least, but we didn't talk about it much. It was one more disappointment, you know? He wanted Mr. David to take over the business but your dad, he had the yellow fever. Chased after the glory of the gold. And by all accounts, he must have found something, but why he put only that one coin in the flower bed, no one knows. Lots of people looked, but the treasure is poof. Like a ghost."

Sitting down sounded like a really good option all at

once. Sophia braced a hand on the desk as she sank into her swivel chair behind it. "This is all very…"

Educational? Disturbing? Unbelievable?

All of the above. She stretched her neck as she contemplated all the ways her father had ruined her life, starting with abandoning his family and ending with allowing his daughter to inherit a piece of property that came with a legend attached.

"It's information," Ace suggested quietly with a nod. "And we appreciate it."

"Yes, of course. Thank you, Jenny." She glanced at the housekeeper, who still stood in the hall with her stack of towels, her intrigued expression roving over the situation in the office unabashedly. "Mr. Madden is helping me with a special project and the subject of the treasure came up, so the information you've given us is invaluable. Don't let us keep you from the rest of your day."

Jenny's face flatlined. She was obviously disappointed not to be involved in any more gossip. "Let me know if you have any other questions."

She vanished in the direction of the stairs to the upper floors, hopefully to do something productive like hang curtains in one of the guest bedrooms.

Sophia stared at the bottle of ibuprofen in its spot by the corner of her desk. "The rest of the treasure is still out there somewhere, isn't it?"

"That's unfortunately irrelevant," Ace said so matter-of-factly that she lifted her gaze to his in question. "The more important question is, how many people believe it is?"

The implications weren't lost on her. There was a good possibility that she'd just learned the reason Intruder Man had been rifling through her grandpa's papers. And even if it wasn't, other people could be out there with that same intent, which doubled her trouble.

She'd have to think about security way beyond what Ace could provide. Get some dogs maybe. Could dogs be trained to look for treasure while they patrolled the grounds searching for trespassers?

What about the guests? How could she keep *them* safe? This was a disaster.

"I'm literally clueless what to do next," she muttered, her head falling to her palms.

The to-do list on her phone rivaled the written one on her notepad, the decorator had left her swatches in three of the bedrooms for her final decision on the color scheme, which she should have already made, and Jonas had tried to speak to her twice today about the insurance claim on the barn.

If anything deserved her attention more than these, it was a treasure she'd unwittingly inherited from both her grandpa and her dad. The money alone… It could go a long way toward the deductible for the barn, and she could move up her agenda for the dude ranch. Offer spa services sooner, rather than later. The plans she'd looked at for the little detached bungalow that would match the house came with a steep price tag, but Maya gold could buy a lot of massage tables and aromatherapy.

It would be the one positive thing she'd ever gotten from her father.

But her life didn't work like that. Either there was no more treasure, and the rumors were wrong, or her father had hidden it someplace no one could find because he planned to come back for it himself.

"It's pretty simple, actually," Ace said as if he had no clue her brain had just fizzled. "The next steps."

"I'm glad one of us thinks so," she mumbled to her desk, which was a lovely shade of espresso covered in a beige computer mat she'd selected the day after she'd quit her job at Teller Advertising.

So optimistic. The pencil drawing of a sprig of almond blossoms gracing the edge of the mat had seemed so elegant at the time, the symbol of her rebirth as a resort owner. She still wanted to hold on to that hope. But this development would crimp things, no doubt.

"Hey," he said softly, like he had at the door when she'd been crying because all of this was too overwhelming. It was his *I care* voice and she couldn't stop herself from responding to it.

She glanced up, straight into his storm-colored eyes that practically dripped with concern. For her. Because he was a solid, dependable guy who had nothing better to do than sit here with her and figure this out. Or if he did have something better to do, he made her believe he'd picked this over everything else.

It meant more to her than she could have possibly verbalized.

"I'm okay," she said and meant it. "Tell me what you think we should do."

His lips lifted. "As long as you keep on remembering that it is indeed a *we*, things will go a lot smoother."

No, there wasn't a good chance she would forget. Not that or the sound rejection of her fake-dating idea. But it wasn't like he'd chucked that plan out the window because he didn't like spending time in her company or he wouldn't be here.

Maybe it really was as simple as his principles preventing him from crossing any lines. Which she firmly appreciated.

Next time, she wouldn't frame it as fake or hide her interest in getting to know him a little better—or a lot better—behind his white knight routine. They could talk about the challenges of acting on the blistering attraction between them like adults. Work through the issues. Determine some ground rules.

She could only dream of having that healthy of a conversation with a man. Her track record with men consisted of a few surface-level dates, then ditching him before he could do it to her.

"So, I guess you're about to advise me about the type of security system I need to install or something, right?" she asked, injecting as much levity into her voice as she could, given that Ace's suggestion would likely be a very painful hit to her bank account.

"Yeah, I'm already working on that angle in my head, definitely," he said. "But the most important thing we can do first is find that treasure."

Chapter 8

The expression on Sophia's face did not reveal a lot of confidence in Ace's idea.

"You want to look for a treasure that may or may not exist, may or may not be hidden somewhere on a six-hundred-acre ranch with a creek running through the middle, and may or may not also be the same treasure a dangerous man is looking for."

Sophia talked with her whole body, and Ace had no plans to apologize for how much he enjoyed it, even when her green eyes snapped with energy directed at him. Especially then.

"Yes," he responded simply. "That is what I'm suggesting. Even finding clues to where the treasure is—or was—is better than nothing. The more we have in our back pocket, the less someone else can get control of and use for their own gain."

She crossed her arms. "A treasure hunt is the last thing I have time for."

"It's the only thing you have time for," he corrected her and stood, holding out his hand. "Come with me. I need to show you exhibit A."

To her credit, she didn't argue. But she did slip her hand

into his, which immediately turned into something as a current the intensity of a lightning bolt forked between them. When folks talked about sparks, they clearly lacked the vocabulary to put the right name to it because this was way more than a tiny, quick-to-fizzle buzz. It was more like the kind of raw energy that could destroy a building in a second flat.

Bad move.

Because she felt it too. He could tell.

Now what was he supposed to do? It would be forever a lie if he had to deny his forceful attraction to this woman, and honestly, he wasn't sure he could do it. Hopefully she wouldn't say a word about it, or he might be forced to do something very painful, like tell her the truth.

Now would be a good time to kill the connection. And when he dropped her hand, his entire body cooled like lava meeting a frozen sea.

"Sorry, that was inappropriate," he muttered, praying he could get out of this room without embarrassing himself.

"It takes two to close a circuit," she said, her gaze so tightly focused on him that it was unlikely she'd miss a single nuance of his reaction to her.

Yeah, he was in a lot of trouble here. He cleared his throat. "And I won't do it again. I want to show you something outside, so just stick close to me."

Distance didn't end up being a problem. Sophia turned out to be a star at following his suggestion, her body a scant few inches from his back as she followed him through the house to the back door. The vibe between them thickened as he flung open the solid oak and pointed in the direction of the temporary stable the hands were building down the knoll from the splintered remains of the barn.

"See that guy there?" he asked. "In the black hat with the long-sleeved tan shirt? What's his name?"

Sophia peered around his shoulder, her coconutty hair literally right under his nose. Breathing through his mouth, he visualized a cold shower, a HALO drop in January and, finally, plunging through the ice in Alaska, which seemed to finally do the trick even though that was the one he'd never actually done.

"Rick?" she said with so many question marks attached that it was clear she'd guessed.

"Wrong. What about that other guy next to him? In the black shirt."

She glanced up at him, the green in her eyes a different color out here in the sunlight than they had been in the office, and he was hard-pressed to say which one he liked better.

Limpet, Limpet, Limpet.

"I sense there's a lesson coming about how I should know my employees' names," she said wryly. "So maybe you could just get on with it."

"It's not that you should know their names. It's that you *don't* know their names. Because they're new. They were just hired this morning. Jonas has about five more open spots to fill and pickings are slim. It's only a matter of time before he hires someone who is not just looking for a paycheck. Or someone who is not an official employee but blends in like one."

Which he well knew could be the case since he'd easily slid onto the ranch roster with fake credentials. The porous borders of the ranch sat on his nerves wrong too.

"So now I need to worry about dangerous employees

as well as random intruders? Great." Her resigned tone scraped across those already taut nerves.

Ace was failing at his job. The real one. The one he'd been paid a lot of zeros to get right, and he had no excuse. Being a cowboy didn't have a lot of skill to it, not that he'd seen so far, but protecting someone ill-equipped to do it themselves—that he had hundreds upon hundreds of hours of training and experience under his belt. He'd fought off a horde of mercenaries in a village outside Marjah single-handedly, for crying out loud, saving an Afghan family of nine who had been left behind during a sloppy evacuation.

He could manage the security protocol of a six-hundred-acre ranch and reassure the owner at the same time.

"Ms. Lang." She was eyeing the new hands, looking every bit as if she might be dutifully cataloging them in her memory, all because he'd been trying to make a point. "Sophia."

That caught her attention. She glanced up at him, worry and stress lines back around her lips, and it was not okay.

"I like it when you call me Sophia," she admitted, her voice warming.

That made two of them. And was also not the subject they needed to be discussing. "Listen to me, now. You do not have to worry about anything. I'm handling this. Trust me. The two ranch hands are Mark Dombrowski and Bobby Chavez. They both came from Rockland Farm down the way and are totally legit. They are not going to cause problems and if they do, I'll handle that too. Repeat what I just said."

Sophia's eyes were so wide, he wondered if he could actually fall into them. And whether he'd try to stop himself if he did. The draw nearly buckled his knees as it was.

"All of it?" she murmured.

"The important part."

She nodded once. "I trust you."

Ace nearly groaned. Of course she'd pick out that one statement from everything else to glom onto and dig the shiv a little deeper between his ribs. "I'm handling this. That part. You don't have to worry."

"I'm not worried. Do I look worried?"

Now her back was up, and she fairly bristled under his scrutiny. Apparently, he was not going to be good at reassuring the owner of the ranch he'd been hired to protect. "You look capable, fierce and strong. My mistake."

For some reason, that made her laugh, and he liked that too, a whole lot more than might be considered suitable under the circumstances. He busied himself with shutting the door since he'd made his point.

"You're the strangest blend of man, Ace Madden," she said, crossing her arms as she contemplated him. "I'm having a hard time figuring out what to do with you."

"Let me remind you, then. You're letting me do all the worrying. About security. New people on the ranch. Taking care of you."

That last bit had slipped out, his voice lowered a notch into a scratchy range that had nothing to do with the job and everything to do with the forbidden fruit standing within reach but so wholly off-limits that it made his teeth hurt.

With the door shut and the two of them closed off from the rest of the world, everything got a lot cozier and more intimate. Anything could happen and no one would be the wiser. It was already too late to avoid everyone else on the ranch knowing he had Sophia's ear. Her trust.

"I've never had a man take care of me before," she said and cocked her head, a flirty glint in her gaze that spelled a whole lot of danger if he didn't diffuse this situation carefully.

Limpet. Oh, who was he kidding. It would be impossible to cut the wire of this detonator. At this point, his best bet was keeping the explosion contained with as few casualties as possible.

"This is a first for me too," he countered gruffly and stuffed his hands in his pockets. "But just for the sake of clarity, I meant taking care of keeping you safe."

"Uh-huh. I got that."

She was still watching him with this intense, somewhat-heated expression that he very much wanted to understand. Before it took off a layer of his skin. "Are we aligned on searching for the treasure? You understand the importance of us getting to whatever is out there before someone else does?"

"I hear you. The point is to have something to advertise. So it gets out that we found whatever my father hid, which means bad people have no reason to bother us any longer."

He nodded, shoving his hands deeper in his pocket to stop the sudden urge he had to kiss her for being so brilliant. "Yes. Exactly. We make a big splash of it and voila, the danger is eliminated. I can go back to fixing fences and you can get busy bossing people."

"You make it sound easy." Her lips lifted in a small smile. "The treasure, if it exists at all, isn't going to be lying around waiting for us to find. What you're talking about is a full-scale search of a property I've barely started to learn. And that's if it's not in the house, which has a million hidey-holes and a pier-and-beam foundation, so it could even be under the house. That's the most logical place since the first coin was found in the flower bed. That's where we should start."

The woman's brain had chopped through all of that in the course of thirty seconds, when five minutes ago, she'd been skeptical of the plan to the point where he'd been convinced she'd never agree. "You impress me, Ms....Sophia."

"I'll take the compliment, but please, for the love of God, do not call me Ms. Sophia. It makes me sound like a Sunday school teacher," she said with a wrinkled nose.

"What's wrong with that? Some of my favorite people are my former Sunday school teachers," he said. "Besides, it wasn't intentional. I'm still warming up to calling you something other than Ms. Lang."

Because that was step one toward bridging the gap between boss/employee and something else entirely. As soon as he relaxed the formality, it would be that much easier to take other liberties, like smoothing away the dark hair that constantly fell from her severe hairstyle.

And if he didn't stop obsessing over every tiny nuance of his employer, it was going to be a very long, painful treasure hunt indeed.

"Sunday school teachers are old. I might never see twenty-nine again, but I'm not so eager to rush up to thirty-nine and shake hands."

Since he couldn't tell her that she seemed like the kind of woman who would only get better with age, more beautiful with the experiences that she would share with someone, he kept his mouth shut. He certainly wouldn't be the person standing by her side, watching her age gracefully, endearingly.

"You aren't in the nursing home yet," he told her and

cleared his throat. "I like the idea of starting with the house. Though it might make more sense to do it after dark, so it doesn't interfere with your boss duties, and I can still scout around outside during the day when it's light. It would be pretty easy to make up some excuse to ride the property, but really be looking for clues."

Sophia skewered him again with that probing gaze. It gave him the impression she was puzzling something out in her head, and he'd already seen that she had a better-than-average analysis gene. Something told him he wasn't going to like the next bit of logic that popped out of her mouth, though.

"Why are you doing all of this?"

Yeah, there it was. She'd poked at the one flaw in all of this, the one thing he had no ready answer for. "I told you. I work for you. It's my job to do whatever you ask of me."

"I didn't ask you to save me from Intruder Man. I didn't text you and insist that you meet me for a clandestine discussion about a treasure that could be worth millions of dollars. A lot of men would have kept that kind of information to themselves. You literally just told me that you could do your own treasure hunt without anyone knowing, even me." She flipped a hand up in question. "What's your story, Ace Madden, who went to Sunday school and took the time to do a background check on my new employees?"

Ugh. This was the very last time he took a job under these kinds of pretenses. What possible benefit was there to keeping his identity a secret? But the instructions for the job had been clear. He couldn't reveal his true purpose for being on the ranch to anyone, least of all Sophia Lang, or he'd forfeit his fee plus incur a breach of contract penalty.

Then who would pay Stephanie's bills? She was just getting her feet under her after a year of being in and out of the hospital. He had to cross the finish line on this assignment.

What no one had told him was how to do this job without dropping huge clues all over the place that he wasn't a run-of-the-mill cowboy, and he'd just given her about twenty. He shuffled his feet as he tried to figure out the best way to lie without lying.

"Background check?" he scoffed, even though that's exactly what he'd done and if he'd thought Sophia was impressive before, his scale for judging that had just been knocked right off the table. "Those boys are open books. They'll tell you anything. All you have to do is say howdy and off they go, spilling their life stories to anyone who will listen. That's how I know they're good guys."

She didn't look convinced. "So you're a good guy too? Doing all of this out of the goodness of your heart."

"Not everyone is out to scam people," he told her sincerely, since this was one thing he could be completely honest about. "I have a protective streak. It's been there since I was little, when my sister got stuck in a tree and I found out how good it felt to be the one who saved her. That's all there is to it. Don't make me out to be something I'm not. I have plenty of flaws."

"Let me know when I've hit one," she said wryly. "I might need the hint."

She'd find some soon enough, of that he had no doubt. The pile of lies he'd fed her would be a great example. Also, a lot of women had accused him in the past of having a hero complex. Of manufacturing a situation where he could be the one to save the day, when they hadn't needed saving in the first place. It was a fine line and he wondered sometimes if they were right.

Was he doing that here too? Imagining the need for a treasure hunt when in reality, it was nothing more than an excuse to be close to Sophia?

Two days, he promised himself. He'd take two days to chase this wild goose and then, if nothing came from it, fade back into the woodwork to watch from afar, like he'd planned to do all along.

"Well," Sophia said and dusted her hands off. "I can't say I'm excited about the idea of taking time out of my schedule to look for a Maya treasure, of all things. But I am happy to be doing it with you."

Chapter 9

True to his word, Ace materialized at Sophia's front door at nine o'clock that night to start their first round of searching the house for gold. Or clues to where it was. Or something.

She'd lost track of what exactly Ace expected to find. Her father wasn't the type to leave a lot of himself behind. And how tragic was it that she'd actually started nursing a tiny spark of hope that they might find something of his? Something she could keep and point to when reminded that he'd abandoned his family in favor of this thing future Sophia would have found.

At least then she'd know what was so much more important than her and her sisters.

Sophia let Ace into the house without turning on the porch light, and yes, it was a little thrilling to be plunged into something so secretive with someone who set her skin on sizzle with nothing more than a stray glance or brush of his elbow as he skirted her to stand in the foyer.

"Hey," she said brilliantly, because her game was strong with this one.

"Hey," he returned as if he hadn't noticed she'd flubbed a perfectly good opportunity to dazzle him with her sparkling wit.

But then, this clandestine meeting wasn't about giving her a chance to flirt with him, as much as she'd like to practice a bit for the real thing later—when she might get up the courage to try again with expressing her interest in a calm, measured way that wouldn't result in another rejection.

Maybe she should create a spreadsheet matrix with relevant strategies, then weight them according to her existing skill level and probability of executing successfully.

Or she could stop standing there like a bump on a log and get this party moving.

"I thought we should start with the attic," she suggested.

Ace nodded. "Fine by me. This is your house and should be searched according to your rules and timetable. I'm just kind of along for the ride."

"I hope you're also along to provide expert treasure hunting advice, because I've never done anything like this before," she called over her shoulder as she led him to the first set of stairs, the wide ones that curved up from the foyer to the second floor in an impressive show of wood and grandeur she hoped would be the hallmark of advertising beauty shots of the property.

"I hate to break it to you, but this is my first treasure hunt too. We'll figure it out together."

A reference to her parting comment from earlier? He hadn't said anything after she'd told him she was happy to be in this with him. Which she'd spent a good bit of time wishing she could take back when he hadn't immediately responded in kind.

He followed her up the stairs and pulled even on the landing, his boots shushing across the gleaming hardwoods, the sound reassuring and somehow familiar, as if she'd heard it a hundred times. This old Victorian was made for a man like him, one so at home in his own skin, so solid and down-to-earth.

"Your house is beautiful," he commented, reading her thoughts, because of course he could.

"My grandpa was born here," she told him, playing the part of tour guide. "Everything is original and hand-crafted, a lost art. I never thought it would be passed to me. But I love it."

Truth. She'd never considered herself anything other than a city girl, a corporate-ladder climber who would eventually get to the top one day. The top of what, she'd questioned many times during the worst part of burnout.

Here, she could breathe at least.

The stairs to the third floor weren't nearly as grand as those in the entranceway. They lay hidden behind a closed door, the narrow corridor dark and a little forbidding. She hadn't been up here since the first day when she took a long tour of the property she'd just inherited, but it seemed the most likely place for something to be hidden by either her grandpa or her father. It had been daylight the last time, though.

Cobwebs shone silver in the flashlight she switched on. She must have hesitated, or Ace was practicing his mind reading again, because he rested an encouraging hand at the small of her back. What he'd meant to encourage her to do, she wasn't sure, but it was fifty-fifty on whether she'd keep leading the way and let the monsters get her, or she turned and curled into him.

Ace took the decision out of her hands, as well as the flashlight, then maneuvered around her with sure steps so that he was in the lead. Which left her back vulnerable, and she didn't like that, either. She scurried after him, probably way too close for his comfort, but not close enough for hers.

At the top of the creaky stairs, pitch-black met absolute black in an unending sea of nothing. The tiny glow from the flashlight did nothing more than cast a reddish tint on Ace's hand. This was not going to work. She couldn't see a blessed thing and her heartbeat thumped painfully in her chest, driving her toward a mild panic attack. He reached out with his non-flashlight-holding hand, and she thought he might be about to enfold her into his embrace, which she would take all day long.

Instead, he snapped on the overhead light she hadn't realized existed.

"That's much better," she said, her breath coming a little easier now along with the deep pang of disappointment that he hadn't segued their surroundings into an excuse to get closer.

He grinned. "I thought we were starring in our own slasher movie for a second there. Expected a guy with a chain saw to appear in the corner."

"Nothing up here but a lot of junk," she said, glancing around at the hodgepodge of items that had been stored away up here for years. A faded velvet sofa with missing buttons and a dusty dresser with peeling paint sat against the far wall, along with a Shaker-style rocking chair with a broken armrest.

"Might as well dive in," he said. "I wish I knew what to tell you to look for, but I don't know. Maybe we start by trying to establish whether the treasure is still on the property or not."

Ace prowled to the left, while she took the right. As she delved deeper into the attic, Sophia came across piles of clothing and linens, musty from years of being stored away in a place with no ventilation. Toys and games were scattered throughout the space, including an old wooden train set with missing pieces, a set of tin soldiers and a few worn-out board games. Her father's? He'd grown up here.

Rusty hammers, wrenches and screwdrivers, as well as old paint cans and brushes, had been shoved over into one corner. Why that stuff hadn't been moved to the shed she'd had torn down, she'd never know. Probably her grandpa had considered them valuable. Dust covered everything, so it was hard to know if any of these things had value.

She ignored the readily identifiable stuff that sat in precarious stacks, opting to start looking through the boxes. The first one was open, full of Christmas decorations. The second had been taped shut, and since this was her first treasure hunt, she'd come unprepared.

She tugged at the tape, hoping the temperature extremes might have worn out the adhesive, but it wouldn't budge, and she couldn't get a fingernail under it. The box shredded her nail, though, an indictment of her calcium intake. She made mental note number 375 of the day to pick up a calcium supplement at the grocery store next time she made it into town.

"Let me." Ace materialized at her side, holding something black in his hand, which he thumbed with a flick, revealing a wicked-looking blade.

Wide-eyed, she watched him slice the tape on both sides. "That is some heavy hardware you're using as scissors."

Ace flicked the blade closed and pocketed the knife, his expression unreadable in the low light. "Would it make you feel better or worse to find out it's seen its share of non-box-related uses?"

Like he'd used to peel an apple or a human? Suddenly very unsure she wanted to know the answer, she shook her head. "You're just full of surprises."

"Well, one thing I don't want to surprise you with. I'm capable of using a knife in a lot of situations but I usually don't. I've got no problem defending you if it comes to it, though. Whatever it takes."

She believed him wholly in that moment. Not that his ability to keep her safe was ever in question. But it did make her feel marginally better to know that he wasn't the type to pull his knife as a first resort, even as she registered that he'd wanted her to know he had it on him, or he wouldn't have bothered with it. A guy with biceps like Ace's could have ripped the box in half without breaking a sweat. No knife needed.

So why had he made such a big show out of it?

He went back to his side of the attic, apparently oblivious to the fact that she was still watching him instead of returning to search her own designated area. The man moved like a precision machine, as if designed to have only the barest necessity of motion, and it was a pleasure to witness.

He did nothing superfluous, organizing his search methodically, and she had the impression he missed nothing. Her ranch hand's talents were ironically wasted as a cowboy, and she wondered if he had ever thought about doing something else with his life.

Military, she remembered. Former. Obviously, he'd left the service at some point. Recently? Was that why he carried the knife still? Actually, she had no idea if that kind of weapon made the list of required gear for a soldier. In her head, they all carried guns and dressed in camo after greasing their faces.

Probably he had a dress uniform too, like they did in the movies, and she'd bet every dime in her checking account that it looked incredibly hot on him. Too bad she'd never get to see it.

Sophia was so busy fantasizing about Ace, his uniform and some decidedly non-military-approved scenarios involving both that she almost missed that the box she'd just opened was full of newspaper clippings. Not the kind that you used to wrap breakables, like she'd originally thought, but full articles someone had cut from the paper deliberately.

The one on top had a photograph of a very young David Lang.

His haircut was the same as in the few printed pictures her mother kept in an album hidden in a drawer. Charli had found it once and pulled it out when their mom had gone to the store. Veronica never had cared one whit about their father. She didn't remember him at all, and refused to look at it, but Sophia had memorized his face, in case she passed him on the street. It seemed like something you should be able to do, recognize your father if you stumbled over him in public.

All the articles were about David Lang. Maybe her grandmother had cut these out and saved them before she'd passed over a decade ago. Sophia pulled out a full-page color article ripped from a magazine dated just five years ago. *After* her grandmother had passed.

It was the only one that didn't feature a picture of David Lang, but it mentioned him under a photo of what must be the Maya coin her grandpa had found. The article was from a magazine called *Ancient Treasures* as noted in the footer of the page, and as she skimmed the print, whoever had written the piece laid out in clear detail that the coin had been traced to the burial site of K'inich Janaab' Pakal, also known as Pakal the Great, one of the more noted Maya rulers. The coins—and the author felt quite certain the term should be plural—had been stolen at some point in the past, then taken by Conquistadors back to Spain.

"Holy crap," she called to Ace. "You have to come look at this."

Ace crossed the attic in a matter of seconds, his gaze flitting over the article as he stood at her elbow, then whistled as she tapped the paragraph of note. "The coin your grandpa found was worth twenty-five thousand dollars?"

"I'm starting to feel a whole lot better about that knife in your pocket," she said faintly.

If there were more of these coins on her property, Intruder Man might be the least of her concerns.

Ace kept reading. "The article says that the king of Spain returned the coins to the Mexican government in the early nineteen hundreds, but then they went missing."

He said the word with giant implied air quotes. She got it. They were dealing with something so valuable, the treasure had changed hands multiple times, likely not without its share of bloodshed in the process.

"So, if nothing else," she concluded, "we missed an opportunity to research this online instead of digging through boxes in the attic. I had no idea Grandpa's find had gotten any press."

Easily rectified. She'd spend a couple of hours in the morning reading more about the treasure, which at least they'd verified did in fact exist. And apparently her father had found it, or at least part of it.

"Is your father an archaeologist or an opportunist?" Ace

asked and when she lifted her brows, he shook his head with a laugh. "Is he Indiana Jones or the Nazis in this scenario?"

"You mean, is he interested in the history and doing the right thing, or would he rather profit?" She started to answer that her father cared about nothing, but obviously he'd spent his life dedicated to the pursuit of treasure, even past the point when he'd found what some might argue would be the cache of a lifetime. "He doesn't have any formal training that I'm aware of, but that doesn't mean he didn't pick up an appreciation for the culture. He'd likely have studied relentlessly to know where to dig."

"Well, that was my real question." Ace tapped the magazine page, which had started to curl at the edges but otherwise seemed unaffected by time and harsh environmental factors. "Whether it was likely he'd found the treasure himself hidden somewhere in a historical site or had gotten it via nefarious means. Because if it's the latter, we could be dealing with a much darker group of mercenaries than I would have assumed."

Aghast, she stared at him. "You think he might have stolen the treasure from someone who legitimately had a claim to it? Like from a museum or something?"

"Or something," Ace said grimly. "But I don't want to accuse your father of anything without more facts. We know there are more coins that appear to be unaccounted for. It's reasonable to assume that they might be hidden here at the ranch if your father came into possession of more than one. We need to thoroughly search the house for the coins, and then start on the property. Sooner rather than later, not as a side project when we have time."

The reality of the dauntless task in front of them set in. "We can't do all of that at night."

"No," he agreed readily. "I can't imagine anything I want to do less than look for a treasure in the dark, one potentially worth six figures or more that your father may have taken under less-than-legal circumstances. On property I don't know well."

Because he couldn't look for a treasure and keep her safe at the same time under those conditions. And she fully believed the latter was his top priority. Maybe she shouldn't. Maybe she should be completely wary of a guy she'd just met, who carried a knife in his pocket that he clearly had some skill wielding.

But she did trust him. That was the gist of it. Who else could she possibly turn to in this situation?

Chapter 10

Sophia and Ace spent another two-plus hours in the attic, finally emerging dusty and exhausted—at least on her part—near midnight. Obviously, Ace had a lot of experience with after-dark activities, as he didn't seem too worse for wear, despite their finding nothing else of use.

But then, nothing much affected him as far as she could tell. He never seemed flustered or unsure, plus he'd taken off his hat at some point, exposing his wheat-blond hair that he kept clipped short, which was a wholly different look on him that she liked, so it was no chore to keep studying him.

Maybe she'd discover one of those flaws he insisted he had. That was the purpose of the knife show earlier, as best she'd reasoned out in the hours of searching they'd done, during which she'd had nothing to do but think about Ace. He'd pulled out the knife to give her the impression he was a dangerous guy who'd done dangerous things with a deadly weapon. She got it. Joke was on him if he thought the idea scared her. It stood to reason that he'd witnessed unsavory scenes during combat and likely had participated in his share.

War wasn't pretty and she didn't want to know what she

didn't know about it. But she did want to know more about the man behind the knife.

"Get some sleep," he murmured on his way out the front door, pausing only for a second to meet her gaze in the low light.

A ripple passed between them, and she swayed into it, drawn to him inexplicably. But he stepped in the opposite direction, through the space into the outside, shutting the door firmly in her face.

Yeah, that's what was supposed to happen. But she didn't have to like it.

Sleep came fitfully and she dreamed about her father, who seemed to be always flipping a gold coin along the backs of his fingers like the pirates in the movies did. Near dawn, she gave up, throwing herself into the shower she'd been too tired to take before going to bed.

Ace showed up at the back door around 7:00 a.m., apparently over his clandestine approach, which made sense given the urgency of their task and the switch to daylight hours. They weren't going to be able to hide their activities too well, but she'd still like to try to avoid an uproar of the whole place if possible.

"Come in," she said and shut the door behind him with a sharp click, thumbing out a quick text to Becky.

"Did you eat breakfast?"

"I had coffee," he said with a shrug. He'd forgone the hat entirely today, his hair still damp from his own shower.

"Then let's test all of the floor joists first and see if we can find a false one that might have a hidey-hole beneath it." His brows lifted. "What? It was in a movie I saw. It could be a thing."

"It could be. That wasn't a vote of no confidence, it was an 'I'm impressed.' Am I allowed to say that?"

She grinned. "You never have to ask permission to compliment me. You can start in the dining room, and I'll take the living room."

They worked in silence, ears keen on the floor for telltale creaks or places where it sounded hollow. Occasionally one of them would call out, "Anything?" and the other would reply, "Nothing." Or a variation thereof.

They met up at the base of the wide, curved staircase in the foyer, Sophia already frustrated and bored with this approach, her to-do list growing by the second as emails and texts poured in, judging by the vibrations from her pocket. "We're never going to find anything this way."

"It's a tedious business," he agreed, shoving his hands in his pockets. "Do you think there's anything in your grandpa's papers that might be a schematic of the house? Possibly with something helpful like an arrow pointing to a hidden room behind the wood paneling in a bedroom or something?"

They'd already looked in her office once, but to be fair, she'd had no clue what to look for and her eye might have skimmed over something like house blueprints because she'd had no idea such a thing would be of value the first time.

But what were the odds that something would be easy?

She threw up her hands. "Maybe?"

"The office is the most logical place for your grandpa to have kept something like that."

She nodded because why not after the lack of progress thus far? Sophia led the way, handing him the key to the desk drawer, which he took without comment as she drifted to the far wall, contemplating. Had the twenty-five grand from the sale of the one recovered coin ended up in the account she'd inherited or had her grandpa spent it all? Or, door number three, did he have a safe hidden somewhere that she hadn't found yet because she'd never thought to look for one?

Tapping on the walls and lifting framed prints, she tried to imagine where her grandpa would have hidden something valuable that wasn't also the same place as in the last five thrillers she'd watched.

The third print she lifted must not have been secured to the wall all that well. It teetered on its nail, then crashed to the floor in a shower of shiny shards and wood.

Ace shot across the room, his arms snaking around her before she could blink. He lifted, pulling her clear from the splintered glass, and straight into a semi-embrace that sent a shiver over her entire body.

Adrenaline. And Ace. It was a heck of a one-two punch.

His gaze swept her with an assessing eye before finally landing on her face. "Are you okay?"

Given that his arms still lay snug against her waist, and they were aligned from hip to torso, she'd never been better in her life. Heat pumped from his body. It was delicious and paired nicely with the fireworks going off inside her. It took all her will to stop herself from stepping more fully into his embrace.

"Define *okay*," she murmured throatily, and that's when something flashed in his expression.

He'd registered their position too. Their gazes locked, singeing the air between them.

But he didn't drop his arms, thank goodness, though he should. They were treasure hunting partners. Strictly professional. The thing between them shouldn't feel like it was about to blaze into a fire hazard. And telling herself that didn't seem to make it fizzle.

What did it say about her love life that this was the most excitement she'd had with a man in ages?

"Oh, I'm sorry!" Becky stood at the door to Sophia's office, flinching as if she'd gotten an eyeful of something she'd rather not have seen. "I didn't mean to interrupt. I heard the crash from the front door just as I was knocking and rushed in to see what in the world had happened."

"No worries," Ace returned smoothly, stepping away from Sophia without jerking like a marionette—which was more than she could say for herself. "The picture frame fell off the wall. I was ensuring Ms. Lang hadn't been injured by the glass."

"Oh, okay." Becky eyed him curiously, not paying attention to Sophia at all, mercifully. "We haven't met. I'm Sophia's accountant, Becky."

"Ace Madden. Ranch hand," he explained with a head jerk toward the back acreage. "Currently repurposed as sweeper of glass. So I'll get to it."

Without a backward glance, Ace vanished in the direction of the kitchen, presumably in search of a broom and dustpan, which Jenny would help him locate. Sophia beelined for her chair, sliding into and swiveling around to face Becky from behind the desk, praying that she came across as calm and professional and not like she'd been about to test out the feel of Ace's lips for herself.

"That man is the definition of smoking," Becky said with eyes wider than a Texas horizon. "If you've got any more of them lying around, send one in my direction. I could use someone to sweep my glass."

"It's not like that," Sophia protested. "Stop making broken glass sound like a euphemism. Did you have a reason for dropping by?"

One that didn't involve almost catching Sophia in flagrante delicto with an employee, preferably.

Thankfully, Becky didn't comment on the snippiness in Sophia's tone and slid a sheaf of papers over the top of the desk. "Signatures. This is the loan paperwork I texted you about."

Oh, for crying out loud. She'd forgotten all about it. That's how things had gone lately. The second she'd read the message on her phone, it had exited her brain faster than water down a drain. Thankfully, it was a small slip, one Becky had covered, which was what Sophia paid her for.

But if she didn't watch herself, this treasure might end up costing her more than time.

"The interest rate came in a little higher than we were hoping," Becky said conversationally as if she hadn't just dropped a big wrench in the conversation.

"Wait. What?" Sophia paused, pen poised over the dotted line. "How much more? I can't afford even a dollar over the repayment amount we discussed with Ken on Friday."

"Well, it's complicated. The ranch isn't pulling in income yet." Becky tapped her index finger on the clause with the interest rate and the refigured monthly payment. "So it's a riskier loan for the bank. Ken said he tried to get the rate lowered but the lender wouldn't budge."

Dismayed, Sophia stared at the number. It would be lovely if a Maya treasure dropped in her lap right about now. Especially one with about six zeros attached. If she didn't take this loan, she wouldn't have the operating capital to open the doors and then she'd never have the money to pay off the loan. It was a vicious catch-22.

"I guess I don't have a choice," she muttered.

"Not unless you have some kind of collateral," Becky agreed. "And since you already told Ken you didn't have anything of value, he assumed that was still true."

"It is for now."

But maybe not for long, depending on what she and Ace found. Anything historical might work for collateral, especially if she could tie it to the treasure. Or barring that, she could just find the actual treasure and then she wouldn't need a loan. Easy.

She rolled her eyes and signed the loan paperwork with her eyes screwed shut, sincerely worried that she might start hyperventilating at any second if she stared any harder at that repayment amount.

"I'll let you get back to sweeping glass," Becky said with a sly grin that faltered a tad when Ace came back into the room with a broom in hand and a trash bag tucked into his back pocket.

He smiled politely and brushed past Becky to show off exactly how good he was with his hands, sweeping almost all the glass into the dustpan in one shot. The shards went into the trash bag, then Ace expertly picked up the larger pieces that hadn't shattered, following with the wood until every last speck of the wreckage had been cleared.

"Ma'am," he said to Becky, in a drawl that almost had the accountant tittering.

"Nice to meet you, Ace Madden, ranch hand," Becky said with a wave and gathered her paperwork to jet out of the door.

"I thought she'd never leave," Sophia muttered in a complete reversal of what should be her attitude when it came to dealing with ranch business.

What was wrong with her? The loan should have been first and foremost on her mind, instead of focusing on her embarrassment at almost being caught with a ranch hand.

Well, technically, she *had* been caught. There couldn't have been a more compromising position to be in when someone stumbled over them, and still be dressed. And what had Becky done? Leaped to the worst possible conclusion. Then asked for one of her own.

Maybe her accountant wasn't silently judging Sophia to quite the degree she'd been imagining. After all, Ace had handled the interruption like a pro—*and* cleaned up the mess without preamble. Any mortification came from the deep-seated conflict Sophia had over whether she should be mixing business with pleasure. So far, Charli and Becky seemed to be in the pro camp. Possibly even Jenny, too, which marked three people who knew she had a thing for Ace.

Three too many. But that ship had sailed. She could no sooner stuff the women's knowledge into the garbage disposal than she could make the treasure materialize on her desk.

Nor could she stop herself from wondering what it would be like to not have to jump apart if someone surprised them in a less-than-professional situation. What it would be like to have a man as principled and dedicated as this one by her side for a much bigger slice of life than treasure hunting.

Ace wouldn't bail if things got hard. She'd always worried she'd wind up attracted to the same kind of man as her mother. Or worse, that all men were like her father, and she had nothing to choose from but weak-willed, spineless men who would abandon her at the earliest opportunity.

Clearly not all men were like that.

"We should get back to work," Ace suggested gently. "If you're sure you're okay."

A hysterical laugh almost bubbled to the surface. "I wasn't okay the first time you asked. But we'll pretend that's not true."

"Since I'm guessing you don't actually mean you cut yourself and need medical triage, I'll step away from that very carefully," he said with a wry twist of his lips, hands spread wide.

"If I *was* bleeding, you'd rip a bandage from your shirt and do some kind of MacGyver thing with chewing gum in place of stitches, wouldn't you?" she grumbled, which made him laugh.

"Do I win or lose points if I say yes?" he said, throwing her a glance from under his lashes as he took a stack of files and settled on the floor to thumb through them since she hadn't moved from her chair.

She might never move from this chair again if he kept looking at her like that. It turned her spine to jelly. "Jury is still out."

"How about now?" he said and held up a plain white envelope, dumped it upside down and poured a key into his hand.

"Is that—"

"Safety deposit box key," he confirmed, his grin widening. "Any chance you know where your grandpa did his banking?"

Chapter 11

Ace drove to the center of Gun Barrel City with Sophia riding shotgun in his stripped-down, late-model pickup truck. It had seemed like a good vehicle for an undercover security specialist playing the part of a cowboy, at the time anyway.

It was rough around the edges, the opposite of fancy. Not the kind of transportation a woman like Sophia would be used to. But when he'd bought the truck, never once had he imagined a woman would see the inside of it.

Especially not one he couldn't stop reacting to every time they were in close quarters together. If he'd thought being closeted in her office made it tough to ignore the pull between them, the cab of the truck made that seem like a picnic.

The scent of her fruity shampoo filled every nook and cranny. The product probably had some expensive French name, but at the end of the day, reminded him of good old-fashioned apples. Which prior to this job, had not seemed particularly sexy, but Sophia somehow kept his brain in a constant state of awareness, so pretty much everything seemed sexy when connected to her.

"This the one?" he asked her as he pulled up to the traffic light in front of what appeared to be the only bank on Main Street, at least on this side of the lake.

She nodded and held on to the armrest as he turned, wobbly on the bench seat she probably wasn't used to. "Let's just hope he didn't do something that will set us back, like drive all the way to Dallas to get a safety deposit box."

As the executor of her grandfather's estate, Sophia did in fact have a very good idea where he'd had an account, and on the drive over, she'd done a lot of grumbling to Ace about how the safety deposit box hadn't been listed on any of the documents.

"It'll be here," he promised her. He could feel it in his gut, though he didn't mention that it wasn't a good feeling. The more they uncovered, the more uneasy he got.

It was one thing to be chasing after a treasure so they could get to it first, and it was another thing entirely to actually find the treasure, whatever it was, only to have some unsavory types try to divest them of it. He had no interest in being a target or painting one on Sophia's back.

Once inside, Sophia asked to speak to the manager, and Ace braced for the long ordeal ahead. They didn't know the box number, and technically, the account was still in her grandfather's name—assuming the box was even at this bank—and the legal tangle of proving her ownership of the asset might even require a warrant or at least a notarized right of transfer.

But when the manager emerged, it was a woman of an indeterminate age wearing a knit sweater who immediately threw her arms around Sophia and fussed over how much she'd grown. Obviously, they'd met. Small town.

"And who is this young man?" the manager cooed as she turned her attention to Ace.

"This is Ace Madden, one of the ranch hands I hired," Sophia said. "Frances was my grandmother's best friend for ages."

Ah. That explained it. Something had finally gone their way.

"She's looking down now, thrilled to pieces that the ranch came to you instead of being sold off," Frances said with a nod. "What can I do for you today? Did you get your grandpa's accounts all squared away?"

"No, ma'am, we were wondering if this goes to a safety deposit box that my grandpa might have had here." Sophia held up the key.

Frances immediately brightened. "Well, he sure did. Let me look up the number for you and you can see what's in it in this room back here. Follow me."

And just like that, he found himself included in the party, no ID check required, just hey, y'all, here's this secure, tamper-proof container meant to store valuable items the owner wanted to keep inaccessible in a vault that you can peruse at your leisure. All because Sophia had connections.

No wonder no one locked their doors around here. Why bother when the homeowner might very well invite a B&E suspect to sit down and have cookies before they took off with their loot?

Frances the bank manager pulled the data from a less than top-of-the-line computer behind her desk and before he could wrap his head around it, she ushered them into the vault, indicating that number 9847 had belonged to her grandpa. The boxes weren't the overly secure kind that required two keys, just the one from the owner, so Frances gave Sophia a nod and went to stand near the door, presumably to give them some semblance of privacy.

"Moment of truth," Sophia murmured to Ace and shoved the key into the lock.

Zero resistance. She twisted and the door popped open to reveal the box inside, which she extracted easily with the small handle attached to the front. It opened with her key as well. White paper covered the whole of the interior.

Sophia groaned. "I hope this isn't just another copy of his will. The man had like twelve copies in a file at home."

But when she pulled it out, it wasn't a stapled sheaf. The paper was large, folded into quarters that Sophia quickly spread out. A drawing covered the entire surface, almost to the edges.

Not just a drawing. Ace sucked in a breath. "It's a map."

Quirking a brow, she glanced at the diagram. "It's the ranch. Look, here's the house, and the barn. Or what used to be the barn."

"This." Ace stabbed a finger at a small square deep in the woods that had a very conveniently placed X in the dead center. "What is this?"

"I don't know. Some kind of deer blind or something, maybe?" She squinted. "It's pretty far back into the woods. I haven't been out there since I was a kid."

A deer blind covered in branches might explain why he hadn't seen it during his tour of the property, but he didn't want to mention that he'd already done a pretty thorough recon job.

"We're going to assume this X meant something important or your grandpa wouldn't have put this map of his property in a safety deposit box. Right?" he probed in case she had any information that would contradict the feeling in his gut.

This was it. The thing they'd been looking for.

"I mean, yeah. Obviously, it's important." She glanced in the box, her expression softening. "Oh, look. My grandmother's ring. I thought she'd been buried with it."

She picked up the only other thing in the box and slipped the ring on her finger. It was a simple band inset with round diamonds and fit Sophia, both in size and style. She curled her hand closed, turning it to let the light flash over the stones.

The look on her face hooked a tender place inside him and he couldn't take his eyes off her. What would he give to be the one who could make her glow like that? But he wasn't the kind of guy who put rings on women's fingers and imagining doing exactly that with Sophia didn't help.

"If this is the only thing I get out of this treasure hunt, I'll be happy," she said with a misty smile. "Thank you."

That's when she decided it would be a good time to launch herself into his arms for a hug to accompany her gratitude, and apples engulfed him as he caught her. Suddenly, he had an armful of Sophia and everything else in the world drained away.

If this went along with a thank-you, maybe he could come up with some other stuff she'd feel grateful for.

"You're welcome," he said gruffly. "But you would have found that envelope eventually. It had your dad's name on it."

She pulled back enough to meet his gaze but not enough to break his hold on her, his new favorite way to have a conversation with her. "It did? I didn't even notice. Surely that means the treasure must be in that spot on the map. Maybe my grandpa was holding the map for my father."

"Maybe." Or it was a dead end because her father had already cleaned out whatever it was on the map. It wouldn't be difficult for someone to sneak onto the property the back way and vanish undetected, booty in hand. "We need to go check it out."

"Well, yes, of course. We should go immediately, before it gets dark. My to-do list will have to wait."

They thanked Frances and Sophia signed some papers to cancel the safety deposit box since she was taking the entirety of the contents with her. The woman's efficiency and attention to detail, despite the huge monkey wrench this treasure hunt must have thrown into her life, was a force to be reckoned with. And he couldn't recall ever being attracted to something like that. It was messing with his head.

"Are you hungry?" he asked her as they climbed back into his truck. "We can run through a drive-through."

"I'm starving," she admitted. "There's a Dairy Queen. But I'm buying since you drove."

Two points to Ms. Lang. He couldn't recall the last time a woman owned up to having an appetite or a time—ever—when one had willingly ponied up money. He'd been fully prepared to split it.

Apparently, they had something in common. A tendency to push toward balancing the scales. He let that sit in the same spot as his growing feelings for her, mostly because he couldn't do anything else. Everything about her worked for him and then some.

They ate cheeseburgers in the car on the drive back to the ranch, a mutual agreement since they were both eager to figure out what the X marked on their newly acquired map. By the time his truck rolled into the back lot where the hands parked their vehicles, he'd fallen into an easy silence with Sophia that he'd never experienced with a woman before. Usually, he was exhausted from whatever mission he'd just been on, mentally preparing for the next one, or just plain bored by the woman's company.

This time, none of that was true. It was different and interesting and complicated. Not to mention impossible to fully enjoy when he constantly felt like the hammer would drop at any second, as soon as he had to tell her the truth.

"Let me just change first," she said as she hopped out of the truck, before he could get his brain in gear and race around to help her down.

Obviously, she didn't need his help. At least not in that regard, but he'd take solace in all the other ways she'd let him be there for her thus far. He liked the idea of being her white knight, even if it couldn't last.

It was the one thing he could take from this relationship without an ounce of guilt.

When she returned, she'd traded her sleek dress for jeans and a T-shirt, with a sweatshirt tied around her waist. The messy bun that he'd started to think of as a permanent fixture on her crown had been replaced by a long, swingy ponytail that his fingers itched to comb through. It was the first time he'd seen her in casual wear and while he really liked her dresses, this side of her put a different hitch in his stride.

Because she suddenly seemed accessible. As if he could actually be with a woman like this, one who ate cheeseburgers in the cab of his truck and filled a pair of jeans as if they'd been custom-made for her frame.

"Come on," he told her more gruffly than he'd intended but jeez.

In the last hour, he'd thought about their relationship status more times than he'd thought about anything else, including the treasure. The answer to the question of who is totally distracted by Sophia and will soon make a mistake if he doesn't get his act together was Ace Madden.

Sophia didn't seem to notice, eagerly falling in next to him as she slung a backpack over her shoulders. At his eyebrow lift, she laughed. "It's snacks and some water bottles. Just in case. Plus the map and my cell phone. And an extra hair band in case my hair starts to annoy me, so I can put it back up in a bun."

"Why did you take it down, then, if there's a chance you'll just put it back up?" he asked, strictly to sidetrack himself from the fact that even her preparedness struck him as sexy.

"I don't know, it seemed more adventurous to do it this way," she said with a shrug, shadows falling on her face as they entered the woods near the new temporary barn the hands were building.

Which he was not helping with and probably should be. While protecting Sophia and helping her find the treasure counted as his primary objective, as well as his real job, he was still taking a paycheck from the ranch. He couldn't refuse or it would raise eyebrows, or even an inquiry into his background, neither of which he could afford at this point.

Great. So he'd found yet another thing to feel guilty about.

"I like the ponytail," he told her, despite knowing full well he shouldn't say stuff like that.

He seemed to have fallen into a rut where he'd keep doing the exact opposite of what his brain insisted was the right thing. Sometimes doing the right thing sucked. She didn't seem to mind the compliment though, her smile bordering on gleeful, which wasn't even close to the same as the look her grandmother's ring had put on her face, but he'd take it.

The ranch wasn't that big by the standard of someone who had traversed twenty miles in full gear, guerilla style, which meant staying off the main road. But he was cognizant of Sophia's lack of physical training, so he kept his pace slow as they took the main trail into the woods.

"It won't take long to get to the X," he assured her. "Maybe twenty minutes tops. Fortunately, it's on this side of the creek."

She nodded, seeming to have no trouble keeping up, which left him plenty of headspace to pay attention to their surroundings. The hands never came into the woods since they focused most of their attention on the flat acreage where the horses grazed, rotating the animals from field to field to ensure they always had enough to eat. The wooded area extended past the boundaries of Sophia's property and her grandpa hadn't fenced this section, likely due to the expense and effort to work around the creek.

It would be a lot easier for an intruder to sneak onto the property from this direction.

The dense trees blocked more of the sun the farther into the woods they walked. He'd like to say the close atmosphere was cozy. The kind of vibe that would allow him to slip an arm around his companion's waist, drawing her closer as they strolled without a care in the world.

That was not a fantasy he could afford to let scroll through his head, let alone act on.

He hadn't been this far into the trees. The last time he'd come into the woods, when he'd found the tarp, he'd been much closer to the house, around the other side of the barn to the north. He'd expected more wildlife, especially if Sophia was right about the X marking the spot of a deer blind. Birds flittered here and there, and an occasional squirrel chittered at them as they passed, but it was eerily quiet for woods.

Fortunate. That's what allowed him to hear the shush of footsteps behind them.

Someone was following them. One of the ranch hands?

Surely not. He knew all of them. A fellow cowboy would have called out for them to wait up if he thought they were off on something they'd allow him to crash.

Ace kept walking, careful to keep his pace identical so he didn't tip off whoever was behind them. His gaze darted around in 360-degree sweeps, preparing for an attack that might come from any direction. Or not. He didn't know this person's intent and it made him antsy.

When he passed a fallen tree branch, he casually hooked it with his hand, breaking off the smaller offshoot branches, then used it as a walking stick. It couldn't hurt to have a weapon.

Their tail got a little closer and a lot more cautious, staying just off the path, which was what had alerted him to the additional presence in the first place since the footsteps sounded different. This was no random person wondering what they were doing. Whoever they were had a bit of skill.

But Ace was better.

Sophia's safety was his number one concern. He had to know what he was dealing with here. The best way to do that was to put a tree between her and their tail while leaving Ace as the primary target—without alerting her to the danger. Which meant an evasive maneuver.

"Want to stop for a second?" he murmured. "Get some water from your backpack?"

Thankfully, she nodded and slipped off the pack, but she was still out in the open. There was only one way to get her up against a tree and he didn't hesitate to use it, even as his conscience screamed at him to think of something else.

The problem was that he couldn't think of anything else but advancing on her, grabbing her hips and backing her up until she aligned with the bark. Which, of course, meant she was sandwiched between the tree and Ace.

Dear Lord, did she feel good.

To anyone else, it would look like he meant to kiss her. It looked an awful lot like that to him too. She peered up at him, her lashes fluttering as she subtly adjusted so that they fit together better, and he bit back a groan.

"This was not what I expected to happen on our jaunt," she said breathlessly, which made two of them.

He didn't want to scare her by alerting her to the stalker's presence. But neither could he let her think he was the kind of guy to take advantage of a woman in the woods when there was no one around to hear her protest. Angling his head, he bent toward her ear, secretly inhaling her scent.

"There's someone back there," he whispered. "Don't flinch. Freeze exactly as you are. Act like you're enjoying my attention."

"It's not an act," she murmured.

That's when a shot rang out.

Chapter 12

Bark splintered from the tree above them, raining down on Sophia's shoulder. Her expression morphed instantly from intrigued to terrified.

Ace didn't have time to fix either one.

"Run," he said through gritted teeth and shouldered her backpack, then grabbed her hand to lead the way. Palmed his knife in the other hand, not that he could throw it with any accuracy unless he turned around. Not happening.

It was more important to get Sophia out of the line of fire. He sprinted off the path, farther into the heavy trees, hoping they would provide enough cover to allow him to put distance between her and the shooter.

Sophia kept up, her hand trembling in his. The fact that she didn't question him, just let him call the shots, went a long way toward allowing him to execute the extraction without worrying about getting her on board.

He headed toward the X, hoping that the original map artist had rendered the diagram to scale. His own skill in estimating the spatial distance he'd memorized wasn't in question, but an error on the part of someone else would be difficult to account for.

Fortunately, the map had it right and none too soon. The

faint outline of a building materialized in the section he'd earmarked in his mind's eye, right where he'd expected it. It was partially camouflaged, which was why he hadn't seen it before, but it wasn't deliberately disguised. The woods had just grown up around it so that you had to know it was there to notice the shape of the structure.

"Almost there," he called back to Sophia, who was huffing a bit and might need some encouragement.

If nothing else, they could use the building as a shield. As they rounded the backside, he hustled her flat up against the south wall. Wood. The building was a brown shed, one of the prefab kinds, larger than he'd first estimated.

Good. He'd been hoping for metal, which would be a lot better at stopping bullets than the rotting wood, but maybe they could duck inside if need be.

For now, they needed to vanish.

Finger to his lips, he hugged the wall in kind, sliding down to a crouch, then motioned for her to do the same. The ground here felt spongy, as if the soil might drain poorly due to the structure compromising the natural flow of rainwater. But the overgrowth of young trees in a ring around the place made it a much more ideal hiding place than it could have been.

A hush stole over the surrounding woods. He strained to hear sounds that would indicate the stalker had followed them, but there was nothing. Either their tail hadn't chased them, or he was holed up a few yards away, waiting for them to make themselves targets again.

That wasn't happening. He could park it here for hours without moving, no problem.

Sophia might be another story, though. She wasn't used to fleeing for her life in combat situations that required stealth maneuvers. Neither could he let her sit down and rest her thighs for a few minutes. If they had to run, she needed to be poised and ready.

Her gaze flicked to the knife in his hand, but he couldn't tell if she appreciated that he had a weapon or if the idea of being protected by a man who knew how to use one bothered her.

One thing for sure, she wasn't breathing normally, and he needed her to. If she passed out from lack of oxygen, he'd have to carry her. It would be a lot harder to defend against an attack if his hands were full of unconscious woman. But he couldn't risk making any sound to tell her to stop hyperventilating.

So he settled for running a soothing hand down her arm, nodding slowly in approval as she began breathing deeper, visibly calming.

Excellent, he mouthed, his thumb skimming over her skin in a circle. Later, he'd think about how nice it felt.

When he estimated that they'd been crouched here for a solid fifteen minutes, he duck-walked to the edge of the shed, then flattened himself to the ground so he could peer around the corner from the lowest profile possible.

Nothing. No movement, no shush of leaves. Even the wind didn't penetrate this deep into the woods. Their tail might have given up. Unlikely, though. It highly depended on the tail's reason for shooting at them. More likely, whoever it was had no small amount of patience and would wait them out.

The door to the shed lay around the other side, unfortunately. They might have to risk it. He would feel a lot better about getting Sophia inside the shelter, where she wasn't quite so exposed. Their tail could even now be climbing a tree far enough away so that Ace couldn't hear the telltale sounds but close enough to take both of them out with a long-range rifle.

That was one of the downsides to civilian security work. He had no clue what type of weaponry he might be up against. In Afghanistan, he was never at a disadvantage thanks to expert intel and a lot of experience he would not benefit from here in East Texas.

After a frustrating round of surveillance that yielded him zero useful information, he rolled to his knees and crawled back to Sophia, his finger to his lips again. She nodded, stretching her back with little side-to-side movements that weren't lost on him. Her muscles hurt. She wasn't used to holding a position so taxing on her body. This situation sucked, no two ways about it.

Just as he started devising a plan in his head to get them from this shed to the tree line where they might be able to make a run for the main house, something groaned, but it wasn't human. It sounded like pressure on wood.

The walls? The shed wasn't about to collapse, was it?

The groaning got louder, and Ace's stomach lurched as if the ground had dropped. Not unusual in an earthquake. Except this was no tremor, or he'd have braced for the shift.

Suddenly, the earth beneath them gave way and he was falling. Sophia cried out. They both hit a hard surface. Dirt and splintered wood rained down from above.

Coughing, Ace rolled to his feet instantly, knife raised, automatically moving to stand guard over Sophia as he assessed the perimeter. They were in some kind of underground shelter. A large one that extended past the area where they'd landed. But the dim light from above didn't penetrate the shadowy edges well enough to see what lurked there.

Sophia moaned, still flat on the concrete, her cheek to the ground. She shifted, a good sign. Concussion protocol scrolled through his mind, even as he tamped back a lick of panic at the thought of having to do any kind of injury triage in the midst of keeping a lookout for the shooter, should he try to ambush them from above.

"Sophia," he murmured and knelt to check her pulse, which was thankfully strong. "Did you hit your head?"

"No," she told him, her voice thick and laced with pain. "I landed on my shoulder. The one Intruder Man injured the other day."

He needed to know how bad it was. And get her out of the light. Pronto. "I'm going to help you sit up."

There wasn't time to stand on principle, not as loud as their untimely crash through the shelter roof had been. He got down and put an arm around her waist, gently lifting her from the concrete, then helped her move out of the circle of dirt and split wood pieces. Near the far wall, which was thankfully well into the shadowy recesses, he helped her sit back against it.

She slumped, drawing her knees up to rest her arm on them. "Where are we?"

"Some kind of shelter under the shed, but it seems like it might be a lot bigger area. Hard to see. It's pretty dark back in these corners."

"Here, use my phone." She fished it from her backpack, which was still slung around his shoulder. "One good thing, you didn't land on this so it's probably fine."

She switched on the flashlight app and handed it to him. Immediately, he tapped it off and pocketed the phone, opting to keep his concern about an ambush to himself for the moment. "In a minute. Talk to me about your pain level. One to ten."

"I don't know, like a five?"

She was lying. Her voice carried a fine thread of distress, and he couldn't see how bad she was hurt while they cowered in the dark, waiting for their tail to show up and shoot them like fish in a barrel.

Remorse soured his throat. She was hurt and it was his fault. If he'd led her into the shed in the first place, they might not have fallen through the spongy places that had rotted—definitely due to poor drainage based on the water-damaged pieces of roof that had hit the concrete along with them.

"I'll live, Ace," she assured him, somehow cluing into his own agony over their situation. "I just don't want to run for a few minutes. Can we just sit here and let me catch my breath?"

"It was a hard fall," he murmured, impressed that she was taking it so well. "And yes, to your question. We can sit here for a few minutes."

Or thirty. As long as it took for him to feel at least semi-confident that their tail wasn't too bright and hadn't figured out where they'd disappeared to. Ironic that he'd maneuvered her into position by the shed wall with the sole intent of hiding them both from view and had inadvertently pulled a decent vanishing act out of thin air.

They may have gotten extremely lucky.

Ace settled back against the wall next to Sophia and nearly bit his tongue when she slipped her hand into his. Okay. She was scared and probably in no small amount of shock. It made sense that she'd want human contact. He could buck up. And he might even be able to keep his brain from short-circuiting.

It was a toss-up whether he did that successfully or not.

Thankfully, the shooter did not show up to demonstrate his ability to track them to their belowground hideout or his skill with hitting a stationary target. At least not yet. Ace had held his position behind a half wall near the road to Kandahar for eight hours once, while waiting on a convoy of terrorists to motor past. When they finally did, he executed the operation with his usual expertise, despite not having moved a muscle in ages.

Patience was a higher-valued skill in stealth combat than almost anything else. And he'd exercise it here too. In more ways than one, apparently, as Sophia let her head drop onto his shoulder.

She trusted him. It was a revelation, even as it felt so easy and normal to be here like this with her, as if they'd been this close-knit team for far longer than a couple of days.

If she'd hesitated back there by the tree for even a second…if she'd questioned his directives, argued with him, the outcome might have been very different. But she hadn't. She'd followed him without question.

It was humbling. And poked at him with sharp prongs of guilt.

He had to move, to do something. To save her.

"Hold this for me," he ordered and closed her palm around the handle of his knife, pointy end raised. "Use it without hesitation if need be. I'm going to check this place out."

She nodded and shifted so he could stand.

The phone's flashlight app wasn't a strong light, but it was enough for him to prowl around the perimeter, noting more cobwebs than anything useful. Several empty barrels stood up against one wall in a line, probably used for storage at one time. An old refrigerator with a missing door sat near a pile of discarded tools, a bolt cutter and a rusted fence pole driver on top.

At the far end of the space, a rotting wooden staircase led to a door at the top. Fantastic. That would be their exit strategy after another couple of hours had passed, long enough for Sophia to recover and for him to feel confident they could run for it without picking up their tail again.

If they could make it up the stairs without the whole thing collapsing. He should test it first. After all, this shed clearly hadn't been used in a long time.

Cautiously, he crept up the stairs, placing his feet in the exact center of each board, expecting his foot to go through one at any second. He didn't touch the railing. The entire structure listed to the side and he thought it likely he'd end up in a heap of broken boards before reaching the top.

But he made it.

Which ended up not mattering in the slightest. The door was locked from the other side. He rattled the doorknob for good measure, noting the hinges were also on the other side. Of course. What fun would it be to have some mechanism available to resolve the situation?

As quickly as he could, he reversed his steps and crossed to Sophia to check on her since it had taken far longer to climb the rickety stairs than he would have liked.

"Doing okay?"

She nodded, barely discernible in the dark, which was good—it made her less of a target. "I'm just mad. Why does someone hate me?"

"I wish I knew." Crouching down, he relieved her of the

knife and closed it with a snap so he could use his hands to assess her. "Can you hold your phone with your other hand for a minute so I can check out your arm?"

"You're a trained medic, too?" she commented wryly, less a question than a statement of her disbelief.

But she held the phone as requested, so he got busy feeling along her clavicle, ignoring her implications since he wasn't sure he was at liberty to say that he had training in a lot of areas courtesy of Uncle Sam.

They didn't send fresh-faced recruits to do certain types of jobs. And an operative who knew a lot about the human body could do a great deal of damage to one.

"Does this hurt?" he asked and pressed on several spots.

"Yeah, but not more than it did a few minutes ago."

"Probably not fractured, then." He sat back on his heels. "Which is shocking, considering how far we fell. If it's bothering you, I can fashion a sling. It'll keep it stationary, which will help with the healing."

"I guess that would be wise."

An old button-up shirt he'd spied a minute ago split apart easily at the seams and in a flash, he had her arm tied up with the knot behind her neck. "It's not much and I'm sorry to say we're trapped for the time being."

He could practically feel her anxiety level ratchet up. "Trapped? As in no way to get out? How did my grandfather get all this stuff down here, then?"

"There's a staircase but the door at the top is locked. I might be able to bust it down, but it could be risky. I'll try in a little while."

After their tail gave up and left. He had no confidence that the roof collapse had escaped the shooter's notice, but if by some miracle it had, he did not want to take a chance on alerting the guy to their location via a second crash. Though whether the door or the staircase would be the cause remained to be seen. There was a better-than-average chance the staircase would give before the door.

"Ace? Thank you."

His mouth turned up automatically. "For getting you trapped in here? Sure thing. It was literally no problem. I didn't even have to try."

"I'm being serious. Everything hurts. I'm scared. It'll probably get cold in a little while when the sun goes down. But nothing seems as bad when you're here."

That hit him sideways. Then settled down inside him with warmth he didn't have the right to feel. He cleared his throat. "I didn't do anything."

"Sure you did. After all, this is the X on the map. Isn't it?"

Chapter 13

Sophia's little crush on Ace exploded into something a lot harder to deal with around the time he busted a locked cabinet into smithereens with nothing more than a pair of bolt cutters.

She could barely see from her position on the floor due to all the darkness, but it sounded impressive, and his brute strength coupled with the gentle care he'd taken with her arm did lovely, silky things to her insides. She was female enough to swoon a little over a capable man while still maintaining her own independence.

Yes, she could take care of herself. Had for a long time. But it was nice to have someone next to her who could also hold his own. And then some.

"Found a lantern," he called gleefully. "And matches."

She had a sneaking suspicion that he liked taking care of her too. It was lovely to not have to do everything for herself. To have someone to lean on occasionally. Who would have thought she'd find competence so sexy?

A snick and then the lantern glowed to life, burning the oil in its base. The underground shelter took shape in the low light. It was sparse and not as small as she'd imagined from her spot against the wall.

"If my grandfather did use this shelter, he must have forgotten about it in his later years," she said with a wrinkled nose.

"I'm surprised there are no existing residents, honestly," Ace said, rubbing the back of his neck. "I thought for sure I'd have to dispatch a rat or a snake and then lie to you about it."

Uh, yeah, that was one thing she'd happily allow him a pass on. She shuddered. "I don't want to know about either of those, dead or alive."

"Deal," he said simply and sank to the ground near her, which was quickly becoming her favorite place for him.

Sure, it was great that he'd done all the recon of the shelter, letting her sit here in misery with a busted arm, but she wasn't so keen on being by herself. Even when he'd left her his knife, it had been small comfort since she'd have to be the one to use it on someone.

Of course, now she had the vision in her head of it being a some*thing* with long teeth and diseases.

"What time is it?" she asked him since he'd long ago taken possession of her cell phone to use as a flashlight.

"Almost eight o'clock."

It had gotten dark an hour ago, then. Ace had used the flashlight sparingly, telling her he was trying to conserve the battery, but she knew he was also worried about someone figuring out they'd fallen into this shelter and coming in after them. They'd have nowhere to go and while she had absolute confidence Ace could handle himself in a close-quarters fight, he wasn't bulletproof. As far as she knew anyway. And she definitely wasn't.

"Surely whoever shot at us is gone. Right?"

He shrugged and she appreciated the simple pleasure of

being able to see the person she was talking to. Never again would she take above ground for granted. Or cell service. She'd checked for bars like forty-seven times at this point, had even sent Ace to the top of the stairs to see if reception was better there. But no. They couldn't call for help.

"You sure you're all right?" he asked her, his gaze flitting over her with concern.

It seemed she wasn't the only one who liked having the light. "I've been better, and I could use a shower. But I'll make it."

"You should eat something," he suggested and pulled out the last protein bar from her backpack, handing it to her.

"Only if you'll split it with me," she insisted and tore open the wrapper, extending it to him so he could take his half.

She didn't think he would. He hadn't eaten anything thus far, opting to give her all the food since she'd been the one to pack it. Which made a selfless sort of sense, until they'd ended up in a precarious situation, trapped for who knew how long.

"You need to keep up your strength too," she told him, and he finally conceded with a flat glance at her that she couldn't interpret as he ripped off a chunk of the bar.

The last of their food disappeared in less than a minute. They'd been conserving the water too, taking sips only every so often, which felt a little pessimistic. Surely someone would find them before too long, right? The ranch wasn't *that* big. A good bloodhound could find people in minutes, or at least they always did in movies.

"Now that we have a decent light, I'm going to search for a key," he told her and before she could protest, he'd rolled to his feet and begun a methodical search through the remaining cabinets.

"If you don't find one, you could always do the bolt-cutter tango with the door," she suggested.

"That's the plan," he confirmed. "Just not too keen on the execution of it. The stairs are pretty rickety."

As was the ladder he'd found. He'd tried to use it to climb out through the hole in the roof but there was nothing to brace it on, and he'd already nixed her idea of climbing it herself while he held it. Apparently, he didn't care for the possibility of her head being used for the shooter's target practice once she poked it up above ground level, and frankly, he'd convinced her it wasn't the brightest plan, either. Not that she thought it was okay for the reverse scenario where his head would be the vulnerable one, but she did admit that he had a bit more training at handling such a situation.

Regardless, it didn't matter. The ladder wasn't suitable for reaching the roof. Neither of them would get to play the part of the target.

So they were back to the locked-door strategy. Which she wasn't allowed to help with, given the state of her shoulder. Ace had pretty firmly insisted she sit tight and stay out of his way.

But when he didn't find a key, she could feel his frustration level climb.

He dusted off his hands as he dropped to the ground next to her, placing the lantern between their splayed legs. "Looks like I'll be trying to pry the door from the doorframe with the bolt cutter. Say a prayer that the force won't disengage whatever is holding the staircase to the wall."

"You don't have to try it, you know. We can hang out here a while longer. It's not going to kill anyone."

He shot her a look full of thinly concealed amusement. "Except you, you mean? I can tell you're dying to get back to the house so you can send a couple of emails."

"I am," she admitted readily with a smile that almost covered her grimace as she thought about the fun in store for her as she tried to work with a shoulder that had performed a rather impressive feat of slamming into concrete without shattering. "But not at the expense of you ending up in a pile of stair treads. Let it be for a while. Sit here and tell me a story to take my mind off how bad everything hurts."

That got his attention and not in a good way. "Everything hurts? Define *everything*. You swore up and down that your head felt fine."

"I don't have a concussion, Ace. Settle down. It was an expression."

He relaxed only slightly, his frame still vibrating with tension. Probably because she'd given him a challenge, then taken it away from him. Twice. She had a feeling he was still itching to have a crack at the doorframe, and he probably could very easily pry the wood from the wall, but the state of the stairs worried her and if they crumpled under his weight, he'd end up a lot worse for wear. Maybe even bleeding or unconscious. If anything happened to him, she'd never forgive herself for letting him get hurt on her account.

"You'll tell me if you start seeing double or feel any kind of pressure in your head, yes?"

She threw up three fingers and rolled her eyes. "You were a Scout, right?"

"Lucky guess," he told her, his mouth lifting up at the corners in a half smile.

"Please. No luck required. You have Boy Scout tattooed across your forehead. Tell me something about you I don't know."

The silence that fell weighed more than the dark. What? He didn't want to get personal? The whole point of her heading in this direction was to get his mind off trying to rescue her when really, she wanted to know more about the man behind the knife. Maybe she could ease him into it.

"Never mind," she said hastily as the silence started to sting a little. "I'll go first. Let's see. Once, when I was in college, I went on a date with Orien Bright."

His brow quirked up. "The rock star?"

"I was young and he hadn't made it big, yet. But yes. It was horrible." Plus, he hadn't adopted his stage name at that point, so to her, he'd always be Salvador Gonzales, the guy who lived next door to her best friend in a low-rent apartment on the wrong side of town.

"I wouldn't have pegged you for a rock star groupie."

"Trust me, it wasn't what you're thinking. We ate fast food and his car broke down on the way home. He was a hard-luck kid until he wasn't. I'm still not sure how he managed to get his career off the ground, let alone to go to become so famous."

"So that's the kind of guy college Sophia went for, huh? Flashy musicians."

He was teasing her. She didn't hate it. "He wore me down. Every time I saw him for a month, he was all, when are you letting me take you to dinner, SoLa? That was probably what did it. He was the only person in my life who had ever bothered to give me a nickname and it was kind of sweet."

Man, she hadn't thought about Salvador in ages, not since the first time she'd seen him on TV and realized it was him. The contrast between that skinny guy, the few other people she'd dated in college and the uber suits who would become her type once she started climbing the corporate ladder was stark.

Neither interested her now. No man had in a long time. Except this one.

"I confess, I'm not sure what you expected me to take from that story," Ace mused. "But I am intrigued at the idea of you being a rock star's girlfriend once upon a time."

She elbowed his arm without a lot of strength behind it, stunned at how much energy the scant movement had sapped. "We're getting to know each other. You obviously didn't want to go first, so…here we are. And he wasn't a rock star at the time. If he had been, I doubt he would have looked twice at me."

"Then he'd be missing out."

The admission hung there between them, and she caught his gaze, half-convinced he'd reel it back. But the vibe between them grew a few teeth and she wished she had a mirror for like five to ten seconds to at least make sure she didn't have a black eye or something from that fall.

"What?" she murmured as the moment stretched out and he still didn't look away. "Do I have something on my face?"

"A smudge of dirt. Near your eye." But as she lifted her hand to the presumed spot in question, he beat her to it, brushing his thumb across her cheek. "Let me."

Oh, she had zero problems with letting him do pretty

much anything he had a mind to. "Adult me is a lot different than college me. Especially this version. Ranch Sophia."

"What were you like before you were Ranch Sophia?"

Given that her cheek still tingled from his touch, she wasn't so sure she still had two brain cells to rub together, let alone enough to answer the question honestly. "I was Ad Exec Sophia, and you would have hated her."

His expression said he found that hard to believe. "I doubt you were too much different than you are now. Driven and competent with a side of wry humor. Right?"

"You make it sound like a compliment," she said with a laugh. "You're being too kind. It's okay if you call me out. It's more like stressed out and liable to make a bad joke to ease the tension and failing at all of the above."

"Don't diminish your accomplishments, Sophia," he told her quietly and there was something about the way he said her name that made her realize it was a deliberate choice to not come up with a cute nickname in that moment.

Because he wanted to differentiate himself from Salvador. As if he needed to. There was literally no contest in her mind between Ace Madden and every other man on the planet, even the ones she hadn't met yet.

The trick wasn't figuring out why she was so struck by him. It was trying to understand why they had such a strong dynamic that he didn't seem eager to explore. The boss-employee thing still stood between them, sure, but it felt like something they could work out, if they chose to.

"I'm not trying to be humble," she murmured, mesmerized by the way the lantern light played over his face. "That's how I operate. High achievers often see what they haven't done as opposed to what they have done. There's always something else to accomplish."

"The infamous to-do list."

She nodded, not so pleased all at once to be reminded of it. "It never gets shorter, only longer. And don't think for a minute that I'm not totally aware you're homing in on me to avoid your own true confession. It's your turn. Spill."

"What? You still want to hear something about me that you don't know? The list is vast. You'll have to be more specific."

It was like a wall came up between them the moment she shifted the focus back to him. Infuriating. What was the big deal? "It's a game, not rocket science. Pick anything. Your favorite color. The reason you went into the military. Why you sign your name with the little flourish at the end."

He eyed her. "How do you know I sign my name with a little flourish?"

A guilty flush crept through her cheeks, and she prayed the lantern light was dim enough to hide it. "I pulled your employment paperwork. I wasn't about to embark on a treasure hunt with someone I knew nothing about."

The reminder put a huge damper on the conversation. Also, she could have gone all night without mentioning she'd checked up on him. Great way to lighten the mood.

But he just nodded. "That was smart. That's what you should have done. You don't know me from Adam and it's only reasonable to take precautions."

Blinking, she stared at him. Somehow, confessing that she'd done her homework on him seemed to have raised her up in his estimation. "That's the whole point of this conversation. So I can get to know you. But maybe I already know everything I need to."

He glanced at her. "I doubt that."

"You're naturally authoritative without being overbearing. You're calm under pressure. Smart, but not like you could go three rounds on *Jeopardy* smart. Something totally beyond that, like you know how everything works and use that to solve every single problem you run across." She ticked the points off on her fingers, saving the most important for last. "I know you'd take a bullet for me. Every bit of that adds up to a guy who intrigues me."

Ace shut his eyes for a moment, squeezing them tight. "You shouldn't say things like that."

"Why not? It may have escaped your notice, so I'll spell it out for you. My father abandoned me when I was a teenager. I have a lot of issues with men who brush off responsibility. You're the opposite of that. Why is it so shocking that I would be attracted to you?"

Well, she couldn't have laid that on the line any more clearly. Obviously, the pain in her shoulder had caused her a bout of delirium or she'd never have been so forthright.

The admission saturated the atmosphere, sucking all the air from her lungs as she waited to see what he'd do with it.

"You want to hear something you don't know?" His voice scraped across her skin, unleashing a shiver, but she nodded. "I'm having a very hard time keeping my hands off you and you're not making it any easier."

"Good thing I don't want you to keep your hands off me," she murmured. "But I do disagree with you on one point. I can make it a lot easier."

She crawled into the space between them and kissed him.

Chapter 14

Ace had never been kissed before.

Sure, he'd participated in kisses. But he'd always been the one to initiate them. A hazard of being the tallest guy in the room. It wasn't often that a woman found herself in a position where she could lay one on him without a precursor.

Clearly, he'd deprived himself of something great by not orchestrating a scenario where a woman could take charge, because he became a huge fan as Sophia's mouth claimed his.

And that was the extent of his brain's ability to string a thought together. The kiss unfolded as she moved closer, still on her knees, still slightly above him and it didn't take much for her to set his skin on fire.

Man, was she a hot kisser. Sophia took no prisoners, and he frankly couldn't think of a better time to surrender to a woman. As if she'd sensed his hesitation fading, she shoved fingers through his hair, splaying them along his neck, urging him forward.

No more invitation needed than that. Ace touched her in kind, running the backs of his hands along her cheekbone, lifting her chin to slant his lips along hers at a deeper angle.

She tasted like sunshine and crisp fall days, and everything forbidden that he shouldn't want and couldn't stop himself from craving. Blood roaring through his veins, he lost himself in the sensations, funneling as much into this experience as he could before his conscience got wind of this.

And then it all crashed over him. *What* was he *doing*? This was not okay.

Wrenching himself free, he scuttled backward faster than a crab at high tide. "I'm sorry."

"I'm not." She tracked him with her gaze, disappointment filling her expression. "Don't you dare say you weren't into that kiss because I'll call you a liar."

Well, she should do that regardless. That would be the least of the nasty names she would be well within her rights to lob in his direction. But he wouldn't lie to her about this. "I wanted to kiss you or I wouldn't have."

"Buuuut…?" Her eyebrows winged up in invitation for him to finish the statement.

"You're tired, Sophia. Hurt. Scared. *Trapped*, most importantly. There are a lot of things swimming through your head right now that are impeding your judgment. I would rather shoot myself than take advantage of this situation."

"So this is you being noble. Noted."

The coolness in her tone said she didn't quite believe the things coming out of his mouth, which rankled since every word was 100 percent true. It just wasn't the whole truth. "I know you think you're making an informed decision about how you want things to go between us, but trust me, this is not the time to be jumping into something we can't take back."

"Wow, I really freaked you out, didn't I?" The wonder creeping over her face didn't help matters.

What was he supposed to do, contradict her? Tell her he wasn't so easy to spook, it was just that he drew a hard line at romancing a woman under false pretenses?

He tried again. "Sophia, I work for you. I'm trying to help you find a treasure your father may have buried on this ranch in some obscure location while keeping an unknown number of bad guys with nebulous agendas from killing you. The last thing you can afford is for me to be distracted. And that was already a pretty big issue before you kissed me."

Good God, could he sound like any more of a prissy coward? He could handle his job and Sophia too. If he was in any position to take control of this situation and put his hands on her the way he wanted to, she wouldn't be disappointed for very long.

But he couldn't.

Worse, his speech seemed to be sinking in. She nodded, a gleam in her eyes making him incredibly nervous.

"I get it. The timing is off. So we table it for now. But once we're out of this hole and back at the house, all bets are off," she said silkily.

Well. Not exactly what he'd been going for, but it was a far sight better than flat out rejecting her, which would only hurt her feelings and would probably sound a whole lot unconvincing anyway.

What had his life come to that he had to desperately grab onto the reprieve? "Yeah, that's so far in the future at this point that I'm pretty sure you're only going to want a hot shower and a bed by then."

"Ha, I want that now, but I definitely like the way you think. It's a date."

He stifled a groan and opted not to correct her deliberate misinterpretation of how many people would be in the shower and bed. Especially since that was all he could think about now that the idea was out there.

There was no scenario where he would even kiss her again before telling her the truth, let alone sleep with her. And if he told her the truth, he forfeited his fee. While she might be worth it to him, he had a payroll. Two other people's names sat next to his on the paperwork for his security company. Stephanie still had medical bills. The list of reasons he would not be getting naked with Sophia at any point in the future was long.

"How is your arm?" he asked gruffly, desperate to get out of his own head.

Sophia blinked at him. "As good as it can be under the circumstances, I guess."

At least she was apparently open to a subject change, a minor miracle. "That's good. Can we focus on the map for a minute or two? I'm still not sure why this place featured so prominently. Maybe whatever is hidden here is upstairs, but my money says it's down here."

Nodding, she got into the spirit, shifting slightly to pull her backpack into her lap with her left hand, and he didn't miss her wince. Yeah, she wasn't in any shape for activities of the intimate variety, which made it all the more important that he'd shut it down. As difficult as it had been.

She didn't have to know it was only one of many reasons.

Sophia spread the map on the ground near the lantern, her finger on the X. They'd been running through the woods with a shooter behind them. It was possible they might not be in the right spot and another building existed somewhere near here. But he didn't think so. There was no reason for a ranch owner to need two sheds of this variety. This one barely felt used in the first place.

Of course, that might have been by design. If David Lang had in fact hidden something here—or near here, since he didn't for a second believe anyone in their right mind would bury a treasure and then pour concrete on top of it—his father may have stopped using the shed for fear someone would discover the treasure.

That would mean they'd been in it together and he wasn't so sure that was a factor. More likely, the son had hidden the treasure and his father had found out about it after the fact.

Which didn't explain why the map had been squirreled away in a safety deposit box.

"You want to share what's going on in that head of yours?" Sophia suggested, resetting more comfortably on the floor. It might have been easier for her, but she'd leaned up against his shoulder and the contact sang through his entire body.

He'd love it if he had the latitude to sling an arm around her, letting her snuggle in. Her shoulder might feel better if she could take some weight off.

But he didn't move. Story of his life.

"I was just trying to piece together whether your grandfather knew your father had hidden something here and that's why the map was at the bank and not in his personal papers at home, or if he hadn't known about the map at all. The key was in an envelope, but you could tell that's what it was. Surely your grandfather knew about the safety deposit box. He had to have been paying for it or your grandma's friend wouldn't have readily known he had one."

Sophia shrugged. "He could have been paying for it

without knowing what was in it. Keep in mind, my dad wasn't super communicative. It wouldn't shock me to find out my dad had the only key and dropped it into my grandpa's files without telling him. You'd have to have a reason to search for it, like we did, to know it was there in the first place. I don't have a lot of answers for you. Sorry."

Unfortunately, he didn't have the luxury of letting any of this go. The sooner they put their time in this shelter to good use, the better. As much as he enjoyed spending this time with Sophia, playing get-to-know-you games and wishing he could start that kiss all over again weren't getting the job done.

And he still firmly believed the best way to protect Sophia was to find whatever the people after her were looking for. There was no way it was a coincidence that they'd found the key to the safety deposit box in the desk where Intruder Man had originally been searching.

"I'm going to look around some more," he told her and carefully eased out from under her lean, wishing he could find a pillow or something for her to use to lie down for a while.

For his second surveillance trip around the room, he snagged the lantern. The first time, he'd been forced to use Sophia's phone, which he left with her instead. The lantern cast a different, warmer glow and had a handle on top, allowing him to hold it up in the shadowy corners.

That was his only excuse for why he now saw the light switch that he'd previously missed.

Rolling his eyes at himself, he tried the switch. A purple light flicked on overhead. Instantly, the white part of his shirt began to glow.

"It's a black light," he called to Sophia.

What a weird thing to install in an underground shelter. Other naturally phosphorescent material glowed blue and green in the surrounding area, and he wished he knew more about what the colors meant, but his experience with black lights started and ended with using one to detect biological and chemical agents that signaled explosives.

"Ace," Sophia breathed. "Come look at this."

"What is it?"

"The map. It's glowing."

Hustling back over to her, he peered over her shoulder. "I don't see anything."

She shot him a look. "That's because you brought the lantern, dummy. Put it over there behind the stairs or something. Haven't you ever been to a blackout party?"

"This is my first one," he said wryly and did as she'd suggested. As soon as the light was hidden, another X with a circle around it appeared on the map in green ink.

But it wasn't here, it was another spot far from here. Of course.

"Guess we just figured out what's special about this shed," he said.

"This is where the treasure is buried," she said, excitement infusing her voice, the dirt across her forehead speckled with neon blue. "I know it. Look, here's the back fence, the one that borders Silver Acres Ranch. We have to dig here."

"As soon as I magic us a way out of this hole, you mean," he commented mildly. "You don't really think it's going to be that easy, do you?"

"Why not? We knew this map was something of note. Why else put it in the safety deposit box?"

Because nothing in life worked out like that. Nothing

was what it seemed, not even him. "Anyone could stumble over this shed. While it's out here a good ways, it's not invisible. No map needed."

"You'd have to know this shelter existed under the original shed to even use the black light to get the next clue," she argued in what was an excellent point. "The door to the underground part is locked. My grandfather probably has the key to the door on his key ring back at the house, but I would have never thought to bring it. There are a million keys on that ring."

But why go to all that trouble? Why have a map at all? Couldn't Sophia's father remember where he buried the treasure? All of the unanswered questions sat heavily with him, and he had to concede that his primary issue with this whole setup was that it felt like one. As if someone had deliberately planted these clues for them to find.

He might be leading Sophia into a slaughter if they followed this map. It had certainly been true when they pursued the trail the first time, landing them in their current predicament.

"We need to be careful," he said. "Do this next bit a little smarter than this round."

"Well, yes," she said with a twist of her lips. "I would prefer not to get trapped in a secret shelter next time."

That was the least of his concerns at the moment. Possibly they were safer down here than on the surface.

"What's the worst thing that can happen?" she continued, clearly excited about the possibilities. "We dig and find nothing. Or we dig and find something."

Sure, while making themselves stationary targets. But this was the whole reason he'd embarked on this mission, to find the treasure. He couldn't ignore the signs pointing to this being the ticket. It just felt off for reasons he couldn't put his finger on.

"Okay," he conceded. "It would be silly to have gone through all of this and then not follow through to the next set of coordinates."

Ace would have to figure out how to get a lot better at his job. His shoddy performance thus far left a lot to be desired, after all.

And that was the real reason he'd had to break off that kiss. What business did he have getting involved with a woman when the only thing he was really good at was sending terrorists off to meet their maker? None. When she found out what he was really like, under the surface where it really mattered, she'd feel a lot differently about that list of Ace's qualities.

Being calm under pressure was how you got good at killing people.

Chapter 15

A ranch dog's muzzle appeared over the edge of the hole in the roof shortly after dawn. Sophia glanced up at the scrabbling sound, never so happy in her whole life to see Jonas's face follow it.

"We're down here," she called, her voice shockingly weak.

It shouldn't have come as such a surprise given that she'd slept maybe two hours, and it felt like a demon slave driver stood behind her shoving hot pokers into her shoulder. Ace had suggested that she could sleep curled up in his arms, using his chest as her pillow, and in her delirium, she'd almost said yes.

But the first time she did that, she wanted it to be under different circumstances—because they were both enjoying being close to each other, not for survival purposes.

It would happen, she had no doubt. But first, she had to admit that Ace's point about a shower and a real bed did hold a lot of appeal, whether he planned to join her or not.

The hinges on the door were remarkably easy to remove from the other side and once their liberators pulled it off the frame, Ace carefully helped Sophia up the stairs. She hated that she needed his strength as much as she loved that he willingly gave it to her, his arm snug around her waist like he'd done it a million times and knew exactly where his hand fit.

Back above ground, it became clear that their disappearance had sparked quite the search effort. A group of cowboys stood off to the left, hands shoved in their pockets and faces eagerly turned toward the action.

The really interesting part was why anyone had thought to look for them. As many people as had seen Ace in Sophia's company, both in the house and out, it wouldn't have surprised her to learn everyone thought he'd whisked her away on a romantic overnight trip somewhere that wasn't here.

Frankly, that sounded fantastic. And completely ridiculous, given the amount of work she had to do to make up for nearly two days of treasure hunting and accomplishing zero ranch-owning tasks. She shouldn't be so thrilled at the idea of the staff gossiping about her and Ace, either.

"Thank you for rescuing us, Jonas," Sophia told him and got a head tip for her trouble.

In Jonas's world, it was practically a whole speech about how grateful he was to find her alive and mostly well.

Ace hustled her to the golf cart that someone had driven out to the shed and insisted she sit in the front, while he drove back to the house. The sun had just started peeking above the horizon, its orange glow lighting up the eastern sky.

"I'll have Jonas get a few of the guys to fix the hole in the roof of the shelter and reset that door," he said, and all she could do was slump in relief that he was taking charge. "Later today, I'll call someone to have a security system installed, the same as the one at the house. Without the map, the shed is useless to anyone looking for the treasure, but they don't know that."

She nodded, annoyed she hadn't thought of that herself. But that was the point of this partnership. She had to let him fill some of the gaps, especially when she didn't know what they were. Even if it sat funny to think of it like that. "If I haven't said this lately, I appreciate you."

He ducked his head, and it was adorable how tough it seemed for him to take her praise.

"Just doing my job."

Since they'd already been over that, she didn't remind him that his job description looked nothing like what he'd actually done over the last few days. She made a mental note to give him a raise. And maybe a promotion. Good grief, she should just flat out hire him to be her full-time bodyguard.

What rabbit hole had she fallen down that she needed one?

If she thought for a minute that she might be overreacting, she just called up the sound of a bullet exploding against the tree above her head, and that sent the notion right back into oblivion.

At the house, she let Ace satisfy himself that no one lurked in any of the shadowy corners, including the attic, and then watched him go back to the cowboys' quarters with reluctance. The alternative was to insist that she wasn't kidding about sharing that shower. Frankly, she didn't have the energy to deal with a hot cowboy anywhere near her bedroom, let alone a wet, unclothed one.

Plus, she'd have to admit that she didn't want to be alone and that felt like a precarious confession. Her emotions were all over the place and dang him for zeroing in on that, then doing the honorable thing by stepping away. She should take a lesson.

The shower went a long way toward making her feel human again, but nothing could be done about the dark area on her cheek. A gallon of concealer just made her look like she had a fake tan, so she wiped it all off and chalked it up to an easily explained war wound that no one would dare ask her about anyway.

Carefully, she tugged on a dress, wincing when she forgot for a second that she couldn't raise her arm above her head. Dressing herself took more effort than it should, and she had to catch her breath for a minute before getting started on her day. In that moment, she chose to keep the sling, despite being sure she'd ditch it today.

Panic started crowding into her head as all the undone things vied for attention. If she couldn't even get dressed without a break, how would she get through the rest of the day? How would she type? Not to mention the critical, exhausting task of tromping back into the woods at some indeterminate time to dig at the spot of the second X. Which would happen today regardless.

When she emerged from her room, Ace stood in the hallway. Waiting for her. Clearly.

Stetson back in place, he was leaned up against the wall, arms crossed, in a pose that she suspected had been totally natural for him to strike but made him look like the poster boy for a perfume commercial. Masculinity dripped from him, spilling into the hall, washing over her as his mouth tipped up in a smile that she felt to her toes.

Good Lord, the man was gorgeous.

Then his smile faded, and he unfolded from the wall, his attention on her face.

And suddenly, the hallway got a whole lot smaller as he reached out and brushed her cheek with his fingertips. "This is not okay."

"It's just a bruise. I'm fine."

Why did she sound so breathless? She'd just spent the night with the man. Granted, not in quite the fashion she'd fantasized about. But it still counted and should have gotten her *more* comfortable with him, not less.

It was him. He was too close. And not close enough. There was way too much space between them and her abused body that desperately wanted his warmth. Stupid. She could have indulged herself in that all night long if she'd accepted his offer to share his body heat.

Thank goodness she hadn't. Things needed to get back to business, pronto.

His stormy eyes met hers. "Your cheek looks a lot worse now that the sun is up."

"Thanks," she said wryly. "You do know how to turn a girl's head."

"Don't be ridiculous, Sophia. A bruise doesn't detract from the fact that you're the most beautiful woman I've ever met." He flicked his thumb down to her chin and lifted, his assessing gaze sweeping down her cheeks, its utilitarian nature not diminishing its power in the slightest. "I'm taking you to the doctor. Please don't argue."

"How did you know I was going to argue?" she countered, shocked her voice worked at all on the heels of learning Ace could sweep her off her feet with a few simple words.

That ghost of a smile flitted across his face again. "Because you have your phone in your hand and you were a millisecond away from opening your email. I know you have a lot to do, but this is nonnegotiable. We need to make sure you don't have a fractured cheekbone."

We. *We* need to make sure. He was aligning himself with her, making them into a unit, even post-shelter, when it didn't matter as much. What was she supposed to take from all of this? He was the one who had put the much-needed distance between them. She needed to keep it there.

"For your information, I checked my email before I got in the shower," she told him. "And I already sent two. Plus, I ordered wallpaper samples from a new place I found, and I scheduled an electrician to give me a quote on adding a generator. I can work and go to the doctor at the same time."

"Great, then it's a date," he said so mildly that she didn't for a second mistake it for a flirty comment. "Get your purse. I'll drive your car. It's more comfortable than my truck."

Walked into that one. "What if I don't want to go to the doctor?"

"Then we're going to find out how you'll take to being thrown over my shoulder and carted outside to be deposited in the passenger seat."

They stared at each other, and she gave in first. Though she absolutely wanted to find out if he would do it but had no desire to give that kind of show to the staff. "I'll go. But when he says I'm fine, you're going to owe me a whole day of being my lackey."

He lifted his brows. "I'm your lackey all day, every day."

"If I thought for a second that I was in charge, you'd strip me of that deluded idea immediately. Most likely with a scene exactly like this one."

"Whatever gets you in the car," he said and steered her toward the garage with a hand at the small of her back.

Why did this feel so comfortable? As if they'd done this dance a hundred times, even the part where they pushed each other to see what would happen. Was this what being married was like? For normal people anyway. She'd never seen a functional marriage up close and personal.

Maybe this was how other people did it. If so, she secretly liked the idea, especially if it meant being able to slide into a bed at the end of the day with Ace in it.

Good grief, what was wrong with her? Thinking about marriage to a man she'd literally just met and had kissed once. Even that had ended prematurely. As it should have.

She glanced at Ace in the driver's seat as he took off toward Gun Barrel City. Maybe when all of this was over, she could figure out a way to make it work. Ask him on a proper date. That would be lovely. She couldn't remember the last time she'd had a date with a guy she liked as much as this one. Actually, she couldn't remember the last time she'd had a date period. The shocking part was that she was considering breaking that streak instead of burying herself in work like she normally did.

Winding up on the business end of a gun did make a girl think. Reprioritize. What's the worst thing that could happen if she took a night off to do something for herself?

"Don't forget to tell the doctor to look at your arm too," Ace reminded her as they left the ranch property and turned right onto the road to town. He glanced at her. "What?"

"I never pegged you as a hoverer. It's sweet."

"It's not hovering. I need you functional ASAP so I can

feel better about forcing you to tromp through the woods later tonight."

Her stupid, traitorous insides danced the Macarena at the thought of spending another night in Ace's company, especially under the cover of dark. When ranch employees would be asleep and not paying attention to either of them. "Is that when we're going treasure hunting? Later tonight?"

He shrugged. "If you're available, yeah. Doing it during the daytime when we're a much bigger target feels like a risk after what happened last time. I don't like doing anything at night where it's more difficult to see a threat, but the reverse is also true."

"Makes it harder for the bad guys to see us too," she concluded. "That makes sense. The doctor is going to give me a thumbs-up. I feel fine."

That was almost true. After her shower, she did more closely resemble a human. The fact that she'd had to rest and questioned her ability to participate in future treasure hunting endeavors notwithstanding. He didn't have to know that.

"You got in the car," he said. "Obviously you recognize the wisdom in making sure."

More like she'd appreciated the excuse to spend a bit more time with him. He didn't have to know that, either.

Ace pulled into the lot of a small clinic near the bank. The waiting room was almost empty, save one tired-looking young mother with an active toddler who squirmed out of her grip four times before she gave up and let him roll around on the floor. After a few minutes, the nurse called the mom and kid to the back, then returned to call Sophia's name.

"You're not going to come with me and speak to the

doctor?" she asked Ace when he didn't stand up. Honestly, she'd expected him to.

"I do have faith in your ability to handle yourself," he countered mildly. "I'm just here to make sure you think so too."

She thought about that all the way to the examination room, where the nurse took her temperature and asked Sophia to step on the scale in the room. Which was where she learned she'd lost some weight since her last trip to the gynecologist. Maybe she'd skipped a few more meals than she'd realized in the midst of all the ranch renovations.

And perhaps Ace might want to retract his statement about her ability to handle everything. What was happening to her independence?

The doctor did an initial exam and asked her some questions about her pain level, then sent her down the hall to the radiology department where the technician scanned both her shoulder and cheek.

Forty-five minutes later, she waltzed back into the waiting room. Ace glanced up from his magazine, immediately tossing it aside in favor of sweeping her with his gaze. Even that little bit of eye contact put flutters in her belly. She was in so much trouble.

"No fractures," she told him and lifted her hands. "Now what are you going to obsess over?"

His quick grin warmed her considerably. "I'm sure you'll present me with something soon enough."

Once they were back in the car, she let the miles stretch out before she asked him, "Just out of curiosity, what were you waiting on me for? Earlier, outside my room. Because I know it wasn't to spirit me away to town."

"Strategy," he responded shortly, tapping his thumb on

the wheel. "As in we needed one, but I made an executive decision the second I saw your face. We'll dig at the second X after dark and make as little of a production out of it as we can."

She sank down in her seat a bit. "I'm a lot tougher than you seem to want to give me credit for."

"That's not the issue. I don't like the way it makes me feel to see you hurt."

The admission put a hum in her chest. "How does it make you feel?"

She shouldn't push the envelope like that, but she really wanted to hear the answer. Except the silence stretched in the car to the point of snapping. Obviously, he didn't want to explain. Because it made him feel things he didn't want to acknowledge? Things he'd already pushed aside due to bad timing?

But when he glanced at her, the storm clouds in his gaze had a lot more emotion in them than she would have expected.

"It makes me feel like breaking the person responsible in half. With my bare hands," he finally said. "I don't like it when violence is my first response."

Before she could figure out how to formulate a reply to that, he pulled onto ranch property. Across the field, she could see a red Mazda parked in the circular drive near the front porch.

Ace glanced at her. "Expecting company?"

"Not even a little bit." The car didn't seem familiar and had that generic look of a rental. "Maybe it's the decorator?"

"Stay in the car," he commanded her and threw it in Park, exiting so fast she didn't have a chance to argue.

She could have saved him the trouble as she spied the familiar dark-haired woman perched on the glider. Spilling from the car, she skirted Ace before he could pounce on Charli.

"Down, boy," she called back over her shoulder. "It's just my sister."

Chapter 16

Sophia threw her arms around Charli. And winced as pain knifed through her, praying Ace hadn't noticed. Stupid sling was supposed to prevent her from doing something dumb.

"What are you doing here?"

Her sister returned the hug enthusiastically, hitting the exact right spot on Sophia's shoulder to light her up. "I came to get in on all the fun."

Fun. Yeah, her sister's timing could be better. How in the world was Sophia going to manage treasure hunting with her sister visiting? "There's nothing but a lot of work at the moment. Maybe come back in a month when I'm closer to opening?"

Charli laughed, smoothing back her long, dark hair that never seemed to be scraggly the way Sophia's was, which was at least half the reason for the perpetual bun. "I'm really not expecting to be entertained. Maybe you could give me some of that work?"

A million things warred in Sophia's chest as she stared at her sister. The same one who had staunchly refused to participate in anything ranch related. The same one who was supposedly waiting around for the ranch to fail so she could collect her share of the profits when—if—Sophia was eventually forced to sell.

What had brought on Charli's change of heart?

"You want to help?" Sophia asked cautiously, in case none of this was what it sounded like. "You want to help. At the ranch. Where we are right now. This place."

Charli smirked. "Yes, the ranch. I…seem to be at a crossroads and figured you were the one person who might get that."

Boy, did she. Her heart softened. There was never a scenario where she'd have denied her sister a place to stay, a job, support, whatever she needed. But there was more to this story that needed to be spelled out before Sophia would blindly dump her sister in the middle of everything going on here at the ranch.

Charli's gaze slid past Sophia to the man standing behind her, interest clearly piqued. "You must be the hot cowboy I've heard so much about."

"Shut it, Charlotte," Sophia muttered, her skin going red hot with embarrassment.

Ace, who had most certainly heard every word of the exchange, stepped up onto the porch, hand extended. "Ace Madden. Definitely a cowboy, but I'm not touching the rest with a ten-foot pole."

"Charlotte Lang, but everyone calls me Charli on account of Charlotte being a horrible name, plus it's the same one as the spider in the book about the pig and the web." She eyed him curiously. "Got any friends?"

"He's my employee," Sophia cut in fiercely. "He has coworkers."

"He could have friends who are not employed here," Charli insisted.

Thankfully, Ace just seemed marginally amused by the whole scenario, tipping his hat to Charli. "I have both co-workers and friends, and if I think of any who would like-wise appreciate being labeled a hot cowboy, I will surely bring them by for an introduction."

With that cryptic comment, he vanished back to his real world, likely to seek out Jonas for an assignment. She missed him already. Inexplicably.

Charli's curious gaze had no place else to land except on Sophia. Which made her squirm for some reason. She was the older sister by three years. There was no reason she should feel both mortified and slightly guilty to have been caught in Ace's company.

"What?" she muttered. "He took me to the doctor."

"He took you to the doctor?" Charli repeated at a much higher decibel than necessary. "That is the coziest thing I've ever heard. When did it progress to the point where you're running errands together? I approve, by the way. He's everything you didn't tell me and more. And the way he charged up here, guns blazing, before you set him straight that I'm not a threat. Whoo, honey. Sizzling."

"You see this thing on my face?" She stabbed in the general direction of her cheek. "It's a bruise. I fell on a concrete slab yesterday. He drove me to the doctor strictly because he feels partially responsible."

Charli's face transformed into a scowl instantly as her body tensed to fly off the porch in the direction of the tem-porary barn. "How did he help your face meet a concrete slab? I swear to God if he touched you, he's going to re-gret the day he was—"

"Whoa, Char." Sophia threw up her hands as if that alone could temper the Valkyrie her sister had just become. "I love that you're ready to so fiercely defend me, but that's not what I meant. There are things going on around here that I need to talk to you about. Especially if you're staying for a few days. Come inside."

Once she'd gotten Charli off the porch and out of earshot of whoever might be strolling by, she led her sister to the kitchen, where she made them both a cup of tea. Sliding into a chair at the breakfast nook, the fatigue that she'd been fighting finally took over.

"Man, I needed this tea." Sophia moaned and shut her eyes for a blink, relaxing for the first time in forever. "How is it already noon?"

And more to the point, how would she make it until tonight without a nap? She wanted to be on point for the next round of treasure hunting. To be an equal partner to Ace.

Charli pulled out her own chair, whumped into it and picked up the second mug. "Start talking. Because I'm probably staying a little more than a few days."

Well, they'd see about that.

Sophia opened her eyes. "Then you should know that I got this bruise running from someone who was shooting at me. Ace was trying to protect me and pulled me around the side of an old building, I guess to use as a cover, and the ground gave way, dumping us into a secret underground shelter. With a concrete floor."

She threw up a hand near the bruise on her face, Vanna White style. Charli got the point, apparently, her brows drawing together.

"What in the world? Who was shooting at you?"

"Million-dollar question." Sophia filled her in on the rest—the treasure hunt, Intruder Man, the barn collapsing. Good gravy, saying it out loud made it sound much worse than it had in her head. "So you might want to think twice about sticking around."

"Are you kidding? You need me now more than ever." Charli sipped her tea and leaned back in her chair as if she'd landed exactly where she meant to be, despite never being the type to ride to Sophia's rescue in the past. "I had no clue any of this was going on. You should have told me."

Sophia had never been the type to tell her sister everything. So it was a little precious of Charli to act like they were buddies. Honestly, she was still a little miffed at both of her sisters for not wanting to go in on the ranch renovations with her. "I've been a little busy."

It felt like she'd been working with Ace on finding the treasure for a month straight, but in reality, it had only been a few days. Look what all had happened in just that short amount of time, though.

Now that she'd spelled out how dangerous it would be to stay, Charli should be making strides toward her rental car and driving away, very fast. Only she wasn't. It was time for a few questions of her own.

"What happened to your job at the…pet store?" It had been a minute since she could recall with absolute clarity what retail establishment her sister was working at this week.

Charli winced. "They wanted me to clean the bird cages and oh, my Lord, can those cockatiels poop like no one's business. I quit that job a few weeks ago. I've been waiting tables at Applebee's since then, but it's not my life's ambition or anything."

Must not comment, Sophia told herself sternly, biting back the multitudes of things she could say in reference to her sister's lackadaisical attitude toward gainful employment. Or worse, a comment about Charli's age, which wasn't nineteen, not that you'd know it to hear her talk.

The woman was almost thirty, for crying out loud. Sophia had gone to college and gained seven years of experience at her first career in that length of time, yet Charli acted like she had all the time in the world to figure out how to be a grown-up.

"So you came here looking for a purpose in life?" Sophia prompted hopefully. "I can give you a job but what I really need is for someone besides me to care about what happens to this ranch. Someone named Lang."

Charli sipped her tea and blinked as if contemplating. "I'm not going to lie. I have a lot of resentment toward dad and being here reminds me of him. He's the reason I can't have nice boys. I'm constantly attracted to losers who will abandon me at the drop of a hat because I have a thing for self-fulfilling prophecies."

"That's easy to fix," Sophia told her. "Stop dating. That's what I did."

But ironically not for the same reason. She'd never worried about someone abandoning her because she made sure to never give someone the chance. Just like she'd done with Ace. That was the root of her waffling with him, after all. As soon as she let herself ignore the fact that she was his boss, the real issue would come out—it didn't matter if he was the sticking sort. She didn't trust him enough to give him a chance to prove it either way.

Huh. It was a day for philosophical revelations apparently.

Oddly, sorting that out in her head gave her the will to concentrate the rest of the day as she tackled her most pressing tasks. Charli sat with her the whole time, dutifully learning the ins and outs of the operation at the ranch. Sophia still wasn't sure why her sister had shown up at the ranch in what amounted to a complete reversal on her initial refusal to set foot at the place. But she'd let herself be cautiously optimistic that this was a turning point.

"What are you calling it?" her sister asked at one point.

"Hidden Creek Ranch," she said and got goose bumps all over again. "I have a whole branding campaign planned around the logo, which will be everywhere, from the towels to the drinking glasses."

"This is going to be a real resort, isn't it?" Charli asked with a touch of wonder in her tone that Sophia tried not to find completely offensive.

"This is what I do," she said mildly. "Or I did when I worked for Teller. Now I'm doing it for me. And you, if you're in."

Charli shrugged. "I'm as in as I guess I can be at this point. I don't have anything else going on."

That was what Sophia would call about as half-hearted of a commitment as her sister could make and still call it a commitment.

"Great," she said without an ounce of irony. She deserved a cookie for it too. "The goal is to create a place that's inviting and luxurious, a place where people can relax and get back to nature."

Nodding, Charli pointed to the list of amenities the resort would offer. "I think I'd like to do something with the horses. Maybe that could be my area."

Biting her lip, Sophia counted to ten before she blurted out that Charli hadn't so much as climbed up into a saddle in almost twenty years. She honestly didn't remember her sister liking the horses that much the scant few times they'd visited as kids.

But things changed. Sophia had hated the ranch back then. She'd spent most of the time her parents forced her to visit wishing they could hurry up and go back home to Dallas. Maybe she could give her sister a break and stop trying to be a second mom.

"Sure," she said. "If that's what you see yourself doing."

And breathe. Don't mention that horses were the one area that didn't need a lick of direction from a Lang. That was Jonas's area, the main reason she'd hired him, so he could manage the livestock and the cowboys while Sophia did everything else. Which apparently would still be her lot.

"I figure we'd do daily trail rides," Sophia continued brightly. "You can think about being the coordinator and maybe lead them?"

"You know," Charli said thoughtfully, wheels turning as she glanced over the multipage document containing Sophia's painstaking plans for the ranch. "It's really curious to me that you didn't revamp the breeding program. That's what Grandpa did. Why turn this place into a resort in the first place? It's so much work."

Unclenching her teeth took more effort than she would have liked. "Because breeding was Grandpa's passion, not mine. And I want this to be something different. Something that's mine. Ours," she amended. "Wiping away what was here before might be cathartic. Don't you want to move on? Erase some of the bad memories?"

"Is that possible?" Charli asked with a sarcastic eye roll that nearly came with its own soundtrack. "Maybe you can forget that Dad was a piece of work and Grandpa was basically an enabler. It's a little tougher for me. I'm not the forgiving sort."

Well, Sophia wasn't, either. She'd carried a lot of resentment toward her father for years. But covering over the remnants of what had been here before would go a long way toward soothing her soul.

But that didn't mean it had happened yet. It was a good reminder. A cautionary tale. She wanted to find the treasure for many reasons, but getting something positive from her father remained the main one. Despite the danger. Despite the very nice bonus of spending time with Ace.

And maybe it would fill some gaps. Her childhood had sucked thanks to her dad, and to Charli's point, it had informed a lot more of her adult decisions than she'd credited. A good dose of anger flooded her heart, emotions she probably needed to feel. To work through, instead of repressing everything behind a facade of business and to-do lists.

"I haven't forgotten anything," Sophia muttered. "Once we find the treasure, then I'll think about everything else. Forgiveness wasn't my goal in all of this."

Charli perked up. "Can I help search for the treasure?"

That was one area she didn't mind playing a little closer to the vest. Since she hadn't mentioned the map yet, she kept that to herself and nodded. "Sure, you can work on the house. Check for secret panels, false floors, a safe behind a painting. That kind of thing. Ace and I are trying out another angle in the woods that we're planning to make some headway on tonight."

"Fantastic." Charli clapped like a little girl being presented with a pony for her birthday. "And I'm a huge fan of letting you do the outside part while I hang out in the place without bugs and snakes."

Yeah, that gelled with her sister's personality. And the second X on the map might only lead to another map or, worse, nothing, because the treasure had already been moved. There was nothing wrong with her sister working back through the house just in case.

It was also safer for Charli inside, where there were no people shooting at her.

Though it was a concern all at once to think of Charli being left alone while Sophia tromped through the woods with Ace. Ugh. Who was going to watch over her sister? Ace already had a full-time job with Sophia.

"Maybe if we find the treasure, we can just live here without turning the place into anything," Charli suggested, her allergy to hard work surfacing once again. "But in the meantime, I guess I'm going to need something else to do besides horses since we won't even have any guests for ages. What if I take over all the decorating?"

Relief spilled through Sophia so fast that she almost went light-headed. "That would be amazing."

Decorating—that was something Charli could do. It was dead in the center of her wheelhouse. And for the rest of the day, Sophia reveled in the fact that Charli had stepped up when she'd needed her.

Chapter 17

"We've got a problem," Ace said as soon as McKay picked up the call. "Grab Pierce and wrap up the research you've been doing. You're both about to become cowboys."

McKay didn't hesitate. "We can be there in four hours. What's the situation?"

That was why Ace had hand-selected Heath McKay and Paxton Pierce to go into the private security business with him. They were solid guys. Better than brothers. The best kind of family who had been through hell and everything else by his side.

"Get here and I'll explain once we're face-to-face."

It would be easier to do it once with both of the guys on his team in person, where they could get the lay of the land themselves. Strategize. Start filling the many gaps that had appeared like rogue bowling balls rolling through all of the pins Ace had set up, knocking his plans into oblivion.

The guys made it to the ranch in three hours.

Ace met them on the road, a mile past the turn-in to the main house, loathe to have a conversation where anyone could overhear them. Both men sat in the cab of an idling pickup truck with visible rust stains and a license plate presumably registered to some untraceable entity.

When Ace approached the driver's side door, McKay rolled the window down with a head tip, his mirrored sunglasses reflecting the light. "You sure this is out of the way enough? Two cars passed us already."

"We're about to add you to the ranch staff anyway. But in the meantime, we can have a conversation without extra ears. Thanks for getting here so fast," Ace said gruffly as a weight lifted off his shoulders instantly.

The three of them had history. There was nothing that could get through the united front of Madden, McKay and Pierce when they stood shoulder to shoulder against the evil of the world. They'd served together in Afghanistan, Iraq and Syria, ridding the world of the terrorist targets that had slithered into the cracks of those places.

When they'd gone into business as civilians, there'd never been any talk of who would be the boss. They were equal partners.

"It helped that you were so cryptic about why you needed us," Paxton Pierce called from the passenger seat. "Otherwise, we might have taken our time jetting to the middle of nowhere."

He and McKay were as different as the day was long. Both made Ace look short, a factor he appreciated after a few days of being the tallest guy around. But where Pierce was wiry with lean muscle and a clean look that he spent time meticulously maintaining, McKay was built like a bar brawler and shaved once a week if he remembered.

Pierce analyzed everything before he made a move; McKay never asked permission and never asked for forgiveness. Ace liked to think he balanced them, falling right in the middle of the extremes.

"That was your cue to start talking, amigo," McKay

prompted, smacking the perpetual stick of gum that had become as much of a habit as the cigarettes he'd given up ten years ago. "We found some good leads on David Lang, which we can continue following from here, pending the reason you pulled us in."

Well, that would have been handy if his teammates had managed to find Sophia's father. Hopefully they could still successfully track him down. If anyone could, it was these two.

"Things got messy, I'm not going to lie," Ace said and pushed his hat back on his head. "The main issue at the moment is the addition of a Lang sister to the mix."

McKay nodded once. "On it. I'm assuming incognito is still the name of the game?"

"It's a requirement." Ace lifted his hands, hating that the answer had to be yes. It was one thing to insert a single undercover operative on a ranch this size; it was another thing entirely to keep three people's professional status on the down-low. "Or we forfeit the fee. So far, I've managed to get Sophia to the point where she trusts me enough to keep a closer eye on her than I was expecting. I'm hoping you can do the same with Charlotte Lang."

McKay's brows rose above the rims of his sunglasses. "It's Sophia already, is it? Fast work."

"Shut up, McKay. It's not like that."

It was exactly like that, and he had a feeling McKay knew it. That was the one problem in working with guys who knew him as well as they knew themselves. They picked up on things you'd rather keep under wraps.

Like the driving need he constantly had to fight to pull Sophia into a corner and try that kiss again.

Pierce hooted. "Defensive much? Sounds like Ms. Lang

might be getting all sorts of preferential treatment, doesn't it, McKay?"

"That's what I heard." McKay grinned. "Maybe I'll try that same tack with the sister. Does she look like Sophia Lang? The other sisters weren't in the dossier."

"Because they weren't supposed to be here," Ace reminded them tautly, annoyed by the direction of the conversation, though why he'd thought his friends wouldn't pick up on his mixed bag of feelings for Sophia, he had no clue. "Charli Lang showed up this morning out of the blue and seems intent on staying awhile. Ergo, you're here for the duration. That's the bottom line. I can't protect two sisters at the same time."

"Is the other one planning to show up too?" Pierce asked, which was a perfectly legit question, but Ace had the distinct feeling he was thinking about staking his own claim on a Lang sister.

"This is not a singles bar," Ace said, channeling his inner calm. "Let's focus on the job."

Getting bent out of shape would only fuel their interest in why he was so bent out of shape over a simple thing like being attracted to an attractive woman. They'd all seen the pictures. He'd known going in that Sophia was easy on the eyes.

He just hadn't known how much he would want to look at her. How hard it would hit him to see that bruise on her face. How many pieces he would like to tear the person responsible into.

More importantly, he'd had no clue she would tie him up in so many knots, or that he'd continually have to remind himself that women like Sophia weren't made for men who had blood on their hands.

Yeah, he'd been talking to himself about focusing just as much as the guys.

"Can't do the job if we don't know all the complexities," McKay said mildly, his fingers drumming on the steering wheel.

Fair. "I don't know if Veronica Lang will become a factor or not. For the time being, Pierce, you're on bunkhouse duty. Slip into the ranks. Keep your ears open. We might be dealing with an infiltration and your job is to ferret that out."

Ace ran down the events of the last few days, and both McKay and Pierce sobered when he got to the part where an active shooter had chased him and Sophia through the woods.

"Assuming Charlotte sleeps occasionally, I can keep my ear to the ground too," McKay said, and Ace nodded.

"She goes by Charli in case that becomes relevant."

Hopefully, McKay wouldn't be introducing himself to Charli the same way Ace had been forced to make his presence known to Sophia—because someone had attacked her. McKay's job would be to prevent it in the first place, now that he was forewarned.

McKay's expression was unreadable. "Charli. Figures. I'll be saying Alpha Bravo in my head every time I look at her."

"As long as you're focused on the tangos, you can do that all you want," Ace said. "I still haven't figured out if the Langs are targets or potential collateral damage. The treasure is a huge draw for less savory types, sure, but how did whoever hired us know its existence would put Sophia and Charli at risk?"

"Do we know anything about the attackers? Same guy?"

Pierce asked, his big brain already whirring over the data. If anyone could uncover a connection, it would be Pierce.

"No idea," Ace admitted. "But if I was a betting man, I'd say, yeah. Or at the very least, it's two guys working together. That's the reason you're here. We need to know what we're dealing with to keep the Lang sisters safe."

The additional eyes on Ace's back helped too.

"We got it," McKay acknowledged, his body vibrating with tension over his lack of momentum. "Let's roll. We'll figure out more by wading into the thick of things than we will by standing around chatting about it."

"There are a lot of new people coming and going around the ranch," Ace cautioned them, appreciating the point about getting a move on, but determined not to send his teammates into battle any blinder than he had to. "A blessing and a curse. You'll be able to slide right into the routine without a lot of questions, but on the flip side, so can anyone else."

His friends nodded. They would be fine. Ace trusted them implicitly or he wouldn't be in business with them. But they'd never expected to be actively dropped into this assignment. It had been tapped as a one-man show from the beginning, and Ace was much more capable of blending than either McKay or Pierce. Hence his initial presence at the ranch, but his plan to lie low had been destroyed pretty much immediately.

This was plan B.

Pierce flipped open his laptop and worked through some last-minute additions to his and McKay's new fictional backgrounds, online presence and work history. Ace's time on the ranch proved to be useful, as he now knew exactly how the employment process worked. As in there wasn't

much to it. Guys showed up and were hired almost immediately, then put to work doing menial labor. The attrition
rate was horrible since most of the hands were drifters,
and more than a couple had legal entanglements they were
trying to avoid.

In short, the ranch was never not hiring.

Ace split from his friends and drove back to the ranch a
few minutes ahead of Pierce and McKay, feeling a lot better about the situation now that he wasn't going this alone.
The rest of the day, he kept close to the house, inventing
excuses to stay within sight of the back door, which left
the front exposed, a situation he didn't like but didn't have
an immediate fix for.

The two new ranch hands were incorporated immediately into the ranch's ecosystem, but in a stroke of bad
luck, McKay and Pierce were both put on perimeter duty,
a task everyone hated, so it was often given to the new
guys. Walking the fence line of a six-hundred-acre ranch
wasn't for the weak and that alone was often the cause of
Jonas shedding personnel.

Ace suspected he did it on purpose. It did weed out those
who couldn't hack it in the physical realm of a working
ranch. Two guys who had survived BUD/S training and
multiple brutal deployments to places where the temperature often topped 120 degrees would eat a six-hundred-
acre walk for breakfast.

But it did put them out of sight of the house, a major
issue. He'd have to figure out how to get Sophia to reas-
sign them without stepping on Jonas's toes. And without
her catching a clue as to why he'd tried to finagle it.

Undercover security was not a picnic, that was for sure.

Later that night, McKay and Pierce finally back at

the bunkhouse pretending to be strung out after a day of fence duty, Ace slipped out to meet Sophia as arranged. He palmed his phone to text her as soon as he hit the circular drive in front of the house, then faded into the shadows in case any curious onlookers strolled by.

Me: Outside in the front

Limpet: Be right there

Her text message even sounded like her voice in his head, slightly breathless, a lot of warmth and laced with something he couldn't describe. It made him think about sunny days with blue skies and little puffy white clouds.

Maybe he should change her name from Limpet to Unicorn. Because she was one. The only woman who had ever kissed him. The only one he'd ever taken to the doctor or gone to the bank with. Granted, neither were banal errands they'd done together because they were a couple, but it was far too easy to forget that.

Well, if he wanted to be honest, he'd done all those things with Stephanie. Especially the doctor appointments. But she was his sister and that didn't count. What did count were the bills from those doctors, not the way Sophia made him feel.

Except when she exited the house and paused on the wide wraparound porch, light from the moon spilled over her in a silvery river, and she was so beautiful that his chest got tight.

Why did she have to be so supremely off-limits?

And he wasn't so far gone that he didn't recognize that might be part of the appeal. He'd long ago accepted that he thrived on challenges. He was built for them. It was what had led him to such an elite branch of the military and drove him into private security.

Of course, he also just really, really liked her.

Sophia peered into the dark, clearly looking for him. He didn't reveal himself right away, grateful for these scant few seconds when he could enjoy watching her without all of the other stuff weighing down the moment.

But she instinctively veered in his direction, apparently as drawn to him as he was to her. That was the only explanation for how she sensed where to find him. If he knew anything, it was how to vanish in hostile territory. You got good, or you died.

"Hey," he called softly as she approached, gratified when she lit up. She made him feel like that too.

"I was starting to think it was never going to be time," she groused good-naturedly.

"Yeah, I was pretty antsy to get to digging too," he admitted.

She stared at him for a long moment, her smile enigmatic. "I meant because I wanted to see you. But yeah, treasure hunting. That's a thing too."

"You shouldn't say stuff like that," he muttered as his stupid, greedy heart latched onto her sentiment and soared.

"Why not? We're not in the shelter any longer. That was your rule. Here we are, not trapped, and if I want to tell you I've had a hard time thinking about anything other than kissing you again, I am one hundred percent going to."

One hundred percent going to kiss him? Or tell him about how much she wanted to kiss him? He couldn't stop his mouth from curving up in pleasure regardless of which one it was, because they both sounded pretty good to his Sophia-starved soul.

This on the heels of vowing not to act on the swirling attraction between them. This woman was like a magnet, drawing him closer, even as he ordered himself to step back.

"We should be focusing on the treasure," he told her gruffly, shoving his hands in his pockets instead of reaching for her. All ten fingers tensed, curling into his palms, tingling with the effort.

"More bad timing?" she said with a frustrated laugh.

The worst. If he'd met her ten years ago, before he had so much blood on his hands, maybe then he could justify touching her. Even meeting her before going undercover might have worked. At least then he'd know he was being honest with her. He'd be able to give her a choice with all the facts.

But today? None of that was true.

"I need to concentrate on our surroundings, Sophia," he said, his hands on her upper arms before he'd scarcely registered pulling them free of his pockets. But he didn't remove them, soaking in the feel of her under his fingers like a blind man inhaling a book via Braille.

Man, he was in so much trouble here. McKay had sniffed it out instantly. Ace would do well to remember that he might be good at vanishing in the dark—specifically when Sophia wasn't around—but he was not good at keeping his emotions hidden.

And he didn't want to lead Sophia down the wrong path, the one that gave her hope for anything intimate springing up between them.

"I need to focus," he continued roughly, his voice carrying all the angst behind his breastbone at not being able to crush her into his embrace and lead her right back inside the house where they could be alone for hours. "We're already a target. Don't think for a minute that we're not being watched twenty-four/seven."

She stared at him, something a little bit dangerous swirling through the air between them. "I'm sorry I'm distracting you. I'll stop. I know you're worried about keeping me safe."

Good, she got it. Why did it feel like he'd been kicked in the stomach?

Chapter 18

Ace had been wafting back-off vibes in Sophia's direction since she'd found him in the shadows of the house earlier. But all of that dissolved when a rat scurried across her foot, and she inhaled sharply. Ace took her hand and held it firmly in his capable grip.

She wished he'd take a lot more than that. But his ultra-calm, ultra-in-control presence soothed her nerves, which had flared to life right around the time he'd earnestly told her to stop talking about kissing so he could make sure they weren't going to die out here in the woods.

It was a sobering reminder. And did nothing to diminish all the squishy things happening in her heart.

What a weird, wonderful thing to be constantly reminded that she wasn't alone.

Ace was here. He'd stand by her no matter what, even if someone started shooting at them. With real bullets. He wouldn't flee like a big coward, leaving her to face the threats alone the way her father had.

Sure, Charli had unearthed a lot of stuff Sophia had repressed, like how hard it was to trust men. How easily Sophia shed them usually, never giving any of them a chance to disappoint her. She'd let Ace into her life because she'd had no choice, but he'd passed all the tests with flying colors and then some.

His hand surrounded hers, a tactile reminder that they were in this together. She liked it. Probably far too much given the circumstances.

Ace threw a glance at her over his shoulder, the finger on his free hand to his lips in the universal *shh* sign. Duh. She hadn't made a peep in at least five minutes, despite the uneven terrain.

They'd circled through the woods past the perimeter fence that separated Hidden Creek Ranch from Silver Acres next door. It had been Sophia's idea and she was very sorry she'd opened her mouth. What didn't seem that far during the day turned into a huge slog in the dark.

She knew better than to even think the word *flashlight*, so they were picking their way through the woods at a snail's pace because while Ace moved like a cheetah through the brush, she could only describe herself as bovine at this point. A big clumsy cow who could draw a bad guy's attention in nothing flat by stepping on every fallen tree branch in existence.

Ace didn't seem to notice, though, carefully helping her over ruts in the ground that he'd somehow seen with his catlike night vision. Her contacts did a lot of things to correct her vision but helping her see in the dark was not one of them. Apparently, this was yet another aspect of Ace's impressive capabilities.

If she mentioned it though, he'd shrug it off like he wasn't anything special. After a decade of exposure to suits with inflated egos, she found Ace's humbleness one of his most attractive qualities.

An eternity later, Ace halted at the edge of a copse of

trees, just shy of stepping out into the wide-open field to their left. It felt like it should be the north pasture, one of the ones Jonas used in rotation to let the horses graze. None of the animals seemed to be in residence at the moment, so they were either in another pasture or she'd gotten completely turned around in their double-back trek through the neighbor's property.

Ace positioned her behind a tree, then held up his finger in the universal "wait here" sign. Then without warning, he vanished back into the woods, leaving her extremely alone.

Black swam through her vision, growing darker the longer he was gone. The forest nearly disappeared, swallowed by the inky night. Had to be a trick of the mind. As in, being terrified sucked light molecules out of existence. Had they done studies on this? Because it felt like a PhD subject any psychologist would be interested in.

Ace materialized at her back. Thank God.

She would recognize him anywhere, even without turning around. It helped that he'd crowded up against her, his heat setting her on fire from head to toe. The darkness switched from foe to friend instantly, binding them together in an intimacy that shouldn't feel so right.

"We weren't followed," he murmured into her ear, and she let her head fall back instinctively, her chin raised in his direction, seeking more contact from his lips, which were right there within reach.

It would have been so easy for him to wrap his arms around her, snuggling her back into his hard body. Why didn't he? She could scarcely breathe she was so aware of him. Surely, he felt it too. Especially since he hadn't stepped back after delivering the message, almost as if he'd struck this pose incidentally and liked it so much, he'd opted to stay.

Well, she liked it too. But had ideas on how it could be better.

She spun, her arms sliding effortlessly underneath his, and for one glorious moment, he engulfed her in the embrace she so desperately needed. Torso to torso, his cheek nuzzling hers in an almost kiss that she felt more deeply than a real one.

"No bad guys," she murmured. "No focus on our surroundings needed."

This time, he didn't wait for her to make the move. His mouth descended on hers hungrily, as if he'd been waiting for the gate to be lifted and once it was, the entire force of his essence sprang to life, driving forward. Into her.

Oh, dear Lord. The man was devouring her whole. Her bones turned to butter, and she wondered how she was still standing. But his sexy, sexy hands splayed across her back, and that was one mystery solved—he was holding her up. Supporting her. Keeping her in place against him in a delicious embrace that righted her topsy world in one swoop.

Then pulled the rug out from under her again as he deepened the kiss to impossible levels. A moan escaped her throat as she got lost in the sensations, the swirl of Ace that swamped her senses. It was more than a kiss, more than an expression of attraction. It was survival. Air in her lungs, blood in her veins, a song in her soul—none of which would exist without this man.

Suddenly, the music stopped. He shook his head and backed up, taking all of that lovely support with him, and she stumbled, a rag doll without anything inside but cotton candy stuffing.

"Don't you dare apologize again," she told him. "We're adults who make our own choices. Own that one."

He nodded once. "I don't seem to have a lot of self-control around you. It feels like a weakness."

Oh, man. That was not the confession she'd been expecting. He was pretty torn up over it too. She swallowed back her retort, choosing to savor the idea that she could make a guy like Ace lose control. He of the legendary calm, who seemed so unflappable. She did that to him.

Preening a little, she smiled. "I'll try to refrain from being so kissable, then."

"It would be appreciated," he said wryly. "Otherwise, we're never going to find this treasure. Plus, it's possible we might attract attention with the goings-on out here. Just because we're alone now doesn't mean it's going to stay that way. So keep your eyes and ears open."

Great. Now all the heat from that kiss had faded in the face of being totally aware of the hostility of their surroundings. Who hid stuff in the woods when there was a perfectly fine house with walls and an attic? David Lang. The worst father and treasure hunter on the planet.

Though if he had found a valuable Maya cache of gold, she'd have to amend the terrible treasure hunter part, which had been the modifier next to her father's name in her mind for almost twenty years.

Ace pointed up. "Earlier today, I hid a bunch of tools in a tree so we wouldn't have to carry them out here in the dark."

So that's what he'd meant when he texted her that he was taking care of supplies. Bless the man. He thought of everything. There might be swooning in her future.

In no time flat, Ace shimmied up the correct tree, no

confusion on his part despite the woods being dark. And scary. He found a solid perch and carefully handed down two spade-shaped shovels with long handles, and she didn't drop either one. Next came a pickax, then a long thin metal bar, a regular ax and finally a saw.

When Ace hit the ground, she held it up in question.

"In case of roots," he explained. "Sometimes you can't cut them easily with an ax."

"Uh, how many treasures have you dug up in your life?" she asked, awed that he seemed fully prepared for everything under the sun—or the moon, as the case may be—while she'd scarcely been able to select the right shoes for the occasion.

He laughed. "None. But I've done a lot of other things in my life that required me to understand what I was about to get into, so I researched what kind of soil to expect in East Texas, especially in a wooded area. The answer is roots. Lots of them. And probably some limestone, though my bet is that your father found a new spot if he hit limestone in his original hole. We'll see."

Dazed and maybe a tiny bit in love with Ace at this point, she followed him to the spot on the map. They'd only seen it under the black light, but he'd memorized the location. She'd argued they should mark the map with visible ink, an idea that was quickly shot down when he'd pointed out that anyone could steal the map, allowing their hard-won information to fall into the wrong hands.

So she'd had to trust that they both remembered the spot correctly.

When Ace was satisfied that they'd found the best place to start digging—reminding her that they didn't know how far down they'd have to go or how big of a hole they needed—he pointed her to an area a couple of feet away.

Careful not to put too much heft on her shoulder, Sophia drove the pointy part of the spade shovel into the ground, expecting it to go at least the entire length of the blade. Instead, momentum nearly knocked her off her feet when the tip barely pierced the ground more than an inch.

Blinking, she glanced at Ace and noted he was stepping on the rolled metal piece at the top of the spade. She tried that and got the shovel into the ground a whole inch more.

This sucked. Digging was a lot harder than she'd anticipated. Especially since she was favoring her shoulder. Not that she'd have had that much more oomph behind her strength if she wasn't. Ace made it look easy, just like he did with everything else.

How big of a wimp was she for not being able to pull her weight?

Resolute, she dug in, pulling some will from somewhere inside that she'd like to say gave her superhuman strength, but really only gave her enough gusto to get the spade into the ground another inch.

"Maybe I should stick to balance sheets," she muttered, drawing Ace's attention from the two-foot-by-two-foot-wide hole already formed beneath his shovel as he scooped out another mound of dirt.

He wasn't even breathing hard.

"If that's where you think your skills lie," he said, pausing to lean on his shovel as he spoke to her. "Then sure. I can dig and you can watch for Intruder Man. But if you want to dig together, you'll figure it out. I have faith in you. You're doing great."

Her heart gobbled up the sentiment, storing it away in

a place that she had no idea any man could reach. Dang it. She couldn't fail him now. Or herself.

She levered the shovel back into the ground for another shot, annoyed enough at her weakness to try again. This time, she jumped on the rolled metal pieces with both feet, driving the spade into the ground halfway this time.

Yes! She repeated the motion, jumping harder. The metal part disappeared into the dirt completely, but then she couldn't scoop the dirt out until she tried stepping on the handle, using the hard-packed earth at the lip of her brand-new hole as the fulcrum.

A big mound of dirt broke free. Sure, she almost face-planted in the middle of it when she didn't compensate for the sudden difference in force, but she didn't care. There was a hole now, barely discernible in the moonlight, but she'd taken a chunk of soil out of the ground all by herself.

"Take that, Texas," she said and kicked the dirt away from her hole.

Amused, Ace grinned. "You did good, Soph. Now do it again."

There was the nickname. Perfectly timed. So much better than SoLa, and the secret thrill over it did a number on her insides, opening the floodgates, allowing Ace to spill into every nook and cranny.

"Yeah, yeah," she groused good-naturedly.

Her shoulder sang with the next round, but she ground her teeth together and got another scoop of dirt out of the hole. Eventually, she had a hole one-tenth the size of Ace's, but it was still a hole, and she was still proud of it.

Without Ace there to encourage her, she might have quit. And he'd apparently be fine with that, based on his comment. That was the great part. He didn't see it as a shortcoming that she'd been clueless at first, but then had given her exactly what she'd needed to rise to the occasion.

She was so in over her head with him. Maybe she should just go ahead and admit she was falling for him. To herself only. Not to him. That would be ridiculous.

All at once, Ace froze. She glanced up at him. The look on his face put her pulse on overdrive.

"What?" she whispered. "Do you see someone coming? Are we in danger?"

"No," he murmured, his gaze catching hers. "Look."

She followed his line of sight to his shovel and watched as he spilled the dirt to the ground in a slow shower. A glint of gold fell along with the dark specks, moonlight reflecting off the flat surface.

A coin. She reached down to pluck it from the dirt, brushing it off.

"It's stamped with zigzag designs like the one in the magazine article," she breathed, awed at the possibilities of what she held in her hand. It was heavier than she would have expected, larger. Twice as big as a silver dollar. "A second coin. How many more are buried here?"

Chapter 19

Enthused and inspired by the find, Ace and Sophia threw themselves into digging, but an hour later, they'd found nothing else. He wasn't shocked.

Sophia was.

"I don't understand," she said, her hands on her hips, her voice low in deference to the fact that she had a coin potentially worth $25,000 in her pocket. "Why bury one coin? The effort alone is staggering, plus it doesn't make a lick of sense."

Ace shrugged. "There are a hundred reasons to bury one coin. Maybe that was all he had left. Maybe he split up the treasure on purpose in case someone came looking for it. Maybe your father isn't the one who buried it."

"You think my grandpa found more than one?" she mused.

"It's possible."

But he didn't think so. His current theory was that it had been left behind accidentally when David Lang moved the treasure, but he didn't want to say so. It might come across as his believing in a boneheaded mistake on the part of her father.

It was just as good a theory as any of the others. Because

he agreed with Sophia. It didn't make any sense, despite the plethora of reasons he could come up with.

Besides, Sophia was flagging. She wouldn't say a word, but Ace could tell. It was time to go. Her shoulder was bothering her, and they'd already pushed the limit of the amount of time he felt comfortable out here in the dark woods. McKay and Pierce were keeping watch a couple hundred yards away, both with one finger on the trigger of their long-range rifles with night-vision scopes, so he wasn't the slightest bit worried about being surprised.

But that didn't mean he wanted to answer questions about why the two new ranch hands were such good shots. Or why they were in the woods in the first place with not-quite-civilian-issue firearms. The longer they stayed here, the greater the odds he'd be doing both.

"There's nothing else here to find," he finally conceded and dropped his shovel on top of the one Sophia had already discarded. "I was hoping for at least another map or some sort of indicator of what to do next."

"It's fine," she said morosely, and he could tell she was disappointed they hadn't found the mother lode.

"Let's get back to the house and figure this out."

She nodded and let him lead her back the way they came. Pierce and McKay melted into the shadows behind them, following at a distance the way they'd done during the first trek into the woods. If they'd been any closer when he'd returned to where he'd left Sophia after getting them into position, he'd never have kissed her like that.

Actually, he shouldn't have done that in the first place. But her point about not needing to focus on keeping her alive right at that moment had been so inspired, he couldn't help himself.

Who was he kidding? He couldn't help himself regardless. She was iron to his magnet. He couldn't resist being drawn to her even if he wanted to. She made him feel like a million dollars, like he might actually be worth something. What he was going to do about it, that was the question.

Tell her the truth.

That was a given. He just couldn't quite figure out when he could do that and not have to forfeit his fee. If the danger to the Lang sisters passed, then he could reasonably say the job was over. But how would he know they were no longer in danger?

It was a maddening circle he couldn't seem to break out of.

At the house, Sophia insisted that he come inside instead of making themselves targets on the porch. Since he couldn't very well tell her that nothing would touch her when the rest of his team stood watch, he nodded and signaled over his shoulder with two fingers, first to the east, and second to the west. McKay and Pierce would get it and move into position as directed.

Yeah, he was breathing a lot easier with backup in place.

Wearily, Sophia sank into the armchair in the living room, the closest room to the front door. He had the feeling she might not have made it much past that.

Tamping down a host of reasons he shouldn't, he crossed the room to stand behind her, sliding his hands along her shoulders to begin kneading them, careful to stay away from the strained area that she'd fallen on.

"Oh, dear Lord that feels heavenly," she moaned, the sound vibrating through his gut.

Add that to the list of reasons he shouldn't have his hands on her. Because he instantly wanted to know what else he could do to make Sophia feel good if that little trill inside would be his reward.

Back off, champ.

Not shockingly, nothing south of his brain listened to that little voice, nor did he lift his hands from her neck.

Ace cleared his throat. "What do you want to do with the coin?"

"Take it to the bank," she said without hesitation. "Though I have a feeling there will be several historical societies that will want to study it or something."

"Maybe that's our best bet," he mused. "We should get it authenticated first. It might not even be real."

She glanced back over her shoulder and then immediately snapped her head forward as if afraid he might stop. No danger of that. This was the most fun he'd had since he'd kissed her at the edge of the forest, which he should regret but didn't.

"Do you think that's the reason why there was only one? It's a forgery?"

"Honestly, I have long stopped trying to form an opinion about this treasure business," he said simply. "My job is to stand between you and whoever is trying to beat you to finding it. You're the brains *and* the beauty of this partnership."

Her quick smile warmed him dangerously fast, and she hadn't even aimed it in his direction.

"I beg to differ. You're the one who brought the tools. You're the one who found the key to the safety deposit box. And you obviously haven't looked in a mirror lately if you think I'm the attractive one here."

The compliment pleased him more than it should. She wasn't the only woman who had ever commented on his looks, but she was definitely the first one to affect him this way. As if she'd reached inside and taken pieces of him each time they were together.

"I guess we'll just be two attractive people trying to solve the mystery of this treasure before someone else does," he told her, which made her laugh for some reason.

Another thing about her he appreciated. She didn't whine about things or complain that something hurt or that she was tired. If anything, she bucked up and forged ahead, no matter what, which made them more alike than he'd have guessed.

She kept doing unexpected things that made him happy to be around her. Like laughing when he mentioned the danger that she was in.

Though, he'd started to wonder if Intruder Man and his friends cared anything about Sophia. They were likely here for the treasure, not her.

"We'll authenticate the coin first," she decided. "That's a good call. We need to know what we're dealing with first."

He moved his hands to the top of her head, gently massaging her temples. "Sure thing, boss."

"How are you so good at that?" she groaned, her eyelids fluttering closed. "I barely even have a headache anymore."

After a beat, he decided it couldn't hurt to be honest. "My sister gets headaches. She's sick a lot. She has something called fibromyalgia."

Sophia went quiet. "I'm sorry. That sounds awful."

It was awful. Painful for him to watch and even worse for Stephanie to go through. The doctors did what they could to help her manage pain and other symptoms, which was why Ace had learned everything he could about massage since his sister's insurance didn't cover it as a medical necessity.

"Is that why you left the military?" she asked.

That was the other reason he couldn't stop thinking about Sophia—she picked up on things other people didn't. "Yeah. I needed to be closer to her and also have a reasonable guarantee of staying alive."

"This is what you call irony," she said with a wry twist of her lips that made him smile in kind. "You should think about moving to another ranch instead of staying at this one and getting shot at. Your sister is more important than my father's legacy of terrible treasure maps and coins of questionable value."

If he was strictly a cowboy—and a coward—another job might be wise, but since he was neither, he made a noise in his throat. "Then who would you fall into a secret shelter with? You'd have no one to harass you into going to the doctor. That would never do."

"I'm serious." She punctuated that by sliding out from under his hands and turning to face him. "This place is dangerous, and you've got someone counting on you."

The fact that Sophia didn't put herself in that category sat funny with him. He should be agreeing with her. Nodding and saying yes, Stephanie was important and had no one else to take care of her.

But he liked being Sophia's hero too. More than he should. More than was expressly necessary to keep doing his job. And that was his real problem.

This was a job. And he'd been skating a line that was at best unprofessional and, at worst, an opportunity to lose his sole source of income.

"I appreciate the sentiment," he told her, his hands hanging uselessly at his sides now that she'd unceremoniously ended the massage session that had been his sole excuse to touch her. "But I'm not going anywhere."

Relief spilled through Sophia's face. "Am I a terrible person for being so happy you said that?"

"No. You're human and terrified because someone has been trying to kill you. My sister will be okay. I hired a nurse who goes by several days a week. I'm exactly where I want to be."

She stared up at him, the vibe between them growing taut and full of emotion that he hadn't meant to put into play, but he couldn't call it back when it was the truth.

"Maybe you should think about going into the body-guard business, then," she murmured. "It would probably pay better than wrangling horses."

Struck all at once at the truth of that—and the fact that he couldn't flat out tell her that she wasn't far off—he scrubbed the back of his neck, at a loss for how to fix this impossible situation of his own making.

"Maybe, but in the meantime, I work for you, and you have a coin that needs to be authenticated. Make some calls, figure out where you want to take it and I'll be ready to go whenever you tell me to get in the car."

She smiled. "I guess it's a given that you're going with me, huh."

It wasn't a question, and he didn't treat it like one. "I'm driving. Don't argue."

The team from the University of Texas's Mesoamerica Center came to them. Dr. Allen, a woman in her late fifties, drove up from Austin within a few hours of receiving Sophia's call. She'd managed to stuff a couple of her colleagues into her hatchback at a moment's notice, apparently, all three of the academics eager to be involved in authenticating Sophia's coin.

Ace hung around at the back of the room, eager to do nothing except stay out of the way and keep an eagle eye on the newcomers. It wasn't that he didn't trust anyone... but these people certainly hadn't earned a lick of his allegiance yet.

Dr. King, a slender man who couldn't stop oohing and aahing over the coin, sat at the kitchen table where he'd decreed the best light in the house to be. He'd parked there the second he'd introduced himself as a numismatist who specialized in ancient coins.

As soon as Ace was sure no one was paying attention to him, he surreptitiously googled *numismatist*, finally spelling it close enough on his third try to get the meaning. It was a coin expert. Why the guy couldn't say that was beyond him.

The other woman, an anthropologist named Dr. Fuentes, who had yet to say a word but had taken approximately 47,000 pictures and texted someone back at the university every single one, stood behind Dr. King. Her sharp gaze missed nothing.

Sophia sat next to Dr. King, leaning toward him occasionally to answer questions as the team asked them. No, she didn't know where the coin had come from. Yes, she was aware that her grandfather had found one, which she learned from Dr. King had been sold to a private collector. Unfortunately, her grandfather had not involved anyone with an interest in the history prior to the sale, so no one at the university had gotten a chance to see it.

"This is exquisite," Dr. King said for the fourth time as he held the coin under a magnifying glass.

He'd donned two pairs of gloves prior to picking it up. Apparently touching it with bare hands was a rookie mistake that he and Sophia had both been taken to task for.

Ace had bitten back a comment about the coin being buried in the ground for probably going on ten years. If that hadn't damaged it, a few fingerprints wouldn't, either. But this was Sophia's show, not his.

"Does that mean it's real?" Sophia asked, her gaze hopeful.

"I'm 99 percent certain," Dr. King said with a nod as he carefully set the coin on a digital scale. "The weight is consistent with what I would expect for a piece of gold this size. I'd like to test the metal composition more thoroughly in a lab, but visually, the color is good. I've assessed a lot of coins in my day, so my eye is pretty well trained."

Dr. Allen pointed with a long, thin piece of plastic, indicating an area of the design. "These markings are commonly found carved into the stones comprising the stepped pyramid of Pakal the Great's tomb in Chiapas. It's a symbol of the Temple of Inscriptions."

"That's fascinating," Sophia breathed. "So this coin came from there?"

"Well, we're not sure," Dr. Allen hedged. "The tomb was looted by the Conquistadors in the sixteenth century and we know they took some artifacts, the coin most likely included. I am not as well versed in Pakal's history as I would like to be able to say for sure. We need to bring in some other teams, particularly one from the National Museum of Anthropology in Mexico City. There are a couple of experts there who can help us trace this coin so we can understand its journey over the last eleven hundred years."

Sophia gasped. "It's that old?"

"Oh, yes, at least. Pakal lived during the Late Classic Period of Maya civilization, which lasted from about 600 to 900 CE," Dr. Fuentes chimed in. "When the archeology team found his tomb in the middle of the last century, it was largely intact, thanks to the Maya engineers who knew a few more tricks to keeping their pyramids sealed than the Egyptians. The Spaniards didn't make off with much. That's why we need to do some more research. This coin could have been part of the official excavation of the tomb. Those artifacts are currently housed in the National Museum. If so, that means it was stolen more recently."

If Ace were a betting man, that was where he'd put his money. Which would mean David Lang was less a treasure hunter and more an opportunistic thief. Crappy news for Sophia.

Sophia glanced at Ace, a wealth of things passing across her face that plucked at strings inside him that he would have preferred stay unplucked, and nodded. "I agree that it really doesn't belong to me even though it was found on my land. I would want it to go back to Mexico and the Maya descendants if it was indeed stolen from the tomb. Involve whoever you need to in order to figure that out."

Jeez. Something bright filled his chest, making it a little hard to breathe. Who was this woman? She'd spent all this time trying to find the treasure, only to offer to give it back at the drop of the hat.

If he hadn't experienced it himself, he would never have believed such a simple act could make him feel this way about another human being.

Dr. Fuentes beamed, as if Sophia had passed a very difficult test. "Bless you, this is very exciting for us and the research we do at the university. Thank you for calling us.

You had a choice, and we appreciate that you made the right one."

"And now we have another request," Dr. Allen inserted firmly, drawing everyone's gaze. "There may be other pieces here on the property. Other coins. Maybe artifacts such as jade beads, pendants, ceramics. The list is infinite, and the pieces are priceless. Would you let us bring a team here to do a proper excavation?"

"Oh, I'm sure that would be fine," Sophia said agreeably. "What does that entail?"

Ace nearly groaned. It meant a lot more people. Machines. Chaos. And that his job would get infinitely harder.

"Sophia," he ground out before anyone else could speak. "A word, please."

Chapter 20

Closeted in her office with Ace definitely topped Sophia's list of things she enjoyed. This was very different from normal, though. He was operating under a full head of steam, pacing around like a caged tiger who hadn't eaten in several days.

Energy rolled off his body in waves, prickling the hair on her arms, and she couldn't figure out why he was infinitely more beautiful when he was like this but so much less approachable. This was the authoritative side of him that she fully appreciated because it meant he would never let anyone get past him when he stood between her and the door.

But she'd grown attached to the gentler Ace, the one who told her she was the most beautiful woman he'd ever met and held her hand as they walked through the woods in the dark.

"I take it I've done something that displeased his highness," she offered wryly. "Maybe you could clue me in before you rip my head off?"

The look on his face almost made her laugh despite the coiled tension arcing through the small room.

"I'm not going to rip your head off," he muttered. "I might rip *something* apart. But it would not be you."

Well, she could think of a few things that might benefit from being torn in two, like the dress she'd changed into before the trio of doctors had arrived from Austin. The slightly dangerous, somewhat breathless vibe Ace had created the moment he'd shut the door lent itself to an out-of-the-norm fantasy, and she wouldn't apologize for thinking about it, not when she'd been dying for him to kiss her again.

And while she had to admit that she might have a soft spot for gentler Ace, caged tiger Ace put a tingle in her belly that she could not ignore. It would be a travesty to waste all that energy.

Now was probably not the opportune time for that. Shame.

She crossed her arms and sank into her desk chair, figuring it was probably wise to keep the desk between them. For now.

"I'm sensing that you're a little worked up about something," she tried again. "Are you upset that I said the coin should go back to Mexico?"

He slammed to a halt, his gaze laser sharp on her face. "What? No. That was the single most unselfish thing I have ever witnessed in my life. You'd be giving up thousands of dollars, maybe hundreds of thousands if they find more Maya stuff. Nobody else on the planet would have made that kind of decision. It was amazing."

Well. That was not the reaction she'd been expecting, and honestly she hadn't even considered a different choice. Something flared to life inside her, glowing just behind her breastbone. Either she was about to have an out-of-body experience or Ace had just touched something she hadn't even known was there.

It was terrifying. And dizzying. Wonderful at the same time. It made her smile, despite the energy, which hadn't fizzled at all after he'd stopped midstride.

"I couldn't have kept it," she murmured. "It wouldn't be right. You saw how earnest all those people are about the history. They want to find the truth, not make a bunch of assumptions about what my father did or didn't do. But if he stole one red cent from a museum, I want to know."

Ace skirted the desk, reaching for her before he'd scarcely cleared it, his palms warm on her arms as he gripped her with surprising tenderness. "Sophia, whatever he did doesn't reflect on you. You know that, right?"

She nodded, her throat tight all at once as she looked up at him. "I never really thought much about the reality of him being a treasure hunter, but if you get down to it, there's not much difference between stealing from a museum and stealing from a historical grave site of an important ruler in a people's ancient culture."

"No," he said, a lightness in his gaze that she hadn't ever noticed before. "There's not."

"I can fix that. If I can help the people of Mexico reclaim even a small piece of their past, I should."

His eyelids fluttered closed for a brief moment and when he opened them, most of the coiled energy had fled. She missed it all at once. Hopefully it was a preview of what she could expect if she got him riled up in a completely different way. That focused intensity called to her at an elemental level.

"Yeah," he muttered, releasing her in favor of perching on the edge of the desk. "That's not wrong. This request for a full-scale excavation, though… Soph, that's a disaster waiting to happen."

If Ace was still calling her Soph, nothing else mattered. She tucked that away, folding it into the glow that hadn't faded one tiny bit, and let just a bit of what she was feeling inside reflect on her face in the form of a tiny smile.

"What would you suggest instead? You keep trying to stave off the Mongol hordes of evil dudes who are going to show up the moment word of this new find gets out?"

Almost all the stubbornness melted from Ace's expression. "I hear you. It would be better to have a sanctioned team on-site who will likely bring their own security to the ranch. If we're not searching for the treasure, I can spend twenty-four/seven making sure you're safe."

"Well, I like where this is going," she murmured and the vibe in the room changed instantly to something with a lot more weight. "Is it time to change your official job title to boyfriend?"

"That's literally the opposite of what I meant." He pressed a thumb to his temple, still clearly torn over what he perceived as his duty versus his desires.

She took mercy on him and laughed, climbing to her feet since it felt like they'd made a decision to move forward with the excavation. "I'm just kidding. Sort of. Door's open any time you want to walk through it. Just saying."

The look on his face made her shiver all at once. "I hope you're not telling me you leave the doors unlocked at night."

"It's an expression, Ace. Jeez." *Mental note: make Ace a copy of the front door key.* "You do know how to make a girl feel wanted."

All at once, the coiled energy returned to his frame in a snap. He had her backed against the desk before she could blink, his mouth crashing down on hers in a kiss that detonated instantly with the force of an atomic bomb.

Oh, my, *yes*. And that was the extent of her brain's ability to processes words, ideas, thoughts. Ace drained everything from her and still kept demanding more. She gave it to him. How could she not?

This was exactly what she'd craved from the moment he'd shut them up together in this room. Oh, who was she kidding? She thought about him taking her into his arms pretty much all the time. But this… This was something else, something different. Slightly perilous, a little scandalous and absolutely delicious.

He ripped his mouth from hers well before she was ready, breathing as heavily as if he'd run a marathon, his gaze dark and searching on hers.

"In case you weren't aware," he ground out, his voice gravelly, "I always want you. Don't you dare think otherwise for a second."

"I, um…won't. Didn't." She blinked. Was that the trick to getting him to cross his made-up line? Tell him that he'd made her feel unwanted?

With what seemed to be a great deal of reluctance, he released her and stepped away, running a hand through his short, cropped hair, giving her the impression he'd been expecting to find his hat on his head.

"Let them know you agree to the excavation team coming to the property but make it clear that all personnel must have a background check," he told her and it didn't sound like a suggestion. "I can coordinate with them once they're on-site, if you want. Act as their point of contact."

"Of course I want that."

He nodded. "I'll support your decision, then. Bring on the chaos."

* * *

This was one of those times Ace wished he'd been wrong. But *chaos* didn't begin to describe what descended on the ranch after Sophia gave the UT Austin team the green light.

The academics consulted with the people at the museum in Mexico all right. All eleven of them. Who had also chosen to collaborate with the Peabody Museum of Archaeology and Ethnology at Harvard. They sent a team of nine, plus more equipment than he could identify, all of which rolled up in an RV painted with the university's logo, followed by a truck hauling two ATVs.

Last time he'd gotten a good head count, there were twenty-three people living in a makeshift campsite in the south pasture, eight vehicles parked nearby, and one of the teams had four drones that constantly flew overhead doing aerial photography.

Then the backhoe arrived. Followed by two generators and a partridge in a pear tree.

"This is insanity," he muttered to McKay in passing as they headed in opposite directions, Ace to check in with Dr. Allen, who seemed to be the leader so far, despite the team from Harvard obviously being much better funded.

"A grad student from Austin just arrived about ten minutes ago," McKay said.

McKay was acting as Ace's second set of eyes and ears, while Pierce, the wizard of the web, ran complicated searches on everyone's backgrounds and known associates using methods better left unexplained.

"On my way to check him out, then," Ace acknowledged. "Allen didn't mention him. I don't like it when new people show up unannounced."

True to his word, Ace played point for all the teams, ensuring they had access to the areas they needed, as well as looking out for the ranch's interest, particularly the horses that didn't like the machinery. Or the people. A sentiment he shared.

Ace found the grad student. Not hard to pick out when the kid was barely old enough to shave and wore shorts like they didn't have the same mosquitoes and chiggers in Austin as they did in East Texas.

"You the new guy?" Ace growled, gratified when the grad student jumped.

"Yes, sir, I'm Quentin. Mallory," he added quickly and stuck out his hand. Then dropped it when Ace eyed him.

They were all so earnest at this age. Ace crossed his arms, which had the not-so-accidental effect of highlighting his biceps. You couldn't be too careful or too untrusting, even with a skinny guy who couldn't weigh more than 125 soaking wet. "Dr. Allen is in the south pasture. You should check in, do not pass go, do not collect two hundred dollars."

Quentin Mallory shook his head, like it had been a suggestion he had the latitude to ignore. "Oh, yeah, I'll get to that. I heard from Dr. Fuentes that the aerial shots showed a promising area near the fence line that I'm—"

"Check in first," he told the kid flatly. These academics and Indiana Jones wannabes hoped to find artifacts and treasure. He got it. But this was his rodeo, not theirs. "This is a working ranch. You don't get to go wherever you please. Step out of line and you're off this project. Spoiler alert. I get to decide where the line is. Don't forget that."

Mallory nodded a bunch of times. "South pasture. Got it. Uh… Which way is south?"

If Ace rolled his eyes any harder, they'd bounce right out of his head. He pointed. The kid skedaddled, but Ace didn't give him the benefit of the doubt. He watched until Mallory hit the gate that led to the larger-than-it-should-be camping area.

When he turned back toward the house, Sophia had just stepped out onto the back porch, wearing a pair of cropped pants and a shirt that tied at her waist. The tiniest bit of skin peeked out and his mouth went dry instantly.

When would it stop feeling like a load of bricks had dropped on his chest every time he saw her across the way? The scant few times he'd managed to corner her in a place with enough shadows to cloak the fact that he just wanted to breathe her in for a minute hadn't been nearly enough.

That was the real shame in all of this. They were both so busy managing everything that they barely got a chance to say hi to each other, let alone a longer conversation. Which he definitely needed to have with her pronto. Or at least soon. Whenever it became clear the job was over.

Weren't they close? The addition of so many people should have made things easier. Better. Safer. Jonas had the hands patrolling the woods regularly to ensure the teams weren't digging up trees and knocking over fences. No intruders could be lurking out there, not without being seen pretty much immediately.

Of course, the problem was that everyone counted as an intruder right now. And no one did. It was often a challenge just to keep track of who was permitted to be on-site, let alone someone who wasn't.

Sophia caught his gaze and he felt it in his gut when she smiled. It didn't seem to matter that she was a football field away, he could almost smell her jasmine body-wash from here.

That would be even better—if he could smell it up close and personal. He'd sent the new kid off to be tagged. Maybe he could sneak a minute or two with the boss.

Apparently, she was of the same mind since she took off, headed in his direction. Meeting her in the middle worked for him and then some.

A rumble from behind him grew loud enough for him to glance away from Sophia. A backhoe rolled toward her, one of the big ones with a wicked-looking scoop on front, teeth extended.

The driver was a maniac going that fast this close to the house. They weren't even supposed to have the heavy machinery here. Annoyed, Ace shot the driver a warning glance.

Only there wasn't a driver. The backhoe kept on rolling toward Sophia unmanned.

Ace's pulse skyrocketed as time suspended, everything falling into a hazy, slow-motion quality. Sophia's gaze stayed stuck on him, her smile his favorite.

But that meant she wasn't paying attention to the backhoe. No one did anymore. There were so many odd machines roaming all over the property now that the noise of one scarcely registered.

She had no idea it was heading in her direction, on a straight path to intercept her.

"Sophia!" he called and threw his hands to the side, hoping it would somehow communicate to her that she needed to move. "Look out!"

He sprinted toward her, knowing he had no shot at getting to her before the backhoe did.

Finally, she glanced to her right, eyes widening. With

something akin to superhuman speed, she jumped just as the teeth of the bucket would have pierced her leg. But she landed right in the path of the giant tires.

Ace reached her then, snatching her into his arms and heaving himself to the ground with her on top of him. His back slammed into the dirt and then Sophia crushed his ribs. But he couldn't focus on that, rolling to be sure they'd cleared the tire tracks.

The backhoe kept going, heading for the house.

He released Sophia after taking a half second to be sure she was okay, then pumped his legs to reach the backhoe. It was difficult enough to scramble into the cab when this kind of equipment was still. Moving, it was almost impossible, but he managed it without getting his leg tangled with the tires.

A second later, he'd pulled the brake and then the key. The backhoe shuddered to a stop inches from the wraparound porch.

Chapter 21

"It wasn't an accident," Ace told Sophia grimly for the third time as she—once again—refused to sit in the chair he'd pulled out from the kitchen table so he could get a good look at her.

"It doesn't make any sense why I would still be a target, though," she said as she stood at the sink, staring out over the back acreage from the relative safety of the house. Which had taken some doing to get her to agree to.

Sophia had brushed off the incident, dusted herself off and expected Ace to agree to let her continue with her plan to have a conversation with Jonas out in the open. Not happening.

"It doesn't have to make sense," he growled. He made that noise a lot lately and he didn't like that this situation had brought out his grumbly side. "You don't have to think about it at all. You just have to do what I say so you don't end up hamburger meat."

She laughed like any of this was funny. "Should I start calling you boss, then?"

"Yes," he told her succinctly. "That's exactly what you should do. The backhoe was the last straw. I'm officially accepting the promotion to head of your security detail. I haven't been able to focus on ranch duties in forever anyway. It's stupid to pretend I'm doing anything else other than shadowing you twenty-four/seven for the foreseeable future."

Her expression heated inexplicably, as if he'd just said he planned to sleep in her bed as a precaution. Oh, if only that was an option. He could see it in his mind's eye perfectly. It helped that he'd had this particular fantasy running in his head for several days now. The one where he used protecting her as an excuse to move into the house, her bedroom, her shower.

But the backhoe incident had brought one ugly truth to light—this was far from over. Sophia was still very much in danger. Which meant he had to keep his mouth shut about his real purpose here.

Though declaring himself her official bodyguard felt like crossing another line that wasn't keeping in the spirit of the job. What was the difference between repurposing himself away from cowboy duty and admitting to her he'd been hired by someone else, who was still nameless? Speaking of things that made no sense...

At this point, he was willing to split hairs. As long as he didn't have to cross a very large plot of land to get between her and danger ever again. If he was already standing next to her, any new threats would have to go through him.

"Have I mentioned lately that I'm a huge fan of Take-Charge Ace?" she murmured. "Which reminds me. If we're going to be spending every second together from now on, I feel compelled to ask. Why do they call you Ace? Is it your real name?"

"What?" He shook his head, baffled at the subject

change when she'd literally almost been killed not fifteen minutes ago. "What does that matter?"

"I'm curious. Indulge me."

Apparently, that was the magic wand he'd needed to get her to sit down in the chair he pulled out. Her new proximity meant she was within touching distance, her gaze avidly fixed on him as if whatever he was about to impart held great significance to her.

If anyone else had asked, he'd have told them no. None of their business.

But it wasn't anyone else. It was Sophia, a woman he desperately wanted to tell everything to. Whatever she wanted to know. Since he couldn't be truthful about the most important things, at least he could tell her this little bit.

He heaved a sigh. "It's short for Andrew Christopher. During my first deployment, my XO sent me on a particularly difficult mission. Let's just say it unfolded successfully. When I returned, he called me his ace in the hole and it stuck."

"Can I call you Andy?" she said mischievously and laughed again when he gave her a withering look. "I'm just kidding. Ace suits you. I like it."

Fortunately, she didn't ask for any details about the mission, which was classified anyway. But the die had been cast and talking about his successes as a SEAL meant the scene in question crowded into his mind. Reminding him who he was.

That was the real secret. The one he couldn't tell her. And that put a wall between them that was insurmountable. She'd never look at him the same again if she knew how good he was at killing.

But she didn't know and she didn't have any issues at the

moment with standing up to crowd into his space, slipping her arms around his waist as she snuggled into his torso. Somehow it became an embrace when his stupid arms refused to stay at his side and eagerly got in on that action.

He should push her away. But she glanced up at him from under her lashes, giving him that smile that she saved strictly for him.

"Thank you for saving my life, Ace. More than once."

"You're welcome," he said gruffly into her hair as the scent of jasmine filled him to the brim. Something pinged around in his heart, looking for a place to land. And found it.

Aw, dang. He'd gone and fallen for her.

Sophia put her head in her hands as she stared at the date printed on the project plan displayed on her laptop.

Charli sat next to her, crunching her way through a bag of Doritos, content to let Sophia do the heavy lifting of the resort planning. She hadn't even asked for a desk or a workspace or anything, so when she thought about it, she showed up to Sophia's office to have an impromptu meeting about the status of things.

"That face doesn't bode well," Charli noted, her eyes on Sophia instead of the project plan they'd been going over. "Are we not going to meet the date?"

"It's less than a month away," Sophia said needlessly, or at least she hoped Charli had glanced at a calendar recently. "I can't even get a firm date out of the seven billion archaeologists in my backyard of when they can wrap up the excavation. The barn is out of commission and the temp barn is not for show. Assuming none of that is actually an issue, where does the decorating project stand?"

Shrugging, her sister glanced through some papers she'd

brought with her to Sophia's office, which weren't even in a file folder or anything. "I think the decorator said he could finish the second suite by next week. Or was it the following week?"

Sophia bit her lip and counted to ten, letting Charli dig through her data until she finally pointed at something that must have meant something to her. "Next week. Then he'll start on the small bedroom. That should take probably ten to twelve days, he thought."

"Business or calendar days?"

Eyes wide, Charli hesitated. "What, like did he include weekends or some such?" When Sophia nodded, she pursed her lips. "Well, he said the team doesn't work on Sundays, so I guess he meant they work six days a week. So, that would put us at…oh."

"Exactly," Sophia confirmed grimly. "It's too close to the launch date, and that doesn't even account for the fact that ideally, I should have opened bookings already. But I haven't because of this mess."

She flipped her fingers at the window where the bright yellow paint of the rogue backhoe stood out in relief against the woods as it chugged merrily through one of the back pastures.

"What if we don't bill it as a luxury resort?" Charli asked, all nonchalant, as if she hadn't just spoken blasphemy.

"What do you mean, don't bill it as a luxury resort? What would we bill it as? Choose your own treasure hunt adventure?" she shot back sarcastically and sucked half a smoothie up through the straw. It was supposed to be her breakfast, but it had been sitting on her desk for an hour and the fruit had started to separate from the protein powder. *Ugh*.

"Maybe it can be a Cowboy Experience instead," her sister said, warming to her subject. "Like, get the guests to move the horses from pasture to pasture. Let them throw out the feed. Clean the tack after the trail ride. Why have staff do all of that?"

Just as she opened her mouth to argue, several things hit her at once. Then no one would care how rustic the surroundings were. She could save some money on payroll. The concept grew on her so fast that she went light-headed.

"Charli," she ground out. "Where in the world did that idea come from?"

"It's not a bad idea," her sister shot back defensively. "You always do this—"

"No, it's not a bad idea. I mean it like, where in the world did that *great* idea come from? You didn't want anything to do with the ranch, and then you show up out of the blue, jump in and actually contribute. It's…" Sophia swallowed, slightly ashamed and a whole lot impressed, now that she'd checked her prejudices in favor of treating Charli like she might be an equal partner in this. "Great."

Charli beamed. "Really?"

Nodding, Sophia opened a new document, ideas pouring out of her brain faster than she could type. "We can have sessions on how to make cowboy fare, like the kind of stuff they eat on cattle drives or whatever. Roping lessons. Jonas can find some guys who can lead that. What if we could find people who wanted to help rebuild the barn?"

And best of all, as already highlighted so eloquently, the guests would be working at the ranch. Getting it in shape. Filling the gaps. And *paying* for the experience. It would be unique too. There were lots of other dude ranches who advertised authentic Western experiences, but they also had golf courses and yachts you could rent for an afternoon.

This concept was different. She could hardly keep her fingers moving fast enough as enthusiasm filled her office.

She and Charli hashed out plans until well past lunchtime. Ace had poked his head in the door no less than five times, just to make sure nothing had happened to her, which was sweet, but where would she go?

Nowhere that he wasn't, that was for sure.

She hadn't forgotten for a second that he'd camped right outside her door, giving her the space and privacy to work, but within shouting distance. Jonas hadn't been thrilled over her commandeering one of his hands, but he'd get over it, especially when she presented him with Charli's newly designed ranch offering.

Ace belonged to her now, in more ways than one. And she was pretty sure he felt the same way about her. It was time to move that forward.

After she and Charli talked for so long that they both went hoarse, she sent her sister off to think about new decorating ideas with the intent of stealing a few minutes for herself. But not alone.

When she opened the door, Ace was sitting in a hardback chair, leaning back against the wall with the front half a foot off the ground. He barely fit in the chair in the first place. It was no wonder he'd figured out a way to give his ridiculously long legs extra room.

"Hey," she murmured and crossed her arms, leaning against the doorjamb as she drank in his beautiful form. "Can I see you for a minute?"

Both front legs thumped to the floor. "Am I being called to the principal's office?"

"Something like that."

But the grin on his face told her he didn't mind so much. "I like anything that means I don't have to try to see through walls to make sure you're okay."

The moment he cleared the door, she shut it and put her back against it. Ace stood near her desk, brows cocked in question, clearly waiting for her to get to the punch line.

She didn't make him wait for it. "It feels like we've turned a corner. So I think it's time you took me on a proper date."

"What corner have we turned?" he asked, scrubbing the back of his neck in that odd, endearing way he had when he was unsure what was happening.

But she wasn't fooled. A man who kissed her the way he did surely wasn't confused about the chemistry between them. A man who protected her the way he did cared. He couldn't possibly be faking that or anything else going on between them.

"This one."

She crossed the room in one stride and pulled his head down to lay a scorching kiss on him. It took him a beat to really commit but when he did, hooooh boy. He incinerated her from the inside out, his mouth pulling responses from her she hadn't previously known she was capable of.

The kiss held all the promise she'd expected it to. Hoped for. Craved.

Breaking off the kiss, she nuzzled his cheek. "That corner. The one where we both know where this is headed and we're both on board. We're well past the point where it matters that you work for me, but if it's still an issue for you, then we can find you another job."

Ace froze, his expression that of someone who had just

walked out on a thin sheet of ice and heard the first crack. In other words, not the reaction she'd been going for.

"I can't find another job, Sophia. I have to be here, where I can make sure no one tries to take you out of the equation," he argued in what amounted to a frustrating but valid point.

"Then I guess we can wait to make it official, but is there anything wrong with giving me some sign that's where this is headed?" she prompted. When he shook his head, her heart suddenly fell out of rhythm. Now she was the one in the precarious position of wondering how she'd wandered out onto the ice. "What? What's the objection this time?"

She'd meant for it come out flirty and carefree, the way she'd managed to do the last few times she'd tried to move their relationship to a place where she felt more secure in its longevity. But this time felt different. The expression on his face felt different.

And she knew. He wasn't going to say okay. He wasn't going to take her on a date. Somehow, she'd misread his interest in her.

"Sophia," he murmured and shut his eyes for a beat. When he opened them, he seemed to realize he still had her caught up in his embrace. He let go so quickly, she stumbled.

But he didn't reach out to steady her.

That's when the first crack cleaved right down the middle of her heart. "I don't like the way you just said my name. What is going on here? You can't kiss me like that and then back off when I start talking about making things official between us. Now is the perfect time. You're my security detail. We're going to be spending a lot of time together anyway, at least as long as the excavation teams are here. How is that not what you want?"

"I do want that," he told her earnestly and she believed him. Wanted to believe him.

"Then why do you look like someone just died?" Oh, man, she was such a moron. Her hand flew to her mouth as she stared up at him. "It's not your sister, is it? Because that's a legit reason you can't commit right now. I'm sorry, I didn't even think—"

"It's not my sister." He stood there, his hand at the back of his neck, refusing to meet her gaze.

Then finally he did, and she wished he hadn't. The bleakness she saw there scared her. Chilled her to the bone. And she wanted to take back everything she'd said thus far, as long as he didn't look at her like that anymore.

He blew out a breath. "I have to tell you something before this goes any further. Though I have a feeling when I'm finished, you'll be happy it never did."

Okay, now he was *really* scaring her. "What is it, Ace? You can tell me anything."

"Except this." His brief smile had not one iota of warmth in it. "I'm not who you think I am."

Chapter 22

Oh, man, now that it was out there, Ace had expected to feel lighter, as if a weight had lifted. But all he felt was blackness and his own guilt for letting it get to this point, plus a healthy amount of self-recrimination for hurting Sophia, who looked like he'd punched her in the face.

"What do you mean?" she whispered. "Are you working for Intruder Man?"

"No," he insisted hotly. But then had to take a step back. What if he *was*? "I guess that's part of the issue. I don't know who I'm working for."

"Besides me, you mean?" Her tone had an acid underlay that made him cringe.

She'd caught on really fast. If he hadn't already been in love with her, that would have tipped the scales.

"Besides you," he admitted. "I was hired by someone to watch you and make sure nothing happened to you. But it was part of my employment agreement that I wouldn't reveal to you that I'd been hired."

"Except you're telling me now," she pointed out. "What changed?"

"You did." He ached to reach out and enfold her back into his embrace, to connect with her in the way that made him feel whole. But the vibe between them said he might pull back a bloody stump if he tried it. "You deserve to understand why I can't be with you the way you would like."

"Because you've been lying to me," she said flatly, understanding dawning in her green eyes. "So this is your heroic effort to make sure your conscience is clean before we get naked together, is that it?"

"Among other things, yes."

This conversation was going either much better than he'd been expecting or much worse. That was the rub. He couldn't read Sophia the way he normally could, and it was gutting him.

"What other things?" Her gaze narrowed.

Worse. This conversation was going much worse. He swallowed. "You didn't know I was here under false pretenses. Now you do. But you also don't know why I'm so good at what I do. You deserve to know that too."

"I do know," she snapped, then all the fight seemed to drain out of her at once. "Or I thought I did. You had me convinced you were a straight arrow. The goodest of the good. The kind of guy who was the opposite of my father, one who would stick with me through thick and thin. Only to find out you're just like him. A liar."

The direct hit hurt but not as much as the hopelessness he saw steal over her expression. He'd done that to her. Made her believe there were men out there who weren't like her father, only to prove her wrong.

"I'm sorry," he whispered. "I never meant for it to happen like this. I never meant to fall for you."

She laughed bitterly and sank into her desk chair, probably to put some distance between them. "Funny, that was exactly what I was praying to hear five minutes ago. I wanted to know if you felt even a tenth of what I was feeling for you. I figured I had a pretty good read on you, so I wasn't walking into this blind. Little did I know."

"I'm not a liar," he said and held up his hands in surrender when she shot him a black look. "It's semantics. But it was a condition of my employment that I not tell you. If it means anything, I'm pretty sure I've just nullified my contract."

"You'll forgive me if I don't have a lot of sympathy for you since that sounds pretty convenient for you." The laptop on the desk in front of her was open and she stared at the screen blankly. "Who puts that kind of stipulation on an employment contract? No one. Or rather no one I'd do business with, if it's even true. It's curious that you thought nothing of it."

Well. He had bills. Bills that he wouldn't be paying now that he'd sacrificed his fee. He'd fight to allow McKay and Pierce to keep their two-thirds, but ultimately that wasn't up to him. It was a crappy situation all the way around, but he couldn't have gone another minute without telling her the truth.

Which he still hadn't done, not fully. And wished he didn't have to, but it would be better to pull the bandage off in one shot. Now, before anything else happened.

"That's because you don't really know me," he said, the harsh words making her flinch. He bucked up under it, though. It was time to lay it all out. "I'm the ace in the hole for one reason. Because I can dispatch terrorists better, faster and more efficiently than anyone else on the planet."

It wasn't a compliment, and he didn't wear it like one. It was a burden. One he'd stood up under for a long time.

Telling her felt less like coming clean and more like he'd piled filth on top of the existing wounds.

"What are you telling me?" she asked suspiciously. "That you weren't really in the military and you were some kind of mercenary instead?"

"No, of course not." Though it wasn't far off. "I was a SEAL, working for the US government. Highly trained. Very motivated to do my job. That meant eliminating targets and I was good at it. More so than anyone else in my platoon, so guess who got the dirty work? I have blood on my hands, Sophia. So much blood."

He could never wash it off. The stain went too deep.

She shook her head. "That's your big secret? You were good at your job? Pardon me while I faint in shock."

Confused, he stared at her. "Are you listening to me? I'm a highly trained killing machine. I killed people. Lots of them. I can't ever wash that stigma away."

"It's not a stigma in war, Ace," she said, brushing it aside as if his greatest shame wasn't something to even consider, let alone worry over. "You were under orders. What would you have done instead, told your commanding officer no? Please. What does that have to do with your post-service decisions? Nothing. You walked in here, fully aware that you'd be lying to me from the outset. *That's* the issue."

"But I didn't have a choice," he explained again, realizing how it sounded, and she didn't give him an inch of grace.

"We always have choices, Ace," she countered, arms crossed over her stomach as if it hurt. "And it sounds like you made yours before we even met."

He had. He'd become a SEAL. Become the kind of man

who would take the lives of others, one who didn't deserve a woman like Sophia.

"Which I can't undo. And I'm sorry for that. But the other choice would have been to not take the job, and I did. That, I won't apologize for. If I hadn't been here, you might have been killed that first day by the man who broke into your office. Or by the sniper in the woods. The backhoe. Possibly even another threat that didn't happen because I am here."

And he'd staunchly defend the fact that he'd done his job as dictated. He'd kept her safe. That had to count for something.

She nodded. "Yeah, one could view it that way. Or Intruder Man was after the key to the safety deposit box all along and because you found it, all that other stuff was set in motion. The guy in the woods could have been shooting at you, after all."

The point wasn't lost on him, and his stomach squelched with a sickening, greasy flood.

Was that what had happened? Had he inadvertently made the threat to Sophia worse? Surely not, or he wouldn't have been hired in the first place. Someone knew she'd be in danger, though.

What if that someone knew because he was the actual threat?

That made zero sense. Ace shook his head. He refused to believe that Intruder Man, or one of his associates, hired him.

"I guess we don't really know for sure," he said. "But I firmly believe that someone had your best interests at heart and handed that job to me so I could stand between you and anything that wanted to hurt you."

Her soft laugh sounded broken. "The irony. Who was supposed to protect me from you being the one to hurt me?"

"Sophia." His own voice broke. "What's happening between us is real. When I kiss you, it's like the rest of the world falls away and I'm flooded with you. There's no employment contract. No treasure, except the one I'm holding in my arms. Focus on that."

"Are you seriously trying to make things be okay between us? Like we're going to pick up where we left off now that I know the truth?"

She stared at him, her gaze boring through him, and he imagined this was Advertising Executive Sophia. The one she'd insisted he would hate, and while he could never hate her, he did feel the chill in his bones.

"No, that's not what I'm trying to say." He could scarcely breathe around the weight on his chest. "I just…don't want you to feel like it was fake on my side. As if you can't trust that what I feel for you is real. I don't want to take that from you."

The wall above Sophia's desk had a spot where the texture hadn't been formed right. It was flat and hollowed out, a metaphor for how he felt. As if he'd scooped out his insides, leaving him with nothingness. It was a fitting punishment for what he'd done. What he'd always known would be in store for him in the long run.

"It doesn't matter anyway," he continued. "I'm not good enough for you. You're right that I made decisions long before we met that make me who I am. I was a good SEAL, but that makes me a bad person. A man who can't erase the sins of the past. For that, I'm truly sorry. You deserve better."

Grimly, she set her mouth in a line, her expression, her

body language, shut like she'd locked herself away behind a concrete wall. "Everything you've ever said to me is in question now. In a lot of ways, you're worse than my father. At least he just left."

"And I'm not leaving you," he told her fiercely, circling the desk, daring to get in her space even though she had clearly wanted the barrier. "I would never abandon you."

"You did, Ace," she said in a small voice that brought him up short before he could take her hand as he'd intended to do. "From the beginning, you never gave me a chance. A real chance. In your head, it was never going to work, or you would have been honest with me way before now. That's the unforgiveable part."

He nodded. It was true. There was never a scenario where he would have made a different decision and that's what he had to live with. "I'm still your bodyguard. That hasn't changed."

"Oh, I'm aware. Regardless of how any of this transpired, the danger is real. I get it. You're going to keep doing your job and I'm going to allow it. But you can do it from that side of the door." She pointed and he recognized a dismissal when he saw one.

Ace walked through the door and shut it, the click reverberating in his heart much more loudly than he would have expected.

So that was done. The weight on his chest didn't abate even hours later, when Sophia finally emerged from her office. The icy silence between them physically hurt, but he took it as his due. She spoke to him by rote, without an ounce of the spirit and fire that he'd grown accustomed to. It was like the woman he'd spent the last few weeks with didn't exist anymore. As if her essence had been sucked out.

And maybe that's what he'd really done with his confession. Drained her of everything that mattered. He'd have to live with that too. But he'd meant what he said, and he'd never walk away, not while there was a chance that someone might threaten her. Or worse.

His conscience would be clear, no matter what.

It was everything else—his heart, his soul, his very marrow—that would bear the black mark of what had happened in her office earlier.

This went on for twenty-four excruciating hours. Sophia shut herself up in her office, sometimes with Charli, sometimes alone, but Ace was always on the outside. That left him at loose ends, running patrols past her window. Coordinating with McKay as he kept an eye on Charli. Working with the archeology teams as the point person. Essentially doing exactly what he'd been doing, but this time with a layer of frost between him and Sophia.

Now it was only a job. Before, he'd been included in the small details of her life, could be easy with her and vice versa. And being cut off from that hurt.

It also made him realize this hadn't been strictly a job from the start. He'd maybe gone into this thinking so, but the idea that he'd stay on the fringes had been eliminated as a possibility pretty much from the first moment he'd laid eyes on Sophia Lang.

She'd speared something inside instantly.

And maybe she'd clued in on that a lot faster than he had. It hit him as he watched her trek to the bunkhouse to speak with Jonas, trailing her because she didn't like it when he walked in step with her. He *had* decided in his head that they weren't meant to be—because it never occurred to him that she wouldn't care about his bloody hands. That it truly wouldn't be a factor in how she felt about him.

He'd used that as an excuse, keeping it between them, all the while pretending the job stipulations were the reason. In reality, it was an easily removed barrier.

This relationship had been doomed the moment he'd thrown up that barrier. He'd ruined anything that might have happened between them with that one simple mistake.

The moment of clarity washed through him, and he wanted to tell her. To apologize all over again. But he had to wait because she'd gone inside with Jonas to discuss ranch business.

Once upon a time, he'd have been included. She'd seen Ace as a partner, someone to share the burden of her life. That's what he wanted. With Sophia. There had to be a way to fix this, to get past his mistake.

What if it was too late?

No, he refused to accept that. She had to see that he'd done it to protect himself, but he was over that now. He wanted to lay it all bare for her and let her make her own decisions.

When she came out of the bunkhouse fifty-eight agonizingly long minutes later, he smiled at her, his face muscles protesting the movement that he hadn't made in a very long time. She didn't smile back.

"Sophia, I need to talk to you," he said without preamble. "It's important."

She blew past him. "I can't talk to you right now."

"Please." He caught up with her in two strides and made the mistake of trying to slow her down by grabbing her hand.

She yanked it free and rounded on him, fire sparking

from her gaze. "Don't. This is not working. I cannot do this with you any longer. I'll hire another bodyguard. Someone without an agenda or the history. But you can't be here anymore. You're fired."

Chapter 23

Sophia slammed the door to the house, the windowpane on the top half rattling. So much for her plan to keep pretending Andrew Madden—if that was even his real name—didn't exist. She'd held out, what, a whole day before blowing her ice princess routine to shreds.

She gave herself points for not peering through the window to see if Ace really left the ranch after she'd fired him or if he would duck back into the bunkhouse to lie low while keeping his eagle eye on everything.

Because she had a feeling she knew. The man could stick.

He'd never leave unless she forced him to, by calling the cops or something. That was the screwed-up thing about all of this. Even as she'd accused him of being just like her father, she'd recognized the problem with that comparison. He wasn't anything like David Lang.

The only thing Ace had in common with her father was that she wouldn't trust either one of them as far as she could throw him. Where her father excelled at making himself scarce, Ace was wired differently.

Or at least that's what she'd believed before his bombshell. Yeah, he wasn't who she thought, not by a long shot.

He wasn't actually her employee. Not *only* her employee, rather.

All this time, she'd worried over dating someone who worked for her. Ironic, right? He was only on her payroll in order to finagle his way into her good graces so he could... Well, she didn't exactly know what his angle was, but he had one all right.

All men did. Even that one. What an idiot she was for thinking he was different.

And she wouldn't waste a second more of her energy on him. That was how men really made you suffer, by plucking at your emotions. Well, not Sophia Lang. She'd cut her teeth on kicking men to the curb.

Too bad she hadn't done that in the first place.

One tear welled up and she let it fall. That was the extent of how much she'd cry over Andrew Christopher, especially since she scarcely knew the man. You couldn't truly be sad about the loss of something that hadn't been real in the first place.

Forge ahead. That was the new plan.

Sophia stormed to her office and did not look up until she'd spent three hours working on the new marketing campaign for the Cowboy Experience at Hidden Creek Ranch. Charli's idea. And it was a good one.

All the reasons she'd been excited after hashing this out with her sister came back to her as she pulled on her considerable expertise to tease out ways to sell the concept to a variety of audiences. Twentysomethings who wanted a sustainable vacation that gave back to the earth instead of stealing from it. Thirty-to-forty-five-ish couples with kids who didn't want to spend the equivalent of a year's college tuition on a spring break trip. Baby boomers who remembered all the great Westerns fondly. Everyone in between who wanted to brag about their unique vacation.

Twice, she glanced up, imagining she'd heard Ace in the hallway. That was the problem with spending so much time with someone. You got used to them being around and when they weren't, it felt like an arm had been cut off.

Plus, she missed him. Sometime in the last hour, she'd let herself admit that.

Despite everything, the man had this smile that she couldn't get over. When he looked at her, she felt *seen*. What was she supposed to do with this ache in her heart?

It was a good thing she had all this work to take her mind off everything else wrong in her life. And just like that, her concentration snapped.

Since the last time she'd looked out the window, the sun had set, plunging the ranch into darkness. Goodness, she'd completely forgotten about eating dinner.

Maybe Charli would like to go with her into town to the Dairy Queen. Just as she raised a hand to knock on her sister's door, she remembered that Charli had told her earlier that day that she had a date tonight. One of the new ranch hands, if she recalled, which Sophia would have warned her about if asked, but really, not everyone was here under false pretenses. This new guy was probably on the complete up and up, and her sister seemed pretty into the idea of dating a cowboy, so who was she to get in the way?

A little morose that her own cowboy experience hadn't worked out so well, she padded into the kitchen, wondering where she'd left her shoes. Jenny had gone to the market apparently, bless her. The makings of a ham sandwich and a small salad would do fine.

The food tasted like sawdust, and she ate as much of

it as she could before deciding she wasn't all that hungry, after all. Good gravy, what was wrong with her? Pre-Ace, she'd never even thought twice about being alone. Or lonely. This would pass. Eventually she'd forget how the man had lit her up inside.

She heard a sound near the front door, like scrabbling. Charli. She rolled her eyes. That girl would forget her head if it wasn't attached.

"Forget your key?" she said as she flipped on the porch light and swung the door open wide.

It wasn't Charli. A man stood on her porch, a gun in his hand, which he leveled at her.

There was a *man* on her porch holding a *gun*. Pointed at *her*.

Fear flooded her stomach in an icy, oily wave. She froze, every bit of her self-defense training sliding right out of her brain. She didn't even have her purse, so how would she grab the Mace on her keychain? Stupid.

She had just enough wits about her to realize it was Intruder Man.

"Appreciate you saving me the trouble, Ms. Lang," he drawled, a sly smile on his face.

His uncovered face. That couldn't be good. Robbers always wore masks so they couldn't be identified, right? So this guy must not care about that. Because he expected her to be dead at the end of this.

"What do you want?" she croaked. "I don't have any money."

He laughed. "Oh, but you do. Specifically, coins. The Maya variety. We're going to have a good long chat about that, Ms. Lang."

He motioned her to the side and when she didn't immediately comply, he reached out and cuffed her across the cheek.

Pain exploded along the already stressed bone where she'd hit the concrete of the shelter. She cried out involuntarily, her palm flying to cover the spot, like that would help anything.

"Move out of the doorway," he snarled, apparently done with being smiley, and grabbed her arm, hustling her to the spot that was apparently acceptable to him. "We don't want any of your watchdogs to know I'm here, now do we?"

Watch*dogs*? Did he think any of the ranch hands cared about what went on at the main house? Well, other than Ace, who probably had left after all since she hadn't seen hide nor hair of him in hours.

"How do you know my name?" she asked. As if that was the most important thing to get straight here. But he'd spoken to her like he knew her, and she most certainly did not know him outside of the incident in her study. And probably the woods—surely, he'd been the one shooting at them.

"I pay attention. That's how I know you found one of the coins. Where? Tell me."

"You mean the backhoe and drones clued you in?" she shot back sarcastically, her cheek still stinging enough to egg on her mood. "You're pretty sharp."

"Don't be mouthy or I'll use my fist on your face next time, little girl," he said, and she believed him.

He wasn't too tall, but he had a beefiness about him that said he might have a heck of a punch. She already knew he could slam a woman into a wall hard enough to leave her in pain. As much as the slap had hurt, she didn't want to find out what else he had in store for her.

Like the bullets in the chamber of that gun he still

pointed at her. He cocked the hammer and nodded once. "Now talk. Tell me where you found the coin."

Sure, and once she did that, he'd kill her and leave her body here for Charli or Jenny to find. The blood would be impossible to get out of the carpet. And that's how you officially figured out you were verging on hysteria, when bloodstains mattered more than being dead.

"It would be easier and faster if I showed you," she improvised wildly. "I'm not quite sure exactly where it was. It was dark and the woods are so big."

"That's an even better idea," he mused. "I was thinking of making you write it down, but this way, if you tell me the wrong area, you can still be convinced to try again."

"Who are you?" she asked, searching for some kind of weapon in her peripheral vision. "You're the same one who broke in here and rifled through the desk in my office."

Something flickered through his gaze. The fact that she'd identified him didn't sit well for some reason. Well, he hadn't worn a mask then, either. What did he expect?

"That's not important. I'm no one to you, other than the last face you'll ever see on this earth if you don't tell me what I need to know."

"I said I'd show you," she snapped. "I need shoes and a jacket if I'm going to be walking through the woods at gunpoint."

"Fine," he allowed wearily. "Make it fast. You have ten seconds. I'm counting down. Ten, nine…"

She raced to find her phone and hid it in her pocket at the same time she threw on a jacket and stepped into her slip-ons, the ones she wore outside when she didn't want to worry about wading through horse manure. Hopefully if anyone was paying attention, they would wonder why she was wearing them at night.

Who she thought would be paying that much attention, she had no idea. Charli probably had no idea what kind of shoes Sophia wore ever, let alone if it was a weird time.

Ace would know, though. He inherently processed details. But she'd sent him away and then forgot about hiring another bodyguard.

Apparently, that would be the last in a long line of mistakes.

"Time's up," he called following her trek through the house, then manhandling her without remorse as he dragged her through the front door.

She had a moment when she thought he'd leave it open, but he shut it, ruining the idea that someone might realize she'd been taken if the door was standing wide.

"Start walking," he commanded.

She did, refusing to acknowledge how hard her legs were shaking. The last time she'd taken this route, Ace had walked alongside her, holding her hand to help her over things, his thumb rubbing over hers companionably.

The tears welled up in earnest now. This man would kill her, she had no doubt, and the last thing she'd said to Ace was *you're fired*. What she wished she'd said, she couldn't fathom, but leaving things in limbo between them wasn't sitting well with her. Not when faced with this kind of an end.

Not that she planned to go down without a fight. But she didn't imagine she'd be much match for a gun.

Moonlight lit the path well enough that she didn't stumble too much, and an eternity later she saw the fence line for the Silver Acres Ranch in the distance. "We're almost there."

"This better be the right place," he said and wagged his gun. "Or I'll shoot you in the arm so you can still walk to the place you should have started with."

"This is where we found it," she told him with a scowl. "Why would I take you to the wrong place? There's nothing else here. The excavation teams started in this area first."

The man stared at the freshly turned earth and swore. The swath extended in a long dark square, stretching more than twenty feet. It couldn't be clearer that someone had dug here recently with heavy, efficient machinery. She couldn't read the look on his face, but it was definitely not happy.

"They didn't find anything else?" he asked and then turned his displeased gaze on her once again. "You're lying. They found the st—artifacts. Someone had to have found it."

Whatever *it* was, that's what this guy was looking for. Maybe had been the whole time.

"No one found anything. Look, the teams are publishing their findings on the Harvard and UT websites. You can read for yourself exactly what they're doing. No kidnapping plot required."

He shook his head, hard, as if she wasn't making sense. Well, she hated to break it to him. There was nothing about this treasure hunt that made sense.

"There was a map," he said. "Where was the other X?"

"The other X?" she repeated carefully. "There was only one. This one. How did you know about the map?"

"Not important. I need that map." His gaze narrowed and she did not like the vibe rolling from him. Dangerous, with a side of evil. "You're going to get it for me."

"You can have the map," she said and meant it. "The

treasure belongs to the people of Mexico and there are almost two dozen scientists on-site who are doing their part to ensure that's what happens to it."

She wasn't worried about this idiot discovering anything that a bunch of really smart people hadn't already learned about the treasure.

Her captor swore again and rubbed his temple. "You've been nothing but a problem. I tried to tell him. This is not the right way."

"What's not the right way?" Who was *him*?

"Stop talking. You've got a mouth that won't quit," he sneered and grabbed her arm, shoving the short barrel between her ribs. The metal scraped against bone painfully. "Move. We're taking another walk."

"To where?" she managed to get out around her clacking teeth.

If he pulled the trigger now, he wouldn't miss. The bullet would tear through her body and there would be no coming back from that.

He didn't answer, just kept hauling her through the woods. But she recognized the shed with the hidden shelter from a hundred yards away. Apparently, he'd found it since the night she and Ace had spent there. Because she didn't for a second believe he'd known they'd been trapped there and left them alone.

The man—whose name she still didn't know—marched her into the shed and down the rickety stairs, shutting the repaired door behind them. It still locked from the other side, but she didn't think that would matter since he didn't seem intent on leaving her there by herself.

The ceiling had also been repaired. Too bad. That might have been a great vantage point for someone to discover she was being held hostage down here in the shelter. If anyone would even think to look for her.

Ace would have. If she hadn't gotten her emotions in a twist and done something stupid like tell him she didn't need his services without securing an actual backup.

He would have looked for her no matter what. Whether he was on her payroll or not. She knew exactly what the expression on his face would be as he searched. How his arms would feel when he found her and crushed her to his chest as he validated for himself that she was safe.

"You've messed everything up," her captor told her derisively. "I gave you a lot of chances to back off. To leave the ranch and never come back. I really thought the backhoe would scare you away for good. Now it's time to do this differently."

The backhoe hadn't been an accident. Ace would never let her live this down. If she got out of this and had a chance to tell him. And he was still speaking to her.

A hysterical sob rose in her throat, and she choked it back. "That's what all of this has been about? Shooting at me in the woods? If you were trying to scare me away, you did a poor job of it."

"Yeah, I'm aware," he said with a frustrated smirk. "Instead of leaving, you invited a lot more people to the party. My boss is very unhappy. So we're going to see if I can get him into a little better mood. I'm going to kill you and leave you here with a note that says your little sister is next if I don't get the map in my hand in twelve hours."

Sophia's pulse scattered. New plan. Hard to come up with one when she couldn't breathe and somehow now Charli's life was in danger. She didn't believe for a sec-

ond that this still-nameless guy would let Charli live after
he got the map.

"You'll never get away with this," she told him. "There
are too many people around. You'll never be able to search
the property without getting caught."

"Oh, good point," he said, nodding as if they were having
a lovely chat. "I'll include that as a stipulation, then. Map,
and everyone has to clear out or the sister dies. Thanks. I
owe you one. Oh, wait, you're going to be dead, so I guess
I'll never have to pay."

He levered up the gun and pointed it at her. The look
on his face put a chill deep down in her bowels. He was
going to kill her.

Just as the muscles in his forearm tensed to pull the
trigger, someone burst from the stairway and crashed into
her captor.

Ace.

Chapter 24

Ace grappled with Intruder Man for the second time. It would definitely be the last.

The gun was easy to dispatch since Ace had managed to surprise him. When he kicked it to the side, he called to Sophia, "Grab it!"

That beautiful woman sprang into action, no questions asked. He didn't have time to make sure she succeeded. During the half second Ace split his attention, Intruder Man got in a lucky swing to his jaw.

Stars exploded across his vision, but he blinked fast and shook it off, rolling up on the toes of his boots to brace for the next blow. Intruder Man didn't disappoint him, coming in low. Ace blocked him easily and went in for the kill, vising his elbow around his opponent's neck and grabbing it to use as a lever to snap his neck.

It was rote. Kill or be killed. This pile of filth had kidnapped Sophia, scared her, probably hurt her. He deserved to die.

At the last millisecond, he checked his strength. And didn't do it. He held this man's life in his hands—which Intruder Man likely didn't even realize—but this wasn't who Ace wanted to be.

This was a choice. He had choices. He didn't have to live in the shadow of the man he'd been. He could be something else if he wanted to. He could choose that right now. For himself and Sophia.

The blackness inside eased all at once. Reconciling the past might take a little longer, but for the first time he felt like he could do it. History didn't have to define his future.

Intruder Man struggled in Ace's headlock, but he wasn't going anywhere unless given permission. Ace was not in a permissive mood.

"Sophia," he called. "Cock that gun and hand it to me."

She obliged and even had the foresight to come up behind him so Intruder Man couldn't grab the gun first. His heart squeezed. Sophia Lang was everything and then some.

In a flash, he released Intruder Man and stuck the gun right at the small of his back where he could take out a kidney and his heart in one shot.

"I wouldn't tempt me if I were you," Ace advised him. "I won't spare you a second time."

"Shoot him in the arm," Sophia advised, her own arms crossed and a glare on her beautiful face. "Then he can still walk and probably won't bleed to death."

There wasn't anything funny about this, but he had to bite back the urge to laugh anyway. This woman slayed him. Even when they were still at odds. The tight band around his lungs eased a fraction, though he didn't think he'd ever get back the years taken off his life when he'd found her missing.

Intruder Man snarled at her. "Shut it, little girl. You're going to get yours, don't worry."

"I'm not worried. You should be, though. I hear Huntsville is a brutal place, but you'll get used to it," she advised him with a brittle smile. "As long as you'll be there, you'll have to."

Ace wrestled his captive up the stairs, Sophia trailing him. He wished he could spend just five seconds making sure she was okay, but he had plenty of time for that later.

Besides, she obviously still had her spirit. Neither Intruder Man nor Ace's boneheadedness had stolen that from her. Good.

The police had finally arrived sometime in the last few minutes, judging by the number of flashing red and blue lights gathered at the main house. When Ace and Sophia rolled into sight, Charli flew from the porch, catching her sister in a giant hug. Several of the scientists stood off to the side, matching smiles as they patted Sophia on the back or calling out that they were happy to see her unharmed.

Ace found one of the state troopers they'd called in just in case Intruder Man had taken Sophia across county lines. He handed over his cargo, along with the gun for evidence, and engaged in the longest conversation on record about the circumstances of his involvement, how he'd captured the assailant, as well as securing his promise to go down to the local station to submit his own prints for investigative purposes.

The last thing he wanted to do was stand here doing official business when he needed to touch Sophia to calm his racing pulse.

An eternity later, he found her standing near the back door to the house, chaffing her palms up and down on her arms as if the chill had finally gotten to her. She was alone, Charli apparently having gone inside.

"Here." He slipped his own flannel shirt around her shoulders, more than comfortable in his base-layer T-shirt.

She didn't shrug it off, a miracle. It wouldn't be shocking to find out she'd rather be cold than wear something of his.

"I thought I fired you," she said, the expression on her face unreadable.

"Well, it turns out you're not my only employer, so..." He lifted his hands. "I still had that backup job to do."

"You told me you forfeited your fee." A line appeared between her brows. "Or was that a lie too?"

"There are more things in this world that motivate me than money," he told her simply. "Making sure I got you back in one piece is a job I'd do for free over and over again."

Her eyes softened then, flooding him with something that had been missing for far too long—hope. He drank in her beautiful face and finally let himself feel the terror he'd held at bay for the long minutes it had taken him to realize where Intruder Man would have taken her.

But she was safe now and he wanted nothing more than to catch her up in his embrace so he could breathe her in. If nothing else, he knew beyond a shadow of a doubt how he felt about her. Rescuing a woman you loved from a kidnapper put a lot of things in perspective.

"How did you find me?" she asked. "Or is that a dumb question? You were still watching the house, weren't you?"

The state trooper took off with a wail of his siren, escorting Intruder Man off the premises for the last time.

"Not well enough," he muttered. "The light in the kitchen was on. I figured you were still in there since you always turn it off when you leave a room. I kept thinking it was so odd that you'd stayed in the kitchen that long and finally I kicked myself into checking. You were gone. That's when I knew something was wrong."

A smile lifted the corners of Sophia's mouth. "Of all things. My anal retentiveness is what saved me?"

"No." He let his own smile bloom. "The fact that I wouldn't have been able to live with myself if I didn't get a chance to apologize is what saved you."

"I'm listening."

Miraculously, she was. He didn't waste the opportunity, and neither could he possibly deny himself the urge to reach out. To finally touch her. When he grasped her hand, she didn't flinch. Progress.

"I'm sorry I didn't believe in us at the time when it was most important. From the beginning. Rookie mistake. You see, I've never been in love before, so I had no idea I was screwing up until it was too late."

That's when the weight lifted. He'd spilled the contents of his heart all over the ground at her feet. All he could do was pray she wouldn't stomp on it.

"That was a pretty good apology," she said, her expression still not giving away much. "But Ace, jeez. I'm still reeling. Give me time to get my feet under me."

"Of course," he interjected quickly. "What like, five, ten minutes?"

Mistake. He knew it the second it left his mouth. Her smile vanished and what felt like quicksand opened up beneath his feet.

"It's not the time for jokes. I'm sorry."

Her hand slipped from his. Along with the hope he'd let himself feel. His heart ached but he made himself nod. "Okay. What can I do?"

"I need space. Obviously, firing you isn't going to work, so just… I don't know. Don't push me right now."

He nodded, his throat tight. It wasn't an outright dismissal but it also wasn't Sophia in his arms forever like the vision in his head. But maybe he could still get there. "I can do that."

And then he had to let her walk away again. But this time, he wasn't going to sit quietly on the sidelines.

When the officer assigned to Sophia's case came by the next afternoon, Ace answered the door with Sophia's blessing and checked credentials or whatever a security specialist did when he wasn't undercover any longer.

Sophia had long lost track of what she was supposed to call the man she couldn't ignore no matter how hard she tried. There was something in the set of his shoulders as he spoke to the uniformed officer that caught and held her attention. Slightly slumped, as if he had a barbell across them with fifty pounds on it weighing him down.

Not that she was spending an inordinate amount of time studying him. The opposite. In fact, she'd say she was going out of her way to not look at him.

Except that was a lie, because her eye kept being drawn to Ace no matter what she promised herself. There was something different about him. Something missing. A… sparkle. Which sounded dumb because he was the most masculine man she'd ever met in her life. But that didn't change facts and before she'd fired him, Ace had always had some kind of je ne sais quoi that she'd found enormously attractive. Obviously.

She cleared her throat.

"Thank you for coming by," she told the officer, whose name tag read Hernandez. "Do you have an update for us?"

Automatically, she'd included Ace and he'd noticed, judging by his quick glance at her face. Well, she wasn't going to take it back. Pretending she didn't see the wisdom in trying to get back to some semblance of their former partnership would be useless. She hated that she needed him. But he was incredibly good at his job. His real job. The one someone who wasn't her had hired him to do.

That was the thing she couldn't stop puzzling over in her head. At first, she'd been convinced he was lying. Who would hire someone and make a rule that it had to be a secret? That was the dumbest thing she'd ever heard of.

But then...if he'd made that up, why? What would be the benefit of lying about being forced to protect her without her knowledge? Wasn't he doing a much better job now that all pretenses were gone?

It was maddening. And that's why she hadn't made up her mind yet on whether she could trust him. Or forgive him.

"I do have an update," the officer announced, glancing at Ace.

Sophia clasped her hands together. "Please feel free to speak candidly. Mr. Madden is head of security at the ranch."

Well. *I guess I just gave Ace his job back.* Or something. The title had just rolled off her tongue so easily. He wisely chose not to say a word, but he did throw up a questioning hand behind Officer Hernandez's back. She made a face at him, and he tipped his hat with a small smile.

For one second, she forgot that she was mad at him and everything sweet and light and wonderful flooded her heart as she soaked up the harmony between them. This was how it had been before, and she missed it.

Officer Hernandez consulted what must be notes on his phone. "The man who kidnapped you is Rodrigo Cortez. He's a known associate of Karl Davenport."

The name struck a chord inside her that rang like a gong. "That was my father's partner."

Without hesitation, Ace came to stand behind her, his presence a solid warmth at her back. He didn't say a word, but she got the message just the same. *I'm here.* Her heart soaked it up. Reveled in it. She wasn't alone and this man was making sure she knew it.

What was she supposed to do with him? He'd *lied* to her. Okay, it was more like he'd misled her. Like her father had. That made them the same.

Except even she couldn't sell that to herself any longer. She was going to have to reframe everything. She just didn't know how.

Officer Hernandez consulted his notes again. "Yes, Davenport did work with David Lang, but we don't have a lead on either of their whereabouts. We're trying to get Cortez to make a deal. Trade info for leniency, but so far he's not talking."

Ace nodded. "You'll keep us informed? Especially if he makes bail?"

"He's not making bail," Hernandez confirmed grimly. "The judge considers him a flight risk since he's a Mexican citizen."

It was over. Intruder Man finally had a name, and he wasn't a threat any longer. Her knees nearly gave out as relief flooded her. Ace and the officer ran through a few more details, none of which she heard. She was too busy trying to sort out her new normal, the one where Ace didn't have to play the part of her bodyguard any longer. Where there were no secrets between them.

What did that look like? Happily ever after, or more like Sophia kicking yet another man to the curb because they were all untrustworthy?

The next morning, Sophia spent a few hours on the new Cowboy Experience plan, doubly excited about executing it since Cortez had been arrested. It bothered her a little that her father's partner, Karl Davenport, was still at large. Hernandez had assured her that several law enforcement agencies were looking for him—and her father—for questioning regarding the coins that had been found at the ranch.

She figured she'd rather them both stay far away from her. The resentment she'd always had for her father leaving her was still there, but it wasn't as sharp. Maybe she could forgive him one day.

Pulling up her accounting software, Sophia plowed through a few dozen entries until a tinkling sound broke her concentration. It was coming from the window.

Mystified, she pushed her chair back and went to investigate, her pulse trilling a little as stray noises still managed to do for some reason despite Intruder Man being behind bars. But it wasn't a threat—at least not to her life.

Her heart, on the other hand… Ace stood outside the window throwing tiny pebbles at the glass. He had an acoustic guitar in his hand and a smile on his face that she couldn't help but respond to.

Levering up the window, she crossed her arms and called out, "What's all this?"

"This—" he gestured in a wide arc around his hips "—is

me giving you space. This—" he held up the guitar "—is my attempt to steal your heart away from Orien Bright. I'm not as good, but I've been practicing."

Ace strummed the guitar and broke into a surprisingly not-awful rendition of "Mammas Don't Let Your Babies Grow Up to be Cowboys." Anyone who had grown up in Texas knew the song, which he must know and chose deliberately.

She tried not to be affected. To call up some of the lingering anger she hadn't been able to get rid of. But all of that ceased to matter as he sang to her outside her window. As grand gestures went, it was pretty simple but so powerful that it filled her to the brim. Tears burned her eyes until she let them fall.

He broke off midverse. "Don't cry, Soph. My singing isn't *that* bad."

"It's not. It's…" *Everything.* And she was so tired of being heartsick. "Come inside before everyone on the property lines up to see what's going on."

In seconds, he'd cleared the back door and stood at the threshold of her office, hat in one hand, guitar in the other. Jeez, what a picture he made. Long, lean legs in boots and jeans, a T-shirt and an unbuttoned flannel shirt. Like every other cowboy on this ranch.

But this one was different. She'd known that from the first moment. How different, she'd had no idea.

"You really learned how to play the guitar so you could serenade me?" she murmured.

He shrugged. "I needed something to do while watching the house. I figured if nothing else I could get a few moments of your time and that was worth it to me."

Another stupid tear worked its way loose and splashed

down on her cheek. What was wrong with her? She never cried, especially over a man. Men were the enemy.

But her heart wouldn't hold on to that sentiment.

Maybe a lot of men were awful human beings. But Ace wasn't in that category. Never had been. He'd kept a secret because he was told to, which was as much of a testament to his character as anything else. He'd apologized, and she'd accepted it.

What she hadn't done was return the favor.

"Please. Come in," she whispered, and bit back the smile as he took two baby steps across the threshold. "All the way in."

When this man committed, he held nothing back. He swept into her office and propped the guitar against the wall, then perched a hip on her desk, a scant two feet from her. His presence filled the room, making her light-headed for a minute as she breathed him in. He smelled like pine and man and everything good in the world.

"I owe you an apology," she said and smiled when he quirked a brow at her.

"I think you have that backward," he suggested lightly. "Hence the serenade. This is me going big and not going home."

"Yeah. I got that. You're not going anywhere." She nodded, contemplating him and his strong fingers wrapped around the brim of his hat. That, he'd kept, and held in front of him like a shield, which stung something inside her. "That's the thing. I kept trying to paint you with a brush that wasn't working. I built up this list of sins in my head that starred you right next to my dad as members of the same club. I wanted to find a flaw so I could do what I do best—abandon you before you could do it to me. I'm sorry."

Ace goggled at her. There was no other word for it. His chest rose on a sharply sucked-in breath as he blinked and swallowed in a combo that squeezed her heart as she realized she'd rendered him speechless.

It was sweet and affecting all at once. And she wasn't finished. "I'm also giving you your job back. You're unfired."

The look on his face slayed her. Apparently, being back on the payroll had done the trick to unstick his tongue from the roof of his mouth.

"Are you sure?" he asked so earnestly, she almost rolled her eyes. And honestly, kind of smile a little. He was so adorable sometimes.

"No, I had to really think about whether to hire the best security specialist I've ever seen in action to keep my ranch safe." She did smile then. "Of course I'm sure."

His storm-colored eyes locked onto hers, so much emotion raging through them that they were almost gray. "I meant about the apology. I'm struggling to understand what you think you did wrong. I'm the one who betrayed your trust and—"

She laid two fingers over his lips. "Shh. You did what you had to do. Your honor is not in question. The issue is mine. I'll say it again. I'm sorry. I didn't believe in us at the most important time, when you needed me to forgive you for keeping a secret you weren't at liberty to divulge. I'm working on getting better at letting things go. If you're willing to stick around to find out how I do, I'm not going anywhere, either."

The storm in his gaze got a lot more heated. But he

didn't rush to sweep her into his arms like she'd expected. He did cup her hand and hold it to his cheek, effectively removing her fingers from his lips, which was a shame. She got it, though. There was a lot more to say and he deserved to hear it.

"I need you, Andrew Christopher." She let the sentiment hang there between them, not pulling it back. "Maybe more than I would like."

"Does that scare you?" he asked quietly and set his hat on her desk, leaving his middle exposed. It was as much a testament to his state of mind as anything.

She did not enjoy hard questions. But he'd probably earned the right to ask them and to be given an honest answer. "It does. In many ways. I'm not used to depending on someone else. I like being responsible for myself. It's doubly hard when I trust someone, only to find out he didn't trust me with all of himself."

To his credit, he didn't flinch. He took it in the jaw, his gaze never wavering. "I know, and I'm sorry. I would take it back if I could. It's hard for me to understand why my past isn't a problem for you. It's a problem for me."

That much was the truth. She could see the ghosts of his previous career flitting through him, even as she appreciated that he understood that was the lack of trust she'd referred to. "It shouldn't be. You have a gift. Many gifts. You used them to make Americans safe, same as you did for me. I respect that. You're one of a kind."

Ducking his head at her praise, he flashed her a tiny smile. "I do believe you might be the only person on the planet who would see it that way, but I'll try to accept that it is your viewpoint."

Something shifted between them then, with an almost palpable shimmer in the atmosphere as he rested his hands on her hips, drawing her forward until she was snug against his powerful body.

Their proximity made her breathless.

"Now, we have another issue," she murmured, the storm capturing her thoroughly as she looped her arms around his neck. "I'm officially your boss again. How do you feel about dating in the workplace? Careful. There is a wrong answer."

His mouth twitched and she realized he was fighting a smile. "That depends. Is there a rule against it? I can't stop being the kind of guy who likes to follow rules."

That, she had a very good answer for. "Since I'm the boss, I get to make the rules and the answer is no. There is not a rule."

"Then I'm a fan of it. As long as I'm the only one dating the boss," he said, his voice dropping down into a rough, gravelly range that rumbled in her belly deliciously. "That's nonnegotiable."

"Man, you drive a hard bargain. Fine." She blew out a breath as if flustered and shook her head. "You're the only hot cowboy allowed in my house. But only if you kiss me right now."

Ace tightened his grip and tipped his chin, so many things flitting through his expression. But he didn't kiss her. "I'll get to that in a minute. If we're going to do this thing differently this time, then I'm not pulling any punches. I love you, Sophia Lang. I will never betray your trust again as long as I live."

Well. He'd gone and one-upped her apology, after all. And now her eyes were stinging again. "In the spirit of true confessions, I guess I have to be honest right back. I love you too."

That's when he kissed her with all the pent-up passion that she'd known from day one lurked beneath that hat.

Epilogue

With all of the university people still on-site, Ace and Sophia didn't have much time to themselves over the next few days. And it didn't look like that would change anytime soon once the team unearthed a set of jade beads that the museum in Mexico authenticated as a piece from Pakal the Great's era, but it was not a previously cataloged find, nor was it from Pakal's tomb.

At least Sophia could rest easy that her father had not stolen anything from the museum or the pyramid. It did appear that he might have legitimately found treasure and hidden at least some of it at the ranch.

Interest exploded over what other Maya artifacts might be buried on the property. When Sophia met Heath McKay and Paxton Pierce, she felt a lot better about the security situation. Not that she didn't have full faith in Ace's abilities, but these guys were obviously cut from the same cloth as her head of security, and it couldn't hurt to have extra eyes and ears.

Plus, it was kind of nice to learn that the three men would continue to work together, even after she'd inadvertently split up their company when Ace had accepted her job offer. No one seemed to hold it against her.

Meanwhile, she and Ace stole what few moments they could together, laughing softly together under the stars and grabbing lunch on the wraparound porch if they both had a break. The Cowboy Experience would open for business in a week and a half and Sophia couldn't be more excited about the future of the ranch as she and Charli checked off the to-do list together.

The following Tuesday, her grandpa's lawyer rang the doorbell unexpectedly.

"Mr. Trask," she said as she opened the door, the latest list of facts and figures draining from her head instantly. The last time she'd received an unexpected visit from this man, he'd told her she had inherited the ranch.

Surely he didn't have more surprises in store for her.

"Ms. Lang," he said with a polite smile. "I have a few things to go over with you, if you have some time."

"Of course." She stepped aside to let him into the foyer, not at all shocked to see Ace materialize on the porch behind the lawyer, clearly having noticed the strange car on the property.

He followed Mr. Trask into the house, his gait easy but alert.

"It's fine," she murmured. "He's my grandfather's attorney. And now mine, I guess."

Ace gave her a look as he drew up beside her, always ready to get between her and anything that might cause harm, no matter what. It made her heart swell every time.

Charli came down the stairs. "Was someone at the door? Oh, hello."

"Ms. Lang. I didn't know you were here. Are you living at the ranch now?" Mr. Trask glanced at Sophia, who nodded. "Then she should hear this as well."

Sensing it would be best if everyone was comfortable, she showed Mr. Trask to the living room, still furnished with her grandmother's sofas and pretty chairs flanking the fireplace. Ace clasped her hand as he settled next to her, Charli opting for one of the chairs while Mr. Trask sat on the other sofa, spreading a few papers out next to him.

"Some events have come to my attention recently," Mr. Trask said and cleared his throat. "First off, I want to apologize if I inadvertently put you in danger, Ms. Lang. It may be my fault you were kidnapped."

"What?" Sophia gasped as Ace made a sound in his throat.

"You're going to want to qualify that really fast," Ace said.

Mr. Trask nodded, his mouth firm. "I'm the one who hired you. It was my stipulation that you remain anonymous. I thought that if Ms. Lang knew there might be trouble, it would scare her away from the ranch. It was Mr. Lang's fondest wish that she remain here and build a life."

"It was you," Sophia repeated in wonder as Ace's grip tightened around her hand.

Of all things. She hadn't needed the validation that she'd been right to trust Ace, but the lingering question of why he'd had to keep his original role here a secret had finally been answered.

Mr. Trask shuffled his papers. "Again, my apologies. I had no idea why your grandfather suspected that someone might come looking for things your father may have left behind, but Mr. Lang entrusted me with looking after you, and I made the best decision I could."

"So, it's really over." Ace rubbed the back of his neck. "I was starting to think maybe we'd never know for sure what had happened. But I don't understand why you made the final payment. It arrived in my account two days ago."

And hadn't that been a shock. He'd told her he was afraid to touch it in case it was a mistake.

"Because you earned it," Mr. Trask said decisively. "Ms. Lang is living at the ranch as Mr. Lang wanted, and her sister is here too. You have done a stellar job looking after them both and I hope I can count on you to continue."

"He's on my payroll now," Sophia said, brows raised. "Along with his partners, so there's no chance of anything getting by them."

"Then my job here is done." Mr. Trask stood. "Please do let me know if you need anything else or have any questions."

Sophia showed the lawyer to the door, her mind whirling with this new information. Oh, yes, she had questions, but they could wait a little while.

"Well, that was informative," Charli said in a way that no one could mistake for sincerity and made a face. "I thought it was Heath at the door. He owes me dinner."

Heath and Charli had hit it off apparently, and since Sophia liked Ace's former teammate, she was thrilled they seemed to be spending more time together. As long as it didn't interfere with opening day, they could get married for all she cared.

Her sister vanished back upstairs, leaving her alone with Ace for the first time in what felt like ages.

"Finally got your answers," she told him, and he grinned, pulling her into a kiss.

"Back at you." But then his smile slipped. "It's still not over, though. Your father's associate, the one Intruder Man worked for, is still at large. The archaeologists are still finding new artifacts. There's a lot going on. I haven't even had time to take you on a proper date."

"You will," she predicted. "In the meantime, I trust that we'll be facing down whatever happens next together."

This was what it looked like to finally have everything she'd ever wanted.

"I love you, Soph," he murmured. "One day, I'm going to make you mine forever."

"Too late. You're already stuck with me," she teased. "Because I love you too and I'm not ever giving you up."

* * * * *

Romantic Suspense

Danger. Passion. Drama.

Available Next Month

Colton Mountain Search Karen Whiddon
Defender After Dark Charlene Parris

A High-Stakes Reunion Tara Taylor Quinn
Close Range Cattleman Amber Leigh Williams

LOVE INSPIRED

Baby Protection Mission Laura Scott
Cold Case Target Jessica R. Patch

Larger Print

LOVE INSPIRED

Tracking The Truth Dana Mentink
Rocky Mountain Survival Jane M. Choate

Larger Print

LOVE INSPIRED

Treacherous Escape Kellie VanHorn
Colorado Double Cross Jennifer Pierce

Larger Print

Keep reading for an excerpt of a new title
from the Intrigue series,
K-9 DETECTION by Nichole Severn

Chapter One

She was making the world a better place one cookie at a time.

And there was nothing that said *I'm sorry that your deputy ended up being a traitorous bastard working for the cartel* than her cranberry-lemon cookies.

Jocelyn Carville parked her SUV outside of Alpine Valley's police station. If you could even call it that. In truth, it was nothing more than two double-wide trailers shoved together to look like one long building. The defining boundary between the two sections cut right down the middle with a set of stairs on each side. One half for the courts, and the other for Alpine Valley's finest.

A low groan registered from the back seat, and she glanced at her German shepherd, Maverick, in the rearview mirror. "Don't give me that pitiful look. I saw you steal four cookies off the counter before I wrapped them. You're not getting any more."

Collecting the plate of perfectly wrapped sweets, Jocelyn shouldered out of the vehicle. Maverick pawed at the side door. Anywhere these cookies went, he was sure to follow. Though sometimes she could convince him they were actually friends. He was prickly at best and standoffish at worst. Good thing she knew how to handle both. His nails ticked at the pavement as he jumped free of the SUV.

"Jocelyn Carville." The low register in that voice added an extra twist in her stomach. Chief of Police Baker Halsey had come out of nowhere. Speaking of *prickly*. The man pulled his keys from his uniform slacks, hugging the material tight to his thigh. And what a thigh it was. Never mind the rest of him with his dark hair, deep brown eyes or the slight dent at the bridge of his nose telling her he'd broken it in the past. Nope. She'd take just his thigh if he were offering. "Here I was thinking my day had started off pretty good. What's Socorro want this time?"

A tendril of resentment wormed through her, but she shut it down fast. There wasn't any room to let feelings like that through. Jocelyn readjusted her hold on the plastic-wrapped plate, keeping her head high. "I'm here for you."

Maverick pressed one side of his head against her calf and took a seat. His heat added to the sweat already breaking out beneath her bra. She was former military. It was her job to call on resources to aid in whatever situation had broken out and stay calm while doing it. To look at pain and suffering logically and offer the most beneficial solution possible. She was a damn good logistics coordinator. Most recently in the Pentagon's war on the Sangre por Sangre cartel. Delivering cookies shouldn't spike her adrenaline like this.

Baker pulled up short of the ancient wood stairs leading up to the front door of the station's trailer. "For *me*?"

"I brought you some cookies." Offering him the plate, she pasted on a smile—practically mastered over the years. Just like her cookies. "They're cranberry-lemon with a hint of drizzle. I remember you liked my lemon bread at the town Christmas bake sale last year. I thought you might like these, too."

"Cookies." He stared down at the plate. One second. Two. Her arms could only take the weight for so long. Lucky for her, she didn't have to wait more than a minute. Because the chief walked right up those stairs without another word.

Maybe *prickly* wasn't the right word. A couple more descriptors came to mind, but her mama would wash her mouth out with soap if she ever heard Jocelyn say them out loud. Well, if her mama made an effort to talk to her at all.

She didn't bother calling Maverick as she hiked up the three rickety steps to the station's glass door and ripped it open. Her K-9 partner was always in hot pursuit of any chance of cookies.

This place looked the same as always. Faux wood paneling on the walls, an entire bank of filing cabinets with files that had yet to be digitized, with the evidence room shoved into the back right corner. Though it looked like someone had gotten the blood out of the industrial carpet recently. Courteously put there by said deputy who'd turned out to be working for the cartel. Jocelyn tracked the chief around one of two desks and moved to set the plate on the end. "Have you had any luck finding a replacement deputy yet?"

Frustration tightened the fine lines etched around those incredibly dark eyes. "What do you want, Ms. Carville? Why are you really here?"

"I told you—I brought you cookies." She latched on to Maverick's collar as he tried to rush forward toward the treats.

"Nobody just brings cookies." Baker locked his sidearm in a drawer at the opposite end of the desk. "Not without wanting something in return, and certainly not when that someone is attached to one of the most dangerous and unrestricted security companies in the world."

And there it was. Him lumping her in with her employer. Seemed every time she managed to get a word in edgewise, Baker couldn't separate her from what she did for a living.

"I don't want anything in return." She motioned to the cookies she'd stayed up all night to bake. For him. Maverick was pawing at the carpet now, trying to get free. "I just thought you could use a little pick-me-up after everything that went down a couple weeks ago. I wanted to say—"

"A pick-me-up?" His dismissal hit harder than she'd expected. Baker faced her fully—a pure mountain of muscle built on secrets and defensiveness. He was a protector at heart, though. Someone who cared deeply about the people of this town. A man who believed in justice and righting wrongs. He had to be to do this kind of job day in and day out. "Let me make one thing clear, Ms. Carville. I'm not your friend. I don't want to pet your dog. I don't want you to bring me cookies or make arrangements for you to check on me to make sure I'm doing okay. You and I and that company you work for aren't allies. We won't be partnering on cases or braiding each other's hair. Police solve crimes. All you mercenaries do is make things worse in my town."

Mercenaries. Her heart threatened to shove straight up into her throat. That…that wasn't what she was at all. She helped people. She was the one who'd gotten Fire and Rescue in from surrounding towns when Sangre por Sangre had ambushed Alpine Valley and burned nearly a half dozen homes out of spite. She didn't hurt people for money, but no amount of explanation would change the chief's mind. He'd already created his own definition of her, and any fantasy she'd had that the two of them could work together or even become acquaintances instantly vanished.

Jocelyn's mouth dried as her courage to articulate any of that faltered. She almost reached for the cookies but thought better of it. "For your information, Maverick doesn't let anyone pet him. Not even me."

She dragged the K-9 with her and headed for the door, but Maverick ripped free of her hold. He sprinted toward the chief's desk. Embarrassment heated through her. Really? Of everything she could've left as her last words, it had to be about the fact her K-9 wasn't the cuddly type? And now Maverick was going to make her chase him. Great. No wonder she'd never won any argument about the importance of bonding as a team back at headquarters. She let herself be railroaded in the smallest conversations. No. She squared her shoulders. She wasn't going to let one tiff get the best of her. She was better than that, had overcome more than that.

But Maverick didn't go for the cookies.

Instead, he raced toward a door at the back and started sniffing at the carpet. The evidence room. Crap on a cracker. She didn't need this right now.

"You forgot your dog." The dismissiveness in Baker's tone told her he hadn't even bothered to look up to watch her leave.

"Thank you for your astute observation, Chief." Jocelyn dropped her hold on the front door. She'd almost made it out of there with her dignity in one piece. But it seemed that wasn't going to happen. At least not today. "You wouldn't happen to have any bomb tech in your evidence room, would you?"

Maverick's abilities to sniff out specific combinations of chemicals in explosives was unrivaled in his work as tactical-explosive-detection dog for the Department of Defense. And here in New Mexico. As cartels had battled over territory and attempted to upend law enforcement and local government, organizations like Sangre por Sangre had started planting devices where no one would find them—until it was too late. Soccer balls at parks, in a woman's purse at a restaurant in Albuquerque, a resident's home here in Alpine Valley. No one was safe. And so Socorro Security had recruited K-9s like Maverick onto the team in the name of strategy—find the threat before the threat found them. They were good at it, too. Protecting those who couldn't protect themselves. Ready to assist police and the DEA at a moment's notice. Founded by a former FBI investigator, Socorro had become the premier security company in the country by recruiting the best of the best. Former military operatives, strategists, combat specialists. They went above and beyond to take on this fight with the cartels. And they were winning.

Frustration and perhaps a hint of disbelief had Baker setting down his clipboard and pen on the desk. Closing the distance between them, the chief pulled his keys from his slacks once again. "Not that I know of. I can't account for every case, but most of what we keep here is from within the past five years. Unregistered arms, a few kilos. Maybe Fido smells the cheese I left in the rat trap last week."

Moving past her, Baker unlocked the door, shoving it open.

"He's a bomb-sniffing dog, Chief, and his name isn't Fido." She barely caught Maverick by the collar as he attempted to rush inside the small, overpacked room. The fluorescent tube light overhead flickered to life and highlighted rows and rows of labeled boxes in uniform shape and size.

A low beeping reached her ears.

Pivoting, Jocelyn set sights on the station's alarm panel near the front door—though it'd been disarmed when Baker had come inside a few minutes ago. "Do you hear that?"

Maverick pressed his face between two boxes on the lowest shelf and yipped. Her skin tightened in alarm.

"We have to get out of the building." Jocelyn unpocketed her cell from her cargo pants and whistled low for Maverick to follow her out. The K-9 growled low to argue, but he'd obey. He *always* obeyed when it counted. She hit Ivy Bardot's contact information and raised the phone to her ear. Someone had planted a device in the police station. She needed full response.

"What?" Baker asked. "I can't just leave, Carville. In case you weren't aware, I'm the only officer on shift today."

They didn't have time for bickering. She grabbed on to his uniform collar and rushed to the front of the station with the chief in tow. "We have to go!"

Fire and sharp debris exploded across her back.

Jocelyn slammed into the nearest wall.

The world went dark.

HE SHOULD'VE GOTTEN out of the damn trailer.

Baker tried to get his legs underneath him, but the blast had ripped some crucial muscle he hadn't known had existed. Oh, hell. The wood paneling he'd surrounded himself day in and day out warbled in his vision. That wasn't good.

The explosion… It'd been a bomb. She'd tried to warn him. *Jocelyn.* Jocelyn Carville.

He shoved onto all fours. "Talk to me, Carville."

No answer.

Heat licked at his right shoulder as he tried to get himself oriented, but there was nothing for his brain to latch on to. The trailer didn't look the same as it had a few minutes ago. Nothing was where it was supposed to be, and now daylight was prodding inside from the corner where the evidence room used to be. Flames climbed the walls, eating up all that faux wood paneling and industrial carpet inch by inch. A weak alarm rang low in his ears. Maybe from next door?

They had to get out of here. "Jocelyn."

A whine pierced through the crackle of flames. He could just make out a distant siren through the opening that hadn't been there before the explosion. Fire and Rescue was on the way. But that wasn't the sound he'd heard. No, it'd been something sullen and hurt.

"Come on." His personalized pep talk wasn't doing any good. Baker shoved to stand, though not as balanced as he'd hoped. His hand nearly went through the trailer wall as he grasped for support. Smoke collected at the back of his throat. He stumbled forward. "Where the hell are you?"

Another whine punctured through the ringing in his head, and he waved off a good amount of black smoke to make out the outline ahead. The dog. Baker couldn't remember his name. The German shepherd was circling something on the floor. "Damn it."

He lunged for Jocelyn. She wasn't responding. Possibly injured. Moving her might make matters worse, but the walls were literally closing in on them. He'd have to drag her out. The shepherd had bitten on to the shoulder of her Kevlar vest and was attempting to pull his handler to safety. Baker reached out.

The K-9 turned all that desperation onto Baker with a warning and bared teeth. His ears darted straight up, and suddenly he wasn't the bomb-sniffing dog who'd tried to warn them of danger. He was in protective mode. And he'd do anything to keep Baker from hurting Jocelyn.

"Knock it off, Cujo. I'm trying to help." Baker raised his hands, palms out, but no amount of deep breathing was going to bring his heart rate down. His mind went straight to the drawer where he'd locked away his gun. He didn't want to have to put the dog down, but if it came to getting Jocelyn out of here alive or fighting off her pet, he'd have no other choice. Though where the desk had gone, he couldn't even begin to guess in this mess.

He leaned forward, moving slower than he wanted. The fire was drawing closer. Every minute he wasted trying to appease some guard dog was another minute Jocelyn might not have. Baker latched on to her vest at both shoulders and pulled, waiting for the shepherd to strike. "I'm here to help. Okay?"

The K-9 seemed to realize Baker wasn't going to hurt its handler and softened around the mouth and eyes.

"Good boy. Now let's get the hell out of here." He hauled Jocelyn through a maze of debris and broken glass out what used to be the front door. His body ached to hell and back, but adrenaline was quickly drowning out the pain. Hugging her around the middle, he got her down the stairs with the German shepherd on her heels.

High-pitched sirens peeled through the empty park across the cul-de-sac and echoed off the surrounding cliffs protecting Alpine Valley. A lot of good they'd done these past few weeks. First a raid in which the cartel had burned down half a dozen homes. Now this.

Baker laid the woman in his arms across the old broken asphalt, shaded by her SUV. Ash darkened the distinct angles of her face, but it was the blood coming from her hairline that claimed the attention of every cell in his body. "Come on, Carville. Open your eyes."

Apparently she only took orders from her employer.

But she was breathing. That had to be enough for now—because there were still a whole lot of people in the trailer next door.

Baker set his sights on Fido. Bomb-sniffing dogs took commands, but he didn't have a clue how to order this one around. He pointed down at the K-9. "Uh, guard?"

Carville's sidekick licked his lips, cocking his head to one side.

"Stay." That had to be one. Baker swallowed the charred taste in his throat as he took in the remains of the station. Loss threatened to consume him as the past rushed to meet the present. No. He had to stay focused, get everyone out.

Fire and Rescue rounded the engine in front of what used to be the station as court staff escaped into the parking lot. Baker rushed to the other half of the trailer. A woman doubled over, nearly coughing up a lung.

He ran straight for her. "Is anyone still in there?"

She turned in a wild search. "Jason, our clerk! I don't see him!"

Baker hauled himself up the stairs, feeling the impact of the explosion with every step. Smoke consumed him once inside. It tendriled in random patterns as he waved one hand in front of his face but refused to disperse. Damn it. He couldn't see anything in here. "Hello! Jason? Are you still in here?"

Movement registered from his left. He tried to navigate through the cloud, fighting for his next breath, and hit the corner of a desk. The smoke must've been feeding in through the HVAC system, and without a giant hole in the ceiling it had nowhere to go. Smoke drove into his lungs. Burned. Baker tried to cough it up, but every breath was like inhaling fire. "Jason, can you hear me?"

He dared another few steps and hit something soft. Not another desk—too low. Sweat beaded down the back of his neck as a tile dropped from the ceiling. It shattered on the corner of another desk a couple feet away.

This place wasn't going to hold much longer. It was falling apart at the seams.

Reaching down, Baker felt a suit jacket with an arm inside and clamped onto it. "Sorry about the rug burn, man, but we gotta go."

Morning sunlight streaming through the glass door at the front of the trailer was the only map he had, but as soon as his brain had homed in on that small glimpse of hope, it was gone. The smoke closed in, suffocating him with every gasp for oxygen. Pinpricks started in his fingers and toes. His body was starved for air. Soon he'd pass out altogether.

A flood of dizziness gripped tight, and he sidestepped to keep himself upright. "Not yet, damn it."

He wasn't going to pass out. Not now.

Baker forced himself forward. One step. Then another. His lungs spasmed for clean air, but there was no way to see if he was heading in the right direction. He just had to do the one thing that never ended well. He had to trust himself.

Seconds distorted into full minutes…into an hour…as he tried to navigate through the smoke. He was losing his grip on the court clerk. His legs finally gave into the percussion of the explosion. He dropped harder than a bag of rocks. The trailer floor shook beneath him. Black webs encroached on his vision. This was it. This was when the past finally claimed him.

Baker clawed toward where he thought the front door might be. Out of air. Out of fight. Hell, maybe he should've had one of those cranberry-lemon cookies as a last meal.

"Jocelyn."

He had no reason to settle on her name. They weren't friends. They weren't even acquaintances. If anything, they were on two separate sides of the war taking over this town. But over the past couple of months, caught in his darkest moments, she'd somehow provided a light when he'd needed it the most. With baked goods and smiles as bright as noon day sun.

The smoke cleared ahead.

A flood of sunlight cut through the blackness swallowing him whole.

"Chief Halsey!" Her voice cut through the haze eating up the cells in his brain, though it was more distorted than he was used to. Her outline solidified in front of him. Soft hands stretched an oxygen mask over his mouth and nose. "Don't worry. We're going to get you out of here."

A steady stream of fresh air fought back the sickness in his lungs, and he realized it wasn't Jocelyn's voice that time. It was deeper. Distinctly male. Another outline maneuvered past him and took to prying his grip from the court clerk. Baker let them. He clawed up the firefighter's frame and dragged himself outside with minimal help. It was amazing what oxygen could do to a starving body.

The sun pierced his vision and laid out a group of onlookers behind the century-old wood fence blocking off the station from the parking lot. A series of growls triggered his flight instinct, but Baker pushed away from the firefighter, keeping him on his feet. The dog. He'd ordered him to guard his handler.

Baker caught sight of the German shepherd from

the back of Alpine Valley's only Animal Control truck. Fido was trying to chew his way through the thin grate keeping him from his partner. Baker's instincts shot into high alert as he homed in on the unconscious woman on the ground, surrounded on either side by two EMS techs. He took a step forward. "Jocelyn?"

They'd stripped her free of her Kevlar vest to administer chest compressions—and exposed a bloodred stain spreading right in front of his eyes. He didn't understand. She'd been breathing when he'd left her.

Baker took a step forward. "What's happening? What's wrong with her?"

"Chief, we need you to keep your distance," one of the techs said. Though he couldn't be sure which one. "She's not responding. We need to get her in the bus. Now."

Strong hands forced him out of the way, but all he had attention for was Jocelyn, a mercenary he hadn't wanted anything to do with but who had insisted on sabotaging his life. Baker tried to follow, but the firefighter at his back was strong-arming him to stay at the scene. Helplessness surged as potent as that day he'd watched everything he'd built burn to the ground, and he wanted to fix it. To fix *this*. "Tell me what's happening."

But there was no time to answer.

The EMTs loaded Jocelyn onto a stretcher and raced for the ambulance. "Let's go! We're losing her!"

NEW RELEASE!

Rancher's Snowed-In Reunion
The Carsons Of Lone Rock
Book 4

**She turned their break-up into her breakout song.
And now they're snowed in…**

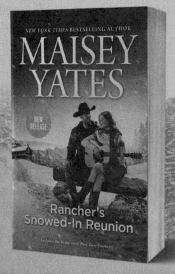

BONUS STORY INCLUDED

Don't miss this snowed-in second-chance romance between closed-off bull rider Flint Carson and Tansey Sands, the rodeo queen turned country music darling.

In-store and online March 2024.

MILLS & BOON
millsandboon.com.au